The Black Diamond and the Witch's Curse

The Black Diamond and the Witch's Curse

Terrence Alexander

Library of Congress Control Number:		2016905408
ISBN:	Hardcover	978-1-5144-8175-2
	Softcover	978-1-5144-8174-5
	eBook	978-1-5144-8173-8

Print information available on the last page.

Rev. date: 04/02/2016

To order additional copies of this book, contact:
Xlibris
1-888-795-4274
www.Xlibris.com
Orders@Xlibris.com
736387

Contents

To Valerie,
  It was great
meeting you and
    sharing a laugh.

        —Terren Alegan

Chapter 1

Arrival

It was hot. This had to be the hottest day of the summer. Even though Move-In Day for the rest of the students was still two weeks away, Derek James was moving into his dorm early, as was the case with the rest of the football team. He was excited to be starting his first year of college at Word University, especially because he was finally getting out from under his mother's overprotective eye.

"Mom, I really didn't need you to help me move in. I got it," Derek said.

"Boy, if I let you move in by yourself, who knows what your room is gonna look like? Besides, I want to meet your roommate," his mother, Valerie James, responded.

"Dad trusted me. I asked him not to come, and he didn't."

"Well, I'm not your dad," Valerie said. "And I gotta make sure that my baby is all right."

"Mom, I'm eighteen. Can you not call me 'baby'?" Derek sighed.

"I'm your mother. You will always be my baby, no matter how old you get."

"That don't mean you gotta call me that," Derek grumbled.

"Whatever. Don't back talk. Now, are we gonna put these things in your room or are we gonna stand here at the car talking all day?"

Derek's room was on the fifth floor, the highest floor in the dorm. Derek looked up at the stately building, with the sun glistening off of the windows, and thought that maybe he could use the help. "Okay, I'll carry the minifridge up. You can take that trunk of clothes. I'll meet you up there. Remember, it's room 510B," Derek decided. As he watched his mom carry the trunk into the building, he wiped the sweat from his brow. Man, he just couldn't believe how hot it was!

Just as he was about to pick up the fridge, he noticed a couple of girls watching him, probably cheerleaders, also moving in that day. He took his shirt off, which by now was drenched, and revealed his impressive athlete's physique. He heard the girls start to giggle. Satisfied, he smirked, tossed the shirt into the car, picked up the minifridge, and made his way up the steps to meet his mom at his room.

As he made his way up to the top of the stairs, Derek could see his mom standing at the door of what he could only presume was his room. As he walked down the hallway, he saw his mom give him a look that made him feel *this* big. When he got to his room, Derek dropped the fridge with a *thud!* and glanced up at his mom.

"Derek, what are you doing with your shirt off?" Valerie admonished.

"Man, it's burning up outside! My shirt felt like I just took it out the washing machine!" Derek said.

"It ain't that hot outside. You know I ain't raise you like that. You ain't the only person out here!"

"Mom, it's like one hundred degrees outside and I ain't want my shirt to be sticking to me. It's not that big a deal," Derek pleaded.

She sighed. "Just open the door," Valerie said as she shook her head in disapproval.

Derek took the key from his pocket and opened the door to his dorm. Inside the room were two wooden desks, two dressers, and two closets. The walls were stark white. It was plain, but Derek had to admit that it was bigger than he had expected. It was bigger than his room at home. He had to keep in mind, though, that unlike at home, he had to share this with another person.

"How much more stuff do you have to bring up?" Valerie asked.

"Well, I got my TV, book bag, the rest of my clothes, and the book," answered Derek.

"Oh my god! I don't feel like going back up and down those steps," exclaimed Valerie.

"Look, you the one that wanted to help me move in. Besides, I could be up and back by myself real quick," suggested Derek.

"No."

"But since I been up here, I can do it. It's not that far and—" Derek started.

"No, Derek! What if somebody saw you? Don't risk it. It's just one more trip. I'm just getting old, is all. Don't mind my complaining," Valerie said. "Come on."

After bringing up the rest of Derek's stuff, it was time for Valerie to go. "Okay, are you sure you got everything?"

"Yes, Mom."

"Laptop? Toothpaste? Deodorant?"

"Yes, Mom."

"Razor?"

"Yes."

"Condoms?"

"What? Come on, Mom!"

"Well, like you said, you're eighteen. I went to college. I know what's up," Valerie said.

"I'm gonna act like we ain't really talking about this," said Derek, desperately wishing his mom would change the subject.

"Okay, I can take a hint. And you're sure you have the book? And anything else you would need?" Valerie inquired.

"Yeah. Positive."

"I still can't believe your dad let you take it with you," Valerie said.

"I guess he figured that I'm old enough for the responsibility," said Derek.

"Guess so," Valerie said as her eyes began to well up with tears.

"Aw come on, Mom, don't start crying."

"I can't help it. My baby is all grown up and leaving me."

"Mom, it's not that far away. And you know I can always pop in whenever I want. It's close enough for me to make the trip."

"I know. Okay, give me a hug before I go." Derek gave his mom a big warm hug. She got into her car and Derek waved as her car slowly faded into the distance.

Derek turned to go back up to his room. As he began to make his way up the steps leading to the front entrance, a black Nissan Altima rolled past a couple of cars filled with other students in the process of moving in and pulled up in the fire lane in front of the building. What was intriguing to Derek about this car was that the driver had Kendrick Lamar's "Backseat Freestyle" blasting from the speakers. Derek could appreciate this guy's taste in music! He walked up to the car as the driver, a stocky-looking guy, got out.

"Ay yo, you ride with Kendrick Lamar?" Derek asked, impressed.

"Of course, my brotha. You a fan?" the driver asked.

"Man, I got *Good Kid, M.A.A.D City* in heavy rotation on my iPod," Derek responded.

"Oh a'ight. I been a fan of Kendrick since *Section.80*," the guy said. "I assume you're on the football team."

"Yeah, wide receiver. You?"

"Running back."

"Cool, cool. I'm Derek, by the way," Derek said as he introduced himself.

"I think my roommate's name is Derek. My name is Bruce. Bruce Graves."

"Yup, I'm definitely your roommate. Well, I just got done putting my stuff up in the room. If you want, I can help you carry some stuff up," Derek offered.

"Okay, good looking out," Bruce said, relieved he had some help.

After Derek and Bruce were finished unloading Bruce's car, they decided to arrange the room to their liking. Bruce said, "Let's put my bed on that wall and yours on the opposite one. That way, we could put the desks right near the windows and the TV can go on the refrigerator in the corner."

"Okay, I'm good with that. I'll put my dresser by my bed. I kind of figured that these walls were gonna be bare so I brought us some posters to liven up the place," Derek said. He threw up some posters of scantily clad chocolate-skinned models and celebrity females.

"Definitely better," Bruce said approvingly.

Derek laughed. "I thought you'd approve."

As the two started to unpack their belongings, Bruce noticed a strange-looking book that fell out of Derek's backpack. "What type of classes are you taking?" Bruce asked. "You already got some of your books?"

"Why?" Derek turned and asked.

Bruce pointed to Derek's backpack. "Did you get to register early? What class takes that book? That jawn looks cool," Bruce said. The book was large and looked about four inches thick. It was a hardback, yet bound in black leather. On the cover was a picture of a majestic roaring golden lion, with a clawed paw raised toward the sky. Bruce thought the book looked *old*.

Derek quickly moved to pick up the book and put it back in the backpack. "Nah, this book is mine. My dad gave it to me. It's kind of a family heirloom," Derek nervously said.

"Heirloom?" Bruce asked perplexingly.

"Yeah," Derek responded. "It's been passed down in my family since before we came over here from Africa on the slave ships. It means a lot."

"Yo, that's cool. Can I see?" Bruce asked.

"Um," Derek hesitated. "It's just my dad has this thing about nobody else handling it. Like I said, it's real old and real important."

Bruce looked slightly disappointed. "Oh. No problem. I understand." An uncomfortable and awkward silence settled between the two.

"So where you from?" Derek asked, trying to lighten the mood.

"I was born in Pittsburg," Bruce answered. "I've lived in Philly for the past seven years though. You?"

"Oh, I'm from right here, Pottington. I actually live, like, a couple miles from here."

"Oh, so you know your way around this city. Know all the places to go where all the honeys at, am I right?" Bruce joked.

"Of course. This is my city. I got you covered," Derek said. "But I got a feeling that you won't have to go far to find a lot of bad chicks, if you know what I'm saying," Derek suggestively offered.

"You think the girls at this school will look that good?" Bruce asked.

"Look, dawg. Not only do they look good, but you gotta remember that Word U is the best HBCU in the nation. These chicks got their heads on straight and the looks to match," said Derek.

"Shit, well, if that's the case, I think I'm gonna have a very fun year," Bruce said. Bruce's stomach began to growl. "I'm about to go get something to eat," he said.

"Okay, I already ate. I'll holla at you later," Derek said.

As soon as Bruce left the room, Derek booted up his laptop. Once he was logged on, he opened up a Skype chat; and soon enough, a man appeared on the screen on the other end of the call. In the background were a few portraits and a TV. It appeared to be a living room. The chocolate-skinned man, the same complexion as Derek himself, was wearing a white undershirt and looked to be in his midforties. He had sprinkles of gray in his hair and a neatly trimmed goatee. A thin pair of reading glasses covered a pair of eyes that would lead someone to believe that this man had seen a lot in life.

The man smiled. "I was wondering when you would finally get around to calling me," he said.

Derek laughed. "What's up, Dad?"

***

The sleek black limousine pulled to a stop in front of the capitol building on First Avenue. The building, the seat of power for the state of Delaware, was a surprisingly modern and impressive-looking structure. Two flights of smooth marble steps led up to the entrance facing the street. Grecian columns radiated from the center of the building to the wings on either side. A huge dome sat on top of the building in the center of the roof with a smaller dome made of glass on either side. It took up eight city blocks. The driver stepped out of the limousine and opened the passenger door, allowing two state senators to enter the luxury car. There was a grim slightly off-putting atmosphere that permeated the car and seemed to be emanating from the two new passengers.

"You know where to go," one of the senators said. The driver nodded his head and began to lead the car to its destination.

Approximately thirty minutes later, the limousine arrived at its destination. City hall was a significantly less-imposing building than the capitol. It was half the size of the capitol building. There was nothing significant to distinguish it from the surrounding buildings. It was an old-looking building built of brick and mortar. It did have a couple of statues outside on the lawn depicting Caesar Rodney, Thomas McKean, and George Read—the three Delawareans that signed the Declaration of Independence—but other than that, it was spectacularly unremarkable.

The two senators exited the car and made their way inside. Once they got through security, they climbed a winding staircase and headed to the mayor's office. The mayor's office was located at the end of a long hallway that spanned the length of the building. There were multiple rooms along the hallway as well. When they reached the office, they confidently stepped inside. Angela Wright, mayor of Pottington, was a young woman in her early thirties. Once she sensed that she was no longer alone, she looked up from the document that she was perusing. "John. Alex. Can I help you?" she asked.

"We've been given instructions to give you this letter," John said.

"By who?" Mayor Wright asked. She took the letter from Alex.

"We think you know who," said Alex.

A look of concern immediately adorned her face. The major quickly and thoroughly read the letter. Her look of concern immediately morphed to a look of fear.

"She can't be serious," she said, incredulously.

"We can assure you that she is *quite* serious," John ominously shot back.

"How does she expect me to do this without compromising myself in the process?" Mayor Wright asked in disbelief.

"That's up for you to decide. We have simply been assigned to monitor and report your progress. You have until the end of next April to accomplish the task," Alex said.

The mayor asked a question to which she already knew the answer: "And if I refuse?"

John leaned in and whispered into her ear, "Then let's just say that your political career will be cut rather short, if you catch our drift," he said threateningly.

Mayor Wright could only watch in dread as the two senators then exited the room. After a brief moment of frustration overwhelmed her, she quickly composed herself and picked up the phone. She had a lot of work to do.

***

"So, you all moved in?" Derek's dad asked.

"Yup, I just finished. Room's all set up," Derek replied.

"Good. Your roommate come yet?" his dad asked.

"Yeah, he came right after Mom left," Derek answered.

"Oh okay. Y'all talk at all? How does he seem?"

"Well, he helped me set up the room. His name's Bruce. He's pretty cool. He's from Philly. Plays running back," Derek said.

"Good. Well, at least it seems like y'all gonna get along," Derek's dad said.

"Well, you know, I'm a pretty hard guy not to get along with," Derek jokingly said.

"Okay, wise guy," his dad said.

Derek quickly shifted to a more serious tone. "But I did have one slight problem."

"What?"

"He saw the book."

"What? How?" Derek's dad asked, slightly alarmed.

"It fell out my book bag."

"He didn't see anything else, did he?"

"No. Everything else is locked in the trunk in my closet," Derek said.

"Well, that's good at least. Why wasn't the book with the rest of the stuff? What was you thinking?" Derek's dad reprimanded.

"I don't know."

"What did he say when he saw it? What did you tell him?"

"He was curious. Thought it was a book for a class. I told him he couldn't see it 'cuz it was a family heirloom. He seemed to accept that answer."

"Good. Derek, you know you gotta be more careful. Don't make me regret letting you take that thing," his dad warned.

"I won't. I will be," said Derek.

"All right," said Derek's dad. He sighed. "You know, your mom is here whining about 'losing her baby.' Have to put up with that for a while. How does it feel to be out on your own now? Big man on campus?"

"I'll tell you when I got something interesting to say about it." Derek laughed. "I think I'm just glad to get out the house. Meet new people."

"And by *meet new people*, you really mean *meet new girls*," Derek's dad knowingly said.

"What you mean?" Derek playfully asked.

"I was eighteen once."

"That's exactly what mom said."

"Okay, but I was an eighteen-year-old guy once. But I ain't hating on you. Go do you. Have fun. That's a part of what college is about. Just don't also forget what you are really there for. Play hard, study hard, get your education," Derek's dad advised.

"Come on, you know me. I will."

"I know. And do me a favor, Derek."

"What?"

"I know I don't have to tell you this, but I will anyway. While you up there having fun, don't get nobody pregnant. You did take that box of rubbers I bought you, right?" his dad asked.

"You mean, the economy pack of Magnums you gave me? How could I forget those? It's like thirty condoms in there," said Derek good-naturedly.

"And you'll probably run through those before Christmas. I know how you be. And like I said, I was eighteen once." Derek just laughed. "I would just feel better knowing you're being safe while you're *meeting new people*," Derek's dad said.

"You have got to be the coolest dad," Derek said.

His dad smiled as he seemed to be listening to something in the background. "Your mom's calling me. Gotta cut this a little short. What you got planned for the rest of the day? Practice?"

"Nah. My first practice ain't 'til tomorrow. I'ma just walk around the campus. Learn where everything is," Derek replied.

"Okay, I'll talk to you later," his dad said.

"Okay." Derek signed off of Skype and closed the laptop. He just had to shake his head. His dad knew him way too well. Derek got up, grabbed his iPod, and went to go explore his new campus and enjoy the only day without football practice that he would be having for a while.

***

Why was the bus late? Derek had to take the school shuttle to get to Rashad T. Brooks Stadium for football practice since it was a couple of miles from the dorm complex in which he lived. But he couldn't understand why the shuttle was late. There weren't any students on campus, for crying out loud! He knew he should have taken the earlier shuttle with Bruce! Just as he was about to give up on making it to practice on time, he saw the shuttle, painted in the school colors of blue and silver and marked on the side with a wildcat, speeding around the corner. Finally! When the bus pulled up to the stop located just outside the main entrance to Liberty Dormitory Complex, Derek and a couple of other football players quickly hopped on board and began the fifteen-minute ride to the stadium.

Derek gazed out of the window as the buildings passed by. The library, student center, a few conferences halls, and other buildings all whizzed by. Word University was located on the southern outskirts of Pottington; therefore, the campus had an interesting blend of urban and suburban architecture. Many of the buildings looked like they belonged to the suburbs, with their old-style brick facades and white colonial exteriors. The layout of the streets, however, looked like they were plucked right out of the inner city. There wasn't much space. The city blocks were small and closely confined. It was because of the lack of space in the immediate area that the sports complex that held Brooks Stadium had to be built off campus.

The shuttle pulled up at the stadium at 2:55 p.m. He made it just in time. He entered the locker room and looked for his locker. He found it in the corner next to a couple of other wide receivers. "Man, you better hurry up and change into your pads and uniform. Coach don't like players being late. Especially freshmen," one of the receivers said. "He will definitely make you run laps on the first day."

"Shit!" exclaimed Derek. He quickly began to rip off his clothes and throw on his equipment as the other players made their way out to the practice field. Despite his best efforts, Derek was the last player out on the field and arrived at the team huddle after Coach Steve, head coach of the Word Wildcats, began his preseason speech. Derek tried to be inconspicuous and knelt on one knee in the back. No such luck.

"This leads me to my two main rules, men. If you follow these rules, we gonna be all right. Be on time and hustle. You in the back," the coach said as he pointed directly at Derek. Every player turned and looked at him. Derek felt eighty pairs of eyes looking intently at him. At that point, Derek wished he was invisible.

"Yes, coach?" Derek asked.

"Stand up, will you," the coach requested. Derek dropped his head and slowly stood up. "What's your name?" Coach Steve asked.

"Derek James, sir," he replied.

"And what do you think happens when a player breaks one of my two rules?" the coach said.

Derek's desire to be invisible only intensified. "I don't know," Derek said sheepishly.

Coach Steve addressed the rest of the team. "This school has made the playoffs ten years in a row. It has won three championships during that time. I can guarantee you it's because I keep things simple with only two rules. But that means, men, that I am not forgiving if those rules are broken." He looked back at Derek. "Mr. James, I want you to run ten laps around the practice field," the coach commanded.

"Ten laps? I was only a minute late," Derek protested.

"Oh, you're right. Ten laps is the wrong amount for only being a minute late. I must be trippin'." Derek slightly nodded. "Fifteen laps," Coach Steve said.

"Fifteen?" Derek asked in disbelief.

"Care to push your luck and make it twenty? Run fifteen laps, then come see me when you're done," Coach Steve said with an air of finality. Derek lowered his head and began to run his laps as the coach finished addressing the rest of the team and they began to stretch and warm up.

When Derek finished running his laps, he saw the coach standing with the water boy over by the coolers. He begrudgingly made his way over to them. "Mr. James, what was your GPA in high school?"

Derek was surprised and a little confused at the question. "Three point eight, coach," Derek responded.

"That means you must be fairly smart, is that right?"

Derek shrugged his shoulders, still trying to figure out where coach was taking this. "Yeah, I guess," he said.

"Did you have a tutor?"

Derek said, "No, I didn't need one."

Coach said, "I saw you play in high school. When I was recruiting you, do you know what I thought of you?" For some reason, Derek sensed that this was a rhetorical question and just decided to listen. "I saw a supremely talented six-foot-three 230-pound receiver that had issues. I saw a player that was built like a Greek god. But I also saw a player that was arrogant. That sometimes he didn't give his all because he knew he was better than the player covering him across the line of scrimmage. Now, I rarely extend scholarships to players with attitude problems, but I saw something in you. Don't make me regret it," the coach said.

Derek said, "I won't. I'm sorry for being late, sir. It won't happen again."

Coach Steve nodded. "Now go join your position meeting." Derek jogged over and finished practice with the other receivers.

Once it was over, Derek sat with Bruce on the shuttle home from practice. "Man, coach did you dirty by calling you out at practice in front of the whole team like that," said Bruce sympathetically.

Derek agreed, "He told me not to make him regret recruiting me."

"Damn, after the first day?" asked Bruce.

"Something tells me he gonna stay on my case all year," Derek mused.

"Fuck ya life," Bruce said jokingly. "I'm sure it'll get better," he said. Derek remained silent. "Listen, a couple of the homies is gonna go get something to eat then chill at one of the seniors' crib. You in?" Bruce asked.

"Nah, I'm straight. I'ma just cop something to eat and head back to the room and study the PlayBook," said Derek. The shuttle stopped at the student center.

"A'ight, homie, I'll catch you later," said Bruce as they shook hands. Derek got off the bus, got some pizza at the student center, called a couple of his friends to see what they were up to, and headed back to his dorm.

It was late by the time Derek got back to his dorm. Just as he was about to open his PlayBook, he heard a knock on the door. Peeved that he was interrupted just as he was about to start studying, he went to go open the door. His frustration immediately dissipated like a balloon when he saw that it was the cheerleader from the previous day.

"Well hello there, pretty lady," Derek said.

"I thought this was your room," she said.

"Now if I didn't know any better, I'd think you was stalkin' me," said Derek.

"Well, it's a good thing you know better then."

"So what brings you all the way up to the fifth floor?"

"I saw you on the football field earlier. Having to run all those laps," she said.

"Man, that was nothing. I ran fifty laps in a fuckin' rainstorm before," Derek boasted. The cheerleader laughed.

"Oh really? And here I was thinking you might need some cheering up," she said flirtingly.

Derek gave her a sly grin. "Well, my roommate's out so I am kinda lonely . . . ," said Derek suggestively as he opened the door more to let her in.

"Well, I guess I'll have to do something about that then," she said as she walked into Derek's room. His dad was wrong. He wasn't going to run though those condoms before Christmas. He was probably going to run out of rubbers by Thanksgiving at the latest.

***

Looking at the chaos of Move-In Day, Derek was grateful that he got to move in early. There were people everywhere! The Liberty Complex was the largest dorm complex at Word U and it showed. Cars were lined up as far as the eye could see. The traffic lights were out, making movement in and out of the complex even more perilous than it would have been normally. Students and parents were hurriedly moving to and fro. There seemed to be no order to this madness, however. From his window on the fifth floor, Derek thought all those people looked a little bit like ants crawling in and out of an anthill. He had to admit, though, that he welcomed the arrival of the rest of his classmates. With so little people at the university, the past two weeks had quickly become a boring routine of eating, football practice, and studying the PlayBook. He hooked up with the cheerleader-- Jasmine, he later learned-- a few more times, but he was already bored with her. Derek James was not one to stay with one girl for too long. He needed variety. It was the spice of life.

There was another reason why Derek was glad he got to move in early. He got a head start on registering for classes for the upcoming semester. Not that it helped. Simply put, Derek didn't know what classes to register for. He had no idea what he wanted to major in. He knew he didn't want to pick a major, just to switch it later. No, if he was going to declare a major, he wanted it to be the one he would graduate with. He called his sister, who went to college in California for nursing, for advice, but she was of little help. She told him to pick a major that was both related to a topic he was interested in and could be used in the real world in a practical way. But that was the problem. He didn't know what he was interested in! He knew he liked football, but how was that practical? He liked music, specifically Hip-Hop and R&B, but he didn't think majoring in music was practical either.

Eventually, Derek decided that he would register for classes that were requirements for graduation and not declare a major. This would allow him to get the required classes out of the way while also giving him more time to decide what he wanted to major in. Thus, he chose Pre-Calculus, Spanish II, First-Year Experience, and English 100, giving him only 11 credits. Normally, a student had to take no less than 12 credits per semester to be considered a full-time student. However, because he was a football player, he was allowed to take as little as 10 credits during the fall semester as long as he took classes over the winter to make up the difference.

Emerging from his reverie, Derek decided to venture out into the madness around campus and exited his dorm room. *Whoosh!* Derek ducked as he barely missed a football sailing past the spot where his head previously resided. "What the hell?" Derek angrily asked as he slowly arose.

"Oh snap, my bad. We didn't see you coming out," the boy who threw the football said, walking down the corridor toward him.

Derek turned to look at him. The boy looked to be slightly smaller than Derek. If he had to guess, Derek would say about 5'10" and maybe 180 lbs. He had caramel skin and wore distinctive silver glasses. "Watch where you throwing that shit! Almost took my head off!" Derek yelled.

"Sorry, dawg," the boy who caught the football said, walking up to him. "You good?" he asked.

"Yeah, I'm all right. Just watch it next time," said Derek as he walked past the boy, made his way down the stairwell, and left the building.

He decided that he would grab a bite to eat and then get the jump on everybody else and get his books for his classes before practice. This was the first day that the dining halls on campus were open, so Derek chose to get lunch there and check out the food he would be eating for the next semester.

Each complex had its own dining hall. Liberty Dining Hall was right across the street from Garrette Hall, Derek's dorm. He walked into the dining hall, swiped his student ID, and got in line for his food. There was a pretty bland and standard offering today, probably because it was the first day. Derek decided to get some pizza, fries, an apple, and some chocolate milk. After he got his food, he migrated to the dining room and looked for a place to sit. The room was filled with students and parents eating with their kids, before or after they helped their kids get settled, no doubt. Derek spotted Bruce seated by a window table along with a few girls and a couple of members of the football team. He made his way over to them.

"What's going on, Derek?" Bruce asked.

"Nothing. I guess you decided to try out the food too, huh?" Derek responded.

"Yeah, I figured I might as well," Bruce said as Derek sat down with them.

"What's good, CJ, Lamont?" Derek said as he nodded to the football players.

"Just getting something to eat before practice," one of them said.

"I heard that," Derek said as he continued eating his food. "The food's not bad."

"As far as dining halls go, I guess. Nowhere near as good as my mom's cooking," one of the girls said.

"That's not saying much," Bruce joked. The girl playfully slapped him on the shoulder.

"Shut up," she said as they all laughed.

Derek finished his food and began to get up. "All right. I'm about to go get my books," he said.

"Already?" one of the girls asked.

"Yeah. Y'all know the bookstore is gonna be crowded tomorrow. It was nice meeting y'all," he said to the girls. "Bruce, CJ, Lamont, I'll see y'all at practice in a little bit."

"All right," they said in unison. Derek dumped his tray on the conveyor belt, left the dining hall, and went to the bookstore. It wasn't crowded at all, just like Derek hoped. He picked up his books, took them back to his dorm, and went to practice.

After practice, he had dinner and looked for something to do. He noticed that there was a crowd of people at the basketball court that was in the back of Garrette Hall. *Probably a pickup game*, Derek thought to himself. Thinking that he hadn't played ball in a while, Derek decided to go over and see if he could join in.

"Yo, I got next," Derek shouted to no one in particular.

"You can take my spot, actually. I need to go anyway," said one of the guys playing in a current game.

"Cool," Derek said as he took his shirt off to join the skins team in the shirts-versus-skins game. He also took off his chain and the charm that was dangling from it so he wouldn't risk damaging them during the game and placed them in a side pocket of his backpack.

Immediately upon entering the game, his team was put on defense. Looking for someone to guard, he noticed a guy rocking dreadlocks and wearing a sleeveless blue shirt with a matching headband. It was difficult not to notice him, seeing as though he was the tallest guy on the court. He was even a couple of inches taller than Derek. This guy looked like he had some game, and Derek liked a challenge. "I got this guy," said Derek as he went over to guard the guy. The boy just shook his head and smirked.

"Man, that boy's been smoking everybody that guards him all night," said one of his teammates.

"That's 'cuz he ain't guard me yet," said Derek with a bravado that he didn't fully feel. He was supremely confident in his abilities, but he was slightly out of practice and might be a little rusty.

Derek checked him up. As he did that, Derek could have sworn that the temperature slightly increased, but he shook it off. He watched the boy dribble the ball and attempt to cross him up, but Derek didn't fall for it and kept his position. "It ain't gonna be that easy tonight," Derek said to him. The boy just nodded and passed the ball off. Derek proceeded to chase him around the three-point line, but fell slightly behind. He saw the guy begin to move toward the basket so Derek made a sharp cut to the basket to cut him off. Suddenly, he saw the boy call for the ball, catch the pass, and run toward him. Before he reached Derek, he leapt into the air. It was quite a majestic leap. Derek went up to meet him in the air and stop the attempted dunk. Bad idea. *Boom!* Their bodies collided with a force that could be felt by the spectators that were standing all along the court. But as strong as Derek was, he couldn't stop the guy. The boy slammed the ball through the hoop with a thunderous dunk, posterizing Derek. The small crowd assembled around the court went wild.

"What was that you was saying, nigga?" the boy taunted as he headed down the court.

"That's what he been doing to us all night," said one of Derek's teammates as they jogged back down the court to go on offense.

"You know who this guy is?" Derek asked.

"Nah. I don't got no idea," the boy responded.

One of Derek's teammates had the basketball and passed the ball off. Derek received it and immediately wanted to take the guy that posterized him in order to get some payback. The guy ran at him. Again, that feeling of the air temperature rising. It seemed to only happen to Derek when the boy got close to him. Derek did a couple of crossover dribbles and ran around a screen. He had a slightly open shot. Knowing that nobody liked a ball hog and wanting to endear himself to his teammates, he resisted the urge and passed the ball to a seemingly wide-open teammate. *Swat!* The ball went flying off the court as if it had been shot out of a cannon. The guy had come out of nowhere and blocked the pass.

How did he get all the way over there so fast? Derek thought to himself in disbelief and a little awe.

"Get that shit out of here, son," the boy yelled.

"This might be a long night," Derek said to no one in particular.

***

Bruce entered the room on a mission. He walked over to the window and gazed down intently at the scene below him.

Good, he thought to himself. Derek seemed to be fully engrossed in the game taking place on the court. *Hopefully that game'll take a while longer,* he hoped. At least long enough for him to finish what he needed to do. He had to find that book! But even though Derek was currently playing a serious game of basketball, he knew there was no time to waste. Bruce didn't know how long they had been playing. The game could be almost over. Besides, he knew that Derek had the ability to be up there at any minute. He left the window and began to search the room.

First, he looked under Derek's bed. Nothing but Derek's quite extensive sneaker collection. He then searched in Derek's desk. The desk had two drawers along the side and a couple of cabinets at the top. He proceeded to look in each one. In the bottom drawer was a couple of notebooks, pencils, pens, and papers. In the top drawer, Bruce found a few pictures, a yearbook, a box of condoms, and some hip-hop and sports magazines. Bruce quickly migrated to the cabinets up top. In the cabinet on the left was some hair grease, a jar of pomade, a couple of brushes, and a durag. Still no book, though. He looked in the other cabinet but found that one empty.

"Crap," Bruce said, frustration growing. He quickly scanned the room, trying to think of another place where Derek could have hidden the book. He saw Derek's equipment bag and quickly ran over to it. He opened it and ruffled through its contents. Water bottles, mouth guards, athletic tape, Ace bandages, PlayBook, but not the book Bruce was looking for. He went over to the bathroom to see if he put it in there, but it wasn't. Now Bruce was starting to get frantic. The last place to look was the closet. In the closet were an ironing board, iron, and various clothes hanging up. At the bottom of the closet, however, was a large black chest with gold trim.

Bingo, Bruce thought in triumph. He pulled the chest out of the closet. It was a little heavy. Bruce's feeling of triumph was fleeting, though, as his face fell. The chest had a lock on it. He examined the lock. The keyhole was in the shape of a cross.

Wait, Bruce realized. *Wasn't the charm on Derek's chain a cross? That's probably the key.*

Bruce went back over to the window. An even larger crowd had gathered around the court. From his vantage point, Bruce spotted Derek's shirt and backpack lying on the ground on the bench behind the crowd. The chain was probably in the backpack since it wasn't around his neck. Bruce would have to go down there and retrieve it. He quickly left the room, ran down the steps, out of the backdoor and over to the court.

With all these people, he won't notice me, Bruce thought. He quickly, but quietly went over to Bruce's belongings and opened the main compartment on Bruce's backpack. There were a few schoolbooks, but no chain. He closed it and looked in the smaller compartment on the front of the bag. He found the chain lying inside.

It was a pretty large and expensive-looking charm. It barely fit into the palm of his hand. It was a cross made of what looked to be solid 24 karat gold. On each point of the cross was a shiny white diamond. In the middle of the cross was a small lion's head. The chain glistened under the lights that lit up the court. He grabbed it, zipped the bag back up, and went back up to the room. Once he got inside, his phone rang. It was his girlfriend back in Philadelphia.

"Hello?"

"Hey, babe. You got a minute?"

"Um, no, not really. I'm kind of busy."

"Busy doing what," she asked suspiciously.

"Nothing like that, girl."

"Well, Lamont really wants to talk to you." Lamont was Bruce's four-year-old son.

"Okay, put him on." Bruce heard rustling on the other end of the line.

"Hey, Daddy."

"What's going on, little man?"

"I miss you, Daddy."

"I miss you too, buddy, more than you know. You start school tomorrow, right?"

"Yeah."

"Remember what I told you. Be good to the teacher. And don't let nobody punk you, all right?"

"Okay. When I'm seeing you 'gain?"

"Soon okay. I promise. Take care of Mommy. Love you."

"Bye." Bruce hung up the phone and put it back in his pocket. He pulled the trunk back out of the closet and went to place the charm in the keyhole when he heard voices outside the door.

***

Maybe it wasn't so smart to get in this game after practice, Derek thought to himself as he huffed and puffed his way back on defense. The game had gone much like Derek's first few minutes in it. But as much as he tried to not get into a personal battle with his opponent, his competitive instincts dragged him into one as he began to get more into the flow of the game. He began to call for the ball more often as the game wore on, and he began to jack up more shots. On the other end of the court, the dude in the headband showed off more and more of his skills. He unleashed flashy handling of the ball, deceptive no-look passes, and even unfurled a few highlight reel alley-oops. The crowd around the court had grown considerably throughout and was thoroughly enjoying the fast-paced action on the court. The personal battle that unfolded captivated everyone, including the other players on the court. But now, Derek was getting tired.

"Next two shots win," yelled one of the players. This sent a surge of anticipation, like electricity, through the crowd. Derek's dreadlocked nemesis got the ball and drove to the hoop. Derek was too tired to stay in front of him, and the guy slammed it home.

As they ran back down the court, the guy said, "That's one down. Need to get your game up or else we takin' this game." Despite his pride, Derek was also smart. He knew he was too tired to shoot the ball accurately, but because he was a hot shooter, he thought that everybody would key in on him. He ran to a spot behind the three-point line on the left wing and called for the ball. Once it arrived, he faked like he was measuring up a shot. Two guys ran at him in an attempt to contest the shot. That's when Derek made a sharp pass to a cutting teammate, who laid the ball up. He and Derek slapped hands as they went back down the court. "That's how we do it, baby!" Next basket won, and everyone knew it.

The skins team needed a stop. A member of the shirts team walked the ball up the court. Every member of the skins team dug in and guarded their opponent. The ball carrier then drove to the basket. In the lane, his defender stripped him of the ball as he was going up for the lay-in. As the ball was on the ground, Derek's man went over to retrieve it. Derek also ran over to retrieve it. In the ensuing scrum, Derek's man got the ball and kicked it out to a boy who was open on the wing. Derek noticed this and went to block the shot, but he was a step slow and therefore too late. The ball went up into the air, and time seemed to momentarily stand still. *Swish!* Nothing but net, and the crowd went wild. Derek briefly lowered his head in defeat but quickly raised it again and joined his team at half-court to congratulate the winning team.

"Ay yo, good game, dawg," Derek said as he congratulated the guy with whom he just finished waging an entertaining and hard-fought battle with.

"You too. That's the most I had to work in a pickup game in a while," he said.

"You played ball in high school? You too good to just be a pickup player," Derek inquired, impressed.

"Yeah. I'm actually on the varsity team here, too. I'ma be the only freshman starter," the guy said confidently.

"Impressive," said Derek. "A'ight, dawg, I'll catch up with you later," Derek said as he grabbed his shirt, backpack, and headed into the building and up to his room. When he reached his room, a girl sauntered around the corner.

"Well hello there, handsome," she said as she slowly walked up to Derek. Derek discreetly examined the girl. He had to admit, she was good looking. Not really in a sexy way, but more of a beautiful way. She was light skinned and came up to Derek's chin. Derek thought she had a nice-sized chest and a pretty big booty. Her brown hair cascaded down to her shoulders where it coalesced into soft curls.

"What's going on?" He noticed her staring at his shirtless chest. He laughed. "Like what you see?" The girl blushed.

"You know, there is a rule against indecent exposure in the public spaces of the dorm. That includes the hallways, and it also includes shirtless boys. I wouldn't let the RA catch you," she said matter-of-factly.

"Well, I won't tell her if you don't," said Derek.

"Something tells me she already knows," she said as she laughed.

"How? I don't see her, and I didn't pass anybody on the stairs. What, she got a secret spy camera or something?" Derek joked as he looked around.

"No, because she's standing right in front of you. I'm Monica, the fifth-floor RA," she said. She smiled as she extended her hand. Derek shook it, slightly embarrassed.

"Well, this changes things. I'm Derek."

"Nice to meet you, Derek. I'll tell you what. Because it's Move-In Day and we haven't had our floor meeting yet to establish the rules, I'll let you off this time."

"Thank you."

Monica nodded and began to walk away. After a few steps, she turned around and began to slowly walk backward so she could face Derek. "Oh, I didn't answer your question," she said. Derek looked at her quizzically. "I very much enjoyed the view. I do love me some chocolate," she said as she walked off.

Derek smiled and opened the door to his room. "Oh hey, Bruce. I didn't know you was in here," Derek said, a little startled.

Bruce was sprawled out on his bed with his laptop open. "Yeah, man, just chillin'. 'Bout to start my fantasy draft," said Bruce.

"I never really got into fantasy football. I'm more of a fan of fantasy baseball myself. Anyway, I'm 'bout to take a shower," Derek said as he dropped his backpack and shirt off at his closet and went into the bathroom.

Bruce soon heard the sound of the shower come alive and J. Cole's "Power Trip" playing in the background. This gave him the perfect opportunity to slip Derek's chain back into his backpack. So close! He didn't know if or when he was going to have another opportunity to get that book. He hoped this didn't ruin *her* plans too much. He really didn't want to get on her bad side.

Chapter 2

Discovery

"Man, I ain't had waffles in a minute," said Derek as he hungrily eyed the brunch spread. He was one of the first ones in line waiting for the dining hall to open up. The dining halls on campus usually were open from 7:00 a.m.–9:30 a.m. for breakfast, 11:00 a.m.–2:00 p.m. for lunch, and 5:00 p.m.–8:00 p.m. for dinner. On days where there were no classes, mainly weekends and holidays, the dining halls skipped breakfast and served brunch from 10:00 a.m.–2:00 p.m. Derek wasn't used to this. He had to have breakfast. It was a Derek James rule. Needless to say, he was starving.

"My mom makes pancakes and waffles every weekend," one of the guys on Derek's floor said. Derek had met up with a couple of students from his floor at the dining hall when he got in line.

"I'm gon' try this spaghetti," somebody else said.

"Spaghetti? At ten o'clock in the morning?" somebody else asked.

"Why not? It's brunch. That means breakfast *and* lunch. So I'm going to get some spaghetti, some muffins, and some orange juice," she replied.

"See, that's just weird, Turquoise," came the reply.

"Whatever, Porsche. That's your problem: always worried about what somebody else is doing," Turquoise jokingly reprimanded.

"Who you think you talking to? Check yourself, honey, 'cuz I am not the one," said Porsche.

"Are y'all really arguing over some damn breakfast? Y'all are so ratchet," said a boy named Travis.

"It's not breakfast, it's brunch, first of all. Second, who asked you?" asked Porsche.

"Whatever. You know what I meant. Can we just get our food and go sit down?" After the group got their food, they found a table and started to eat.

"Y'all going to the freshman orientation today?" Turquoise asked them.

"There's a freshman orientation?" Travis asked.

"Didn't you read your e-mail?" Turquoise asked.

"Well obviously not. What time is it?"

"Seven," Turquoise replied.

"Isn't it mandatory?" Porsche asked.

"Yeah, but how are they gonna know if you go? It's not like they take attendance or nothing," said Turquoise.

"Wait, don't we have our floor meeting tonight? I thought I saw that on the board in the hallway," asked Derek.

"That's after the orientation," said Turquoise.

"Well, I don't have nothing better to do. I might as well go," said Travis.

"Well, since we got practice 'til five, I guess I'll head to dinner after practice then go to the orientation before the floor meeting. I guess our day is now fully booked," said Derek to Travis.

"Well, ours is too," said Porsche. "We still have to register for courses."

Derek said, "I'm glad I already registered or else this day would've been too much."

"What classes did you register for?" asked Turquoise.

"English 100, FYE, Spanish II, and Pre-Calc," answered Derek.

"What's your major?" asked Travis.

"I have the feeling that I'm gonna get the question a lot," Derek said, shaking his head. "I haven't declared a major yet. I'm undecided. What about you?"

"Business administration," Travis said. Derek nodded.

"I'm thinking about majoring in psychology. You should take Psyc 101," said Porsche.

"Maybe next semester," said Derek.

Travis pulled out his cell phone and checked the time. "I'm about to head out and get my books for class tomorrow. All right, boss, I'll see you at practice," Travis said.

Porsche and Turquoise watched Travis put his tray away and exit the building. "I should go too," Porsche said as she followed Travis out the door.

That left Derek and Turquoise. A comfortable silence descended on the two as they continued to eat. Derek decided the break this silence. "So, Turquoise, where you from?"

Turquoise responded, "Call me Turk. And I'm from here in Delaware."

"Me too. What school did you go to?"

"Howard."

"Really? I went to AI," Derek said.

"Oh okay," she said. "What did you do this summer before coming here? Anything interesting?"

"Nah, not really. Went to the beach for a few days with some of my friends. You?"

"I went to the Made in America Festival in Philly," Turquoise said.

"I really wanted to go to that! How did you like it?"

"Oh, it was crazy! I mainly went for my girl Beyoncé. She did her thing as usual."

"Yeah, she's a great performer. I like her too," Derek agreed. He and Turquoise finished the last of their food and prepared to leave. "So what you got planned for the rest of the day?" Derek asked as they put their trays on the conveyor.

"I'm going to register for my classes and then go visit some of my friends in Smith Hall." They walked out of the door. It creaked shut behind them. "Okay, let me go. See you later, Derek," Turquoise said as she ambled toward the dorm.

Derek started to walk to the bus stop, but turned to look back at Turquoise walking away. *Something tells me she's going to be . . . interesting,* Derek thought to himself.

***

Knock! Knock! Knock! Bruce went over to open up the door. Once he saw who was on the other side, he got *really* nervous. "Angela! What are you doing here? I thought you were giving a speech at the orientation tonight? Shouldn't you be preparing for that?" he asked.

"Don't play dumb. You know exactly why I'm here." Mayor Wright walked in the dorm room. "So? Where is it?"

"Where's what?" Bruce asked, trying his best to be evasive.

"Don't make me slap you. Now where is the book?"

"Um, he didn't bring it here," Bruce lied, hoping she would fall for it.

She gave him a look. "Why do you lie to me when you know I can tell when you're doing it? Haven't you learned anything over the past ten years?" She shook her head. "You know I can read you like an open book and yet you still test me. And time and time again, you fail." She walked over to Derek's closet and pulled out his chest. "So the book's in here."

"Yeah, but see that lock? Derek has the key around his neck."

"And that's a problem?"

"Well, he never takes it off! He wears it in the shower, at football practice, when he sleeps. What did you want me to do? Rip it off his neck?"

"And yet you had it yesterday." This time, it was Bruce's turn to give her a look.

"I really wish you'd stop doing that," he said.

"Who cares what you wish? Why didn't you open the chest?"

"He was about to walk in on me! You know how fast he can be. I'm lucky he didn't look in his bag before I had a chance to put the chain back in. My cover would have been blown!"

"I'm going to blow you, literally, if you don't get me that book," Mayor Wright warned.

"Why do you want that book so much all of a sudden, anyway?" Bruce asked.

"It holds information that may be important to me. That's all you need to know for now."

"Can't you just, you know, open the damn thing?"

"If it was that simple, I wouldn't need you, now, would I? This chest is protected. Even I can't break through it."

"Well, you know where the key is. Just go take it from him. I'm sure you're stronger than he is," Bruce suggested.

Mayor Wright sighed in exasperation. "Probably. But that would definitely alert him to my intentions, and I don't want to reveal myself to him. At least not until if and when it's necessary. Keep trying. And don't get caught. Just because you're my cousin doesn't mean I will tolerate failure. And you know the type of things I can do to people who fail me." A look of abject terror crossed Bruce's face. With that, Mayor Wright took one last glance at Derek's chest, turned, and walked out of the room.

***

Derek joined the rest of the freshman class as the throngs of students filed into Word University's basketball arena, Jake Turner Arena. At the entrance, every student was given a drawstring bag filled with educational trinkets. Groups of upperclassmen were stationed in the lobby and around the building to direct and assist the students.

"Everybody, make your way to conference rooms J-A, J-B, and J-C down the hall! There, you'll find an activity fair. Around seven thirty, begin making your way to the court for a few remarks!" the helpers yelled above the din of noise the rowdy freshmen were producing. They repeated these directions to each successive group of new students that entered the building.

Derek made his way to room J-B and walked around the activity fair. It was a festive atmosphere with upbeat music playing in the background. There were representatives for every varsity and club sport, fraternity and sorority, and extracurricular activity on campus. There was nothing there that really piqued his interest. He wasn't interested in joining a fraternity, and he was already on the football team. He figured that would monopolize much of his free time anyway. When the time came to go to the court, Derek found a seat up in the stands and waited for the proceedings to begin. Soon enough, a man whom Derek realized was the provost took the stage.

"Welcome, class of 2017. I am John Jackson, provost of this university. I want to personally welcome you to Word University. You are a part of the chosen few who were selected to attend this prestigious university. Word University is the oldest historically black college or university in the United States. It was founded by Joseph P. Word, a Quaker that was dedicated to the education of free African-descended youth. It started out as a one-room building and, over the years, has expanded to the sprawling campus that you now live on. Some of the most famous and distinguished individuals in the history of this country attended college here. We here at Word U remain dedicated to educating the next generation of scholars and continuing that legacy. We receive thousands of applications from high school seniors every year. Out of the thousands of those applicants, you were chosen for your academics, athletics, drive, determination, and dedication. You are about to embark on a journey that will have a profound impact on the rest of your lives.

"During these next four years, you will go about the process of discovering yourselves and setting yourselves up for future success. If you haven't already, you will find out what you are best at and hone your interests. Even if you currently have a good idea about those things, they may change as you begin to experience life as young adults and start to find your way in this world. Get involved. Take advantage of everything that this school has to offer. We have varsity and sports clubs for those that love athletics. Our Greek life is robust and filled with chapters of historic fraternities and sororities. We have a music studio and throw concerts for those students that are musically inclined. We have multiple research labs for those that want to conduct experiments and research. We offer opportunities to study abroad if you want to see the world. We frequently host world-renowned scholars, authors, musicians, politicians, and athletes. This is just a taste of all the opportunities that await you here.

"If you have questions, there are people that are readily willing and able to help. If you ever feel overwhelmed academically, we have tutors and academic enrichment centers on campus to help you. We have counseling services for those that have any personal issues that they may need help with. We are a family here at Word U and are all happy to accept you guys in. As the tapestry that is your life unfurls here at Word U, we ask that you act with honesty, decency, integrity, and respect. Keep in mind that you are a representative of your family, your school, and your community. Do nothing to tarnish the names and reputations of those entities. The faculty here at Word U is excited to get to meet all of you and look forward to interacting with you for the duration of your stay here."

After a light applause from the crowd, the provost sat down and another man walked up to the podium. "I'm Darrell Hicks, dean of the College of Arts and Sciences, and like Provost Jackson said, I very much look forward to meeting all of you who chose majors in the college. Let's keep this thing moving so you can get to your dorm meetings, shall we. Before we leave, we will have a few brief remarks from Ms. Angela Wright, mayor of Pottington."

As the mayor made her way to the podium, Derek happened to glance down at his shirt. *What?* he thought, surprised. The diamonds on his charm, usually white, had turned as black as onyx. The mayor began to talk to the crowd of freshmen, but Derek was barely paying attention as he looked around at the students around him.

"Hello, new students of Word University. It brings me great joy to look out into this crowd and see all of the young faces embarking on their collegiate journey. Provost Jackson told you about the rich history of Word U and the legacy that it has. This university is the pride and joy of this city and this state. The luminaries that have emerged from this school throughout its history have all made major impacts on their communities. This school and its students have an impeccable reputation in this state and nationwide. It is a beacon of optimism and a source of overwhelming pride in the black community. It is one of the most competitive and rigorous schools in the country and the crown jewel of the network of HBCUs. You are the role models that we look to for guidance and to set a good example for the rest of the kids in this city, state, and country. To show them that an education is the most important thing they can acquire to better their lives and the lives of others in their community. Many of you will follow in the footsteps of those that came before you and do great, world-changing things. Some of you already have extraordinary . . . *talents.*"

At that moment, Derek could have sworn she was looking directly at him. "Use these talents to make the world a better place. As mayor of Pottington, I welcome you to our city and I wish you luck in all of your future endeavors."

After some more light applause, the dean returned to the podium. "Okay, that concludes the orientation. As you guys leave, the shuttles are outside waiting to take you to your dorms. Your building meetings will take place as you all arrive. I hope you guys enjoy your first day of classes tomorrow, and good luck this semester." With that, everyone started to filter out of the arena. When Derek got outside, he whipped out his cell phone and called home.

"Hello?"

"Hey, Dad."

"What's going on?"

"This might be a stupid question, but was you at Word U just now?"

"No. Why?"

"I didn't think so. I was at my freshman orientation, and the diamonds on my charm turned black."

Silence.

"You know what this means, right?" Derek said, excitedly.

"Derek," his dad warned.

"Other than us, I ain't never met another one," Derek said.

"You can't just go being all nosy. They may not want to be found."

"It's not like I'm gonna go all detective. I'll just keep an eye out," Derek said.

"Be careful. You don't want to expose yourself to somebody unless you absolutely sure," his dad said.

"It's not like I haven't told anybody before."

"Yes, but those were your friends. This is different. You don't even know this person."

"Dad, I promise I'll be careful, okay?"

"All right. Bye."

He hung up. Derek looked at his charm. It was white for the time being. Derek got on the shuttle that was going to the Liberty complex. When he got to his dorm, he went up to the common room on the fifth floor and waited for the meeting to begin with the rest of his dorm mates. He was shocked to see that his charm was black again. The person that he was looking for was right there on his floor, right there in the room! He scanned the room. There were about thirty people in the room.

I wonder who it is. Just as he began to speculate, Monica walked in.

"Okay, let's get started. My name is Monica. I'm going to be your resident adviser for this year. I'm a sophomore, so I'm only one year removed from being in your shoes. As I'm sure all of you know by now, this is an athletic dorm so all of you play a sport. I'll spend the first half of this meeting explaining the rules and expectations of the dorm. At the end, we'll do a little icebreaker so we can begin to get to know each other.

"First, I'll start with safety. There are four fire alarms on each floor—one in the common room, one at each end of the hallway, and one in the middle. I shouldn't have to say this, but do not pull the fire alarm unless there is an actual fire. Each alarm has a substance on it that leaves a residue so if it's a false alarm, the firemen can check. We've had some problems in the past with false alarms. There will be fire drills throughout the year. I always know the day that we will have them, but never the exact time. They could be during the middle of the day, in the morning, or at like 3:00 a.m. when you're sleep. If the fire alarm rings, you are to calmly make your way down the steps and go to the basketball court behind the building until we get the okay to go back inside. Okay?

"Now, more info about me. As your RA, it's my job to make sure things go smoothly in the dorm. If you guys ever have any questions or issues, you can always come to my room and ask. For the most part, if I'm in there, it will be open. If the door is closed, it means I'm either sleeping, downstairs in the office, or not here. There's a corkboard right outside my room that will serve as a bulletin board for the floor. So if there are any announcements, opportunities that I think you guys need to know about, anything like that, it will be up there. I will be holding a monthly meeting, and I will post that on the corkboard a week or two before it's scheduled. I really want to support you guys, so if you have any games, let me know because I would like to attend if I can and I also want to put it on the board so any of the people on the floor can come if they want to. I think that goes a long way to fostering a family atmosphere here. Let's make this floor as social as it can be. Any questions so far?" Everybody shook their heads. Monica looked down at a sheet she brought in.

"Um, let's see here. Okay, rules and regulations. This is a substance-free dorm. Seeing as we are all under twenty-one, there is no alcohol allowed in the dorm and there are to be no illegal drugs under any circumstances. Now, we're not going to just do random raids of rooms or anything like that. If you give us reasonable suspicion, then we are allowed to inspect your dorm. That means if, like, someone tells me you've got something or I smell it coming from your dorm or something like that. I have to tell you that if we find contraband in your room, both people will get written up and have to appear in infractions court.

"There is no curfew for the dorm, but we do observe courtesy hours and quiet hours. Courtesy hours are in effect at all times. All that means is that you can't play really loud music, don't yell in the hallways, things like that. Quiet hours are in effect from 11:00 p.m. to 8:00 a.m. That means that one of the RAs in the building will conduct rounds throughout the building at eleven o'clock and make sure that all the doors are closed and no one is hanging out in the hallways. During those hours, you have to either be in one of the common rooms, in a room, or going in or out the building."

"Can we get written up if we not?" one of the students asked.

"Good question. As a general policy, we don't unless you are a constant offender. But mostly, if we see your door open, we'll just ask you to close it, or if we see you just hanging out in the hallway, we'll remind you it's quiet hours and ask that you go to where you need to go. If we can hear your music or TV through the door, we'll knock and ask that you turn it down. Look, we don't want to write you guys up. It's just a courtesy to people who may be trying to study or trying to sleep and get ready for the next day.

"In the building, of course, there's no smoking. We also have a rule against indecent exposure. I already had to talk to somebody about this." She smiled as she looked in Derek's direction. Derek just laughed. "We never have a problem with girls breaking this rule, just guys for some reason. Look, I know that you guys live here and we want you to treat this like it's your home. How many of you guys walk around your house at times in only your boxers or at least without a shirt on?" Comically, every guy raised their hand. "I thought so. When you are not in your room, everyone has to have on a shirt of some sort and pants of some sort. Even if it's just a wife-beater and shorts, that's okay."

Someone asked, "What if we coming from practice or from balling outside or something?"

Monica answered, "Well, we're not going to be Nazis about it or anything. If that's the case, just make your way to your room as quickly as possible. That's all. Another good question."

Monica again looked down at her paper. She said to herself, "Okay, I talked about safety, illegal substances, quiet and courtesy hours, indecent exposure . . . All right, that looks like that's everything for now. If there are no more questions, we can move to our icebreaker. We'll go around the room and have everybody tell the room your name, where you're from, and what sport you play. Also, I want everybody to come up and get a piece of paper from this bowl. On each piece is a question or statement that you have to answer. So everybody come up and get a piece of paper."

Once everybody was done, Monica started. "Okay, I'll go first. My name is Monica. I'm from Cleveland. I play volleyball, and my favorite movie is *Dreamgirls*. Now we'll start over here . . ."

A couple of people went before it was Bruce's turn. "My name is Bruce. I'm from Philly. I play football and I don't have any siblings, but I do have a four-year-old son."

A couple of other people went. "My name is Turquoise, but you can call me Turk. I'm from Delaware. I play volleyball, and I like to go to the beach."

After her came Porsche. "Hello, my name is Porsche. I'm from New Jersey. I run track, and I my favorite team is the Eagles."

After her, a couple of more girls went, then Travis. "What's up, y'all. My name's Travis. I'm from Detroit. I play football, and my favorite food is fried chicken."

Two more people went before it was Derek's turn. "My name is Derek. I'm from Pottington. I play football, and I have a dog named Dodger."

The last person to go was the guy who almost decapitated Derek with the football the day before. "Hi. My name is Matthias. I'm from Pottington. I play tennis, and my favorite artist is Usher."

At that time, Monica announced, "Okay, well, that's all I got. You guys are free to stay here and continue to mingle or you can go off and do whatever. I hope all of you had an okay time registering for classes today." The group began to disperse.

When Matthias left the room along with a couple of other people, Derek's charm turned white again. It had to be one of them! But which one? His dad's warning rang in his head. He couldn't risk revealing himself to the wrong person or the results could be disastrous. He had to be careful, and he didn't want to just individually walk up to each of the people that walked out and hope that his charm told him who he was looking for. Derek racked his brain for a plan.

Let's see. My charm turned black at the orientation, so the person was sitting around me both here and there. Which one of those people was sitting near me in the arena! Think! He tried to remember the faces of those sitting around him a couple of hours ago. Wasn't the guy he just learned was Matthias sitting a couple of rows down from him? It was hard to tell because he wasn't really paying attention and didn't get a good look, obviously. It was little to go on, but it was his only lead.

***

There was something empowering about this rather routine activity. Derek was walking with a mass of students to the main campus, where the majority of the classrooms were located. It was the first day of classes of his freshman year, and Derek was actually pretty excited. He wasn't exactly like the stereotypical football player. He wasn't just some jock who was all brawn with little brains. Derek prided himself on being a good student as well as a good athlete. He enjoyed school and the acquisition of knowledge. Growing up, his parents instilled in him not just the importance of an education, but a love of it. As a proud black man, it thrilled him to look around at the large group of students that surrounded him and see a sea of different shades of browns and blacks. Since the school week started on a Tuesday this week, Derek was on his way to Spanish class. On Mondays and Wednesdays, he had Pre-Calc in the mornings. He had Spanish and English on Tuesday and Thursday mornings. His one-credit FYE class was on Fridays. It was a pretty favorable schedule.

Derek reached his classroom and sat at a table in the front of the class. Derek liked Spanish. By the time it was time for the class to start, there were about fifteen students in the course. "Good morning, class. My name is Señorita Pierce and welcome to Spanish 2. Just to let you know, because this is Spanish 2, this class is usually Spanish-speaking only. This means that from the time class starts to the time class is over for that day, I will be conversing solely in Spanish, and I expect you to attempt to do the same. If you are confused about something I just said, I will help you. Being that this is the first day, I will be talking in English today. Just know that this is the last day that I will be speaking in English during the two hours we have class every day. Now, here is a syllabus for the semester . . ." The rest of the class was simply an introduction to the course and a review of basic concepts learned in high school just as a refresher. After class was over, Derek had an hour before his next class. He saw Turquoise walking across the street.

"Hey, Turk, hold on!" he yelled as he ran to catch up to her.

Turquoise turned around to see where the source of the request was located. "Hey. What's going on, Derek?" she asked.

"I just got outta Spanish. I got English in about forty-five minutes," he responded. Derek walked with her for a couple of minutes. "Where you going?" Derek asked.

"On my way to my first class," she answered.

"What class is it?" Derek curiously inquired.

"Psyc 100," she said.

"I'm thinking about taking that class next semester. Tell me how it is," he said.

"All right. See you later," Turquoise said as she quickly walked off to find her next class.

Derek looked at the time on his cell phone. *I might as well go to class a little early today.* When he got to the room his next class was in, he was a little surprised when he found out he wasn't going to be alone. It was not just because he was fifteen minutes early, but because of who was in the room when he got there. She looked just as equally surprised when he walked in.

"Well, you're here early," she said.

"That's a pot calling the kettle black if I ever heard one," Derek quipped. "No pun intended," he said as he laughed at the unintended racial humor.

"I was hoping the professor would be here before class started. Oh well." She sighed. "So why are you here so early?"

"Had nothing better to do," he said nonchalantly. "I'm not looking forward to this class, though. I hate English."

"Why? I kind of like reading and writing."

"Oh, it ain't reading and writing that I hate. I love to read. I like language in general. I like Spanish for some reason. It's English that I hate. That's probably why I butcher it at times. It's my subconscious protest against the language," Derek surmised. The girl giggled.

"Oh my gosh, that's so funny. I'm Kelsey, by the way," she said as she formally introduced herself.

"Derek."

"Where are you from, Derek?"

"Here. You?"

"DC." Derek looked at her hesitantly.

"What?"

"Can I ask you a question?"

"What?"

"Not that it means anything, I'm just curious, but why you did you decide to come to Word U? I mean, it's a historically black university and you're white."

"Well, I used to live in the suburbs before I moved to the city after elementary school. I was in the public school district, so both my middle and high schools were mostly black. I have enough experience being around black people to know that people are just people. I didn't just see this school as a black school, but also a good school. This is one of the best schools in the country. It's crazy hard to get into. Besides all of that, I think it's good for a person in the majority to experience life as a minority. It lends perspective and empathy."

"Did you put that on your admissions essay?" Derek joked. Kelsey laughed.

"Maybe." They both shared a hearty laugh.

"I can respect that. You a football fan?" Derek asked.

"No, not really. I can watch it though. I know what's going on during the games," Kelsey responded.

"You should come to my game this weekend. It's our first game of the season," Derek offered.

"You're on the football team?"

"Yeah. I'm a wide receiver. So, you gonna come?"

"You're not inviting me on a date or anything, are you?" she jokingly asked.

"While I do find you cute, no I'm not. Just as a friend. You seem like you really cool."

"Well, in that case, I'll think about it," Kelsey said, somewhat noncommittal.

"Well, all right then," Derek said, pleased with himself, as the rest of the class started filing into the room. Derek hated English, but maybe having Kelsey there would make the class a bit more bearable.

After the class, Derek decided to take the elevator to descend the five floors needed to reach the ground floor of the building. He was alone as he entered the elevator. On the fourth floor, the elevator stopped and opened to let a passenger on. "Hi. Derek, right?" Matthias asked as he boarded the elevator.

"Yeah. Comin' from class?" Derek asked.

"Sure am. Look, I'm sorry again for what happened the other day. Are we cool?"

"Yeah don't worry about it," Derek answered.

"Wow! What kind of chain is that? How does it change colors like that?" Matthias asked curiously.

Derek furrowed his brow. "What?" Derek looked down at his charm, and sure enough, it was black. "Oh snap, it is you!" Derek exclaimed.

"Who's me?" Matthias asked.

"The diamonds only turn black when I'm around another warlock!" Derek said excitedly. At Derek's mention of the word *warlock*, a strange look came over Matthias's face. The elevator reached the ground floor, and Matthias walked out of it. Derek quickly trailed him.

"Warlock? What are you talking about?" Matthias asked.

Derek said, "They turned black yesterday at the orientation and did it again at the floor meeting. I thought it was you, but I couldn't be sure . . ."

"Be sure of what exactly?" Matthias asked agitatedly.

"That you're a warlock!" Derek said. Derek could have sworn that there was a slight hitch in Matthias's gait as he said that, but it was fleeting.

"I'm a warlock? Do you know how stupid you sound right now?" Matthias asked as they crossed the street.

A sobering thought suddenly crossed Derek's mind. *What if he don't know that he a warlock yet?* Was that even possible at his age?

"Come on, you don't gotta front with me 'cuz I have powers too and—" Matthias turned around and cut him off.

"Look. I don't know if I'm being punk'd or if you're recording this and going to post it on YouTube or something, but all I know is that you sound like you have a few screws loose. Don't come at me talking about warlocks and powers and whatever else. Now, excuse me, I have a class to get to," Matthias said dismissively as he quickly retreated into the crowd of students.

Derek allowed a frustrated sigh to escape from his lips. *Great. Now he probably thinks I'm certifiably insane.* Derek slightly shook his head, looked around to see if anybody was paying attention to the conversation that just transpired between them. Derek had just taken a huge risk and could only hope that it didn't come back to bite him.

With those thoughts swimming around his head, Derek headed off to lunch.

***

"Slow down and run that by me one more time, Bruce."

"I just ran into Derek talking to some guy on our floor. Matthias, I think his name is," Bruce replied into the phone's receiver. He was on his way to class when he saw Derek chasing after Matthias and Matthias looked none too happy. Something told him that they were talking about something important so he quickly ducked around the corner and carefully eavesdropped on their conversation, hoping to get any information he could about that book. What he heard was potentially more important.

"And this is important because? Are you going to call me after every move he makes? You should be focused on finding a way to get that book. Besides, I'm the mayor. I'm too busy to talk to you every five minutes. If you haven't found a way to get that book, then—"

"But this might be about the book. Or at least could be even bigger."

The mayor was intrigued. "What did they say?"

"Well, I don't know exactly, but—"

"*WHAT? You interrupted my conference call to supposedly tell me something important but don't even know what was said?*" Mayor Wright bellowed over the phone.

"I was standing around the corner, give me a break. I said I didn't know *exactly*, but I did hear some stuff. Something about warlocks and powers. And Matthias looked and sounded pretty mad, and he stormed off."

"And you're sure you didn't hear much else?"

"You're the one who reminded me that I can't lie to you." The other side of the line went silent for a few moments. "Hello?"

"Yes, I'm still here, Bruce. I'm just thinking, is all."

"What do you think this means?"

"Well, if this means what I think it means, it simply complicates what I have to do. Nothing more and nothing less."

"Which is?"

"Boy, didn't I tell you it's none of your concern? I have to get back to this conference call. Keep me posted. And keep working on that book."

"Okay, but what should I do if—" Bruce abruptly heard the line go dead. "Did she just hang up on me? All this better be for a good reason," he said to himself as he walked off.

***

Derek was glad he came home to an empty room. This whole day was frustrating. At practice, he learned that the game plan the coach was putting in place for their game against the University of Delaware, one of their rivals, called for him to be the number 3 receiver. He knew he was a freshman, but Derek had never been that low of an option before. When he asked coach about it, he said that he had to "earn his playing time." But how could he do that if he wasn't given a fair chance? In his mind, Derek had outperformed the two starters at his position in practice. It was so unfair! On top of that, he was pretty sure that he had freaked Matthias out earlier that day. But his charm told him Matthias was indeed a warlock. Had it been wrong? His dad told him that it was foolproof. Was he mistaken? Was it possible that Matthias didn't even know he was a warlock? And if he didn't, that meant that Derek just outed himself to a stranger. The whole thing didn't make any sense. "Aargh!" Derek yelled as he threw himself on his bed. Just then, he heard a knock on the door. "Who is it?" he yelled.

"It's Matt," the voice said.

"Who?"

"I said it's Matt. Matthias," the voice said. Derek quickly rose from his bed. He didn't think he'd be hearing from Matthias anytime soon. He went over and opened up the door.

"Can I come in?" he hurriedly asked.

"Yeah, sure," Derek said as he stepped aside to let Matt come in. "Listen, if I freaked you out today, I'm sorry. That wasn't my intention. I guess my imagination can get out of control sometimes," Derek said.

Matt nodded. "Do you mind locking the door?" he asked. This confused Derek.

"Ooooookay," he said as he went to lock the door. "So what's up?"

"All that stuff you were talking about earlier. Did you really believe what you were saying?"

Derek looked Matthias in the eye, saw something, and said, "Yeah."

"You said I was a . . . warlock and said you had powers. You have to know that sounds ridiculous."

"Yeah, I guess it does." Derek thought Matthias looked as if he was struggling internally with something. It showed all over his face.

"Theoretically speaking, if you did have these powers, could you show them to me?" Matt suddenly asked.

Derek just looked at him. It was at this point that he made a decision. He was about to pass the point of no return. "I do have powers. I can prove it to you if you want."

"Let's see it then." Matthias didn't really know what to expect. Suddenly, he felt the air ripple in front of him. He heard a faint sound of sucking wind, like air filling a void in space, as Derek disappeared in front of him in the blink of an eye. "Oh my god," Matthias said, stunned.

"Behind you," Matthias heard from behind him. He whipped his head around to find Derek there, and the space where he previously occupied was completely empty. "So you were telling the truth." Derek nodded. "You really are a warlock, just like me."

"So you are a warlock," Derek confirmed.

"Yeah. But you just ambushed me with all this talk about magic, and it kind of put me on the defensive."

"My bad," Derek said as he chuckled a little. "So do you have any powers?"

"Sure do. Watch." Matthias rubbed his hands together and slowly spread them apart as a string of electricity crackled between them. It seemed to snake along his wrists before it began to dance along and in between his fingertips. Derek stood there, transfixed. "It's called electrokinesis. I can generate and control electricity. I assume your power is teleportation."

Derek nodded. "Well, that, and I am a limited telepath. Very limited as a matter of fact."

"Two powers. What does that make you, a level 4?" Derek nodded. "Impressive," Matthias said. "So how did you know I was a warlock again?"

"My cross. The diamonds on my amulet turn from white to black when I'm in the presence of another warlock. My dad gave it to me when I was younger. It's been in my family for generations. One of my ancestors made it," Derek explained.

Matthias walked over to get a closer look at the amulet dangling from Derek's neck. "This thing must cost a fortune. This is legit gold and diamonds."

"Nope, it's priceless. I would never in a million years even entertain the thought of sellin' this thing," Derek said.

"Now that I'm concentrating on it, I can feel the mystical energies emanating from it. It's really powerful," Matthias said.

"Family legend says that it's imbued with the magic of our entire line and because of it, it's never wrong. That's why I was so sure you was a warlock."

"I wish I had something like that. I can think of a couple of times where it would have come in handy," Matthias admired. Derek thought of something at that precise moment.

"Wait here. I want to show you something." Matthias saw him go over to a closet a pull out a chest. He used his cross to unlock the chest and pulled out a black and gold book.

"Is that . . . ?"

"Yup," Derek said as he made his way over to his desk and set the book on it. Matthias joined him. "This is my family's grimoire."

Chapter 3

Companion

These past few weeks were some of the most fun Derek had in a while. The football team was off to a 3–0 start. Despite not starting any of the games, Derek was emerging as a big play threat in the early going, catching ten passes for 170 yards and four TDs. His classes were going relatively well considering it was his first semester of college. They were much more difficult than high school, but nothing he couldn't handle. Even his least favorite subject, English, was going well enough. He suspected that had something to do with Kelsey's presence. He had to admit that he was spending more time with her than he initially anticipated, particularly away from class. She had indeed attended his game. She even surprised him by showing up at his second home game this past week. He told her that he was not interested in her romantically, but that wasn't entirely true. He thought she was cute. She was smart and chill. But Derek had never really had a girlfriend before, so he didn't really know how to be a boyfriend. Sure he had plenty of girls he fooled around with in the past, but none more than a few weeks. Truth be told, Derek couldn't imagine being in a monogamous long-term relationship. It was for this reason that he never foresaw himself getting married. The thought of being tethered to one girl for that long unsettled him. Even the very thought gave him a slight shiver. Kelsey was nice. Derek thought it would be in both of their best interests to just remain friends, at least for a while.

By far, the most fun Derek had, though, was hanging out with Matthias. Up until now, Derek had never met a warlock outside of his own family. It was nice to share his magic with somebody else for a change, somebody his own age. It was also nice to have someone that could fully relate to him as a young black warlock. After Derek showed him his grimoire, Matthias showed him his. It was a little different, though. Matthias had found a way to upload a digital replica to his tablet. The original was kept at his house. It was ingenious, really. He even found a way to upload the covers, which were dark green with an elephant's head in the middle of the front cover.

As he found out, magic was just one thing that they had in common, however. They had similar tastes in music—Matthias was more of an R&B guy than Derek—and both liked to learn. They weren't completely alike. For one, Matthias had a girlfriend. He also was somehow a Dallas Cowboys fan. As a self-respecting and proud Philadelphia Eagles fan, Derek found it in his heart to forgive him for what could only be described as a severe lack of judgment in a person that seems to rarely have such a thing.

Right now, though, Derek was in the library trying to complete his paper for English that was due the next day. Why did he wait so long to do it? The due date just kind of crept up on him. It had taken him about an hour, but he was already halfway through the five-page paper. Just then, he spotted Bernard walking into the library.

"Yo, Bernard!" Derek yelled.

"Shhhh!" the librarian scolded him.

"Sorry," Derek said sheepishly. Derek got up and went over to his friend.

"What're you doing here, Derek?" Bernard asked.

"Trying to finish this paper I got due tomorrow. I figured I might as well come to the library since I don't have a printer," said Derek. "You have a paper due too?"

Bernard said, "No, I work here. Work-study program."

"Oh okay," said Derek. Just then, a beautiful girl walked into the library and right past the boys. "Yo, do you see that?" Derek asked.

"What, you mean the chick with the big-ass booty that just walked by? Nah, I didn't notice," Bernard said sarcastically.

"I dare you to go holla at her," Derek said.

"You think I won't?"

"Nope."

Bernard felt challenged. "Okay. Not only will I holler at her, I bet you I can pull her number."

"Now this I gotta see," Derek said.

"Watch and learn."

Derek watched Bernard walk over to the girl and start to talk to her, but they were too far away for him to make out what they were saying. After a brief back and forth, the girl laughed at Bernard and walked away shaking her head. Bernard walked back over to Derek in defeat.

"Smooth," Derek said as he chuckled.

"Shut up and get back to your paper!" Bernard said as he walked away. Just as he was doing that, Derek got a phone call.

***

"Rhonda, I really should be studying," said Matthias, exasperated. He had his first test of the year the next day, and instead of doing some last-minute studying, he was at a bowling alley.

"Oh please, I bet you know that material inside and out. How often have you studied for that test by now?" Rhonda asked as she gave him a knowing look.

"That's not the point," Matt retorted back.

"That's exactly the point. You can only study so much. It's like I told you back at Glasgow—sometimes you just have to trust your knowledge and preparation. You listened to me, and you were valedictorian."

Matt shot back, "But this isn't high school. I just don't want to be wasting precious time."

"And spending time with your girlfriend on her birthday is wasting time?" Rhonda asked as she rolled the bowling ball down the alley. The ball knocked down seven pins. "Yes!"

"That's not what I meant," Matthias said as Rhonda knocked down the final three pins to complete the spare. "I just really want to ace this test," he said as he got up to take his turn.

"You will. Stop worrying so much. Now concentrate on the game. You're losing," Rhonda said as she gave Matt a loving slap on the butt as they crossed paths on her way back to her seat.

"Girl, there is no way I'm losing this game." They had split the first two games, so this game determined the winner. *Buzz!* Rhonda casually looked at Matt's cell phone as it vibrated, indicating that he had just received a text message.

"Matt, you just got a text from some guy named Derek," Rhonda said just after Matt got a strike. She handed him his cell phone and proceeded to take her turn.

"Thanks, babe." He opened the message.

Derek: You @ da dorm?

Matt: No Im @ da bowlin alley wit my girl. Y?

Derek: I jus got a call from one of my boys. I mite need ur help wit sumthn asap. Hit me up as soon as you done

Matt: Cool

Matthias wondered what that was all about. He knew it was hard to tell on a text, but it sounded slightly urgent. "Matt. Matt are you listening? It's your turn," Rhonda said. Matt got up to finish the game, but Rhonda got the feeling that from the moment Matthias got that text message, his mind was somewhere else.

After dropping off Rhonda at her dorm after their time at the bowling alley, Matthias made his way back to Garrette Hall. Once he parked, he sent a message to Derek.

Matt: I'm here

Derek: Come up to the lounge. Nobodys in here rite now

Matthias made his way up to the lounge. Sure enough, Derek was in there alone, but he had his grimoire, which surprised Derek. "So what's going on? What did you need me for?" Matthias asked.

"I got a call earlier from one of my boys. He told me about a problem he been havin'. Apparently, he been hearing sounds in the walls and finding holes in stuff all over his house. At first, it was like once every couple of days, but now it's like every day," Derek explained.

"Sounds like he has an infestation of rats."

"That's what he thought, especially when he saw a rat scurrying across the floor one day. So he called an exterminator."

"Okay, so what's the problem?" Matthias asked.

"When the exterminator came, he said he didn't find any rats. He didn't see anything."

"So they left on their own?"

"Nope. If anything, it got even worse. It's to the point where he can't get no sleep," Derek said, shaking his head.

"So why is he calling you? You aren't an exterminator. And why did you bring your grimoire?" Matthias asked, confused.

"A couple of my close friends know that I'm a warlock. He's one of them. He said—"

Matthias interrupted him. "Wait, you told mortals that you're a warlock?" Matthias asked incredulously.

"Well, my boys, yeah. I didn't want to hide nothin'. You mean you ain't tell nobody other than your family?" asked Derek, surprised.

Matthias responded, "No, not a soul. It was always stressed to me not to, that keeping my secret was of the utmost importance. Not even Rhonda knows. How did they respond when you told them? I'm curious."

"Of course, they was freaked out at first, but it ain't last long. Like I said, we boys. Soon enough, they thought it was cool and it allowed me to be myself around them, my entire self. Sure, they don't fully understand since they not magical, but it's all cool," Derek said.

Matthias nodded. "So what were you saying?"

"Yeah, so like I was saying, he decided to call me when he saw one of those critters scurrying across the floor then just seem to vanish into thin air," Derek explained.

"Oh. Well, that certainly doesn't sound normal."

"No, it don't, do it? But when he told me about all this, I thought I remembered something like this in my grimoire. Sure enough . . ." Derek passed his grimoire, lying on the table and open to a specific page, over to Matthias for him to read.

Rykiens

These small ratlike creatures are pests that tend to live in the walls of houses, barns, etc. They are known to be quite noisy and feed on substances that are commonly found around the house such as fabric, wood, metal, leather, and of course, food. Rykiens especially love dog food. While they are not particularly deadly to humans, they multiply extremely quickly. Therefore, it's best to get rid of one as soon as you see it in order to prevent the infestation from getting out of hand.

"I see. But what did you need me for?"
"Keep reading," instructed Derek.

It can be difficult to kill these creatures, as they have the ability to turn invisible. They might be somewhat sensitive to electricity, though, as they have been known to be highly visible when lightning lights up the sky during thunderstorms. The only way to kill them is with a wand, crafted from the twig of a sycamore tree and activated with the incantation, "Richanus dustructe coy portatum." Once the wand is activated, point it at a rykien and say, "Creatis dustructe."

"So that's it," Matthias said as clarity dawned on him.

"I already made the wand before you got here, but I can't kill what I can't see. I figured we could stop by my house and pick up some dog food to lure them out, you could use your powers so I could see them, then I can kill them."

"I'm going to assume we're going to take my car?" He already knew the answer to the question before he asked.

"Seeing as I don't have a car and I can't teleport us both to his house, yeah."

"So not only did you need my powers, you needed my ride." Derek looked a little embarrassed. "Ah, so now I get to the heart of the matter."

"I wouldn't ask if I didn't need you. He really needs those little bastards taken care of."

"I have a test tomorrow. I already had to take my girl bowling. Now you want me to go out to some dude's house somewhere to help you kill a bunch of invisible rats?"

"It's only nine thirty. By the time we swing by my crib, get to my boy's house, and kill those suckers, you'll be back no later than like midnight. That'll give you a few hours to get some late-night cramming in."

Matthias sighed. "Fine. The quicker we go, the faster I can finally prepare for my test."

After the boys stopped by Derek's house, they made their way to the house of Derek's friend. "You didn't say your friend lived in Riverdale," said Matthias. Riverdale was one of the shadier neighborhoods of the city. It was infamous for its open-air drug market.

"Technically, he doesn't live in Riverdale, he lives near it," Derek retorted.

"Close enough. Is my car going to be safe?"

"Of course. Ain't you been to the hood before?"

"No. Never had a reason to come over here."

"Well, I been here plenty of times. Devon lives just outside Riverdale, and my barber actually lives in Riverdale on Spruce Street. My dad's car ain't been jacked yet."

"Let's just get this over with as soon as possible," Matthias worried as they got out of the car and made their way up the steps. Derek rapped on the door, and a dark, rotund teen opened the door.

"Derek! What's going on, my nigga," the boy said as he greeted Derek with an elaborate handshake.

"Nothin', Devon. Just came to take care of your little pest problem. Anything new?"

"Nah, they just starting to make those sounds again," Devon complained.

"Well, we'll take care of them." It was then that Devon seemed to register Matthias's presence for the first time.

"Who's this?" he asked.

"Oh, this is Matt. He gonna help me get rid of those things. Devon, we got some dog food in the car. Can you go get it while me and him go check out and see what's going on?"

"Dog food? What the fuck?" Devon wondered.

"It's a long story."

"As long as it helps get those things out my house, I don't care."

Devon went out to the car as Derek and Matthias went inside. When they took a look around, they were slightly shocked. There were holes in all the furniture. The rykiens had really done a number on Devon's house. "What's that sound?" Matt whispered. There was a sound coming from the walls that sounded like a bunch of nails tapping on a chalkboard. The sound seemed to be coming from all around them.

"See what I mean? You try sleeping through that," Devon said, walking in with the dog food. "Okay, let's dump some dog food in each corner of the room. Matt, you know what to do." As soon as they were done setting up the bait, they moved to the middle of the room, and Matthias sent out gentle waves of electrical currents throughout the room.

"How you doing that? You a warlock too?" Devon asked Matt.

"Yeah."

Derek scanned the room for any sign of life. Soon enough, he could make out the faint brown silhouettes of a bunch of what appeared to be giant rats huddled around each of the bait stations. "There's got to be at least thirty of them things. Well, here goes nothing." He took out the wand and pointed it at one of the feeding rykiens.

"Creatis dustructe!" Almost immediately, the thing let out a mangled "Scriiiiiii!" as it burst into blue flames. This seemed to alert the rest of the creatures as they immediately began to scatter across the floor in utter chaos! They even began to scale the walls.

"This is so nasty!" Devon yelled. Derek wildly flung the wand around trying to kill as many rykiens as he could. Just then, Matthias felt something big and furry jump onto his back and start to creep into his shirt.

"Ahh!" he yelled as he began to fumble with his shirt, trying to get the creature out. This temporarily stopped the electrical current around the room, and the remaining creatures began to disappear.

"I can't see them no more!" Derek yelled.

"Help get this thing off me!" Matthias ordered as Devon went to go help him. He got the rykien off Matthias, and Derek killed it.

Matthias went back to sending a current through the room. Derek only saw two left. He killed one, and just as he was about to kill the last one, he felt a bite on his ankle. "Ow! Damn thing bit me!" The rykien grabbed the wand in its mouth when it fell out of Derek's hand and began to head for a hole in the wall.

"We can't let it get away," Matthias said.

Derek quickly said, "Matt, stop so I can get it." As soon as Matthias stopped using his power, Derek teleported in front of the hole just before the critter got there. He grabbed the wand from its mouth and destroyed it.

"Wasn't there one more?" Devon asked. Derek teleported back to Matthias, and Devon and Matthias used his power to uncloak the last remaining rykien. Derek vanquished it as it let loose one last mangled scream and disappeared in a plume of blue smoke. The three of them took a deep sigh of relief.

"See, that wasn't so bad," said Derek. Matthias gave him a dirty look.

Devon thanked Derek and Matthias for getting rid of the rykiens, and they made their way back to campus. On the ride back, Derek examined the bite mark he had on his lower leg. It was bleeding and was starting to itch.

"It did say that those things wasn't harmful to people, right?" Derek asked, concerned.

"I think so, yeah. Why? What's wrong?"

Derek said, "'Cuz this bite is bleeding kind of bad, and it reeeally itches."

Matthias took a quick glance down at Derek's leg. "Ew. That looks kind of nasty. I got a spell that might fix that," Matthias offered.

"Cool, 'cuz I don't think it would be a good idea to go to student health. I want to go as a last resort." They parked in the parking lot adjacent to the dorm and walked up to the building. As they walked into the building, they bumped into Travis.

He asked, "Hey! What's going on, you two? Where y'all coming from?"

They looked at each other, trying to think of a good explanation. "Uuuum," started Matthias.

Derek decided to settle on a version of the truth. "We just came from my friend's house. He wanted to show me something, and Matt came along to see what he was talking about."

"Oh okay. What was it?" asked Travis, intrigued.

"What was it?" Matthias repeated, trying to think of something. He looked at Derek in uncertainty.

"It was some funny-looking rat he found in his house. Thing was nasty looking," Derek answered.

It was at that time that Travis noticed the bite mark on Derek's leg. "What happened to you?" Travis asked, pointing at Derek's leg.

At this point, the wound was not only bleeding, but also beginning to emit yellowish pus.

"Yeah. I got too close to the thing and it bit me."

Travis had a look of concern on his face and said, "That thing might have had rabies or something. You should go to Student Health. They open 24-7."

Derek replied, "Nah, I'll be all right. Put a Band-Aid on it upstairs. Well, we'll catch you later." Matthias and Derek rushed past Travis and up the stairs.

When Derek and Matthias arrived at Matthias's room, his roommate was watching television. Matthias went over and retrieved his grimoire tablet from the drawer. He scrolled through a couple of pages before landing on a healing charm.

"My mom used this on me a couple of years ago. All we need is some water," he said. He pulled a bottle of water from his minifridge. He went with Derek into the bathroom. Derek sat down on the toilet and held his leg over the shower. Matthias began to pour the water over Derek's wound while he chanted, "Rigomortis inglotum." As the water cascaded down Derek's leg, the blood and pus began to wash away and subside. The wound started to stitch itself back together as if it were a loom made of skin. In the matter of about a minute, Derek's leg was as good as new.

"Wow, it don't even itch no more!" said Derek.

"My mom created this spell when we went hiking. I fell over a tree stump and tore up my arm pretty good. There was a creek nearby, so she put a charm on some water to heal my arm and added the spell to our grimoire."

Derek asked, "Have you made up any spells of your own yet?"

"No, it takes a lot of experience to make your own spells. If you don't do them right, they can easily backfire on you. No, I just stick to spells that I know have worked before," Matthias explained.

"Yeah, me neither. I see a few things my dad added to our grimoire, though. If you don't mind, I think I'm gonna add this charm to my grimoire. The book said rykiens wasn't harmful to humans, but I'm finna change that entry. That bite was plenty harmful," Derek said.

"Go ahead. Knock yourself out."

"All right, cool. Thanks again for helping me out with that. Stay breezy," Derek said as he walked out the bathroom.

***

"Let's go, Wildcats!" yelled Anton. A couple of people from Matthias's physics class decided to attend the football game against Penn State together. Even though Matthias wasn't a huge fan of college football, he decided to tag along. Normally, he wouldn't be all that interested in the game, but having a friend on the team gave the game intrigue. Besides, it wasn't often that schools like Word U played big-time programs like Penn State. Despite the tough times that Penn State was going through with the NCAA sanctions, it was still quite exciting. There was 2:03 left until halftime, and Word U was trailing 16–14, but they had the ball on their own 34-yard line.

Matthias looked to see if Derek was on the field, but he was standing on the sideline. Matthias followed the team enough to know that Derek was having a pretty good start to the season. Up until this point though, he was having a quiet game with only one catch for just seven measly yards. On first down, the quarterback completed a pass to the tight end in the middle of the field for ten yards and a first down at the 44-yard line. They decided to save the one timeout they had left by going to a hurry-up offense. With 1:40 left on the clock, they handed the ball off to the running back for a 2-yard loss.

"Why would you run the ball in a two-minute drill?" cried Anton in frustration. Anton, Matthias's lab partner, was a fervent football fan. With the clock still running, the quarterback snapped the ball and was immediately chased by defenders. "Throw the ball!" yelled Anton. After a lengthy scramble, the quarterback was sacked at the 35-yard line for a 7-yard loss on second down. The crowd noise dropped precipitously in disappointment. Now third and nineteen with thirty-seven seconds left, Matthias noticed that Derek was running onto the field. "Let's go, Derek!"

With 25 seconds left, the quarterback snapped the ball and made his reads. Just before the rush got there, he fired the ball deep down the seam to Derek. Despite being double covered, Derek leapt high in the air over both defenders and made a spectacular highlight reel catch at the 25-yard line. The crowd went wild. Word U used their final timeout to set up a 42-yard field goal attempt. It was good, and the Wildcats went into halftime leading 17–16.

At halftime, very few people left their seats. Like many HBCUs, the band's halftime performance was the show within the show. Word U had one of the best bands in the area. The crowd stood at their seats in great anticipation, waiting for the band to take the field. After a couple of minutes, the band arrived on the field to great applause. They knew what the crowd wanted and were more than happy to give it to them. The band ran through a medley of current popular hit songs and had the crowd eating out of the palm of their hands by the time the ten minutes allotted for halftime were up.

Both teams came out at halftime firing on all cylinders. It was a back-and-forth game. Matthias was emotionally spent from all the lead changes and momentum swings. Every time one team seemed as if they had snatched momentum, it slipped through their fingers like water and flowed to the other team. Following his catch at the end of the half, Derek was having an even bigger second half. It was as if the coaching staff woke up and realized it might be best to give their best playmaker the ball. In the second half, Derek had six catches for 120 yards and two touchdowns, giving him eight catches for 167 yards total. Now, with five minutes remaining in the game, the Wildcats trailed 37–31 but had the ball. Starting their drive on their own 20-yard line, they began to march down the field. The crowd was getting into a frenzy, anticipating a late game comeback. On third down, from midfield, Derek got behind the safety and was streaking toward the end zone. The quarterback saw this and heaved the ball down the sideline. The crowd stood on its feet. That was it! That was going to give them the lead! As the ball was in the air, Matthias thought the trajectory was a little too long, but hoped that Derek could catch up. His hopes went unrealized as Derek dove for the ball, but it tantalizingly landed just past his reach. So close! Matthias and the crowd let out a collective groan.

With 2:48 left in the game, it was fourth down. The crowd wanted them to go for the conversion, but with all three of their timeouts left, the coach decided to punt the ball off and gave Penn State the ball on their own twenty. They started their drive with a long run up to the 39-yard line. They would advance no further, but Word U was forced to use all of their timeouts to preserve as much clock as possible. However, the long run had allowed Penn State to flip field position. With less than two minutes left and no timeouts, they would have to drive the length of the field and score a touchdown. The crowd was growing restless. They needed a miracle.

"Is that Derek?" Matthias asked out loud. Sure enough, Derek trotted out to return the punt. This was the first time Derek would return a punt all season. When the punt came down, Derek dropped the ball! He recovered it, but by this time, there were defenders all around him. In an amazing display of improvisation, he made a couple of defenders miss initially and then streaked up the sideline. He cut toward the middle of the field to elude one tackler and saw that there were blockers out in front.

"Go! Go! Go!" yelled Anton in excitement.

"He's got it! We're going to win the football game!" Matthias said as he hugged one of his classmates. Derek followed his blockers all the way to the end zone as the spectators were delirious. It was 38–37 Wildcats with a just a little over a minute left in the game.

On the ensuing kickoff, the return man got the ball out all the way to the 49-yard line. The kicker made the game-saving shoestring tackle. The stadium all of a sudden got much quieter. A couple of completions put the ball on the 15-yard line with seven seconds to go. There was enough time to attempt a game-winning 31-yard field goal—a chip shot. At this point, the stadium was deathly silent, all the euphoria of the punt return touchdown erased. Matthias couldn't watch. As Penn State lined up for the field goal, he literally covered his eyes. Then Matthias heard a huge raucous roar erupt from the crowd.

"What happened?" he asked.

Anton was jumping for joy. "They blocked the kick! They blocked the kick! It's over!" he yelled. Matthias looked at the scoreboard in disbelief: 38–37 Word U.

In the locker room after the game, it was a madhouse. Players were hugging each other, high-fiving, dancing, and some even just sat in disbelief at what they just accomplished. After a while, Coach Steve came in to address the team.

"All right, all right, settle down for a minute, men. Now that was a good hard-fought win out there. I was proud of the way that each and every one of you fought and persevered through adversity. This is just a taste of what this team is capable of when we practice hard, play with passion and poise, and execute together as a team. Now you guys know that I'm not one to usually assign game balls because I believe that every win is about the team and not an individual. Today, I'm making an exception. Derek James, where are you?" Amid whoops and hollers, Derek made his way to the center of the room.

"Today, Mr. James epitomized what this team is all about. Despite not being a starter, he practices and prepares as if he is one so he is prepared whenever his number is called. When things got tough today, he made plays to give us the spark we needed. When he was asked to return a punt at a crucial spot in the game, something he had never done before, he accepted the assignment without complaint. He did it with enthusiasm, and his return turned out to be the winning points. For that," he said as he held up the football, "Derek James." He handed the football to Derek and left the room as his teammates congratulated Derek.

Dion, one of the juniors and captains of the team, spoke up. "Everybody, party at my place to celebrate! Derek, you definitely better be there, rook!"

After he got dressed, Derek emerged from the celebratory locker room to find Kelsey waiting for him. "Kelsey! What are you doing here?"

"I just wanted to catch you before you got too busy celebrating and stuff. Good game today," Kelsey said.

Derek replied, "Why, thank you. What you doing tonight?"

"I have a test on Monday so I think I'm going to study for that."

"We having a party to celebrate the W. You should come."

"I don't know. I think I should probably get ready for this test," she said.

"Oh come on! You can at least stop by for a few minutes to help me celebrate. You got all day tomorrow to study. What do you say?"

Kelsey relented. "Well, I guess I could drop by for just a few minutes."

Derek smiled. "Good. His house is on Pennsylvania Avenue. Text me when you get there." As Kelsey walked away, Derek saw Matthias walk by with a crowd of people. "Matt!" Matthias heard Derek calling him and went over.

"What's up? Good game by the way. That punt return was clutch!" Matthias said as he congratulated Derek.

"Thanks. Hey, what you doing tonight? Got anything planned?"

"No. Rhonda's going out with her girls so I'm free. Why?"

"One of the captains is throwing a party. You should come on over, come chill with us."

"Isn't it just for the football team?" Matthias asked.

"It's supposed to be a small get-together, but you with me. They'll let you in."

"Well, I could use a little down time from all the studying. And that rykien problem you dragged me into," Matthias said as he gave Derek a look and rolled his eyes. "Okay. I'll be there."

***

Kelsey walked up to the house. It looked like it was packed! Definitely more people than she was expecting. She sent Derek a text message: "I'm outside."

He responded, "Okay come to da door. I'll get 'em to let u in." Kelsey went up to the doorman.

"Can I help you?" he asked.

"Oh, I'm just waiting on Derek," she said. She heard a voice come from behind the doorman.

"That's okay, Russell, she with me." The guy stepped aside and let her in. Derek was standing there waiting. "Glad you could make it, Kels."

Kelsey said, "I only just stopped by for about a half hour. Then I really have to go." She had to lean in and speak up to be heard over the blaring music.

"That's fine." He led her through the house. "Want something to drink? We got beer, vodka, fruit punch, Pepsi, lemonade . . ."

"Um, I guess I'll take a fruit punch," she said.

"Spiked?" he slyly asked.

"If you do that, I will kill you. I will hunt you down and I will kill you," Kelsey said, laughing.

Derek laughed. "All right, I'll be right back. Make yourself comfortable," he said as he disappeared into the crowd. He came back a few minutes later with her drink. Kelsey smelled it before she drank it. "What, you don't trust me?" Derek asked incredulously.

Giggling, she said, "Just making sure." After sometime talking to Derek and meeting some of the players on the team, Kelsey looked at her watch. "Okay, I really should get going. This test is going to kick my ass if I don't study for it."

Derek walked her to the door. "Okay, well thanks for coming out. I'll see you in class on Tuesday."

As Kelsey disappeared around the corner, Derek saw Matthias approaching from the opposite direction. Matthias walked up the steps and met Derek on the porch. Derek put his arm around Matthias and said jubilantly, "What's up, dawg! Come on in!"

They pushed through the crowd. "I thought you said it was a 'little get-together'?" Matthias asked as he bumped into somebody.

"Yeah, it was supposed to be, but I guess it got out of hand," Derek said casually. "You got here just in time. We about to start up a game of Smash. You want in?"

This piqued Matthias's interest. "Y'all don't want any of this. I will kill somebody in *Super Smash Bros.*," he boasted.

Dion happened to be walking by on his way to the basement, where the game was going to be played, and overheard this. "Nigga, you must be crazy. Ask anybody here. I am by far the best Smash player in this house."

Derek begged to differ. "Stop lying, I just beat you the other day," he said.

"That was pure luck. Won't happen again," countered Dion.

Derek said, "Well, let's go then."

The three went downstairs and joined a couple of other guys and got engrossed in the game. Matthias more than held his own over the course of the game's duration. Eventually, the players started trickling back up to the party until just Matthias and Derek remained.

"One last game between just us?" Matthias challenged.

"I accept your challenge!"

After Matthias won the game, Derek said, "When you first got here, I noticed this girl in a pink dress standing off to the side, checking you out."

"You saw that? I thought I was the only one who noticed."

"She might still be here. Why don't you go find here and talk to her?"

"You know I have a girlfriend, right?"

"So? Don't mean you can't talk her. It's not like I said go bone her or something. You ain't have nothing to drink so you know you can trust yourself."

"That's because I don't drink."

"Yeah, I feel you. I don't really drink either. At least not after my dad told me a story about the time he got drunk and telekinetically lifted a couple of shot glasses, trying to impress some chick he liked. He had to erase her memory. I like being in control of myself. Don't want something like that to happen to me. Besides, I like to partake in *other* substances, if you know what I'm saying."

Matthias got a puzzled look on his face. "Like?" Derek pulled a small, clear plastic bag out of his pocket. In the bag were a couple of joints. "You smoke weed?"

"Don't act so surprised. Smoking weed is a lot less harmful than cigarettes. And it's better to smoke weed than drink alcohol. You don't lose that feeling of control, and I ain't never heard of nobody dying from weed poisoning or being an angry pothead. We just chill, relax." Upon seeing Matthias's slightly skeptical look, Derek asked, "You ain't never smoked before, have you?"

"No. I don't like weed."

"I didn't think so. You look like a choir boy, literally. How do you know if you like it or not if you ain't never tried it?" Derek questioned.

"Okay, I don't *want* to like weed. I'm surprised you get away with it. Don't they test for it? You can get suspended."

"Man, coach don't care about weed. As long as it don't interfere with your ability to play well, he looks the other way. Plenty of people on the team smoke. It's not even really a secret at this point. Even the team captains do weed. Didn't you notice those bongs upstairs?" Derek put one of the joints in his mouth, pulled out a lighter, lit up, and took a drag. He looked at Matthias and offered him one of his joints.

"Nah, I'm good."

"Just to let you know, I'm just gonna keep pestering you until you smoke with me at least once. I will make it my mission to get you to try weed," Derek said jokingly.

"So you want to turn me into a drug addict? Some influence you are." Matthias laughed.

"It ain't even like that. That's the good part. Weed's not addictive. Ain't you even a little curious? Don't you at least want to try it once, even if it's just to know for sure that you don't like it?"

Matthias gave in. "If I smoke this one time, does that mean you will leave me alone? You won't ask me again?"

"I promise."

"Fine. Hand me one." Derek gave him a joint, and Matthias started to smoke it. After a few puffs, a thought flashed through Matthias's head. "You sure the owner of the house is okay with this?"

"Yeah. He smokes too, so it's cool."

After a few more minutes of idle chitchat, Derek and Matthias finished their joints. "Want to go back upstairs to the party?" Derek asked.

Matthias checked the time. "No, it's eleven thirty. I already stayed here a little longer than I thought I was going to. It's about time for me to head out." They both rose from the couch. "Are you going to come back to the dorm?"

"Since I spent so much time down here, I think I'ma spend a little more time upstairs. This party was partially for me, after all. I'll head out a little later." They made their way up the steps and to the front door. "So how was your first time getting high?" Derek asked.

"Not bad, I suppose."

"Wasn't what you was expecting, was it?"

"Eh."

"So, do you like it?" Derek coaxed.

"I don't dislike it. It's not something I would be opposed to doing again on a special occasion. As a regular thing though, I think I'll pass."

"I can respect that. Take it easy on your way back to Garrette. Your eyes are kinda glazed over. I would just go straight to your room, being in your state."

"Will do. Check you later."

Chapter 4

Diamond

Matthias loved this time of the year. He looked forward to early October every year. The weather was beginning to change, but wasn't too cold just yet, making it really comfortable. The leaves were beginning to change, bathing the area in a stark and brilliant burst of seasonal oranges, browns, and reds. Football season was in full swing, and the baseball playoffs were starting. This year was particularly exciting for Matthias because his favorite team, the Los Angeles Dodgers, were in the postseason tournament. Most of all, he always began his training for the upcoming spring tennis season.

Matthias fell in love with tennis when he was about seven years old. On a day trip to New York, his dad took him to the US Open, and he watched Venus and Serena Williams play in the finals. He decided to try it himself and loved it. Even as a youngster, he was very aware of the difference that existed between him and many of his fellow players. He didn't care that as a black boy, he was often the only player of color in a tournament. He looked toward Venus and especially Serena for inspiration. If two girls from Compton, California, could not just play but also dominate a predominantly white sport, why couldn't he?

Ever since he started playing tennis when he was little, his dad was his coach and hitting partner. Matthias had mixed feelings about his father. Obviously, he knew his dad loved him more than life itself. But Matthias found it extremely hard, if not nearly impossible to please the man. It seemed like anytime Matthias accomplished something, his dad was never satisfied. He was a taskmaster. He was hard on Matthias. He demanded nothing but excellence. If Matthias earned even one B in a class, he was on punishment. This extended to the tennis court. Matthias had to be the best. If he missed one shot, he had to hit a bunch more of those shots. If he lost a match, he had to do extra practice. Matthias figured that all this was probably related to the fact that he was his father's only child, his only son. It didn't make it any easier, though.

As his coach, his dad started off every preseason with endurance and strength training to get him in shape. They did that for about a month. Then they moved on to the actual hitting, which lasted for another month. They then took time off for the holidays, with Matthias doing just light maintenance work. January was about playing competitive games against his dad. His dad was always his toughest opponent. He never went easy on him, even when he was a little boy. His dad kept himself in excellent shape, and just after the New Year, he always beat Matthias like a drum. As he got older, Matthias became more competitive in their matches in the latter half of January. He even remembered the first time he actually beat his dad when he was fourteen. The feeling was indescribable. He even detected a hint of pride on his father's face at the time. This led to invitation tournaments around the country in February to kick off his regular season, playing the high school season from March to May, and then a few more invitation tournaments in June before his season ended.

Once he got in college, Matthias thought of parting ways with his dad as his coach and hitting partner, but ultimately decided against it. As tough as he was, under his tutelage, Matthias won the state championship in singles play all four years he was in high school. He consistently went deep in every tournament he entered, winning extremely often. He owed much of his success to his father's training methods and wanted to continue that in college. There was a brief discussion of Matthias perhaps going pro, but it went nowhere. His father was big on getting an education first and foremost. Besides that, Matthias liked tennis, but not enough for it to be his life. The NCAA had a fall tennis season, but Matthias and his dad decided against playing it his freshman year. They weren't properly prepared for it, and Matthias wanted to get acclimated to the jump in competition before participating in elite invitation tournaments.

As a player, Matthias featured a powerful forehand and a versatile one-handed backhand that he could slice or flatten. Most players nowadays used the two-handed backhand. This gave Matthias an advantage because he featured a shot that many players hadn't played against before, and it almost always threw his opponents for a loop. His slice allowed him to stay in points and gave him time to use his speed to recover, making him a capable defender. His best shot, though, was his forehand. He could use that shot to pound winners from any spot on the court, including behind the baseline. He excelled at transitioning from defense to offense, often getting his opponent off balance using a slice backhand, then unleashing his forehand or flat backhand for a clean winner. Most tournaments were on hard courts, but his best surface was grass. It was difficult to find grass courts in the United States, though. His toughest surface remained clay. It neutralized some of his power, and his speed worked against him at times because he still hadn't gotten fully comfortable sliding on the dirt.

Today, Matthias was meeting his dad at the practice field. He had three miles to run to start his training. He didn't know why his dad insisted on being there with him. He didn't need him to run his miles. If he was worried about times, he could always time himself and report those to him. He was in college now. He thought it was time for his father to realize that and loosen the reins a little. When he arrived at the track, his dad was already waiting in the middle of the field.

"Hello, son," his dad, Isaac, said.

"Hey, Dad," Matthias replied. He gave him a nice, firm handshake in greeting.

"How have you been? Your mother and I haven't heard from you since you started school," Isaac asked.

"You know me. I've been so busy with papers and tests and stuff."

"How's Rhonda? Are y'all good?" Isaac asked.

"Yep, everything's fine on that front. Went bowling for her birthday. Had fun with that."

"Well, anything interesting happen so far?"

"Very interesting. There's another warlock that lives on my floor."

"Really? How do you know?"

"Actually, he approached me. He has an amulet that detects witches and warlocks."

"So you've met him," Isaac said.

Matthias started to stretch. "Yeah. Dude's pretty cool. He's a level 4 warlock with the powers of teleportation and telepathy."

Isaac whistled. "That's impressive."

"I know. It's nice to have somebody my age that I can share my magic with. You know, he showed me his grimoire. It has rituals in there from Africa, from before his family came over here in the slave ships. They have to be hundreds of years old. And they seem complex and unlike any spells I've ever seen before. But they're written in some weird language that neither of us understands. It's quite fascinating, really," Matthias said in wonder.

"Sounds like this guy's family is pretty powerful."

"Yeah." Matthias finished stretching. "Okay, I'm done, coach. What did you have planned for today?"

"Twenty laps."

"Twenty laps? But that's five miles," Matthias protested.

"I understand that. I can count, Matt, thank you."

"But I thought I was going to run three miles. I always start off with three miles."

"That was before you got to college. You're older now, and the competition is tougher. We have to up your training to compete." Matthias dropped his head and began his laps.

***

Mayor Wright walked into Derek's room in triumph. It took her a while, but she finally found what she needed to get Derek's book. The Key of Tutbar was the answer to her little dilemma. The chest that housed the book was locked, and only one key in the world opened it, the one around Derek's neck, which he never let off his person. At least, that was what she thought. However, there were two keys that could open that chest. The Key of Tutbar was a universal key that was guaranteed to open any lock, mystical or otherwise. It had taken a week's sojourn through the Nile valley, but she had found it. It was currently 4:00 p.m. Derek would be at football practice, making this the perfect opportunity to steal the book. She didn't want to get directly involved yet if she could avoid it, but she didn't trust Bruce with the Key. It was an ancient priceless mystical object. It would fetch a pretty penny on the black market.

Mayor Wright walked over to Derek's closet. The chest was in the exact same place it was in last time. She knelt down and placed the Key on the lock. She listened as the Key briefly glowed red before she heard a satisfying *Click!*

Bingo, she thought as she twisted the built-in lock and opened the chest. Her target was sitting right there, surrounded by herbs and other trinkets that she could only guess were Derek's spell ingredients. She went to pick it up, but was stopped by some unseen force just a couple of inches from the book. "That's funny," she quietly said to herself. She tried again, but the same thing happened. "What's going on?" There seemed to be some invisible force field that was preventing her from touching the book. She used her telekinesis to help her try to break through the force field, but to no avail. Try as she might, she couldn't touch it.

"Damn it," she said in frustration. Just then, she heard the toilet flush in the bathroom. *Somebody's here.* She quickly shut the chest as she heard the bathroom door open up across the room.

"What are you doing?" Derek asked when he came out of the bathroom.

"Uuuh," said Mayor Wright.

"Bruce, what you doin' in my closet?" he asked suspiciously.

"I can't find my . . . brush. I thought I might have put it in your closet by mistake," Mayor Wright said, quickly thinking of an alibi.

"Okay. Was it in there?"

"No. Guess I gotta keep looking."

"Oh. Hope you find it." A thought then occurred to Derek. "Wait, why ain't you at practice?"

Mayor Wright desperately racked her brain for a suitable excuse. "My group for my class project was meeting at three thirty so Coach Steve gave me the day off."

"I didn't even know you had a class project."

"Yup. Well, I gotta go," Mayor Wright said as she hastily made her exit from the room.

Once she was outside the door, she began to walk down the hallway, thinking to herself. She wasn't expecting Derek to be there. It was a good thing she cast that masking hex on herself before she came to the dorm. It didn't actually physically change her appearance; it only made people see someone else when they looked at her.

So the book protects itself. She had to admit, it was ingenious. It also took an advanced level of knowledge and magic to pull something like that off. Certainly more than Derek possessed, she was sure. In any case, the grimoire was a lost cause. She would just have to make do without it.

***

"Okay, are you sure he would like this?" Kelsey asked, unconvinced. Her dad's birthday was Sunday, and she had to get him a gift. She was going to be going back to Washington DC on Saturday, so it was the last real chance she would have to get him something nice since it was already Friday. She decided to go to the mall but wasn't sure what to get a man, even if it was her dad, so she asked Derek to tag along and give her his input and opinion as a man. Since Saturday was the last home game they would have for a while before they came back off the road for homecoming, he should have been back at the dorm getting his rest, but he didn't want to leave Kelsey high and dry.

"You said he liked cologne, right?" he asked.

"I said he was shopping for colognes the last time I was home," she replied.

"Well, this cologne smells nice. You should get it," Derek suggested.

"Okay, if you say so," she said.

After paying for the cologne, Kelsey and Derek walked out the store and headed for the food court to get something to eat. After getting their food, they sat down and started to eat. Once he saw what Kelsey had to eat, Derek remarked, "Ew. You like Arby's?"

"What? Arby's is soooo good," she said.

"No, it's not. Besides, how are you gonna come to the mall and not eat Sukihana?"

"I'm not a huge fan of Chinese and Japanese food."

"You would like this though. Wanna try some of mine?" Derek asked.

"No, I'm okay."

Derek shrugged his shoulders. "Suit yourself."

"Derek, is that you?" somebody said from behind Derek's back.

"I think someone is calling you," Kelsey said. Derek turned around and saw Devon walking toward them.

"What you doin' here, Devon?" Derek asked.

"I was at Gamestop." He looked at Kelsey. "Sorry for interrupting your date. My bad," Devon said.

Derek was quick to say, "It's not a date. We just friends. She in my English class."

Kelsey said, "I assume you're Derek's friend."

"I'm Devon," he said as he introduced himself.

"Kelsey."

"Nice to meet you, Kelsey. Why don't you give me your number and let me call you sometime?"

"Well damn!" Derek said.

"Well, you said y'all just friends so I ain't cockblocking or nothing," Devon said, defending himself.

"If I was trying to holler at her, you certainly ain't helping!" Derek said.

Kelsey laughed at their bickering. "That's okay." She turned to Devon. "I don't think that would be a good idea."

"Eh, I tried," Devon said, hesitating before continuing. "It's 'cuz I'm black, ain't it?" Derek sighed loudly and covered his face with his hand in embarrassment.

Kelsey giggled. "You caught me. I just don't find you very attractive because you're black. Maybe if you were Derek's shade, you'd have a chance," she said, a smile growing on her face as she said it.

Devon shook his head in mock disappointment while saying, "The light-skin dudes always get the girls."

Derek looked at his arm and said, "I'm not even light skin."

"You light skin compared to me," Devon said.

"You got a point. You make a chalkboard look pale."

"Man, shut up with ya crusty hairline. You need to go to the barbershop and get all them naps cut off. I got Brillo pads that look softer than that shit," Devon taunted.

Derek swept his hand through his hair, which hadn't been cut since he started school. By this point, it was a few inches long and, Derek had to admit, slightly unruly. "A'ight, I'll give you that one. I do need a fresh cut."

"The shop only got two barbers right now."

"What? Why?"

"Because Gus in jail right now, Fred tore his Achilles playing ball, and Cedric in Florida for the next two weeks. I got Cedric to give me a cut before he left," Devon said.

"What's Gus in jail for?" Derek asked.

"You know the drama Gus got with his girl. She found out he was cheating on her so she slashed his tires. He went upside her head, and she called the cops on him. He couldn't afford the bail, so he in jail until the court date," Devon explained.

Derek just shook his head. "So it's only Lamar and Rich?"

"Yup."

"I'll hit Lamar up then."

"Let me go before I miss my bus. It was nice meeting you, Kelsey."

"Nice meeting you too. See ya."

"See you, D." Devon walked off.

"He's certainly . . . interesting," Kelsey said.

"That's a nice word for it," he said. They shared a laugh as they finished eating their food.

On his way back to the dorm after he and Kelsey parted ways, Derek passed by Matthias talking on his cell phone. "How much? . . . That's too much. Why? I've been coming there for a couple years, can't you make an exception? . . . Well, I'm not paying that much. You're good, but not $25 good.. . . That's not good enough! . . . Sure. Whatever, bye." Matthias ended the call and grumbled in frustration.

"Everything okay?" Derek asked.

"That was my barbershop. I called to make an appointment, and they told me they raised their rates to $25 per cut. I asked why and they said because they've had less people coming in the past few months. I asked them to make an exception for me since I've been going there for a few years and they said no. Then they said what they would do for me was give me my next cut at current price before raising rates for me," Matthias explained in anger.

"Why don't you just go to a different barbershop?" Derek asked.

"Because I really like this one. I just don't want to pay $25, but I might have to," Matthias said.

"Why don't you come with me to my barbershop? I'm going in for a cut on Sunday," Derek offered.

"I don't know. I'm really finicky about who I let touch my hair," Matthias said.

"They do a good job on me. Besides, I only pay $10 for my cut even though he charges $15 normally. That's a lot less than $25."

Matthias said, "Really, $15? Right now, I pay $20. I just might have to take you up on that offer."

"Okay. I'm leaving here at three o'clock on Sunday," Derek said.

***

She wasn't looking forward to this little meeting. Mayor Wright had failed in her attempt to secure Derek's grimoire and knew that she would have to answer for it. At that precise moment, the two senators strode into her office without warning.

"Gentlemen! What an unwelcome surprise."

"How are things going?" one of the senators asked.

"Well, we're making progress. With a few more tweaks, I believe that the city's budget will—" she started.

"We don't care about your pathetic city's economic troubles, witch! What of the task you have been assigned?"

Angela closed her eyes and braced herself for the inevitable reprimand before slowly beginning, "I haven't exactly—"

"So you have not completed it? What have you been doing for all these weeks?" one of the senators asked.

"My plan was to acquire the boy's grimoire, but I was unable to."

"Why is his family's book of magic so important?" the other senator asked.

"I felt that it might contain some information that would make my task a little more . . . discreet," she said.

"Being discreet shouldn't be your focus, but to simply get it done."

"In any case, I was unable to secure the book. It has a protection on it that even I was unable to break through."

"If you couldn't even steal one lousy book, how do you plan on accomplishing the much more difficult task you have been given?" one of the senators asked.

"My plan A may have been a bust, but don't think for one second that I don't have a plan B, or even a plan C if necessary. This was nothing but a momentary setback," Mayor Wright offered.

"I think we should report this," one of the senators said to the other.

"Wait! There's no need to do that. Telling her of this will only make her angry."

"Yes, we imagine she would be very angry with you. Why should we care about that? Sounds like a personal problem."

"Because she may also get mad at you. After all, you guys would be the ones delivering the message, and she has no problem shooting the messenger. We both know how angry she can get," Angela said, trying to dissuade them. It appeared to be working as the two senators shared a worried look with each other. "Look, I was given until the end of April. It's only October. Allow me to use the time I was given to go about the task the best way I see fit," Mayor Wright pleaded.

"Fine," one of them said. Mayor Wright let out a premature sigh of relief before she was caught off guard as her desk was violently slammed back into the wall, pinning her. She cried out in pain as one of the senators said ominously, "We strongly suggest you move on to your supposed plan B, witch. We want progress, not excuses!" they said as they made an abrupt exit from the office. Angela knew she escaped this time, but she wasn't sure if she would be able to the next time. When they came again, she would need to have something concrete to show them. Maybe it was time to become a little more hands-on.

***

"This is where you go to get a haircut?" Matthias asked as they approached the barbershop. It was relatively nondescript. It was sitting on a corner with glass windows facing the sidewalk.

"What were you expecting?" Derek asked.

"I don't know. Something a little more fancy, perhaps. This place doesn't even have that little red, white, and blue rolling column thing that most barbershops have," Matthias said as they walked in the shop.

Matthias looked around the shop. It looked like a typical barbershop, nothing out of the ordinary. There were about six stations that lined the walls, each one with a bunch of equipment on the counters and a big mirror on the wall behind it. There was a TV that was mounted on the wall in the back corner and doorway in the middle of the back wall, which Matthias speculated must have led to a backroom of some sorts.

"Derek! Man, what's going on with you?" the barber asked of Derek. He was sitting in the barber's chair by the station in the back corner.

"Nothing, man. Just came to get my haircut," Derek answered.

"Yeah, I can see you wolfing over there. That's 'cuz you ain't been here in a while."

"That's 'cuz I been so busy. Football, tests, papers. You know how it is," Derek said as he walked over to the station and took a seat in his chair.

"I think I remember. It ain't been *that* long, now," the barber said, laughing.

"Lamar, is it okay if you give my boy a cut after me?" Derek said, pointing to Matthias, who had taken a seat in one of the visitors' chairs.

"Sure 'nough is. Any friend of yours is a friend of mine. What's your name, man?" Lamar asked Matthias.

"Matthias, sir. You can call me Matt if you want."

"Okay, Matt it is. And don't call me 'sir.' Makes me sound older than I am already, you feel me? Call me Lamar."

Matthias laughed. "Got you, Lamar."

"So, Derek, what you getting today?" Lamar asked Derek as he put the cape around him.

"Nothing special this time. Just my usual," Derek said.

"Light black and even all-around it is," Lamar said as he got started. "No designs shaved in or anything?"

"Maybe next time. Although you can put a part in, I guess."

"Straight or curved?"

"Put a bit of a loop," Derek said.

"Gotcha," said Lamar as he got to work. "You know, Devon was in here the other day."

"Yeah, he told me. He also told me about Gus."

Lamar shook his head and said, "Man, we been telling Gus to stop fooling around on that girl. Everybody know she crazy. See, he thought he could get away with it and not get caught. I got the money to bail him out, but I was like 'Nah, I'ma let you sit in jail. That's what you get for messing around with all them chicken heads. Maybe now you'll learn your lesson.' He ain't like that too much."

"I know Cedric in Florida and Fred had surgery. Where's Rich?" Derek asked.

"His car's in the shop. Yep, it's only me today. It's been pretty slow today."

Soon, Lamar was done trimming Derek's hair and moved on to shaping him up. "So what you decide to major in?"

"I haven't declared yet. I can't decide."

"What about you, Matt?"

"I'm a communications major," Matthias said.

"Oh okay. Cool." After Lamar was done with Derek, he cleaned him up and dusted him off. When Derek stood up to pay him, he reached in his pocket. "Uh-oh. I forgot my money at the dorm."

"That's okay. You can just pay me next time."

"Well, I might forget next time too. That's okay, I'll go get it. I'll be right back." Derek teleported out.

Matthias had an alarmed look on his face as he quickly looked toward Lamar. Lamar took this to mean that Matthias was shocked at the display. How could Derek just teleport out like that in front of a mortal? It was okay when it was just him and one of Derek's friends, like Devon or Raheem. Now, he had to do damage control to explain this away.

"I can explain—"

"You don't look too surprised," Matthias said, interrupting him.

"Wait, so you know?" Lamar asked.

"That he's a warlock? Yeah. So am I."

"Really?"

"How do you know? Are you a warlock too?" Matthias asked. At that moment, Derek teleported back in.

Derek handed Lamar the bill and said, "Here's your $10."

Lamar accepted it from him and said, "Why didn't you tell me Matt was a warlock?"

"Oh. Matt's a warlock," Derek said.

"Well, thanks for telling me now. When you teleported out, I almost had a heart attack. I thought I was gonna have to jump through hoops trying to explain it," Lamar reprimanded.

"Sorry, my fault. Damn, it slipped my mind," Derek shot back.

"You ready?" Lamar asked Matthias. He walked over and sat down in Lamar's chair. "So what you getting done?"

"I'll take the same thing as Derek. Without the part though. That's a little too fancy for my taste," said Matthias. Lamar nodded and got started on Matthias's head.

"Tell me more about yourself, Matt. What's your level?

"Well, I'm a level 3 warlock. I have the power of electrokinesis," Matthias said.

"So you can control electricity. That's tight. How long have you had your powers? Derek got his a couple years ago."

"I've had mine since birth. You never answered my question. How do you know about Derek?"

"I'm not a warlock, I'm a kintano."

Matthias said, "A human who studies magic."

"I been studying magic since I was eight. I met Derek's dad when we was fifteen. I helped him kill a werewolf. We been close ever since."

"I come to Lamar for a lot of my spell ingredients. He still won't tell me where he gets most of the stuff," Derek offered.

"Kintano's secret," Lamar said cheekily. "Have y'all thought about forming a warlock's diamond?"

"A who?" Derek asked.

"A warlock's diamond. I only asked because I did a tarot reading for you, Derek. It revealed danger and death in your future. I told your dad first, but he made me promise not to tell you so you wouldn't worry."

"What's a warlock's diamond?" Matthias asked.

"It's a blood-bonding ritual performed by four warlocks. It links them together, providing both power and protection."

"I've never heard of something like that," Matthias commented.

"That's 'cuz it's real rare. You know how witches and warlocks can't cast spells together?" They both nodded. "Well, this allows them to. Once linked, warlocks can cast spells together to increase the effect. There are some spells that specifically require more than one person to cast. This opens the door for more powerful spells, obviously."

Derek looked intrigued by this. "I like the sound of that."

"If it does all that, why don't more people bond themselves?" Matthias wondered, sensing a catch.

"Probably because once linked, a warlock's individual spells become a little weaker and less controllable over time. Not drastic initially, but noticeable. Eventually, they wouldn't be able to cast much of any spells without another member of their diamond. Besides that, it's dangerous.

Once you link yourselves, you can't undo it. You bound for life. The four witches or warlocks become more than family. They lives, they magic is permanently intertwined," Lamar explained as he moved on to Matthias's shape-up.

"That doesn't sound very powerful to me," said Matthias.

"Even though a warlock's spell casting might wane, their active powers increase in potency."

"Do you know the ritual?" Derek asked.

"You're actually considering this?" asked Matthias.

"Come on, you can't tell me the idea of getting stronger don't excite you? What kind of warlock are you?" remarked Derek. Matthias smirked.

"Slow your roll, Speedy Gonzalez. I only told you this as an idea, a precaution. The quest for power is every warlock's weakness. Your kind is drawn to it, like moths to a flame. But you know what happens when they get too close to that flame, don't you? Don't let your natural lust for power consume you as it has consumed so many others before you. Besides, you need four willing warlocks. Each one has to consent. Where you gonna find two more?" Lamar cautioned as he finished up with Matthias's haircut.

"Do you know the ritual?" Derek asked again, this time more forcefully.

Lamar gave Derek a long look. "Wait here." Lamar disappeared behind the doorway on the back wall and reappeared a few moments later with a piece of parchment in hand. "All the instructions are on this paper," he said as he handed it to Derek. Derek took it. "Seeing as you eighteen now, I won't tell any of this to your dad. I figure you a man now, old enough now to make your own decisions."

"I appreciate that."

Matthias looked at his head carefully in the mirror. "Color me impressed. I think I'm going to come here from here on out, if that's okay with you."

"Of course, brotha," said Lamar.

"So how much do I owe you?" Matthias inquired. Lamar shook his head.

"The first cut is free. Next time is $15," said Lamar. Matthias thanked him as he and Derek left the barbershop.

Once they were outside, Derek couldn't contain himself. "So?" he asked.

"So what?" Matthias answered.

"What you think?" Derek asked impatiently.

"About that bonding ritual? I don't know. Sounds kinda gay. Not that there's anything wrong with that if you're into that particular thing . . .," Matthias said.

Derek shook his head. "Stop playing around, this is serious. I think this is something we should consider," Derek said.

"Why?" Matthias asked as they hopped in the car.

"Didn't you hear what he said? He said death is in our future," Derek started.

"Correction. He said death was in *your* future. He didn't say anything about me. And a warning like that is vague. It could easily mean something like you're going to watch somebody get hit by a bus or something. Then we just linked ourselves for nothing," Matthias countered.

Derek said, "Tarot cards are notoriously personal and accurate. I want to be prepared."

"Can't you just get your family to help? Wouldn't that be the safer and more prudent thing to do?" Matthias asked.

Derek shook his head. "No, I'm a man now. I don't want to keep running to my parents for help. It's about time I learned to fend for myself. Besides, my mom's not a witch, and my dad don't have his powers no more. I'm not sure what they could really do."

"You're only focusing on the positive. If it were that easy, every group of witches and warlocks would do it. What about the cons? What if something goes wrong? You heard what he said. Once linked, our spell casting gets weaker," Matthias reasoned.

Derek was getting frustrated. "He said *over time*. That would give us enough time to make that adjustment. And it would be offset by our stronger individual powers and ability to cast spells together."

Matthias was beginning to cave. "Even if I agreed to do it—which I'm not, necessarily—we need four warlocks. Where are we going to find two other people to agree to something like this?"

Derek crossed his arms. "That would be a problem. But let's just say we did find two more guys. Would you do it?"

Matthias pulled into the parking lot. After what seemed like an eternity to Derek, he finally said, "Yeah. I'm in."

After saying goodbye to Matthias, Derek retreated to his room and headed straight to his closet. He took out his grimoire and opened it to a blank page in the back. "Copio." In an instant, the instructions for the blood bonding ritual were copied from the parchment to Derek's grimoire. It still amazed Derek how the book never seemed to run out of blank pages near the back to add stuff. Derek knew he was being a little forceful with Matthias about the bonding ritual, but it was with good reason.

Truth be told, Lamar's warning terrified him. Magic was not all fun and games. Having powers, casting spells, and the like was cool, but there were other aspects of the mystical world that were not so benevolent. There were supernatural phenomena, magical creatures, and mystical artifacts out there that could do some serious damage to you. That said nothing of all the nonmagical dangers out there. Derek had multiple brushes with death before and had no desire to test his luck again. If this bonding ritual offered a layer of protection, he would take it, potential consequences be damned.

***

"Absolutely not!" Even though Matthias agreed to perform the ritual with Derek, he was still struggling with the decision. Rhonda had noticed that he seemed distracted and asked him what was wrong. Of course, he couldn't tell her the whole truth so he opted to give her a version of it. After telling her he recently agreed to something that he's not sure he should have, she suggested he talk to his dad about it and get his advice. It was a great idea, and Matthias was a little embarrassed that he hadn't thought about it first. During his tennis training, Matthias explained the situation to his dad. Needless to say, he wasn't exactly enthusiastic about the prospect.

"Why not?" he asked his dad.

"How well do you really know this guy? You're talking about binding yourself to him and two other strangers for the rest of your life. Aside from sounding asinine, it sounds kind of homosexual." Matthias chuckled. "What?"

Matthias said, "I said the same thing to Derek."

Isaac chuckled too. "Well, it does!"

"Do you think it's too dangerous?" Matthias asked as he continued to stretch.

"That's an understatement. The very fact that it uses blood magic should have tipped you off. You know that type of magic is ancient, dark, and dangerous. It's not to be messed with."

"What about Derek? This could really help him."

"His protection isn't your problem. The last thing I want you doing is getting caught up in his issues. If he's about to start going through some dangerous times, I think that's your cue to distance yourself. Best to protect yourself," Isaac said.

"I can't just leave him high and dry. I don't think I could live with myself if he got hurt and I could have done something about it."

"Well, you're about to turn nineteen so I can't make this decision for you. But just ask yourself—is potentially helping this Derek worth definitely hurting yourself?" That gave Matthias a lot to ponder as he finished his stretching and moved on to his weight training.

***

"What the hell was that?" Coach Steve screamed. The locker room was deathly silent you could hear a pin drop. They just finished playing a game that was not just bad, it was embarrassing. After starting the year undefeated, Word U played a game against New Jersey State College, a team that had just a solitary win on the year. It should have been a breeze. The Wildcats lost the game 23–12. They were held without a touchdown for the first time all year. It was a sloppy game. Untimely penalties, blown coverages, missed tackles. Derek had a particularly bad game, with multiple dropped balls and a noticeable avoidance of contact.

"That had to have been the absolute worst game we have played in a couple of years! This should have been a piece of cake! That team's not good enough to hold our jockstraps! These are the type of losses that we can't afford. Not a single unit played good. Lee, what were you seeing out there? You had two picks and should have had two more! Did the secondary go deaf and mute? 'Cuz there wasn't no communication. Receivers running free all over the field! James, where were you? I thought I was in Florida with all them alligator arms you had. I ain't never seen a receiver so afraid of contact!" Coach Steve paused to gather himself and reined in his anger. "Y'all better get a good night's rest, men, because this will not happen again. I promise you that!" Coach Steve walked out of the room.

Derek felt personally responsible for the loss. He had two surefire touchdown passes that he didn't catch because he felt a defender bearing down on him and short-armed the ball. Ever since he learned of the tarot reading, he was hyper aware of the dangers that surrounded him. He hadn't used his powers at all since that Sunday for fear that he would accidently teleport into a wall or into the path of an oncoming truck. In addition to supernatural dangers, he was cognizant of the everyday hazards he encountered on a daily basis. He carefully crossed streets, avoided sharp objects such as knives, and tried not to walk outside alone at night. This extended to the football field. He had a poor week of practice. Every collision in football was the chance for a catastrophic injury. Before now, he had never thought about it. He just played football. Now, he had his head on a swivel on almost every play. His pride didn't allow him to admit that he was scared, but whatever was wrong with him, he had to get over it. He could deal with it if it only impacted his own life. But now, he was hurting his teammates and costing them football games, which was something he absolutely could not let go on for much longer. He had to fix this.

Chapter 5

Omar

This was so frustrating! Bruce had a paper due the next morning and needed to print it out. He got all the way to the library before noticing that he had left the flash drive that contained the document in his room. That meant that he had to go all the way back to Garrette Hall to pick up his stupid flash drive and then turn around to go right back to the library. Unfortunately, the shuttle didn't run that late. He had taken the last shuttle that was going to run that night. If he had been able to print out his paper when he had first gone to the library, that wouldn't have been a problem. Now, not only would he have to walk to the library, but he would also have to walk back. All of this was on his mind as he made his way up to his room. He was so absorbed in his thoughts that he didn't notice the rubber band around the doorknob as he opened the door to his room.

"Whoa!" Bruce said, gawking at the sight that greeted him. Right there in front of him was Derek in a rather compromising position.

"Bruce, what the hell?" Derek asked in shock.

"My bad, dawg. I didn't know you was in here," said Bruce.

"Didn't you see the rubber band?" Derek asked.

"Nah. I wasn't paying attention," Bruce said slowly. He was still looking at Derek and the girl, mostly out of astonishment and surprise.

Derek shook his head. "I knew I should've put a sign on the door." He didn't seem angry, or even embarrassed in the least. He actually seemed a little bemused. There had been no immediate attempt to withdraw from the girl. As a matter of fact, he was in the same position that he was in when Bruce opened the door.

"Derek, maybe I should go," said Derek's guest. This seemed to wake Bruce up.

"No, that's okay. Y'all just go back to what y'all was doing. I just gotta grab my flash drive and I'll be out of here. Don't mind me," Bruce said, turning his head to get a better look at the girl.

After some time had passed and Bruce made no attempt to get his flash drive, Derek said, "Bruce?"

"Yeah?"

"The flash drive?"

"Oh yeah. Right. Sorry." He quickly went over to his desk, grabbed the flash drive, and began to make his way out of the room. While he was doing this, Derek and the girl started up again. "Just text me when you done."

"Uh-huh," Derek grunted and Bruce left the room.

***

"Sorry we were interrupted earlier," said Derek, apologizing for Bruce's intrusion. He was standing in the doorway, seeing his lady friend out.

"That's okay," she said. "I am surprised that you were so cool about it with him, though. You barely missed a stroke."

Derek chuckled. "There ain't no shame in my game."

The girl agreed. "That's a good attitude to have. You definitely don't have anything to be ashamed of," she said suggestively, glancing at Derek's pants. They both laughed. "And on that note, I'm going to head out. I'll see you later," she said.

Derek briefly watched her walk down the hall before closing the door. Derek needed that. It felt good to get back into the swing of things. He had been off his game lately. He was skittish, hesitant. His jumpiness and uneasiness was both uncharacteristic and unsettling. He remembered the phone conversation he had with his big sister that set him straight.

***

A few days ago . . .

"Hello?"

"You busy, Naomi?"

"Just washing clothes, why?"

"I need some advice. I got a problem and don't know what to do about it."

"Okay. Shoot."

"I been a little . . . off lately."

"Off? How so?"

"I been really jumpy. Really cautious. Overly cautious. You should see me trying to cross the street."

"That sounds odd, but nothing really to worry about."

"It gets worse. I been playing real bad the past week or two."

"Everybody goes through ups and downs, Derek. Just stick with it and I'm sure it'll get better."

"But I ain't never played this bad. I can't catch a ball unless I'm wide open. I mean, I'm visibly flinching whenever a defender gets near me. We lost a game because of it."

"Wow, that does sound pretty bad. Well, why do you think this is happening?"

"This all started when Lamar told me about this tarot reading he did for me."

"Tarot reading?"

"Yeah. It's kind of like getting your fortune told, only it's using these mystical cards."

"Well, what did he say it said?"

"He said there was danger and death in my future."

"Oh come on, Derek."

"What? This is serious stuff. You can't just ignore something like that."

"If you say so. I'm not a witch. Magic is yours and Dad's thing."

"What do you think I should do?"

"Is it possible that the reading could be wrong?"

"I don't think so. Tarot cards are known to be really accurate."

"Well, was he at least a little more specific than that?"

"No, not really."

"So he told you death was in your future, but he didn't give you a method, time frame, nothing? Derek, you realize that could mean you will die tomorrow or you could die ten years from now. Hell, it could mean you simply die from old age. You don't know if you are murdered, die in a car accident, or get some disease or something. You get what I'm saying?"

"No. Connect the dots for me, sis."

"What I'm saying is, a warning like that is entirely too vague. You can't possibly prepare for something based on such little info. Whatever is going to happen is in God's plan. It's going to happen, whether you want it to or not. Let him worry about it. If you start worrying about something that you have no control over, you're going to worry yourself sick. It might even become a self-fulfilling prophecy."

"Huh. I never thought about it that way. I get what you saying. You saying that I should only worry about something when it happens because that's when I can do something about it."

"Exactly. Until then, just live your life like you normally would. Get back into a normal routine and trust that if something were to come up, you can handle it. Catch the ball in traffic and trust that if you take a big hit, you'll get back up like you always do. If you normally don't look fifty eleven times before crossing the street, then don't. If you haven't cut yourself yet, then knives are probably okay for you to be around. You can't live your life in fear. That's not really living. That's just existing."

***

He knew talking to Naomi would set him straight. She always knew what to say to calm him down. The two of them were very close, both in age and relationship. She was right. Why worry about something if you couldn't do anything about it yet? That didn't mean that he couldn't be a little more aware of his surroundings. But until if and when he knew what exactly he was in danger from, it did him little good to agonize. Therefore, he took her advice. He was the rare wide receiver that loved contact. At practice, he asked for a couple of passes over the middle and for the defender to act like he was an opponent. His coach was hesitant initially, but obliged. When the throw came, he forced himself to hang in there, caught the ball, and got absolutely lit up. And just like Naomi suggested, he got up fine. That encouraged him to get back to normal in other aspects of his life. That's what led him to the female companion that he had his sexual liaison with. Derek was very sexually active. He noticed that he hadn't had sex since his first week of school, meaning it had been about one and a half months. For him, going a month without sex was an eternity, and it was unusual for him to go more than two weeks. He was more than happy to get back in the saddle, so to speak. Afterward, he felt much better about facing whatever was in his future.

***

Woo! That feels good, Derek thought as he stood at the urinal. He had needed to use the bathroom for a while, and he was happy to finally relieve himself. They were going over present participles in Spanish class so Derek didn't want to leave during class. As he was at the urinal, he noticed someone walking into the bathroom out of the corner of his eye. The guy went to a urinal a couple of units away, and Derek stole a quick glance to see who it was. The guy looked familiar, but he couldn't quite put his finger on how he knew him. When Derek got done and went to go wash his hands, he continued to rack his brain. It was going to bother him until he figured it out. The guy approached the sink and greeted Derek with, "What's going on, boss?" That's when it hit Derek and he remembered where he knew the guy from.

"Hey, ain't you that guy I played pickup with way back when?" Derek asked.

"Huh?" he asked.

"Yeah, you are. Remember the day before classes started? In back of Garrette?"

"Ah. I remember now. Yeah, what's been going on?" the guy asked in realization.

"Nothing much. Struggling to get through some of these classes," Derek said.

The guy laughed. "Yeah, I hear you. I think a lot of people feel that way."

"I don't think I caught your name that night," Derek said. "I'm Derek."

"Omar," the guy said. He looked at his watch. "Look, I gotta go. Nice talking to you."

"You too," Derek said as he turned back around toward the sink and saw his reflection staring back at him in the mirror. Something was off. He didn't notice it at first, but there it was, clear as day. The diamonds on his amulet were jet-black again! He turned around, but Omar had just walked out the door. He ran out the door to catch him, but lost him in the crowd of students.

***

"Are you sure?" Matthias asked skeptically. Later on that day, Derek asked Monica about Omar. She told him that she did believe that there was a guy named Omar that fit Derek's description on the second floor, but that he had to ask the second floor RA, Jay, to be sure. When Derek got confirmation from Jay that Omar lived in room 205A, he could barely contain his excitement and quickly went to go find Matthias, who was in his room down the hall.

"What do you mean am I sure? The diamonds turned black, and he was the only one in the bathroom. What else would that mean?" Derek asked.

"Well, for starters, are you sure that you were the only two people in the bathroom?" Matthias asked.

Derek responded, "Yes. I would have noticed a whole 'nother human being in the bathroom, don't you think?"

"Isn't it possible that the amulet could have detected somebody outside the bathroom?"

"That just so happened to leave the area just as Omar left the room? Pretty big coincidence, don't you think. Now that I think about it, I think I remember something weird happening when I played him in a pickup game before. I swore it was slightly hotter around him than normal. It was hot that night so I just ignored it, but now I'm not so sure," Derek explained.

"You could have been imagining that," Matthias said.

"Anybody ever tell you that you're a huge skeptic? If you put that together with what happened earlier today, you got pretty good evidence, correct?"

"Fine. But I'm going to come with you. And let me do the talking. The last thing we need is for you to do to him what you did to me and practically jump the guy," Matthias said as he began to walk with Derek to the second floor.

"That makes three warlocks. We only need one more to make the diamond!" Derek said.

"Not so fast. Sorry to burst your bubble, but firstly, we don't know if he is a warlock for sure just yet. Secondly, if he is, we don't know anything about him. And lastly, what if he doesn't want to join?" Matthias asked as he ticked each point off his fingers.

Derek grumbled. "There you go being a skeptic again. O ye of little faith!"

"It's not about having faith. You seem to think that this is going to be easier and smoother than it's going to be, and I'm just trying to inject a much-needed dose of realism to the situation."

"That's just a fancier way of saying that you are indeed a skeptic, a downer, a wet blanket, a buzzkill, a—"

Matthias interrupted him before he could go on. "Okay, I get the point!"

When they arrived at room 205A, Matthias paused. "What is it?" Derek asked.

"I didn't actually think about what to say when we got here."

"Wing it."

"What do I do now?" Derek rolled his eyes and knocked on the door. *Knock! Knock! Knock!* No one answered the door. "How do you know he's even in here?"

"I don't," Derek said. He knocked on the door again.

"Let's go. He's not here," Matthias said. As soon as they turned to leave, the door opened up and there stood Omar.

"What's up?" Omar asked.

Matthias and Derek looked down at Derek's amulet, whose diamonds were pitch-black. Whispered Derek, "I told you."

"Don't gloat," Matthias whispered back.

"Is that a mood-changing chain?" Omar asked.

"Um, no. It just changes colors sometimes," Matthias said quickly.

Omar gave him an odd look and said, "Oh. And who are you?"

"This is Matthias. Just call him Matt," said Derek. Matthias gave him a warning look before extending his hand toward Omar for a handshake. Derek shot him a defiant look right back.

"Nice to meet you, Matt," Omar said as he shook his hand. "So what do you want?"

"We think that maybe you can help us with something," Matthias started.

"Really? What is it?"

"Well, um, something strange has happened and you might know something about it."

Omar looked perplexed. "Something strange?"

"Yeah. Something . . . unexplainable; almost . . . unnatural. Know what I mean?" Derek threw up his arms and rolled his eyes in exasperation at Matthias.

A quizzical look crossed Omar's face. "Nah, I don't know, homie. What was it?"

"We saw this dog outside, a stray dog, and one minute it was there and as soon as we blink, *Poof!* it's gone. It's like it vanished into thin air. *Like magic.* You wouldn't happen to know anything about that, would you? Do things like that ever happen around you? Because things like that tend to happen around us often. If you understand what I mean." As he said this, Matthias gave Omar a hard look.

Omar slowly shook his head. "Nope. I can't say that it has. Although you're right. That does sound kinda weird."

Matthias comically hung his head in defeat. Derek grew impatient and blurted out, "Look, we know that you a warlock 'cuz we ones too." Matthias slapped his forehead, frustrated at Derek's bluntness and lack of tact. Omar's eyes got as big as saucers, and he quickly emerged from the doorway into the hall and shut the door behind him.

"I'm sure I have no idea what the hell you talking about."

"No, it's good. You don't have to front with us. See this cross?" Omar looked down at it. "It's a mystical amulet whose diamonds turn black when I'm around a witch or warlock. Other than me, of course," Derek said.

Omar looked down the hall to check to see if anybody was there. "Follow me." They followed Omar into the deserted lounge.

"Are y'all crazy? You can't just walk up to people accusing them of being warlocks. People gon' think y'all insane."

"But you are a warlock, right?" Derek asked.

Omar hesitated before answering, "Yes."

"You gotta forgive Derek. He can come on a little strong," Matthias said sympathetically.

"Okay, so we established that we all warlocks. What do you need? Is something wrong?"

"Not really, we just—"

Derek cut Matthias off and said, "Well, now that you ask. We actually came to you to see if you would perform an ancient blood ritual with us that would bind us together for the rest of our lives." Matthias could do nothing but close his eyes.

"What?"

"It would help us do more powerful spells and your powers would get a nice boost. Of course, your individual spells would get progressively weaker, but it would totally be worth it. So what do you say?" Derek asked.

Omar just stared at them in disbelief before walking out the room. "Good job," said Matthias.

"What? It was better than watching you drown back there," Derek said.

Matthias sighed and said, "This is not good."

"I don't know. I think that went rather well."

***

Omar walked into the dining hall and shook his head. *More Elvis. Is that all people can think of?* he thought. An overall festive mood enveloped the campus. The homecoming game was on Saturday, so it was officially Spirit Week at Word University. The school was overrun with blue and silver. A heaping dose of school spirit was the order of the day, and it seemed that everyone was caught up in it. Each day of Spirit Week was a dress-up day relating to a certain decade. Tuesday was the sixties, Wednesday was the seventies, Thursday was the eighties, and Friday was nineties. Today, Monday, was the fifties. A lot of the women were dressed as either pin-up girls or housewives, wiggle dresses and all. There seemed to be a lack of creativity on the men's side, however, as there were a lot of men that dressed like Elvis. He had never seen so much leather. The second most popular costume seemed to be the zoot suit, which Omar thought was hilarious because zoot suits were more associated with the 1940s than the 1950s. Beyond that, he just thought they were eyesores.

Omar got his food and sat down at a table in the corner by himself. This would allow him to both eat and do a bit of reading for his history class undisturbed. As he got more engrossed in his book, he began to tune out the outside world.

"Omar! What's going on, man?" Derek said, slapping Omar on the back. Omar was so into his book that he didn't notice Derek approaching his table. This allowed Derek to sneak up on him and greatly startle him.

"Shit! Come on, homie, you can't just be sneaking up on people like that. I almost swung on you," Omar said.

Derek waved that off while saying, "Oh please! I wish you would. What you doing?"

"Trying to study. What are you wearing?" Omar asked as he got a better look at Derek.

Derek had on a pair of gray slacks, an old-style flannel blazer, and a white golf cap. "It's an old-timey sweater my dad had in our attic somewhere. It was probably my poppop's or something. I knew everybody was going to do the whole *Grease* look and I didn't wanna dress in a zoot suit."

"My eyes thank you," Omar said.

"Mind if I join you?"

"Yes."

"Thanks," Derek said as he promptly sat down. Omar rolled his eyes in annoyance.

"¿Qué joder?" Omar said with his palms turned up.

This surprised Derek. "You speak Spanish? What class you in?"

"No soy ninguna clase. Soy medio puertorriqueño."

"You half Puerto Rican? Can't really tell, especially with the dreads," Derek said.

"That's what everybody says. My mom is Puerto Rican, but I don't look nothing like her. People tell me I look just like my dad. I wouldn't know since I never really met the guy," Omar said.

The mood got noticeably somber. Looking to change the subject, Derek asked in a much peppier tone, "So have you thought about our offer?"

"What offer?"

"To do the ritual with us?"

"You mean that was a real offer? I thought that was a bad joke."

Derek shook his head. "No we was being serious. So what do you say?"

"Hmm, let me see," Omar said as he pretended to give the idea some thought. "Uh, no."

"Why not? It'll give you a power boost. Speaking of which, what is your power?" Derek asked.

Omar said succinctly, "None of your business."

"If you tell me yours, I'll tell you mine," he offered.

"Dude, I don't really care what yours is," Omar said.

"When I played you, I felt like it was hotter around you. Is it related to that?"

"Maybe."

"Can you at least give me a hint?" Derek asked.

"That was your hint."

"Can't you just tell me?"

"Nope."

"Please?"

"Nope."

Derek finally relented. "Fine." He got up from the table. "But think about that offer we made. We really need you." Omar watched Derek walk away from the table and went back to his book.

***

Omar was so glad that the student center had a Chik-fil-A in its food court. It was his favorite fast-food place. It looked like he wasn't alone in that because it seemed like the line for Chik-fil-A was always the longest one. That caused Omar to rush from class to make sure that he got there before the lunch crowd arrived. He ordered what he always got, a chicken nugget meal with a cookies-and-cream milkshake. Once he got his meal, he sat down at a table and began to dig in. Halfway through his meal, he made eye contact with Matthias as he was walking through the student center. Matthias nodded to him before making his way over to Omar's table.

"What's going on, Omar?"

"Did y'all two get together and decide to ambush me while I'm eating?" Omar jokingly asked.

Matthias laughed. "I take it you had a visit from Derek?"

"Let's just say he might have found me in the dining hall last night," Omar said.

Matthias sat down. "Let me guess—the ritual came up."

"Man, you're good," said Omar.

Matthias shook his head and said, "One thing I'm learning about Derek is that he can be very persistent when he wants to be."

"Ya think?" Omar rhetorically asked. They both laughed.

"So what exactly did he say?"

While smacking away on a waffle fry, Omar said, "Well, he asked if I had given his offer some thought."

"Have you?" Matthias asked.

"No, not really. I got no idea what this ritual is or how it's gonna affect me. I don't even know y'all," Omar said.

"It's a blood ritual. Apparently, the ritual needs four warlocks to work. It links them together, allowing them to cast spells together. It'll increase the power of said spells and also open up possibilities for the casting of spells that can only be cast by multiple warlocks," Matthias said.

"That sounds too good to be true. What's the catch?"

"What makes you think there's a downside?" Omar gave him a knowing look. "Okay, so maybe it'll be harder to cast spells on your own," he mumbled.

"Say that again."

Matthias sighed. "The spell is permanent. Also, your individual spell casting gets a little less predictable over time."

"And you agreed to something like that?"

"Derek has his reasons for wanting this to happen."

"Which are?" Omar inquired.

"I think that's a question you should ask him. Just know that it's a pretty compelling reason. Besides, I'm a little intrigued by being able to cast more power spells. It'd be like we'd be making our own little fraternity, if you think about it," Matthias said.

"I never liked fraternities," said Omar.

"That's why I said 'like' a fraternity. So what else did Derek want?"

"He wanted to know what my power was," Omar said as he finished drinking his milkshake. "He got mad when I wouldn't tell him."

"What is your power?"

"Come on." Matthias followed Omar outside and to the side of the building. Omar carefully looked around. "Watch this." He took out a lighter and lit the flame. With his free hand, he pulled the flame from the lighter and cradled it. After putting the lighter back in his pocket, Omar began to juggle the flame between his hands.

"How are you doing that?" asked Matthias in awe.

"I can manipulate fire. I can also generate it, but that's a lot harder to do. It's much easier for me to work with fire that's already there."

"That's kind of like me. I can make and control electricity. Why didn't you tell Derek?"

Omar shrugged. "I just wanted to mess with him."

Matthias let out a hearty laugh. "Just ain't right, just ain't right," he said, shaking his head.

Omar laughed right along with him. Through the laughs, he managed to get out, "Man, he interrupted me when I was reading this book for class. I ain't appreciate that."

"So you needle him by not telling him your power."

"You should've saw him. He practically begged me to tell me. It was so sad."

Matthias couldn't stop laughing and said, "Stop it! I'm rolling!"

"Yo what is his power anyway?"

"He's a teleporter and telepath. Why?"

"'Cuz he thought by telling me his powers, I would tell him mine. I told him I ain't care about his power. Next time, imagine how salty he gonna feel when I know his powers and he still don't know mine!" Omar said.

Matthias started laughing again and asked, "You are going to tell him eventually, right?"

"Yeah, but don't tell him. I want to see him squirm for a little while longer. Plus, I know he still mad that I beat his ass in basketball. This is going to be something else I got over him."

Matthias saw a group of students leave the student center. "Well, I was on my way to my professor's office hours. Don't got much time left. You should really think about the ritual. No pressure, just an earnest suggestion. I'll see you later." He walked off.

Now feeling unsure, Omar called his mom a couple of days later. When Omar was accepted into Word University, his mother stipulated that he had to call her every Friday night in exchange for her blessing. Omar looked forward to their conversations. He loved his mother dearly and relished the opportunity to stay informed on what was going on back home in Los Angeles. Usually, their talks were pretty short and straightforward, but this time, he had much to tell her.

"Hola, hijo," Omar's mom, Esperanza, said.

"Hey, Mom. God, I have so much to tell you."

"What is it, *hijo*?"

"I met these other two warlocks at school."

"Wow. That's great, Omar!"

"If you say so," Omar said unsurely.

"¿Qué problema?"

"They wanted me to perform some binding ritual with them."

"A diamond?"

Omar was a little surprised. "I don't know. Do you know what they talking about?"

"Your *abuelita* was a part of a coven back in Puerto Rico. I imagine a diamond is the warlock equivalent," she revealed.

Omar had never met his grandmother. She died before he was born. He had only ever heard stories about her from his mom. She was a witch with the power of precognition, meaning she had visions of the future. Tragically, she had even foreseen her own death due to breast cancer.

"How was it?" he asked.

"My mom loved the women in her coven. It's the reason why she didn't move to America with me and your aunts." Esperanza's voice took on a soft tone, as if she were reminiscing about a fond memory. "They were like family to us."

"Did she tell you what being in a coven was like?"

"Before joining the coven, your *abuelita*'s visions were not as accurate and much more difficult to control. They would frequently come to her against her will. After she bonded with the other members, they became much more precise and controlled over time. Eventually she could call them on command, look farther into the future, and was much more accurate."

"They did say I would get a power boost. But they also said something about my individual magic getting weaker?"

"Oh yes. My mother's spells did suffer a power dip. In her later years, she cast only really simple spells as a result. Whenever she needed to cast a slightly more advanced spell, she always did it with another witch. They became dependent on one another in that way."

"I don't know, Mom. What do you think I should do?"

"Why do these boys want you to join?"

"I don't know. They didn't say."

"I would find out what their motives are. If everything checks out, I say go for it. Your *abuelita* found the power the coven gave her invaluable and the bonds she formed with her coven-mates an irreplaceable part of her life. If you have the opportunity to experience something similar, that would be a rare gift that I'm not sure would be smart for you to pass up."

Omar remained silent for some time while he processed what his mother said. "Okay. Thanks, Mom. *Te amo.*"

"Y tú, hijo. Adíos." Omar ended the call.

***

Derek was a guy who was always comfortable and confident on the big stage. It was safe to say that homecoming was such a stage. The whole week had gotten him hyped for the festivities that were to take place the next day. The Spirit Week dress-up days, all the blue and white, and the upcoming parade made him excited to play that Saturday. Besides that, a couple of the fraternities were going to be throwing parties that night. It was a fun time to be on campus. Right now, though, Derek was walking with Turquoise back to the dorm. They were coming from the POD, one of the university convenience stores, for a postdinner snack. Derek spotted Omar walking toward them, probably on his way to the POD himself.

"Derek. Just the man I wanted to see. Can I talk to you for a minute, homie?"

Derek glanced back at Turquoise before saying, "Sure. Let me just walk Turk back to the dorm—"

Turquoise interrupted him. "That's okay, Derek. The dorm is right over there."

"Are you sure?"

Turquoise rolled her eyes. "I'm a big girl. I'm sure I can walk a block by myself at night at this point." She walked off.

"So what is it? Have you thought about our offer?" Derek asked.

"Actually, I have."

"Have you changed your mind?"

"Before I answer that, I need to know something first. Why do you want to do this so bad? Why did you ask me in the first place?"

Derek debated whether to be truthful with him or not. He slowly started to say, "I have it on good authority that I might be in some type of serious danger although I don't know from what. Doing this ritual may be the best way for me to protect myself."

Omar had to admit he didn't know what answer he was expecting when he asked that question, but that certainly wasn't it. He considered this answer before finally saying, "I'm a pyrokinetic."

"What?"

"I can make and control fire. That's my power."

"That's cool. Well, not really, but you know what I mean. I—"

"Can teleport. I know," Omar said.

Derek looked surprised. "You must've been talking to Matt. So now you know why I need your help. Can I count on it?"

"Yeah. If we can find one more warlock, I'll do the linking ritual."

Chapter 6

Grounded

It was a perfect day. The sun-splashed day featured temperatures in the midsixties, no wind, and nary a cloud in the sky. Matthias was on his way to the tailgate down by Brooks Stadium. After that, he was going to attend the homecoming parade and game later on with Rhonda, Omar, and a few of Omar's teammates on the basketball team. His parents were going to attend the game, but Matthias wanted no part of going with them. Hopefully, he wouldn't even run into them. He looked at the clock: 11:00 a.m. Time to go pick up Rhonda.

"I told you we should have taken the bus!" Rhonda said as they reached the stadium. The only trouble was that they now had to find a parking spot. By the looks of all the cars, that was going to be a challenge.

"Did you see the lines at the bus stops? It would have taken us forever to get down here," Matthias countered.

"We've been driving around for ten minutes. Just park on the side here. It's homecoming so I'm sure they won't tow you," she said.

Matthias pulled over and parked on the side of the road. "If we come back and this car isn't here, you're paying to reclaim it." Rhonda rolled her eyes as they got out and made the trek to the stadium parking lot where the tailgate was happening.

As expected, it was packed. There were a lot of people enjoying the festival-like ambiance. There was music blasting from speakers located all around the lot. The smell of food was wafting through the air. Chicken, burgers, hotdogs, ribs, and more were at nearly every station. There was also a lot of alcohol flowing, and with a lot of regular townsfolk intermingling with the students, it was hard to tell who was who. Matthias was slightly surprised that there were so many people that were drinking so early in the day, but not really. He knew that people needed only a weak excuse to drink and party.

After hanging out for about thirty minutes, Matthias spotted Omar and his buddies walking by. "Omar! Over here!" he yelled. Omar heard him, turned toward him and Rhonda, and made his way over to them.

"I was wondering where you were. Couldn't find you in all these people," Omar said.

Matthias said, "It is a lot of people, isn't it? And a lot of people are drinking. Why am I not surprised?"

Omar said, "I can't stand beer. It's so bitter."

Rhonda cleared her throat as if to get Matthias's attention. "Oh yeah. Omar, this is my girlfriend Rhonda. Rhonda, Omar," said Matthias, introducing them.

"Nice to meet you, Rhonda," Omar said.

"Same here."

Omar introduced his two buddies to Matthias and Rhonda. "This is CJ," he said as he pointed to the guy on his left. "And this is Donnelle," he said, pointing to the guy on his right.

Since the parade wasn't for a couple of hours, the group decided to mill about until then. They ate some food and enjoyed the music. Just before the parade was to begin, they ran into Matthias's mom and dad.

"Oh no," Matthias said.

"What?" asked Omar.

Matthias said, "Just turn around. Quick!"

CJ was confused. "Why? What's up?" he asked.

Rhonda laughed. "Because his mom and dad are right over there," she said, pointing to a couple lounging by a Camaro.

Donnelle whistled in appreciation. "That's your mom and pop's car?"

Rhonda reveled in her boyfriend's obvious discomfort and yelled, "Hi, Mr. and Mrs. Johnson!" The couple looked to where the greeting had come from, saw the group of students, waved, and walked over to them.

As they were making their way to them, Matthias asked Rhonda, "Why would you do that?"

Rhonda, not backing down, said back, "Come on, babe. Your parents aren't that bad."

Matthias snorted. "Easy for you to say."

"Hi, Rhonda," said Matthias's mother, Shawnette. "How have you been? Belated happy birthday."

"Well, that's certainly belated, but thank you," said Rhonda.

Isaac asked Matthias, "Don't be rude, Matt. Who are your friends here?"

Matthias said, "This is Omar and his friends CJ and Donnelle. Everybody, this is Shawnette and Isaac Johnson, my parents."

Omar extended his hand for Isaac to shake. "Wait, Omar!" Matthias said, but it was too late. Once their hands connected, Isaac violently closed his eyes for a brief moment before reopening them.

"Are you okay, Mr. Johnson?" Rhonda asked as Omar, CJ, and Donnelle looked on in concern.

Shawnette moved over to her husband and placed a hand on his shoulder. "What is it, honey?"

"Nothing," he said. "Matt, come over here for a second." Matthias hung his head before following his dad away from the group.

"Is there something you want to tell me about Omar?" Isaac asked.

"Yes. He's a very good basketball player. Think I could take him in tennis though," Matthias said.

"Matt," Isaac said in a no-nonsense tone.

"Okay. Yes, he is a warlock. What did you sense?"

"I only got a long enough look to know that he's a level 3. What are you doing hanging out with him?"

"Well, if you must know, he's agreed to perform the ritual with us."

"You mean that binding ritual? You mean that's still happening?" Isaac said in alarm.

"We still need one more person, but yes, that's the plan."

"Did you not listen to a single word I told you?"

"Yes. Every single word, as a matter of fact. You said, and I quote, 'You're about to turn nineteen, so I can't make this decision for you.'"

"That's because I trusted you to make the right one. Did you not hear the rest of my speech about messing with dark magiks being extremely dangerous?"

"Of course I did. But you raised me to be both smart and independent. And above all, to do the right thing, even if it's hard. I believe that helping Derek out is the right thing to do. And with all due respect—and that is a lot of respect, sir—I think you should listen to your own words and leave this decision to me. That's one of the reasons I wanted to live on campus instead of at home. Let me mature into my own person, Dad. Loosen the reins," Matthias pleaded.

"It's hard to do that when you clearly don't know what you're getting yourself into. You're making a mistake, Matt."

"A part of growing up is making mistakes and finding a way to correct them. If I am making a mistake, then let me make it. Please."

Isaac gave him a long, hard look before acquiescing. "Fine. But don't say I didn't warn you."

They went back over to the group. "Come on, Shawnette," Isaac said as he walked away from the group, clearly perturbed.

"It was nice meeting you all." She followed after her husband to settle him down.

Once they were out of earshot, Omar asked, "What was that all about, homie?"

"I'll tell you later. Come on, the parade's about to start."

Once the time came for the parade, they decided to grab a spot near the middle of the route, figuring that most people would opt to go to the very beginning or very end. The parade began, and the spectators thoroughly enjoyed all the floats that passed by. The homecoming court was featured amid roaring cheers. Soon enough, the parade was over, and it was time to enter the stadium.

"They better win this game. You can't lose homecoming. It's an unwritten rule," said CJ.

"Don't worry. Howard is sorry. They should win this game, no problem," said Donnelle.

"Are we gonna stand here talking about the game or go in and actually see it?" Rhonda asked. The group followed the crowd into the stadium. This was going to be fun.

***

"Mitos yoanic brion gaia." Angela slowly dropped the dirt into the bowl as she chanted, "Mitos yoanic brion gaia." Next, she grabbed the

matches, lit one, and raised it above her head. "Mitos yoanic brion gaia."
She lowered the lit match to the dirt, and lit it on fire in several places.
The dirt slowly began to burn. It started off slow before it began to build
in intensity. Before long, the blaze engulfed the entirety of the dirt in
the large bowl. At that moment, Mariah, Angela's assistant, walked out
into the yard.

"Angela, the director of urban affairs is on the phone."

"Why is he calling me on a Saturday? Tell him I'm in the middle
of something. I'll return his call later," Angela said as she watched the
flame intently.

"He says that it's urgent."

"He always says it's urgent. I don't have time for his petty concerns
at the moment. This has to be done while the sun is at its apex in the
afternoon sky. Tell him I'll call him back."

Mariah shook her head. "He won't like that."

"Then don't tell him for all I care! Just hang up. Now quiet. I need
concentration," Angela said impatiently. Mariah ended the call and put
the cell phone on silent.

"What are you doing?"

"Plan B."

"Excuse me?"

After reaching their peak intensity, the flames began to subside.
Angela raised her hand toward the back door. A pitcher of water that
was resting on the step began to quickly and carefully float toward her.
When it reached her outstretched hand, she grabbed the handle and
walked over to the bowl. As she poured the water onto the simmering
dirt, she chanted, "Solar outre rhemus." The steam that spewed from
the dirt began to fan out and blanketed the area around the bowl.

Can you go get those totems that I left on the kitchen table, Mariah?
Angela asked telepathically. Mariah went into the house and looked
around for the totems. *Hurry before the smoke clears!* Mariah went into
the kitchen and found the totems lying on the table. They were rocks,
held together with vines. She grabbed them and went back outside to
Mayor Wright. "Place them in the bowl." She put them in the bowl,
and Angela buried them in the smoldering dirt using her telekinesis.

"Moldem animus humana. Moldem animus humana. Moldem
animus humana. Moldem animus humana." The dirt covered each of
the totems and formed crude miniature dolls. Angela took the totems

from the bowl and buried them within the area that was covered by the steam.

"What was that all about?" Mariah asked.

"Hopefully, a solution to my dilemma. But it will take a few days for them to gestate. What's today's date, the twenty-sixth? They should be ripe by Halloween. Fitting, really," Angela answered.

"What'll you do with them when they're ready?"

"I got a task in mind. Call Stanley back. Let me hear what nonsense he's talking about now. Urgent, my ass."

***

> Omar: U gonna watch game 6 2nite?
> Matt: Ima have to miss the first part. Gotta lecture at 7:30
> Omar: Me too. Gore Hall.
> Matt: Mines in Gore too. Room 218
> Omar: Yup. Same lecture. Meet you there
> Matt: U eat yet?
> Omar: No y?
> Matt: Wanna get dinner and go to the lecture after?
> Omar: Sure. Meet u @ Lib after practice @ 6:15

After dinner, Matthias and Omar made their way to Gore Hall. The lecture that they were attending was entitled "The New Jim Crow." The guest speaker was Michelle Alexander. She was promoting her book of the same name.

"So what class do you need to go to this lecture for?" Matthias asked.

"My intro to criminal justice class. I'm a criminal justice major. You?"

Matthias said, "My anthropology class."

"You have to go to this lecture for anthropology?"

Matthias answered, "It's cross-listed with Black American Studies."

"Oooooh. Now I get it," Omar said, understanding dawning on him. The two warlocks got there just as the lecture was starting. They slipped in and tried to be inconspicuous as they grabbed two seats near the back.

Throughout the lecture, Matthias could only pay attention just enough to record notes that he would need to write a quick two-page summary of the lecture. Other than that, he kept watching the time, hoping that the lecture would end with enough time left for him to catch the second half of the World Series game that night. Omar, however, found himself engrossed in what Mrs. Alexander was saying. He found her research findings and conclusions illuminating. According to Alexander, the American criminal justice system was a modern-day Jim Crow system. She revealed how it created a permanent undercaste of black and brown people, mostly young and male. She laid out the history of the criminal justice system and made compelling comparisons between the legal Jim Crow segregation system of yesteryear and the de facto segregation system the modern-day justice system created.

"Shit no!" Omar whispered during the middle of the lecture.

"What's wrong?" Matthias asked.

"My computer's about to die. I forgot to plug it up today."

"Just plug in the charger," whispered Matthias.

Omar shook his head and said," I didn't bring the charger or anything to write with."

"Let me see your computer," Matthias said. Omar slid his laptop over to Matthias. Matthias put his finger over the jack where the charger would normally connect to the laptop and sent a jolt of electricity through the computer. He then slid the computer back to Omar. "You forget that I'm a human backup generator," he whispered.

"Oh my god, you just saved my life," Omar said in relief.

"Don't worry about it. It was nothing." Soon, the lecture was over. "Good. Let's get out of here," Matthias said as he put his notebook in his backpack. Omar didn't appear to be in as much of a rush to leave.

"Hold up. I want to get a copy of the book and have her sign it," Omar said.

Matthias looked toward the table where the books were being sold. "Do you see that line? Look, it's just after nine o'clock. If we leave now, we should get back around nine fifteen, which means we'll have only missed the first couple of innings," Matthias said.

"How about you go and I'll just walk back?" Omar suggested.

"And let you make a twenty-five-minute walk by yourself in the dark?" Matthias asked.

"I could always take the bus back," Omar countered.

"You won't make it. It's going to take you about twenty minutes to get the book bought and signed. The last shuttle runs past here at nine fifteen," Matthias argued.

"Look, just go. I'll be fine," Omar said as he stood in line.

Matthias shook his head and said, "It's Mischief Night. Who knows what kids are going to be up to? I'll wait. Just make it snappy."

***

He knew he shouldn't be in the park this late. But he was running late, and he had to be at his house before 9:45 p.m. or else his ankle monitor would record that he violated a provision of his probation. He couldn't let that happen, seeing as he was so close to getting it off. Cutting through the park was a quicker route. He would just have to speed up the pace. He followed the path through the trees until he got to the clearing in the middle of the park. Surrounding the field was a jungle gym, swing set, and basketball court. As he made his way across the field to take the path that lay beyond it, he thought he felt movement under his feet. *What was that?* Had he just imagined it? There it was again. *That can't be an earthquake. In Delaware?*

He looked around to see what could have possibly been causing the miniquake. He didn't see anything out of the ordinary initially. Out of the corner of his eye, though, he thought he saw movement. He turned around and saw what looked like a mound of dirt, but it seemed to be getting larger. It kept getting larger until it towered over him. He couldn't believe his eyes! After the mound stopped growing at about eight feet, it started to coalesce and harden into a vaguely humanoid figure. He was terrified!

What the fuck? The menacing creature that was now in front of him was a sight to behold! It had rocks for feet. Its body seemed to be a convoluted mess of earth, rocks, and tree bark. One of its forearms was a collection of vines. The head, which seemed to rest on its torso with no neck to support it, was misshapen and deformed.

In the back of his mind, he knew he should be running for the hills. But he was too scared to move. He tried to tell his legs to move, but they wouldn't obey. The monster quickly lashed out with its vines. They wrapped around his waist in a viselike grip. The monster then launched him across the field as if he were a football.

"Ahhhhhhhhh!" he screamed through the air as he landed with a *thud!* He tumbled across the ground before he hit up against the chain-link fence surrounding the basketball court. The creature charged toward him. He was so focused on the monster coming at him that he didn't notice that another one had sprung up from the ground and was coming at him from the side. With the fence behind him and the creature in front of him, he was trapped! Just as the monster was about to crush him into the fence, his mind kicked into gear and he ducked the attempted sandwich by tucking and rolling out of the way. The earth creature ran into the fence and toppled it over.

It was at this time that he noticed the other creature. *You gotta be kidding me!* He was so preoccupied with the new creature that he didn't notice the other one get up. Suddenly, he felt what seemed like a whip snake its way around his neck from behind. It was constricting his breathing, it was so tight! He dropped to his knees and began to feel himself being slowly dragged along the ground. His vision was starting to darken around the edges as he started to lose consciousness. At the last moment, he reached into his pocket and pulled out a pocket knife. He plunged it into the vines around his neck. The monster let out a *roar!* and the monster stopped dragging him along the ground. At that time, the other monster reached into its thick body and pulled out a small boulder. It hurled it straight at him! Coming like a locomotive, he raised his hand at it. Just before it was going to decapitate him, it abruptly stopped! It not only stopped, but it also seemed to be in suspended animation. He raised his hand at the monster in front of him, and the same thing happened to it. The creature completely stopped, as if it were frozen.

By this point, the creature behind him had recovered and began to drag him toward it again. He stabbed the creature again, this time plunging the blade deeper into its vines. The creature roared again and released its grip of him. The boy flung both of his hands at the monster, and it too froze in place. He noticed that since the creature was directly behind him, he was the only thing blocking the path of the boulder and the creature. He got out of the way and flung his hands at the boulder. It resumed its motion and hit the creature square in its knees. The earth monster was knocked back. This was his chance! He took off running toward the path and out of the park. As soon as he reached the other side of the field, whatever affected the other creature wore off. It looked across the field, but it was too late. Its target was well on its way out of the park. He had gotten away. Both creatures sank back into the ground and disappeared.

***

Matthias looked at his watch impatiently. *I knew I should have drove.* Omar was taking a little longer than usual, and he had resorted to waiting by the door. It wasn't until about 9:30 p.m. that Omar came over, signed book in hand.

"It's about time. Come on. At this point, maybe I'll get back in time to catch the last three or four innings."

Omar said, "I told you to go without me. You didn't listen so stop complaining." Matthias grumbled under his breath as they both exited the building and began the trek back to Garrette Hall. "So what did you think about the lecture?" Omar asked.

"It was good, I guess."

Omar scoffed. "You guess?"

"Yeah. I mean, it was pretty provocative. It just wasn't that revelatory to me, personally. I knew that the corrections system was profoundly racist because it always has been."

"But to actually compare it to Jim Crow? To expose the widespread systemic racial bias was genius. What really brought it home was how she broke down the effect that it has on us as a community. It's certainly unsettling to think that in America, the supposed 'land of the free', there is a system that intentionally creates a permanent undercaste in 2013. I was thoroughly entertained," Omar gushed.

"Oh, trust me. I know," Matthias said, still a little peeved at how long it took Omar to leave.

"Shut up." The guys began to approach the park. "Let's cut through the park. It'll save us some time. That way, you can catch as much of the game as possible. I would just hate to cost you any more time than I already have," he said, sarcastically.

They entered the park and began to make their way through the trees. Matthias noticed that there was somebody in the park, walking across the field. "I'm surprised somebody is in the park this late," remarked Omar.

"Probably for Mischief Night," Matthias speculated.

"By himself?" asked Omar.

Matthias changed course. "He could always be a drug dealer or something."

Omar said, "Out in the open like that. Aren't they normally a bit more conspicuous than that?"

"Look, I don't know why he's here. Why are we in the park this late?" Matthias asked in annoyance.

"I was just asking a question. You didn't have to fuckin' jump down my throat," Omar said in defense of himself. Suddenly the boys felt a tremor. "Okay, did you just feel that?" Omar asked.

"Yeah. Weird," Matthias said. They felt another one. "There goes another one! What is that?"

Omar looked around to see if he could make out what was going on. His eyes laid on Matthias. His eyes were fixed on the field. He looked spooked. "What?"

Matthias just pointed at the middle of the clearing. Omar turned to look at the clearing and saw what had Matthias so spooked. The guy that was crossing the field earlier was no longer alone. Behind him was the ugliest thing that Omar had ever seen, and that was saying something. It appeared to be some type of rock-dirt thing. Whatever it was, it certainly wasn't normal.

"What is that thing?" Omar asked.

Matthias replied, "I have no idea."

"Where did it come from?"

"It grew right out of the ground," Matthias said, still gazing at the clearing. Suddenly, they both witnessed the monster grab the boy and fling him across the field. "Ohhhh!" Matthias exclaimed in a panic.

"Shit just got real," said Omar. The monster began to run after the boy, who lay trapped up against a fence. "Let's get outta here!" said Omar.

Matthias shook his head. "We should call the cops," he said.

"Oh, and tell them what? Some supernatural creature just rose from the earth and attacked some guy. Please send help?" Omar asked incredulously.

Matthias asked, "What if he needs help?"

"Sucks to be him then. What do you expect us to do?" As soon as he said this, they saw another one of the creatures rise from the ground. "Look, now there's two of them. I reeeeeally think we need to go. They might come after us when they done with him. And I'm too young to die," Omar said.

The old creature grabbed the boy and began to choke him and drag the boy toward him. "I can't believe they're about to kill him," Matthias said.

The new creature pulled a large rock out of its body and threw it at the boy, who was kneeling on the ground in the old creature's grip. It would surely take his torso off. They both gasped, anticipating the gruesome sight. However, just as the rock was about to reach its intended target, the boy raised his arms at it and it magically stopped in place. "What?" Matthias asked in shock. Omar could only comically rub his eyes, as if to make sure that he saw what he just saw. The boy then did the same thing to the newer creature. "Are you seeing what I'm seeing?" Matthias asked. The old creature resumed dragging the boy along the ground before the boy stabbed the creature's vines that were around his neck and did whatever he did to the previous creature to the old one.

At that point, Omar and Matthias were thoroughly frightened, shocked, and confused. They watched from afar as the boy got out of the way and threw his hands at the rock. It resumed its flight and smashed into the older creature, knocking him back. The boy took off running before the creatures could react. The monsters saw that the boy had gotten too far away and melted back into the ground. The boys were dead silent as they tried to process what they just saw.

Matthias was the first to react. "Okay, what was that? What were those monsters? And what did that guy do to them?"

Omar said, "I don't know, but I don't want to stick around to find out." With minds sufficiently blown, Matthias and Omar quickly passed through the park and made their way back to the dorm.

***

Derek was beginning to reconsider his choice in costume as he looked in the mirror. For Halloween, he decided to be an angel. It was an untraditional outfit, though. He had on white slacks and a pair of white Nike Air Force Ones. His wings, which featured multiple layers of white feathers, protruded out past his shoulders and down slightly past his waist. They were attached to a white sleeveless vest. On his head rested not a halo, but a large afro wig. When he saw the costume in the store, he knew he had to have it because he was sure no one else would. It was certainly unique. He wanted to wear the costume as he had seen it modeled in the picture in the store and that was with no shirt on under the vest. It was a little chilly outside though. He was giving serious consideration to slipping a shirt under the vest. Ultimately, he chose not to. It wasn't too cold, and besides, he wasn't going to let a little cold ruin a great costume.

He was excited to see what other people were going to be wearing. Bruce was a pirate, in honor of the Pittsburgh Pirates, his hometown team. Derek walked out of his room. Down the hall, he saw someone else coming out of their room, most likely on their way to class. She descended down the stairs, and Derek chased after her.

"Hey, Monica, wait up!" He caught up to her at the bottom of the steps on the ground floor. She turned around, and he got a good look at her. He had to admit, if he didn't see her come to her room, he would have had a difficult time knowing who she was. He looked her up and down. "Let me guess. You a butterfly," he said. She was wearing black tights with orange and white designs on it. She had plastic wings like a monarch butterfly. She had a huge butterfly mask that covered most of her face.

"Lucky guess. I like your costume, by the way," she said.

"Thanks. I picked it out myself," he said.

"I bet. So where you off to?" Monica asked as she began to walk out the door.

Derek followed her and said, "Kirkbride. My first class is there. You?" Monica just started to laugh. "What so funny?" Derek asked.

"Kirkbride Jesus should have a field day with you dressed like that. I would pay money to see him tell you off if he sees you today," she said as the two of them walked to Central Campus. There were quite a few people dressed in costumes. Derek was glad he didn't stand out too much.

"I completely forgot about him," Derek said, laughing right along with her. Kirkbride Jesus was a local man who stood outside Kirkbride Hall every day and preached to everyone who passed by although nobody really paid him any real attention. The students all considered him comedic relief.

"Oh, you have to record him if he sees you. That would be gold!" Monica said.

Derek thought that would be a good idea. It would certainly provide a few laughs. "Okay. I promise. God, now I hope he see me!"

***

Matthias was sitting on a bench outside the building, waiting for his anthropology class to start. After he got back from the lecture of the previous night, he was pretty shook up, but managed to bang out the paper that he had due that morning. It was only a two pager, so Matthias was grateful for that. Suddenly, his vision went black.

"Guess who," said a voice coming from behind him.

"Let's see here. Small hands . . . sweet perfume . . . Faith!"

The hands covering his eyes fell by the wayside, allowing his vision to return. Rhonda gave him a playful tap on the shoulder. "Boy, you know it is not no Faith!"

Matthias laughed as he turned around to face Rhonda. "You know I knew who you were," he said.

Rhonda smiled and enveloped him in a big hug, at least as big as her smaller frame could muster. "Happy birthday, Matt!"

Matthias said, "Thanks, babe. When I checked my phone for texts this morning and didn't see one from you, I briefly thought you might have forgotten. Glad you still remember me."

She scoffed. "You know I would never forget my babe's special day. It's kind of hard, seeing as it's on Halloween. Have I ever told you how freaky that is?"

"You may have mentioned it once or twice in high school," Matthias said, amused.

"The beginning of your last year as a teenager. So how does it feel to be nineteen?"

Matthias appeared to give it some thought. "About the same as I felt when I was eighteen . . . a couple of hours ago. I'm not a year older, I'm a day older. Wait, I just thought of something. What are you doing here? Don't you have class?"

Rhonda shook her head. "Nope. Our professor cancelled class for today."

"Halloween?" Matthias asked.

"No. Apparently, he had some family emergency to take care of."

Just then, Anton walked by them on his way to class. "Yo, Matt!" he said.

Matthias welcomed him over to join him and Rhonda. "On your way to class?" Matthias asked.

"You know it," Anton responded.

"This is my girlfriend, Rhonda," Matthias said, pointing to Rhonda. They exchanged greetings.

"Don't tell me you ain't got no costume," Anton said.

Matthias shook his head, "Uh-uh."

"What? You don't celebrate Halloween?" he asked.

Matthias shook his head. "It's not that. I mean, yes, I am a Christian. But I have worn costumes in the past. I just didn't feel like wearing one this year. Guess I wasn't inspired enough." Anton shook his head in mock disapproval. "Well, where's your costume?" Matthias asked.

"I'm wearing it," he said.

Matthias examined him. "What are you?" he asked.

Mark looked at him like he had two heads before saying, "Isn't it obvious?" Matthias gave him a blank look. "Long white tee. Baseball cap. Durag. Grill. Saggin' pants. Air Force Ones. Ring any bells?"

"You're a drug dealer?" Matthias asked.

"No. I'm a rapper. You mean you really can't tell?"

It was Rhonda's turn to interject. "What rapper dresses like that anymore?"

Anton threw his hands up. "Man, what do y'all know? I'm about to be late for class. Bye." He walked off.

"Well, I guess I better let you get to inside. Don't want to be late," she said.

He pulled her closer to him. "Aw, do you have to? Come in and sit in on the class with me," he said.

Rhonda laughed dismissively and said, "I don't think so! I'll pass." She laid a chaste peck on his lips. "Stop by my room later on tonight. I want to give you your present."

Rhonda didn't have a roommate, so this gave him ideas about what his present was going to be. "My present, huh? And what, pray tell, is this gift?"

Rhonda noticed the suggestive look on his face. "I guess you'll just have to come and find out. All I will say is it's something you haven't had before and I'm sure you'll like it. Now get to class." He gave her another kiss and made his way inside.

***

After his Spanish class, Derek made his way to the courtyard outside the building. He had gotten plenty of compliments on his costume already, and he had just been to one class. He definitely had chosen right. Before he turned the corner, he heard a voice that let him know he was maybe about to question that belief. He went around the corner and noticed that a crowd was in a semicircle. Kirkbride Jesus was in the middle. It seemed that Derek arrived right in the middle of one of his rants.

"For you do not know what it is you do! You all celebrate Satan's holiday! Turn away from his wickedness! Do not embrace him. Repent! It isn't too late. For he can be a forgiving God, even of sinners. But you must repent!" Derek tried to blend in with the crowd by hanging out near the back of the crowd. No such luck.

"You! In the back," Kirkbride Jesus said, pointing at Derek. The crowd began to snicker as they turned toward him. The students in front of him parted ways so Derek and Kirkbride Jesus had a direct line of sight to each other. "Do you know that you are going to hell?" Derek should have been offended by this, but he was only amused. He decided to agitate Kirkbride Jesus. He had a little time to kill.

"And why is that?"

"Because you are a blasphemer! You dare to disguise yourself as one of heaven's warriors on a day reserved for Satan himself. The almighty will find a way to smite you. Repent!"

Someone from the crowd could be heard saying, "Oh snap. You gonna let him talk to you like that?"

"And how do you know what God thinks?" Derek didn't believe what he was saying. He was just trying to anger Kirkbride Jesus.

"It is not I who speaks for the Lord our God. It is right here," he said as he grabbed a copy of the Bible. "It is in his word," he said to the crowd.

"So it literally says in the Bible that I will be smitten and sent to hell for dressing up like an angel on Halloween? Care to try that again?" At this point, Derek was just being argumentative, and the crowd loved it. This was so fun!

"Not in those words. But to associate a holy entity with the devil's day is sin! That's why you must repent! You must all repent!" he yelled at the congregants.

"It seems to me like you're putting words in God's mouth. Isn't that like being a false prophet? So in actuality, you're being the sinner! It wouldn't surprise me if he struck you down right now." The crowd started laughing. Derek could see Kirkbride Jesus's face begin to turn beet red from anger.

"I don't even believe in God!" someone jokingly yelled from the crowd. This gave Derek an idea that would really set Kirkbride Jesus off.

"Yeah. What if we don't believe in God? Then all of what you saying is one big joke," Derek posited.

Kirkbride Jesus looked as if he had just been shot. "O ye of little faith. That is in God's word as well. He addresses the infidels. If you should believeth in him and accept Jesus as your Lord and Savior, he will grant you everlasting life!"

"You have to admit, though, there's no evidence of God's existence."

"The absence of evidence is not the evidence of absence, my friend," Kirkbride Jesus countered.

"Oh, come on. You stole that from the boondocks!" The crowd got another laugh out of that. Just then, Porsche happened to walk by. She was dressed in a sexy devil costume, complete with horns and tail. This was too good!

"What's going on here?" she asked Derek.

"See, people? Like this misguided young woman, you worship demons on this day! Young woman, why do you insist on dressing like a satanic whore? Have you no relationship with the Almighty? Are you drifting through the wilderness that being without God's love creates?" Kirkbride Jesus exclaimed as he shook his head at the sight of an angel and a demon standing side by side.

"Oh, I know you did not just call me whore! Don't test me, 'cuz I will—" Derek put his arm around her and led her away before she could tear into the man.

Kirkbride Jesus called out to Derek as they walked away. "Remove those garments! They are an affront to God!"

Derek yelled back, "Nah, I don't swing that way!"

After they got about a block away, Derek asked, "You good?"

"Yeah," Porsche responded. "What was going on back there?"

Derek chuckled. "He called me out on my costume. Said it was blasphemy. I was just trying to get under his skin. Man, he was trippin'," he said.

Porsche giggled. "You are too much. Leave it up to you to mess with Kirkbride Jesus."

"He's such a sad little man." Derek whipped out his cell phone. "I'm 'bout to be late for class. See you later."

Porsche said, "See you." As Derek began to walk away, she said, "And, Derek . . ." He turned back around to her. "Good costume. It's quite heavenly." He smiled at her and continued walking to class.

***

As Omar walked through the lounge, he noticed Matthias scrolling through a tablet. He walked in. "What you doing?"

"I can't get what we saw at the park out of my mind. That was some serious stuff," Matthias said.

"Who you telling? I actually had a nightmare about it last night. Which is weird because I almost never remember my dreams," Omar said.

"In any case, I'm sure those things were magical. I was just scrolling through my grimoire to see if they were in here," Matthias explained. He scrolled past another page.

Omar sat down at the spot across from Matthias. "Any luck so far?"

"I don't think so. I've run across a creature or two that are similar, but no dice," Matthias said. "I still can't believe we just sat by and watched that guy almost get killed by those things."

"You saw them. Realistically, what could we have really done?"

Matthias temporarily stopped scrolling to say, "I don't know. We do have these things called powers. I'm sure we could have done something. Even if it was just to distract them long enough for him to escape without getting hurt."

"How do we even know our powers would have even worked on those things? And in the end, he really didn't need our help. What did he do to those things? Do you remember how that rock almost hit him, but then it completely stopped in midair? And how he stopped those monsters dead in their tracks? What was that all about?"

Matthias rested his hand on his chin. "I have no idea. Something about all this isn't quite adding up. We're trying to put two and two together and coming up with everything but four."

Matthias scrolled through a few more pages on his tablet before he stopped on a page. "Wait. Here they are! Look at this!" Omar went over to Matthias's side of the table. On the tablet was a drawing of the creature that they saw at the park. Matthias glanced at the door to make sure they were alone before he read the entry aloud. "Golems. Creatures made completely of enchanted earth. Relentless monsters that will not cease until their master's will is done. Usually created to protect towns and villages from external threats or act as intellectually dull hit men due to their lack of free will and durable frame. No known spell to vanquish them or ward them off."

Just as Matthias finished reading the entry, Derek walked in the lounge. "What up?" he asked.

They looked up from the tablet and almost laughed. Matthias asked, "What are you wearing?"

"Don't y'all two ever get tired of asking me that? I'm an angel for Halloween. Where's y'all's costumes?"

"I'm in costume. I'm a warlock," Matthias said cheekily.

"Hardy har-har." Derek looked down at the table. "So what are you two up to?

"Nothing," Omar said a little too quickly.

Derek gestured at the tablet on the table. "Look, by now I know what Matt's grimoire looks like. So what are y'all looking for?"

"Mind your business! Damn!" Omar said.

"Did you forget I'm a telepath? I could always just read your mind. I'd rather not though. It'd be easier if you just tell me, but I'ma find out either way," Derek said, hoping they'd buy it. He actually couldn't read their minds, at least not yet, but they didn't know that.

Omar and Matthias gave each other a look before Matthias said, "We might as well tell him. Besides, he might be able to help."

Omar turned to Derek and said, "Last night, we saw this guy being attacked by these scary-looking"—he paused—"things in the park on Elm Street. He got away, but we were still pretty shook up about the whole thing."

Matthias took over from there. "So I looked up those things in my grimoire to see if they were in there. Sure enough . . ." He passed the tablet to Derek, who read the page it was displaying.

"Golems? So y'all saw these things attacking some random guy?"

Matthias said, "Not just attacking. They nearly killed him. But here's the good part. Guess how he got away."

Silence.

"He stopped them," Matthias said.

"Yeah, I get that. But how?"

Omar explained, "No, you don't understand. He literally *stopped* them. Homie raised his hand at them just as they threw this big rock at him, and it just stopped. Completely. In midair just feet from his chest. It, and those monsters, did not move an inch. They was statues."

Derek paused for a bit to process this new information. "So are you saying this guy is potentially, what, a warlock?"

"It's certainly in the realm of possibility," Omar said.

"Both of you are missing the bigger issue here," Matthias said.

"Which is?" asked Derek.

"The book said that these things were created with the sole purpose of carrying out its master's bidding. It also said that they are traditionally made for one of two reasons: protection or assassination. I'm guessing the latter. Which means that someone made those things and sent them to kill this guy," Matthias pointed out.

"We don't know that they were specifically targeting him. They could have been protectors of some kind and mistook him for somebody else or thought he was gonna hurt the park or something," Omar countered.

"I guess. But they looked pretty sure to me. They showed up exactly as he got to the middle of the field and began to attack him immediately. That sounds like a targeted attack to me."

"So not only is there another potential warlock out there, but he could be in some deep shit," Derek said. Matthias and Omar nodded. They lapsed into silence as they each contemplated what these revelations meant.

***

He rapped on the door of the apartment and anxiously awaited for it be answered. Nothing. He knocked once more, but again, there was no answer. "Deandre?" he shouted out. No answer. He put his ear to the black door to see if he could hear any sounds coming from within the room. Silence. He must have beaten him home. He would just have to wait outside the door for him to arrive. He took a seat next to the door and listened to J. Cole's *Born Sinner* on his iPod. About twenty minutes later, he heard somebody enter the apartment building downstairs and begin to make the climb up the stairs. The guy reached the second floor, saw somebody sitting beside his door, and asked, in surprise, "Tre?"

Once he saw who it was, Tre'Vell let out an impatient breath. "It's about time. I been waitin' for like twenty minutes," he said as he put away his iPod and stood up.

"You know I don't get out of class 'til three. What you doing here, anyway? You know it's not okay for you to be here with that thing on," Deandre said, pointing to the ankle monitor wrapped around his leg.

Tre'Vell waved his hand dismissively. "The thing only records stuff at certain times. Besides, my PO knows you. I'm sure I won't get in too much trouble if he knew I was here."

Deandre opened the door to his apartment, and they went in. The sparsely furnished apartment was very modest. There was just one bedroom, along with a small bathroom, living room, dining room, and kitchen. In the living room were a small sofa, old recliner, and a thirty-two flat-screen television. The dining room contained the only table in the apartment. Tre'Vell went to go sit down on the sofa. Deandre put his backpack in his bedroom. When he reemerged from his room, he sat down in the recliner and turned on the television.

"So what's up? Everything good?" he asked Tre'Vell.

"Nah. I was attacked on my way to my crib last night," he said.

Deandre said, "For real? You look all right. What happened?"

"I'm not even sure myself. I was running late, so I decided to cut through the park on Elm Street on my way home. And I was attacked by something," Tre began.

"Something? What, was it an animal?" Deandre asked.

Tre'Vell shook his head. "I don't think so. No."

"So you was jumped by somebody," Deandre surmised.

"You can say I was jumped, but I don't think it was by some*body*," Tre'Vell said.

Deandre had a puzzled look on his face. His friend was thoroughly confusing him. "So you was attacked, but not by an animal and not by somebody? Did you not get a good look at 'em?"

Tre seemed to stare off into space, as if he was thinking about something. "Oh, I got a great look, all right," he said.

"You lost me, man," Deandre said.

"I don't know how to describe them. This is gonna sound real strange, but I swear I ain't making this shit up. I was walking through the park and these . . . these things rose up from the ground and attacked me," Tre'Vell explained.

"What you mean when you say 'things'?"

Tre'Vell stood up and began to pace. "I mean, they was big. About two feet taller than me. They looked like they was made out of dirt and rocks. They tossed me around the park and almost choked me to death."

Deandre looked skeptical. "Made out of dirt? You wasn't drinking, was you?"

"I told you this sounded crazy. I wasn't drunk, I swear on my daddy's grave this really happened. They flung me around like a doll baby, then almost choked me to death. One of them almost took my head off," Tre'Vell said.

Deandre knew his childhood friend. He looked in his eyes to see if he was pulling his leg. The earnest look in his eyes told him all he needed to know. He believed every word Tre'Vell was saying. "So what happened? How'd you get away?"

"I did that thing I can do."

Deandre nodded. "That's good. What do you think they wanted?"

Tre'Vell shrugged his shoulders. "I ain't got no idea. What you think I should do?"

Deandre offered, "Well first, avoid that park. Second, keep your head on a swivel, especially at night. It's just like when we was bangin'. If whatever you saw comes at you again, just do your thing again and run the hell away."

Tre'Vell nodded. "Enough about this. How was campus today? I know it must've been bananas with Halloween and all."

Deandre blew a breath through his lips. "It actually wasn't. Yeah, there was some crazy costumes, but it was all in fun. But get this. You know that guy who always preaching outside Kirkbride?"

Tre'Vell nodded. "Yeah."

"Well, some guy dressed as an angel started arguing with him. I was rollin'," Deandre said.

Tre'Vell laughed. He looked at his watch. "A'ight, well, let me get to work. I'll see you, dawg," said Tre'Vell.

"See you. Be careful out there."

Tre'Vell turned around and said, "Of course." He left the apartment.

***

Maria knew that something was up with her friend. She seemed both a little happier and more nervous than normal. She went to her dorm to study for the test they had the next day, but throughout the study session, Rhonda seemed slightly distracted. Near the end, Maria had finally had enough.

"Okay. What's going on with you?" she asked.

Rhonda was taken aback. "What do you mean?" Rhonda asked.

"Come on, girl, I know when your heart's not fully in something. You ain't really focusing on this test. So spill," Maria said.

Rhonda released a nervous breath. "It's Matt's birthday."

Maria said, "Oh, I didn't know that. What did you do for his birthday?"

"Well, I didn't do anything yet. I asked him to come over tonight though," Rhonda responded.

"Oh reeeally," Maria said provocatively. "Gonna give him some birthday sex," she sang.

"No, Jeremih. We've never done that, anyway. I'm not even sure I'm ready to go that far yet."

Maria asked, "Haven't y'all been going out for like three years?"

Rhonda shook her head. "Two years, but I'm still a virgin and I'm pretty sure he is too. Sex is just a big step that I'm not 100 percent positive that I'm ready for yet."

"Okay. Then why is he coming over?" Maria asked in confusion.

Rhonda giggled and said, "Because I'm going to surprise him by giving him some head."

Maria gasped and said, "Girl! That is so ratchet!" They shared a hearty laugh.

"Oh, I know. But I know that he wants to take our relationship to the next level," Rhonda said.

"Has he told you that?" Maria inquired.

"He don't have to. He's a guy. A nice, sweet guy, but a guy nonetheless. His mind's only on one thing," Rhonda said.

Maria began to follow Rhonda's train of thought. "And you think that this is a way to satisfy him without going all the way yet."

Rhonda sheepishly nodded. "Do you think he'll like it?"

Maria said, "Like you said, he's a guy. Of course he'll like it. Just don't gag. I heard that ain't cute."

When it was approaching time for Matthias to arrive, Maria excused herself from the room and returned to her dorm. As the time got closer, Rhonda's nervousness lessened, and gleeful anticipation replaced it. She really, really liked Matthias. Pleasing him would please her by proxy. She had nothing to be nervous about. She soon heard a knock on her door. Showtime. She opened it up, and there stood her man.

"Well hello there, kind sir," she said.

Matthias closed his eyes, held out his hands, and said, "I'm ready for my present. What you got for me?" Rhonda shook her head, grabbed Matthias's shirt, and yanked him inside.

Chapter 7

Completion

"Don't forget your projects are due next week. No late work will be accepted," the professor said at the end of class. This course, History of Hip-Hop, was Omar's favorite class. Omar always had a love of rap music, but never truly delved into the intricacies of the art form. This class traced the history of rap from the early Negro spirituals to present day hip-hop. It was the rare class that was both academically interesting and culturally stimulating. Listening and analyzing music both in and out of class was also pretty cool.

"So what's your project going to be?" asked Brian, one of Omar's classmates. The professor was giving the students a lot of latitude with the project. It just had to be in some way connected to some aspect of the history of African-American spoken word. This leeway was both a blessing and a curse. On the one hand, it allowed each person to tailor the project to their strengths instead of forcing a format onto them. On the other hand, it placed the task of focusing the project squarely on the individual. Without set guidelines, it could meander into an incoherent mess if you weren't careful. Or worse, fall woefully short in creativity on a task where that was a part of the grade. It had taken him a couple of weeks to come up with an idea, but he liked what he eventually decided on.

"I'm going to make a mixtape. Each song is going to highlight one of the units we covered in class. I already made the beats on my Mac and wrote the lyrics to all the songs. Now I just gotta put it all together," he said.

Brian asked, "How you gonna do that? You got a program on your computer?"

Omar said, "No. I'm going to go to the campus theater. There's a music studio inside."

"Man, I wish I had thought of something like that," Brian said as they exited the classroom. "I made a fuckin' poster. God, that's so wack!" They both chuckled.

After bidding adieu to Brian, Omar made his way back to Garrette Hall to prepare for basketball practice. Their first game was only a week away. That meant that Coach Spinder was beginning to tailor the practices to their upcoming opponent. It also meant more time in the film room. Omar knew that the film study would only increase as the season wore on and more game tape became available. Seeing as this was the first game of the season, they had to resort to watching tape from the previous season. Since some of the players were different, it wouldn't be beneficial to examine the film too closely. For the first couple of games, they would probably have to rely on just being outright better than their opponents.

As Omar rode the shuttle to the arena, his mind briefly drifted back to the scene at the park a couple of days prior. He just couldn't get the images of those terrifying monsters out of his mind. As soon as he found out what they were, something deep inside told him that wouldn't be the last time they encountered those monstrosities. He didn't know what that something was, but he just couldn't shake the feeling. There were so many questions. Who sent those things? Why were they after that guy? Who and what was he? And what was his connection to all of this? As the bus pulled up to the stadium, he pushed those musings to the back of his mind and began to focus on practice.

***

Today marked the next step in Matthias's tennis training. It was the first day of hitting practice. The first shot they always worked on was his serve. After watching players like Pete Sampras and Serena Williams, his dad developed the belief that the serve was by far the most important shot a player could possess. It was the only shot that was completely controlled by one player. This was both a good thing and a bad thing. On the plus side, a good serve was the only shot that could dominate a match on its own. On the minus side, for many players, this was the first shot to go awry when they were losing it mentally. It also determined the direction the point would take. Having a powerful, accurate serve not only allowed the server to take early control of a point but also freed up the rest of their game and allowed them to be more aggressive on the return of serve. Having the confidence that you will hold your service games gave a player more leeway to take chances on their opponent's service games.

Matthias didn't have the fastest serve ever, generally being clocked around 115 miles per hour, but it was fast enough to be effective. He didn't hit a ton of aces, but was very good at hitting his spots at a high percentage and moving it around the service box. It also was fast enough that opponents couldn't necessarily return it very deep very often, setting up his next shot. Isaac was instrumental in cultivating this by having him hone his simple serve mechanics. He had very few moving parts and was extremely fluid, leaving very little opportunities for his serve to break down. His ball toss was not very high in the air and was always in the same place, slightly in front of him. From the same ball toss, Matthias could hit every corner of the box using just a simple rotation of his wrist at the point of contact. This gave him great disguise, which also helped make up for his serve's lack of punch.

"So how's it going, son?" Matthias heard his father ask as he walked up behind him, interrupting his stretching routine.

"Fine," he answered simply.

"Good, good," Isaac said as he patted Matthias on the head.

"Why you insist on continuing to do that is beyond me. You know I hate when you do that," Matthias said.

"I can sense that you're worried about something, or someone. What's wrong, Matt?" Isaac asked.

"Nothing." Isaac just gave him a look. He clearly didn't believe him. "Well, it's not exactly nothing, but it's not anything that you need to be worried about."

"If it's worrying you as much as I sense that it is, I think I do need to worry."

"Dad, can you please just trust me when I say that I can handle it?"

"Can you at least give me a general gist of what it's about? Just because I agreed to give you more independence doesn't mean you just stop being my son."

Matthias debated internally how much he wanted to divulge to his father. "I saw someone get attacked, and I'm not sure what to make of it."

"Was the victim seriously injured?" Isaac asked in concern.

"No. It was just an unusual attack, is all."

"Was it somebody you know?"

"No. Like I said, it's no big deal. I got it."

"Okay," Isaac said, convinced that his son was fine. He began to practice with Matthias on his ball toss.

***

"An F?" Derek whispered as his paper was handed back to him. This was unacceptable. It had to be some kind of mistake, a misprint. Sure, English wasn't his favorite subject, but he had never gotten a failing grade before in his life. Once the class was dismissed, he made his way up to the professor.

"Excuse me, Mrs. Tatum? Do you have a minute?"

The professor stopped packing up her things. "Sure, Mr. James. What's on your mind?"

"Um, I just wanted to know why you gave me an F on this paper. I thought it was a perfectly decent paper. Maybe not my best work ever, but definitely not F worthy," he said.

"At the back of the paper is the grading rubric that I used to determine your score. This way, my scoring is transparent."

"Yes, I know. I looked at it. I guess I don't agree with the marks I got for some of the categories."

"All right. Which specific ones do you want to discuss?"

"For example, I got a 0 for 'formatting.' Why?"

"May I see the paper again?" she asked. Derek handed her the paper. After briefly perusing it, he said, "Well, that's simple. This was a research paper, and you used the wrong formatting style."

"Huh? I'm pretty sure I used APA," he protested.

"Yes, you did. However, the assignment was to use MLA format. It was clearly stated on the Wordkai Web site." Wordkai was the name of the internal Web site that Word University professors used to post assignments, announcements, grades, etc.

Derek was dumbfounded. He must have skipped over that part when reading the assignment and assumed it was in APA format since that's the only format he used in high school. "Well, is there any way that I can at least get a couple of points for using a proper citation style? It was an honest mistake," he bargained.

"I was thinking of doing that, but that wasn't the only problem with your formatting. If you had used correct APA style, I would have given you half credit."

"What's wrong with it?"

"You used an outdated version of APA. You used the fifth edition, which is old. The most up-to-date edition is the sixth one." Derek covered his face with his paper in shame. "I wouldn't worry too much, Mr. James. This is just a momentary setback. Even with this, you should still currently have a passing grade. As long as you do well on the remaining assignments, you'll be fine. Okay?"

Derek nodded and said, "Thanks, Professor."

"Glad to help. You know, Derek, if you ever have any questions about an assignment, you can always come to my office hours. I could have told you that you were using the wrong format if you did," she said.

"Yeah, I know. But it's just hard because I either got class or practice during your office hours."

"If you e-mail me some times that work for you, I'll make myself available. I truly want you to succeed. No professor delights in handing out failing grades."

"I'll keep that in mind," Derek said as he began to leave the sterile room. "Thanks again. See you on Thursday."

***

Omar walked up to the receptionist at the front lobby of the theater. The four-story building had the look of an old-style opera house. It featured Second Empire–style architecture, with a distinctive facade of cast iron adorned with lively Masonic images.

"Can I help you?" she asked in a soft, welcoming tone.

"Hopefully. I have a project for school, and I need to make a mixtape. I already got the lyrics, CD, and beats on my computer. I just need to put it all together. I don't know my way around the studio equipment, and I was hoping that somebody could help a brotha out," Omar said.

"One of our students in the work-study program uses the studios pretty often," the receptionist said. She looked at a clipboard. "It looks like Studio C is free. You can head on down there, and I will send him in there to help you out." Omar thanked her and headed down the hall to the recording studios.

When he walked into Studio C, it was just as Omar had seen in the movies. There was a small room behind a window where he assumed the recordings took place since there was a microphone in the room. Outside of the recording room were panels of buttons and knobs and levers. There were so many of them that his head started spinning just looking at them. As he sat down, he heard the door to the studio open behind him. It must be the person the receptionist sent to help him.

"What's happenin'? Mary said you needed some help," he asked.

Omar just continued to examine the tools in front of him, so he didn't turn to address the newcomer. "Yeah. It looks like I'm in *Star Trek* or something. I'm completely lost, you feel me?" he said.

"Well, I'm in here all the time so I got you," the employee said.

As he turned around, Omar said, "Good, 'cuz I needed this CD done, like, yesterday." When he got a good look at the guy, Omar felt he had seen him before but couldn't put his finger on where. Then it hit him. This was the guy that got attacked in that park the other day!

"What you lookin' at?" he asked warily.

This woke Omar up. "Nothing. Just thought you looked like somebody, is all. I'm Omar," he said.

The guy nodded to him. "Tre'Vell. Call me Tre," he said.

"Cool, cool. So do you have any idea how to make a mixtape?" Omar asked.

"Yeah. Now do you already have the beats, or are you finna make 'em in here?" Tre asked as he moved toward the panel.

"Nah, I already got the beats and lyrics. I just gotta record them, put them with the beats, and burn the songs to the CD," Omar said.

"Good. Then this should be pretty easy then." Tre'Vell began the process of producing the CD. Omar thought he looked like a blur, pushing this, raising that. He really knew his way around that studio, and for that, Omar was supremely thankful.

After they were nearly done with the mixtape, Omar decided to broach the topic of the incident at the park. "Can I ask you a question?"

"Depends on what it is," said Tre'Vell.

"Was you in the park the other day?" Omar asked hesitantly.

A pregnant pause invaded the room. "Why do you ask?" Tre'Vell asked slowly.

"You just look like somebody I saw one night. Just some crazy out-of-this-world shit happened that night in that park," Omar said.

Realization dawned on Tre'Vell's face. "You saw that?"

"Yeah. Me and my homeboy was walking back to our dorm that night and saw the whole thing. What was that all about?"

Tre'Vell sat down in the chair. "I don't know. You saw those things, how they rose up out the ground. Now, I done seen a lot in my life, so it takes a whole lot to scare me. I was scared shitless."

"Do you know why they was after you?" Omar inquired.

"I ain't never seen those things before in my life. I ain't got no idea why they came at me. Glad I got away," he said.

"How did you get away anyway? We saw what you did to those things. What was that?"

"I don't know. It's somethin' that I started to be able to do about three years ago. This is gon' sound strange, but when I get real scared, I raise my hands at somethin' and it just stops."

"It just . . . stops?" Omar asked, confusion clouding his face.

"Here. Let me show you." Tre'Vell pulled out his cell phone and casually tossed it over his shoulder. He then spun around and flicked his hands at it. The phone abruptly stopped its descent and just seemed to linger in the air, frozen in time.

Omar walked over to the phone and circled it, examining it. "Wow."

"You don't seem that shocked, Ain't you freaked out?" Tre'Vell asked, walking over to him.

"Nah, I'm a warlock too," Omar said.

"What?"

"I'm a warlock, like you," Omar clarified.

Tre'Vell furrowed his brow. "A what? What you talkin' about?"

"Yeah. See . . . look." Omar snapped his thumb and middle finger together, and a flame appeared, hovering above his thumb. Omar smiled and looked back toward Tre'Vell. However, he was confused to see a shocked look on his face. "What's the matter? You ain't seen another warlock before?"

"Why do you keep callin' me a warlock?" he asked.

"That's what you are, right?" Omar asked, suddenly uncertain. The look on Tre's face told Omar that he really didn't know what Omar was talking about. "Look, me and a couple of the homies are forming this kind of group, but we need one more member. You should think about joining."

"Um. Your mixtape is pretty much done. I'm finna leave 'cuz I got somethin' to do. Peace," Tre'Vell said as, in his haste, he practically tripped over himself leaving the studio.

"Was it something I said?"

***

Derek was still attempting to process what Omar was telling them. "But that don't make no sense." Omar had just finished telling him and Matthias about his time in the studio with Tre'Vell.

"I know. But that's what he said," Omar said.

"He has to be lying," Matthias offered.

"Maybe, but I don't think so. I didn't get the impression that he was being untruthful. I'm telling you, he looked pretty surprised when I showed him my power. If he was acting, just give him the Oscar right now," Omar countered.

"It's just, Derek is right. Why would he show you his power and be all shook when you reciprocated?"

"It wasn't just when I lit that flame. When I said he was a warlock, he seemed real surprised," said Omar.

"That's not a whole lot different from Matt denying he was a warlock when I asked him," Derek argued.

"Or you, for that matter," Matthias chimed in.

"True. But then why would he show me his power? He didn't deny he had a power, just acted surprised when I told him I was a warlock."

"Again, that don't make no sense," Derek said.

The three of them lapsed into silence, each trying to unravel this mystery. Suddenly, a thought struck Omar. "Maybe he ain't a warlock. Maybe he something else. Do either of you know of something that can stop time?"

After some time, Derek shook his head. "Nope. You?"

Matthias said, "I can't think of anything . . . hold on."

"What?"

"What if he is a warlock, but just doesn't know it?"

"At his age? How do you not know you a warlock? Didn't you say he said he got his ability a couple years ago?" Derek asked Omar.

"Unh-hm."

"I guess that could be a possibility, but unlikely."

"Okay, so we got two options. Either he is something other than a warlock or he's a warlock and doesn't know it," Matthias summed up.

"And how do the golems fit into all this?" Omar asked.

"I got no idea, but I'm sure it has something to do with it. How much you wanna bet that if we find out what he is, we'll start to find out more about the golems?" Derek said.

"That's a reasonable deduction. But how do we figure that out? Derek, what if you read his mind, find out if he was acting or not?" Matthias suggested.

Derek let out a nervous laugh. "Yeah, I don't think that's gonna work."

"And why not?"

Derek struggled to come up with a plausible explanation. "Well, . . . it's just that . . . digging into somebody's mind is dangerous. Who knows what you'll find out?" Matthias and Omar just stared at him, neither one really buying his explanation. Finally, Derek caved. "Okay. I actually know it won't work because I can't read his mind."

"What do you mean you can't read his mind? You told me you were a telepath," Matthias asked in disbelief. Had Derek lied to him?

Derek raised his finger in opposition. "No, I said I was a *limited* telepath. My power only works on immediate family and really close friends. My whole life, I can count on two hands whose mind I been able to read."

"Well, that's helpful," Matthias said sarcastically.

"Who you tellin'?" Derek said in agreement.

"Well, that plan's a bust. Now what?"

Omar looked at both of them like they were slow. "Really?"

"What?" both Derek and Matthias asked.

"Isn't the answer obvious?"

"No."

"Do I have to do all the thinking around here?"

"Look, are you gonna tell us or keep being a smart-ass?" Derek asked with a hint of impatience.

"Just find out the same way you did with us."

A look of understanding dawned on both Matthias and Derek. "My amulet."

"Exactly. All you gotta do is just let me borrow it. I'll stop by the theater, and if it activates, we got our answer."

"Not gonna happen," Derek quickly dismissed.

"Why not?"

"Because I ain't giving you my amulet. None of the men in my family have ever given it to someone else. It is to remain in the possession of its owner at all times. Besides, I don't even know if it'll work for you."

Omar began to protest. "But—"

"Nope. I'm just gonna have to do it. What does he look like?"

"Well, he about Matt's height and size. Mohawk. Same shade as you. Oh, and he got a neck tattoo."

"What's the tattoo of?"

"A pair of fangs with 'BBD' between them," Omar described.

"All right, cool."

"Wait! You two should go together," Matthias interjected.

"Why?" Derek asked.

"Because if all three of us went, it could look like we're ganging up on him. Omar should be the one to go with you since he knows him. Tre might feel more comfortable. I don't want you going by yourself, *capisce*?"

"No, not *capisce*. I don't care what the fuck you want, fool. You ain't my daddy."

"You are bad at these types of things. Tact isn't exactly your strong suit. It'll be easier if Omar goes with you, is all I'm saying. Agreed?"

Derek just stared at him before nonchalantly shrugging his shoulders and finally saying, "Yeah. Sure. Whatever you say." He turned and began walking to the door.

"I mean it this time, Derek! Don't you go down there by yourself!" Matthias yelled as the door shut behind him.

***

Derek disembarked from the shuttle and made his way inside the theater. After walking through the red oak double doors, he found himself in a quiet lobby. He scanned the area, but there was seemingly no one in the building. He walked up to the receptionist's desk and rang the bell. It emitted an odd, shrill sound that seemed to reverberate throughout the lobby longer than expected. A lady soon emerged from a doorway behind the desk. "Yes, can I help you?"

"Yeah hopefully. Does a person named Tre'Vell work here today?" Derek asked.

She looked down at a notebook on her desk. "Yes. Why do you want to know?"

"Can I talk to him?"

"I'm sorry, but he's not allowed to have visitors during work hours. He has to be available to help those who need to use the facilities."

"But that's why I'm here. Yesterday, he helped a student named Omar with a CD. I'm his group partner, and I just had some questions about what they did. He said to ask Tre'Vell because he wasn't sure."

"All right. I'll see what I can do." Derek wandered around while the receptionist made a few calls. "Right now, he's busy. He said that he'll meet you here in about ten minutes. You can wait over there." She pointed to a sofa on the opposite side of the room.

"Thanks," he said and sat down on the sofa. He pulled his reading book for his English class out of his backpack. He figured that he might as well get some reading done while he waited.

After finishing up the chapter he was on, he noticed some movement out of the corner of his eye. He turned to see what was coming out of the door that led to a stairwell he assumed connected all the floors of the building. From the door emerged a man with a mohawk and a distinctly noticeable tattoo.

"Tre, this young man would like to speak with you about a project he's working on with a student you assisted yesterday," the receptionist said. Tre looked at him warily.

Derek stood up and introduced himself. "Hi. I'm Derek," he said, extending his arm. Tre'Vell didn't accept it. Derek withdrew his hand, slightly embarrassed.

"What you want?" Tre'Vell asked.

Derek glanced down at his amulet and was excited to see that the diamonds were black. At this point, he gave a passing thought to just making up something and leaving, content to know that he was indeed a warlock. The thought was only fleeting and was soon replaced by eagerness.

"I'm Omar's partner for a group project. He said he came in here yesterday and you helped him," Derek said.

"He ain't mention nothin' about a group project," said Tre'Vell.

"Weird. Anyway, can you show me how to work the equipment? I want to make some revisions."

Tre'Vell stared at him for some time before asking for the keys to Studio F, knowing it wasn't booked for the day. "Follow me." They made their way to Studio F. Once inside, Tre asked, "Okay, I know you don't want to make no revisions so what's this all about? What did he tell you about yesterday?"

"He just wanted me to confirm what he suspected you was, that's all. See, you are a warlock after all," Derek said.

"Am I bein' punk'd? He said the same crap yesterday. What is with y'all? I ain't no warlock. That's some crazy bullshit," Tre'Vell said.

"With what you can do and what you saw him do, is it really out the realm of possibility? How else do you explain being able to stop things in midair? That ain't normal. It ain't crazy, it's true. My amulet proves it," Derek said excitedly.

"What?"

Derek held his cross in the palm of his hand. "This cross is an amulet that detects witches and warlocks. The black diamonds tell me that you a warlock," he said. Tre shook his head and tried to leave. Just as he reached the door, Derek desperately yelled out, "Don't you want to know about those things that attacked you the other night?" Tre'Vell paused with his back still facing Derek. "Those things are called golems, and it probably won't be the last time you see them," Derek said.

"How do you know that?" asked Tre'Vell.

"Because Matt looked them up in his grimoire."

"Grim what? What the hell is that?"

"His family's spellbook, of course. You mean you really don't know what that is?" Derek took his silence to be a no. "How do you not know about that? Whatever, don't worry about it. The point is, those things are going to come after you again, and you might not be so lucky next time."

"I can handle myself."

"From what I heard, barely." Tre'Vell gave him a look that could kill. "All I'm saying is that I know a way that can protect you from them."

"Oh really?" asked Tre'Vell, unconvinced. "And what's that?"

"It's simple, really. All's you gotta do is perform this blood ritual with the three of us. It'll bind us together, giving all of us a power boost."

"And exactly how long do this ritual last?" asked Tre'Vell.

Derek closed his eyes and revealed, "For the rest of our lives."

"OH HELL NO!"

"Just hear me out," Derek said.

"I heard just about enough out of you. Out!"

"I really think—"

"Either you gonna leave or I'ma throw you out," Tre said threateningly.

"Fine, damn." Derek began to leave. "Just give what I said some thought. The basketball team's first game is tomorrow and Omar's on the team. You should go. I heard they gonna be real good this year." Derek left the studio, hoping Tre'Vell would reconsider—not just for his sake, but for Derek's too.

***

Matthias looked around in the stands, looking for any signs of Tre'Vell. He knew that Derek wouldn't listen to him, and after confronting him earlier in the day, he divulged that he indeed went to the theater to talk to Tre'Vell. Derek told him that Tre'Vell was a warlock but declined to perform the ritual. He also told him to look out for him at the basketball game, just in case he made an appearance. Derek couldn't be there since the football team had a Thursday night road game.

"Who you looking for? Your girl?" asked one of the friends that he was attending the game with.

"No. She don't like basketball. Just scoping out the scene. A season opener only comes around once a year, you know," said Matthias.

"Whatever, dude," his friend said.

During the pregame introductions, Omar was announced as the starting point guard. He was the only freshman in the starting lineup.

Once the game started, the Wildcats took a big lead early with a 12–0 run to open the game. Omar, as the point guard, was tasked with distributing the ball to his teammates, which he did very well during the first half. Toward the end of the first half, Omar had five assists with a few of them being quite flashy. Matthias noticed that once he got on the basketball court, Omar seemed like a different person. He was more intense and also seemed to love entertaining the crowd. Even though he was the only freshman on the floor, his play made him stand out. Even a layperson could see that he was dominating the game. At the half, with Word U leading 41–29, Omar had twelve points, four rebounds, five assists, and two steals.

The second half went much the way the first had. Already leading by twelve points at the half, Word U began the second half on a 10–0 run to increase the lead to 51–29. From that point onward, their opponent never got to within fourteen points. With the game firmly in hand, Omar seemed to free up his game even more. He flew around the court, and the crowd ate it up. A couple of acrobatic alley-oops, breakaway dunks, and no-look passes had the student section chanting his name. Coach Spinder removed him from the game with about five minutes left in the game to a standing ovation. He finished the game with twenty-five points, seven rebounds, eleven assists, four steals, and even threw in three blocks for good measure. Word U won the game 83–57.

After the game was over, his friends declined his offer of a ride back to their dorm. Matthias made his way to his car, which he parked a couple of blocks away in the opposite direction of where the crowd of students was flowing. Once he was a few blocks from his car, he felt a slight tremor from the ground. "That can't be good," he murmured to himself.

"Helllp!" he heard someone yell from the alleyway across the street. Matthias ran across the street to the entryway of the alley. On the far side of the alley, Tre'Vell was lying against the wall with his hands bound together behind his back. A golem was slowly advancing on him.

Panicking, Matthias scanned the alley, thinking of something to do. He ran over to a trash can and hurled it at the golem. It bounced off him like a pebble hurled at an elephant. It did succeed, however, at getting his attention off Tre'Vell and onto Matthias! "Uh-oh," he said. The golem hurled his arm out at Matthias, wrapping his vine-like whip around Matthias's midsection and tossing him over his head to the opposite end of the alley near Tre'Vell. He landed on his back, and a wave of pain shot through him. "Ow!" Matthias quickly rolled over and scrambled over to where Tre'Vell was sprawled.

"Who are you?" Tre'Vell hurriedly asked.

"I'm a friend of Omar's," Matthias answered. As the golem came toward them, Matthias fired off a burst of electricity at the beast. It barely affected the thing, only momentarily halting its momentum. "I was afraid of that. It's made of dirt. My power is going to have little to no effect," Matthias said.

"So what you sayin' is we about to get killed?"

"Maybe not. *Aero pritus*," Matthias said. A sudden burst of wind engulfed the alley, knocking the golem back toward the entrance. Matthias looked down at Tre'Vell. "It seems to take a while getting up when knocked down. We might make it if we make a run for it. Can you get up?"

Tre shook his head. "Nah. When that thing slammed me, I think he broke my ankle. It's killin' me."

"Well, we gotta try or else we're sitting ducks. Give me your hand," Matthias said as he helped Tre'Vell to his feet. He draped his arm around his shoulder in order to alleviate the pressure put on Tre'Vell's injured leg.

On the other end of the alley, a man happened upon the scene taking place. "What the hell?" he said in fear and confusion. The golem, who at this point had risen to its feet, whipped around and grabbed hold of the stranger. "What's going on? Get the fuck off me!" he said, trying in vain to break free. Tre'Vell and Matthias watched in absolute horror as the golem violently ripped the man in half, blood spurting as if launched from a geyser. The monster tossed the man's torso to its left and dropped the man's trunk in a trashcan. He refocused on the two of them again and began making its way to them once more.

"I think I'm gonna be sick," Tre'Vell said, growing slightly nauseous.

"If it makes you feel any better, you might not be alive long enough for it to matter," Matthias said.

"That's not funny," Tre'Vell said.

"Who's joking?" Matthias countered.

As the golem got closer, Matthias again tried knocking it back with a gust of wind. This time though, the monster was ready for it. His rock feet burrowed into the ground, preventing it from being sent flying. He continued his advance.

"Can you do what you did to it last time?" Matthias quickly asked.

"Nah. He tied my hands behind my back. In order to freeze him, I would have to turn around, and I can't freeze what I can't see," Tre'Vell explained.

"Great," Matthias said.

He again fired a stream of electricity at the beast, and it had the same noneffect as the previous time. They were trapped with their backs against the wall, literally! Matthias looked around the alley in desperation. He noticed a pipe running along the wall and got an idea. Once the golem got close enough, he pointed at the pipe and said, "Agueus liberan." The pipe burst, and water spewed out of it and onto the golem, drenching it and momentarily halting its progress.

"I'm going to need both my hands," said Matthias as he let go of Tre'Vell.

Tre'Vell stood on one leg and leaned against the wall for support. Matthias took a big breath and let out as much electricity as he could muster. Tre'Vell had to close his eyes as the blinding light from Matthias's powers lit up the alley and spilled into the night sky. Once Matthias's attack landed on the golem, a howling screech erupted from the beast. Matthias continued his assault even though he felt himself beginning to tire. He had never generated and released anywhere near this much electricity before, and this was pushing him past his limits. The electrical current was starting to weaken precipitously. However, the creature was soon brought to its knees in anguish. This brought a second wind to Matthias for one last push. With all his might, he fed one last burst of electricity to the monster. With one last *roar!* the golem collapsed to the ground and exploded, leaving nothing but leaves, dirt, and rocks.

Once Tre'Vell felt the heat that was generated by all the electricity subside, he slowly opened his eyes. Matthias dropped to his hands and knees in exhaustion. Tre'Vell felt a different emotion: elation. The monster was no more! His elation was dampened, however, when he put his injured leg on the ground and attempted to walk. He immediately collapsed to the ground as a sharp pain surged through him. "Ahh!" he cried out.

Matthias saw that water was still trickling from the pipe. First, he helped untie Tre'Vell's hands before saying, "Come on over to the water. I can do something about that bum ankle." Matthias helped Tre'Vell get to his feet and hop to the wall.

"Hold your ankle under the water," he commanded. Tre'Vell shot him a look of protest, but Matthias said, "Trust me." Tre'Vell did as he was asked and sucked in a breath as he gingerly removed his sneaker and slowly let the water hit his ankle. "Rigomortis inglotum." Tre'Vell was amazed as the pain in his ankle dulled considerably.

"That's amazing!" he said as he lowered his leg to the ground. He was pleased to see that he could walk on it. It still hurt a bit, but it was tolerable.

"That should help. Your ankle was probably broken. The charm didn't heal it fully since it looks like you still have some swelling, but at least now you can walk on it," said Matthias, pleased with his work.

"Yo, man, good lookin' out. I thought I was a dead man back there," thanked Tre'Vell.

Matthias dismissively waved his hand and said, "Don't mention it. I wish I had helped you the last time. So where you headed?"

"I was on my way home from the game before that thing came after me."

Matthias said, "Let me give you a ride home. Just to make sure nothing else funny happens."

Once they arrived at Tre'Vell's apartment building, Tre'Vell didn't immediately make a move to get out of the car. "What?" asked Matthias.

"That was amazin' what you did back there," Tre'Vell said.

"Like I said earlier, don't mention it," responded Matthias.

"So I guess that you a . . . a . . . warlock like Omar said we are, huh?" asked Tre'Vell. Matthias nodded his head yes. "So that nigga wasn't lyin' after all. Ever since I got this . . . ability, I knew it wasn't normal, but I ain't know nothin' about all this." Tre'Vell chuckled. "Trippy. Some guy came to my job yesterday talkin' about how those things—golems I think he said—would come back after me."

Matthias sighed and said, "That was Derek. I told him not to go to the theater alone. He has a hard time listening, obviously." Matthias rolled his eyes.

"But he was right. Which makes me think if he might be right about what else he said," said Tre'Vell.

"What did he say?"

Tre'Vell said, "That the best way to protect myself is to perform some ritual with y'all."

Matthias smirked. "Yeah, that sounds like him. Look, it's no pressure. It's totally up to you. Don't let Derek strong-arm you."

Tre'Vell lingered before he opened the door to the car. "Hold up," Matthias said. He wrote his number down on a piece of paper. "Here goes my number." Tre'Vell took the paper. "Hit me up if anything else happens or if you want to talk about any of this," said Matthias. Tre'Vell nodded, exited the car, and disappeared into the apartment building. Before he could pull off, Matthias's cell phone started ringing. It was Derek.

"Hello?"

"You will never guess what just happened." Matthias thought Derek's breathing sounded ragged over the phone. Maybe it was the connection?

"Funny. I can say the same thing to you."

"Mine's pretty bad."

"I bet you I got yours beat by a mile."

"I got attacked by a golem."

Matthias paused. "I got attacked by a golem."

"I barely got away."

"I barely got away."

"Why are you copying me?"

"I'm not, but I wish I were. I ran into Tre'Vell getting attacked by a golem after the game tonight. We barely got away. I managed to kill it, though."

"How?"

"I soaked it in water from a pipe running along the wall and electrocuted it."

"That's smart. After the game was over, I realized I forgot my cell phone in the locker room. I snuck out to go pick it up. The golem chased me through the school. For some reason, all the doors was locked. I had to keep teleporting just to stop from getting caught. This poor janitor though. He got in the way and the golem ripped his heart out. It actually punched through his chest, ripped his heart out, and showed it to me."

"There was this guy that walked into the alley, and the golem ripped him in half. I don't think I'll ever be able to get that image out of my head. I'm going to be having nightmares for a while."

"Tell me about it."

"So what happened? You all right? How'd you end up getting away?"

"I'm straight. I tricked the thing into knocking one of the doors down, and I teleported the hell out of there. Thankfully, it didn't follow me."

"Thank God. This can't have been a coincidence—all three of us getting attacked at the same time. Somebody needs to call Omar and see if he's okay."

"I called him before I called you. He fine. Ain't nothing happen with him."

"That's a relief. Tre had a broken ankle, but I healed it."

"He was probably shittin' hisself, I'm sure," he said, laughing.

"We both were, although I tried my best to keep a level head."

"I told him that those things was going to come after him again. I didn't know they'd come after me too. You know what this means. The reading . . ."

"I really don't feel like hearing about your obsession with a vague tarot reading that may or may not have taken place."

"I'm just saying."

"Look, it's late and I need to get home. I'll catch up with you when you get back to campus and we'll figure this thing out then." He hung up the phone.

Chapter 8

Ritual

The first thing that came to her mind was that she hoped he was there. Rhonda had just learned that she was chosen as part of a group chosen by her professor to meet the governor, and she was on her way to Matthias's room to surprise him with the good news. When she got there, she was going to knock, but something told her to try the doorknob first. She was slightly surprised that it was unlocked and slowly opened the door. In the room, she saw her beau sitting on his bed in front of his computer. She could have sworn she also saw a thin stream of electricity migrating from his finger, which was positioned slightly outside the port where the charging cable went, to the laptop. She did a double-take just to make sure she really saw what she saw.

"Matt?"

Matthias immediately jerked his head toward the door and quickly removed his hand from the laptop. "Rhonda! Hey, what's going on?"

"I wanted to tell you something, but I didn't want to tell you over the phone," she said.

"I wasn't expecting you. Why didn't you just text me to make sure I was here?"

"I wanted to surprise you. What was that?" she asked suspiciously.

"What was what?" Derek asked in response a little too quickly for her taste.

Rhonda pointed to the laptop. "Whatever you were doing to that computer?"

"I wasn't doing anything. Darn static electricity." He shook out his finger for dramatic effect.

"Static electricity?" Rhonda asked, unconvinced. That certainly didn't look like any static electricity she had ever seen. It was much too strong and prolonged for that.

"Yeah. I've been having problems like that with this thing for a couple of days now. It's been shocking me all over the place."

Rhonda looked right in Matthias's eyes and didn't like what she saw. She had known Matthias for three years, so she knew when he was lying. More importantly, and dismaying, he was hiding something. She didn't know what, but she resolved to find out. She would drop it for now, though.

"Are you okay?" she asked, approaching him in concern. He waved her off.

"Of course. It's just a bit of static. So what did you want to tell me?"

"Oh yeah. Remember when I told you about that contest in my American Political System class?"

"I think so. Is that the one where you were saying that you could go meet the governor?"

"Yeah, that's the one. Well, the professor e-mailed those people that he decided to take to the capitol. I'm in!"

"Really? Congratulations! When did you find out?"

Rhonda sat down on the edge of the bed. "Just now. Maybe about an hour ago. I was so excited I just had to tell you!"

"Have you told your parents yet?"

"Oh snap! I didn't even think of that. I gotta go!" Rhonda quickly got off the bed and flew out of the room.

Matthias shook his head in bemusement. That girlfriend of his could be so crazy! After that thought, he unconsciously let out a sigh of relief. He knew he just dodged a bullet. Rhonda didn't know about magic, and she had walked in on him charging up his laptop using his powers. If it weren't for his quick thinking, he would have had a lot of explaining to do. He was just glad that she bought his answer. He didn't even realize that the door was unlocked. Deep down, he knew that if he planned on making his relationship with Rhonda long term, eventually the time would come where he would have to reveal himself to her, to "come out." That time was not now, though. He had to make sure he was more careful. Just then, his cell phone vibrated, indicating that he had just received a text message. He looked to see who it was and read the message.

Interesting, he thought to himself.

***

"It's about time!" said Matthias as he watched Omar enter the study room.

"You lucky I came at all! What's this all about anyway? I was in the middle of beatin' up on some fools in *Mario Kart*," complained Omar. He got a text message not too long ago from Matthias telling him to meet him in this study room at the library. It was kind of in a secluded part of the library and took some time to find.

"Omar?" Omar turned around and saw Derek walk in the door. "I ain't know you was gonna be here. I just thought Matt needed something," Derek said. He addressed Matthias. "What's up? You good?"

"Yes. Sit down. The both of you." Matthias gestured to a couple of empty seats at the table while he engaged with his phone. Derek and Omar sat down.

"Derek told me about what happened to y'all two a couple of days ago. I told you we was next!" said Omar.

While not removing his gaze from his phone, Matthias said, "Okay, you might have been correct about that. You want a cookie?" The sarcasm was practically dripping off him.

"Is that why you brought us here?" Derek asked.

"Partially. We can't get started yet. Everybody's not here," he said.

Omar was confused. "Get what started? Who else is coming?" As soon as those words left his mouth, he heard the door open behind him and turn to see who it was. It was Tre'Vell.

"Hey, Tre. Glad you made it okay," said Matthias.

"What's he doing here?" asked Derek.

"'He' is right here," said Tre'Vell with a not-so-subtle hint of annoyance.

Matthias tried, and failed, to stifle a laugh. "After our little run-in last week, I gave Tre my number in case anything else came up. Turns out he has quite a bit of questions that I think we can help him with." Tre'Vell nodded in confirmation and sat down at the table.

"Like what?"

"Let's start with the basics and go from there. My name is Matthias Johnson. This is Derek James." Matthias pointed to Derek. "And this one over here is Omar Brutton. You are?"

"Tre'Vell Hinton."

"Now that that pointless introduction is over, why don't you get to why he really is here?" said Derek.

"Look, I'm getting real tired of you not addressin' me," Tre'Vell said to Derek, pointing at him. "From now on, if you got a question about me, ask me. Not him."

Derek held up his hands in mock surrender. "My bad, dawg. Don't get your drawers in a twist. What did you want to know?"

"First off, what was those things? You seemed to know back in the studio."

"They called golems. Think of them as magical dirt monsters," said Derek.

"Magical?"

Omar nodded. "Yeah. You know, hocus-pocus stuff."

"You mean, that stuff y'all was talkin' about is really real?"

"Yeah. You wasn't joking, was you? You really don't know nothing about this stuff?" Omar said in amazement.

"How's that possible? Clearly, you a warlock. Did your parents keep this stuff from you or something?"

"You could say that," Tre'Vell said vaguely. On the confused looks he got, Tre'Vell explained. "My dad died when I was eight. He ain't never mention or show anything about no magic."

"Oh, dawg. We sorry," said Derek in sympathy. "Well, what about your mom. She kept this from you?" Tre'Vell's face turned solemn.

"My mom ain't in the picture. Bitch abandoned me when I was five. I ain't heard from her since. Probably wouldn't notice her if she burst through that door," Tre'Vell said, a clear edge to his voice. They could tell that there was a lot of pain behind that admission.

"So if you don't mind my asking, what happened? When your dad died, that technically made you an orphan," Matthias asked slowly, trying to tread carefully on a sensitive subject.

"His best friend took me in. Showed me some love."

"If your dad was alive until you were eight and he didn't tell you anything about magic, that probably means he didn't know anything. Which means your mom was probably a witch," said Matthias.

"That would explain how you wouldn't know anything about your magic. The person whom you got it from wasn't around to tell you," Omar reasoned.

"Witches? Warlocks? Monsters? What do all that mean?"

"Okay. We are going to have to start at the beginning with the basics," said Matthias. "We are all warlocks. That means that we can harness magic. A witch is the female equivalent."

"Witches and warlocks are categorized by their level. There are five levels. A level 1 is the weakest. They don't have individual power and can only cast charms," said Omar.

"What the fuck is a charm?"

Derek decided to chime in. "It's a spell. See, there are four types of spells that a witch or warlock can cast. There are charms, which are cast on inanimate objects and result in positive effects. You got jinxes, which are the opposite of charms. They result in negative effects. Then you got hexes, which result in positive effects and are cast on animate objects like animals or people. Lastly, you got curses. Those are the strongest spells and require the most power to cast and control. They cast on animate objects and obviously result in something negative. You with me so far?"

"Yeah, I think so."

"Right. So as I was saying, level 1s have no individual power and can only cast charms. Level 2s have one individual power and can cast both charms and jinxes. Most magical folk are Level 3s. They got one power and can cast charms, jinxes, and hexes. That's what me and Matthias are," said Omar.

"Is that what I am too?"

Matthias said, "We don't know. Have you shown any other powers?"

"Other than stoppin' things, I don't think so."

"Well, that means that you're either a 2 or a 3. We can easily determine it by seeing if you can cast a hex."

Omar continued. "After Level 3s, you got Level 4s. That's what Derek is. Level 4s are kind of rare. They got two active powers and can cast charms, jinxes, and hexes. Some can even cast low-level curses. Then you got Ultimates."

"I'm guessin' Ultimates is the highest level?"

"Yup, Level 5s. Now they are real rare. Supposedly, every family only has one of those come around every couple hundred years at least, but that's only a myth. I think."

"They can do everything. They got three or more active powers and can cast charms, jinxes, hexes, and curses. Pretty powerful stuff," said Derek.

"Okay, I done seen your power," he said, pointing at Matthias. He then moved on to Omar. "And yours. What's yours?" he asked Derek.

"Like Omar said, I'm a level 4 so I got two powers. I can teleport." He teleported to the other end of the table before teleporting back to his chair. "And I'm a telepath. I can read minds. Somewhat. It's pretty restricted."

"What you mean 'restricted'?"

"I can only read the minds of immediate family and close friends. Even then, they can block me if they wanted to." Tre'Vell nodded at this.

"Have you always been able to teleport?"

"Nah. I got my magic when I turned thirteen. But each family is different."

"See, magic can be kind of complicated. For instance, in some families, everyone born into it are magical. In other families though, only warlocks are born or witches. Some families inherit the same set of powers while others get their powers at random. Some kids have their magic at birth. Some, like Omar, get their magic at an early age. Others get theirs during adolescence," Matthias explained.

"That's me. I get magic from my dad's side of the family. In my family, we have three powers passed down: teleportation, telekinesis, and telepathy. My family only produces warlocks, which are the first-born boy, and each one inherits one of those abilities. Since I'm a level 4, I got two of those: teleportation and telepathy. My dad had telekinesis, but he lost his power when I got mines. But that's what happens for us. Every dad loses his active power when his son comes into his magic on his thirteenth birthday."

Omar cut in. "For me, I got my magic from my mom. Magic skips a generation in my family. My mom was a mortal, but my *abuela* was a witch."

"And both of my parents are magical. Everyone born is magical in my family. I've had my powers since I was a baby. You can imagine how that went. Caused quite a bit of problems before I finally learned how to control it," said Matthias.

Omar looked at Tre'Vell in concern. "You all right, homie? You look like your head is spinning."

"Just tryin' to take this all in. Um, let's go back to those monsters. Golems, right? What's the story on those things?"

"Well, like we said, think of them as magical dirt monsters. A lot of times, they protect places or people, kind of like bodyguards."

"So why was they after me? I ain't got beef with nobody," Tre'Vell asked.

"We don't have the answer to that question. And they don't seem to just be after you anymore. I was attacked by one at the same time y'all was," Derek said.

Matthias placed his hand on his chin in thought. "And that's not good. I don't think that was a coincidence."

"What you mean?"

"Golems aren't naturally occurring monsters," Matthias offered.

"Ain't that what you call an oxymoron?" Tre'Vell asked.

Matthias thought about it before saying, "I guess to a mortal, it would seem that way."

Omar jumped in to shed some light on the thought. "What he means is that there is some monster species that are self-sustaining. They reproduce and shit. Like werewolves and vampires."

"Vampires and werewolves is real? Never mind. I got a feelin' that I'ma be askin' that a lot from now on. Go 'head."

"Other monsters can only be made. They ain't born," Omar said, putting air quotes around the word *born*.

"Exactly. Which means that somebody made those things specifically to kill us," said a concerned Matthias.

"That's one of the reasons why I asked you to perform the bonding ritual with us back at the theater," said Derek. "I knew those things might come back."

"Fine. What does this bonding ritual thing do?"

"You know how we barely made it out alive?" Matthias asked. Tre'Vell nodded. "It took everything I had and then some to stop it. If that pipe wasn't there, we wouldn't be here right now. This bonding ritual would make us stronger, which with these attacks might be a good course of action. Who knows how many more golems are going to come after us? We don't know who sent them or how much they made. It wouldn't be the worst thing in the world to be more prepared."

"But how will it make us stronger? That's the part I ain't gettin'," asked Tre'Vell.

Derek said, "It'll allow us to form what's called a warlock's diamond. Witches and warlocks can't normally mix they magic. See, every witch and warlock's magic has a unique signature that don't allow them to cast spells together. There are some spells that require more than one magical being to cast. Those spells are off limits 'cuz we can't cast spells together, see what I'm saying? This ritual solves that problem. It'll meld our magics together, giving each of us the same combined signature."

"Spells that are cast by multiple warlocks are obviously stronger. In addition to that, each of our active powers should get a little boost. That's a nice perk," said Omar.

Tre'Vell still sounded a little unconvinced. "That sounds a little too good to be true. And one thing I learned is if it seems too good to be true, it normally is. What's the catch?"

Matthias looked right in Tre'Vell's eyes. "The spell is irreversible and lifelong. If we do this, we'll be linked to each other forever. Mystically speaking, we'll be closer than brothers until the day we die. It's not something to enter lightly. There's a reason why diamonds are really rare. This could be the best way for you to guard against any future attacks, but it's totally up to you. We can't force you into this decision." Tre'Vell, still deep in thought, arose from his seat to leave and contemplate the offer.

"Hold up. Before you bounce, can I ask you something?" Tre'Vell looked at Derek. "I couldn't help but notice that ankle monitor. Why do you got it on, if you don't mind me asking?"

Tre'Vell looked down at the device. "I was arrested for a robbery. Since I was a minor at the time wit' no record, the judge let me off wit' probation. The monitor is a part of my probation. I get it off in a couple days." He didn't wait for a reaction as he left the room.

***

She was not pleased, she could tell. Mariah watched her boss gazing intently at the crystal ball resting on the table in front of her. She was stewing, staring at the ball as if doing so would change the images she had seen within its depths. Mariah knew that when she got in this mode, it was best to just leave her to her devices. She wished she was privy to the scenes that the mayor had watched, but since she herself was not a witch, the crystal ball would appear to be nothing but glass to her. It was clear that whatever Angela saw was upsetting her greatly. Her curiosity got the best of her.

"What did you see?" she asked cautiously.

"It seems as if my golems have hit a snag," Mayor Wright said.

"What does that mean?"

"Nothing that's not surmountable. At least not yet. I have one less golem available, though."

"I'm assuming the golems are those dolls you buried in the ground back then, correct?"

"Yes, Mariah." She resumed gazing at the crystal ball. Mariah took this as her cue to stop talking. After some time passed, Mayor Wright muttered, mostly to herself, "This is an unexpected and most unwelcome development."

I wish I knew what she was talking about, Mariah thought to herself.

"I'm talking about my golems. It seems their involvement has had the opposite effect of my intent. I thought that it would only take one golem each to do the job, but I underestimated them. Derek got away, and I didn't foresee Matthias coming to the aid of Tre'Vell. If it wasn't for him, Tre'Vell would surely be gone. Instead of killing the boys, the golems seem to have driven them closer together," Angela said, a quiet anger lacing her speech.

"Who are Derek, Matthias, and Tre'Vell? And did you say 'killing'?" Mariah asked.

"They are three of the people I have been charged with . . . eliminating."

"By who?"

"That's none of your concern. Just know that she is very scary, very powerful, and not to be trifled with. I've got until next year to kill these four boys."

"But you're the mayor! You can't be caught up in a multiple homicide! That would launch maybe the worst political scandal in American history!" Mariah warned.

Mariah pounded the table with her fist in anger. The act was so forceful it sent a large crack snaking through the wooden table. Mariah flinched. "Don't you think I know that! I have no intention of confronting them directly. That's what the golems are for," she yelled.

"But you said the golems failed. One of them was defeated," Mariah countered.

"That was the result of a mistake that I will not let happen again. I have three golems left. It will clearly take all three of them to dispose of the boys. I just have to find another opportunity to dispatch them. They'll probably be extra careful now, though. Not be caught alone for any substantial period of time."

Angela refocused her attention to the crystal ball. She stroked the air around the ball. "O crystal ball, I command thee. Your insights now, bring forth to me. Extinguished lives I wish to see. Four warlocks, young, it has to be." The mayor looked intently as a scene began to unfold within the ball.

"Perfect."

***

"Welcome, scholars of Word University!" Sarah T. Bonner, governor of the state of Delaware, stood in the center of the congressional hall as the group of ten students filed in. "Don't be shy. Come in! Come in!" She waited until the collegians and their professor were fully in the room and preparing to listen to what she had to say. A few of them were a little preoccupied with the ceiling, which towered above the hall and was painted with scenes and people from early Delaware history. The governor patiently waited for them to have their fill. When they were done admiring the ceiling, she began.

"Right now, you guys are in legislative hall, which is the meeting space for the Delaware General Assembly. This building actually is not the first capitol building. The first building was much smaller than this one. It was destroyed in the fire of 1892, however. During the construction of this building, the legislature hired the famed French painter Pierré DuBront to paint the ceiling. It took him about two years."

"That's impressive," said one of the students. The governor smiled before continuing.

"Your professor tells me that your class is currently studying the legislative branch of the government. Let me give you a brief overview of the history of the general assembly. It was created by the Delaware Constitution of 1776. One of the first significant acts of the general assembly was the calling of the constitutional convention, which was the first to ratify the constitution in 1787. That's why we are the First State. One of the best moments for the general assembly was its rejection of a secession from the Union in 1861, despite being a slave state at the time. One of its worst moments, however, was its repeated failure to legislate the end of slavery or adoption of women's voting rights. It took federal law to institute those laws.

"Up until 1898, the seats in the general assembly was composed of ten at-large members from each county. After that year, the number increased to fifty-two, and each was elected from districts within the counties. The districts were determined by geography, not population size, which hurt the much more populous New Castle County. In 1965, that was rectified when the Supreme Court Case *Reynold v. Sims* forced the state to redistrict according to population size. In 1972, the number of members was increased to its current size of sixty-two.

"Currently, the general assembly is a bicameral legislature made of two houses—the Delaware Senate, with its twenty-one senators, and the Delaware House of Representatives and its forty-one members. It convenes on the second Tuesday of January in odd-numbered years, with the second session of the same assembly doing likewise in even-numbered ones. The sessions are required to adjourn by the last day of June. Half of the senate seats are up for election every two years, and they serve a four-year term. All of the seats in the House are up for election every two years for a two year term. Members are elected from single-member districts, and elections are held the Tuesday after the first Monday in November."

Rhonda clapped along with her classmates at the end of the governor's speech. This was the last part of the day's itinerary. They had gotten a tour of the entire capitol building, met with a couple of senators and the representative of the district that Word University was in. After a luncheon with a couple of administrators, they spent a couple of hours at the Delaware History Museum. The meeting with the governor and tour of legislative hall was the icing on the cake of a very informative day. The group was granted a few minutes to wander around the hall. Rhonda went to examine some of the paintings on the wall.

"That's Ebe W. Tunnell, the fiftieth governor of the state of Delaware. He served from 1897–1901," said the governor. She had snuck in behind Rhonda. Startled, she whipped around, her hand over her heart. The governor giggled. "I'm sorry. I didn't mean to scare you."

"I just was in my own little world. That's all. So are all these people governors?" Rhonda asked.

"Why, yes. The portrait or painting of every governor since this building was completed in 1896 is hung in this hall."

"I'm sorry, where are my manners? My momma taught me better than that. I'm Rhonda. Rhonda Little." She held out her hand. The governor shook it.

"It's nice to meet you, Ms. Little. Sarah Bonner."

"So, Governor, what got you involved in politics?" Rhonda inquired.

"I was a volunteer for the Clinton campaign back in '96. I loved it, and that sparked my interest in politics. It was a way for me to make a difference. What about you? Is your major political science?"

"Yes. I want to be a—" Her phone rang. It echoed in the hall. "Excuse me," she apologized as she pulled out her cell phone. She took a look at who it was, ended the call, and put it back in her pocket. "Sorry about that."

"Was it a boy?" Governor Bonner teased.

"Maybe."

The governor laughed. "Don't mind me. I'm just teasing."

"No, that's okay. It's my boyfriend actually. Although I don't know why he's calling me. I told him I was going to be here today. He's probably just calling to see if I'm all right or something."

"How sweet. You know, you have no idea how it warms my heart to see young people in committed relationships. There's so much attention on the casual hook-up culture that it's nice to know that there are young people who still believe in loving, monogamous relationships."

"Well, thank you, I guess." Rhonda giggled.

"So what's his name?" the governor asked.

"Matt. We're both freshmen. We've known each other since high school." The governor carefully rested her hand on Rhonda's shoulder.

"You tell Mr. Matt that he is lucky to have you and I wish the both of you the best of luck in your future endeavors. Now go on, before your class leaves you behind." Rhonda thanked her and went to go join the group as it was leaving the room.

As Rhonda was walking away, the governor smirked and said under her breath, "Because he's definitely going to need it."

***

"So what made you decide to do the ritual?" Matthias asked as they made their way to the location the linking ritual was to take place. A few days prior, he got a call from Tre'Vell in which he told Matthias that he wanted to perform the ritual with them. Since he didn't have a car, Matthias offered to pick him up and take him to the ritual site.

"My Intro to Sociology class got me thinkin' about my pops. I don't wanna end up like him. That's the reason I stopped drug dealin'. One of my homies was on the block with me slingin' when a car rode by us and started shootin'. My powers saved me, but he wasn't so lucky. All I could see when my pops was bleedin' out on the street was him. It took me back to that scene, watching him get shot right in front of me. I don't want to die violently. If this helps protect me from that even a little, I'm down," Tre'Vell explained quietly, but resolutely. After a few minutes of an uncomfortable silence, he asked Matthias, "So where we goin'?"

"To St. Francis Cemetery," he replied.

"The cemetery? Why we goin' there?" Tre'Vell asked in surprise.

Matthias turned a corner before answering, "The instructions were very specific. The ritual has to be done in a cemetery at midnight on a full moon. Something about the mystical energies being the most malleable or something." Tre'Vell looked at the digital clock in the car.

"It's already eleven thirty-five. The cemetery's all the way on the other side of town. We gonna make it in time?" he asked.

"Yeah, we should. Omar and Derek are going to meet us there and set up. That way, we can start when we get there."

About ten minutes later, Matthias pulled up alongside a silver Corvette that was parked outside the front entrance to the cemetery. After parking behind it, Matthias and Tre'Vell walked up to the front gate. It was wrought iron and looked to be about ten feet high. A brick wall surrounded the cemetery that was about eight feet high.

"So how do we get in?" Tre'Vell asked. Matthias sized up the gate before beginning to scale it. "I guess that's my answer," Tre'Vell muttered. Once Matthias got to the other side, he turned around expecting to see Tre'Vell right behind him. He was still on the outside.

"Well, what are you waiting for? Come on," he urged.

"This can't be legal," Tre'Vell protested.

"You used to deal drugs and got caught in a robbery and you're worried about breaking and entering into a cemetery? Really?" Tre'Vell was not amused. He scaled the gate, though, and joined Matthias on the other side inside the cemetery.

Tre'Vell looked around at all the tombstones that littered the ground. The light from the full moon cast an eerie glow upon the grounds. The long shadows created by it seemed to come alive, as if they could sense what was to come. Tre'Vell had never been inside of a cemetery before, let alone been there at night. He thought it vaguely resembled Michael Jackson's "Thriller" music video.

"This is creepy," he said.

"I agree. Derek said they would be behind the mausoleum. Do you see it?" Matthias asked. They scanned the cemetery.

"Over there, to the left," Tre'Vell said, pointing to it looming in the distance.

They quickly made their way to the mausoleum and went around to the back of the structure. It was made of stone with a wooden door. It was remarkable for its blandness. They found Omar and Derek right where Matthias said they'd be.

"What took you so long? It's almost midnight!" Derek said.

"Better late than never," said Matthias. "We're here now, so let's get started."

Derek said, "Okay, I got everything set up. Each of us has to stand behind one of the symbols I carved into the ground over there."

Tre'Vell looked to where Derek was pointing. There were four symbols etched into the ground adjacent to each other. In between each symbol was a line of delphinium, forming a diamond, with the symbols as its points. In the middle of the makeshift diamond was a pile of orchids, with a line of delphinium connecting the pile to each of the symbols. They each took their places behind the symbols.

"What are these symbols?" asked Matthias.

"Ancient symbols representing the four elements—Omar's at the southern end representing fire, you're at the western end representing water, Tre's at the northern end representing earth, and I'm at the eastern end representing wind." He looked at his watch. "All right, it's twelve o'clock. Let's get this show on the road." He retrieved an athame as well as his grimoire from his backpack and opened it to the page containing the ritual.

"What's that?" asked Tre'Vell.

"It's my grimoire," Derek answered. Upon seeing Tre'Vell's look, he said, "We'll tell you later."

"What's with the minisword?" Omar asked.

"It's a double-sided ceremonial knife called an athame, not a minisword."

Derek held the athame up above his head and chanted, "Kunai nadal. Yati ono mawel. Hinon thrip covut zen atem." He then cut his finger and let a few drops of blood drip onto the tip of the athame. "Each of us has to bless the athame with our blood. Then once all our blood is mixed together on the blade, each of us traces the symbol in front of us." Derek passed the athame to Omar, who cut his finger and dropped some blood to cover Derek's. Matthias and Tre'Vell did the same. Once Tre'Vell gave it back to Derek, he traced the symbol in front of him. Omar, Matthias, and Tre'Vell did the same in succession.

"Say along with me, 'Cartoosh weldu ponti yvetol brideran.'" They chanted the phrase in unison four times. As they chanted, clouds quickly formed above, and the wind began to pick up. Lightning began to crackle above them in the night sky, and thunder began to roar. At the conclusion of the fourth chant, a streak of lightning descended from the sky and struck the pile of orchids, setting them ablaze.

"Is that supposed to happen?" Tre'Vell shouted.

"Yeah, I think so!" Derek yelled back.

The fire soon spread from the orchids to the delphinium emanating from them to the symbols. Then the fire spread to the delphinium that connected the symbols. The wind snuffed out the fire from the orchids and the lines of delphinium that connected the pile to the symbols, leaving nothing but ash. The fire continued to rage along the rim of the diamond, and the symbols started to glow a dull red.

"The book says that we have to step on our symbols!" Derek yelled, straining to be heard over the deafening sound of the wind and thunder.

"Are you crazy?" Omar yelled.

"That's what it says! We came this far, we might as well finish it off!" Derek shouted back. Reluctantly, each of them stepped onto the symbol in front of them.

"I can't move my legs!" Matthias yelled. Tre'Vell, Derek, and Omar realized that they couldn't either.

"I can't either!" said Tre'Vell.

"None of us can," said Derek.

"What now?" asked Omar.

As soon as the words can tumbling from his mouth, a searing pain began to climb up his body. "Аннннн!" It was a pain the likes of which he had never felt before in his life. It was as if his blood was set on fire and consuming his insides. The pain slowly migrated from his feet, to his legs, to his groin, to his torso and arms, and finally to his head. The same thing was happening to Matthias, Derek, and Tre'Vell, and they all had similar reactions. Tre'Vell tried in vain to move off the symbol, but it was no use. The four warlocks continued to scream in agony as the storm raged around them.

Eventually, their eyes began to emit a reddish glow. This was when the pain reached its crescendo. Derek felt as if his head was about to explode. Tre'Vell thought that his eyes were being ripped from their sockets. Omar silently cursed Derek for convincing him to do this. Matthias wished that he had listened to his father. Soon, however, the thunder stopped, the wind subsided, and the sky cleared up. The fire died down until it went out entirely and the symbols ceased glowing. Once the symbols stopped glowing, their eyes returned to their normal state, and the pain that had just moments before seemed all-encompassing was relieved. All four of them collapsed from the terrifying and draining ordeal.

Panting hard, with tears trickling from his eyes, Omar said, "Derek, remind me to kick your ass later on."

Matthias caught his breath and tried to compose himself before asking the group, "Is everybody all right? Does anybody feel any different?"

"I do feel a tingle. But that could easily be the aftereffects of the pain," said Derek. Tre'Vell remained silent.

After a few moments to catch their breath, they began to rise. Suddenly, the earth began to convulse beneath their feet. The shaking was so violent the mausoleum began to crack. The four of them couldn't maintain their balance and fell to the ground in a tangled heap.

"What's goin' on?" Tre'Vell asked in alarm. "Is this part of the ritual?"

Derek, while attempting to rise and failing, said, "The grimoire ain't mention nothing about an earthquake."

Matthias said, "Maybe you did something wrong."

"I did everything the book said!" Derek claimed in protest.

"Uh, guys. Look!" yelled Omar. A couple of mounds were burrowing their way toward them. As the earthquake subsided, three menacing golems slowly sprouted from the ground.

"Okay, we on the other side of town. How do these things keep findin' us?" asked Tre'Vell.

"Clearly somebody is sending them after us," said Matthias.

"Anybody have any ideas?" asked Omar.

"Let's not get killed," offered Derek.

"Okay, anybody got any helpful ideas?"

As soon as he asked that, one of the golems lashed out it's whiplike vines at Derek, wrapped him up, and hurled him over its shoulder to a point about fifty meters away. He landed on his leg right next to a tombstone. He landed at an awkward angle, causing significant pain to shoot to his right hip. Derek got up and began to hobble away. Once he got up, the golem ran after him.

"We need to make a run for it." One of the two remaining golems then disappeared into the ground. "Where'd it go?" asked Omar.

The ground beneath them trembled, and the golem reappeared behind them. They spun around just in time to see the golem take a mighty swipe with its rock-hard arm and send Tre'Vell and Omar hurtling through the air and into the hefty girth of a nearby tree trunk. Tre'Vell was temporarily knocked unconscious. The golem contorted itself into a boulder of dirt and rock and started to careen toward them.

"Omar! Tre!" Matthias yelled. He turned his attention to the golem that was hurtling toward his two defenseless comrades. He took a step toward them, but the last golem was having none of that. It raised its arm toward Matthias. Matthias felt himself get stuck in place. He looked down and saw tree and plant roots snaking their way around his feet and up his legs. He struggled with the encroaching roots, but made no headway in halting their advances. Once the roots had trapped his entire lower body, the golem began to lumber toward him.

Knowing it would be in vain, but having no other course of action, Matthias let loose a surge of electricity at the beast in a last-ditch effort to save himself. He was shocked, however, at the wattage he was generating. Unlike the last time, when his power had virtually no effect on the monster, the golem was stopped in its tracks by Matthias's assault. The golem, struggling to withstand the electrical attack, used its rock arm to shield itself and its other arm to command another set of roots to subdue Matthias. The roots shot from the earth and wrapped around his arms and began pulling them down. "No!" He tried his best to win the battle with the roots, but it was to no avail. His arms were soon pinned to his side. Without the use of his hands, his attack against the golem ceased. It plunged its arms into its stomach and yanked out a spear composed of tree bark. It was with great horror that Matthias saw the golem chuck the pointy weapon straight at his head. Dramatic scenes from his short life began to flash before his eyes. So this was how he was going to go out? The symmetry of him dying in a graveyard wasn't lost on him. Time seemed to slow around him as he closed his eyes in grim anticipation of being impaled.

***

Derek glanced back as he hobbled along. If he could just get to the gate, he could teleport to the car. He had no intention of abandoning his friends. On the contrary, he wanted to use the car as a weapon, maybe run the creatures over. He was certain that would greatly damage the car, perhaps even total it, but this was a life-and-death situation. He would just have to come up with a way to explain it to his dad, the car's owner. The monster was quickly gaining on him. He would never reach the gate in time. He needed to think of a new plan. Derek quickly made a sharp left turn to barely avoid a tombstone sailing past his head. The golem had just barely missed. The sudden movement, though, caused more pain to shoot through his injured hip, and he crumbled to the ground in a heap. The monster, seeing its window of opportunity open, lashed its vines at Derek and grabbed hold of his ankle. It then tossed

Derek against the sturdy brick wall that outlined the graveyard. The air was knocked out of his lungs as he slid down the wall to the ground.

Derek felt like he couldn't move anything without a gargantuan effort, such was the pain that currently engulfed his body. Desperation set in as he saw the beast morph into a boulder and barrel toward him like a locomotive. It was attempting to crush him against the wall. He looked around for anything that could help. Out of the corner of his eye, he saw something glint in the moonlight. It was the athame!

It must have flown over here during the storm and earthquake. With a yelp of pain, he lunged for the blade and grabbed it. The monster's body was too hard to pierce with it, but there had to be a weak spot. He saw a tree in the distance and got an idea. It was a huge risk, and his life depended on it working in his favor.

Just before the golem would have sandwiched him, Derek teleported out. The creature crashed into the wall and roared in pain, coming out of its boulder stance. Derek reappeared in front of the tree. "Hey, muhfucker! Up here!" The golem's head shot up to Derek. Derek taunted, "Don't be a pussy! Come and get me!" The monster grunted and charged the tree. Derek stood his ground. This would take perfect timing.

As the golem descended on the tree, Derek forced himself to hold his nerve and barely stopped himself from teleporting out. Just before the golem reached him, Derek teleported up into the branches of the tree, and the golem crashed into the tree trunk. A violent ripple ran through the tree, and for a minute, Derek wasn't sure that the tree would hold. But it did and the golem fell to the ground. This was his chance! Derek slid down out of the branches and landed on the monster's back. The beast quickly arose and began thrashing about, trying to shake Derek off, but Derek held on for dear life! The golem ran backward into the tree, smushing Derek between a rock and a hard place, but still, Derek held.

Once the golem began to tire, Derek plunged the athame into its face. The creature let out a bloodcurdling scream before doing a face plant. Derek rolled off the beast in both pain and relief and slowly went to go see how the rest of the group was faring.

***

Omar saw the golem careening toward them and panicked. He looked down and saw that Tre'Vell was out cold. He shook him in a desperate attempt to wake him up. "Tre, come on, man! Get up!" He showed no signs of life other than the slight rise and fall of his chest. Other than that, he was completely motionless. Omar looked back up at the rapidly approaching golem. He quickly pulled out his lighter and lit the flame. Before the golem, who was only about twenty meters away at that point, could get any closer, Omar took a huge breath and blew on the flame. His mouth became a flamethrower, with the small flame produced by the lighter growing to unbelievable proportions. The stream of fire struck the golem. With a howl, the golem stopped its advance and unfurled itself back to its full height.

To protect himself and Tre'Vell, Derek blew a stream of fire in a semicircle between the monster and them. It created a barrier of fire that Omar was sure would deter the creature from coming any closer. This thinking proved to be false, however, as the creature, with its body of dirt and rock, slowly broke through the barrier. As he continued to attempt to awaken Tre'Vell, Omar tried a different approach. He used the flame to create minidarts made of fire and began to hurl them at the golem. They seemed to be having a slight effect on the creature. The creature's hide was too tough to really do damage, but the darts were strong enough to slow its progress. They weren't stopping it, though, and slowly but surely, the beast was getting closer. "Damn it, Tre. WAKE UP!" This seemed to work as Tre'Vell slowly began to stir.

The golem raised its arm, and a bunch of roots rose up from the ground and grabbed Omar's arm, the one that held the lighter. It dropped to the ground harmlessly. Now unencumbered, the beast restarted its march toward them. As the monster drew back its vine whip, Tre'Vell fully awoke. Still a little groggy, he took in the scene in front of him and threw up his hands in panic as the golem's whip came forward. The creature froze—its whip stopped just feet from Omar.

"It's about time!" Omar yelled.

"That's not gonna hold him for long. Let's get out of here!" Tre'Vell said.

Omar burned the roots to free his arm. He and Tre'Vell rushed around the golem, which was still suspended. When they got around the creature, they saw Matthias in the distance. He looked to be trapped by the same roots that claimed Omar's arm.

"Shit, he can't move," commented Tre'Vell.

"We got to help him," said Omar. They began to run toward Matthias, but panicked when they saw Mathias's golem withdraw what looked like some type of sharp weapon from its body and heave it at him.

***

Matthias thought it was taking the spear longer to reach him than it should have. Maybe his sense of time was distorted due to his impending death. He cautiously opened his eyes, hesitant to look at the spear making a beeline to his face. When he fully opened his eyes, his breath caught in his throat. There was the wooden spear, suspended mere inches from his eyes! It was so close he could practically make out the individual shards of wood.

What? Matthias turned his head and saw Omar running toward him. Tre'Vell was standing behind him, his arms raised toward Matthias. He closed his eyes and let out a huge sigh of relief. A few inches. That's how close he had come to certain death!

Omar ran up to Matthias and began to burn off the roots that encapsulated his body. "Hold on. I got you," Omar said. Matthias looked beyond the spear and saw that the golem, who was a good distance away still, was frozen as well. By the time Omar was finished burning all the roots, Tre'Vell had caught up to them.

"You a'ight?" he asked Matthias.

"Yeah. Barely. Thanks for saving my life. I thought I was a dead man for sure," Matthias said, moving out of the path of the spear.

Tre'Vell patted him on the shoulder and said, "No problem. I'm just glad we was just in time."

"I didn't know your power reached that far. You was all the way back there with me and managed to not only freeze the spear, but the golem too," Omar said.

"It don't. At least, it ain't before. When I saw that thing chuck that spear at Matt, I just threw up my hands and hoped, to tell you the truth," replied Tre'Vell.

Right then, Derek teleported in, his hand grasping his waist. "What happened to you?" said Omar, observing Derek in obvious pain.

"Don't ask," he responded dryly. He surveyed the scene. "One of y'all take this wood thing and shove it through its head. That's they weak spot." Matthias grabbed the still-suspended spear, ran to the golem, and thrust the spear right through its head like a shish kebab. It let out a mangled roar before it fell, vanquished.

"Glad that's over," Matthias said, walking back to the rest of the group.

"Wait! Wasn't there three? I took care of mine and you killed this one. Where's the last one?" Derek asked.

While pointing, Omar said, "Over there by that tree." All four of them turned to the remaining golem. "You know, I'm surprised it's still frozen," Omar quipped.

"It won't be for long. We won't get over to it by the time it unfreezes," said Tre'Vell.

"Who cares? Now, we can probably make it out the graveyard. Let's get out of here!"

Derek shook his head. "I'm pretty sure these are the last three golems, or else the rest of them would have come here. If we don't kill that thing, what's to stop it from coming after us again?"

Omar disagreed. "Man, I'm with Matt. Let's roll out. Besides, didn't you hear what Tre just said? It'll unfreeze by the time we get over there."

Derek walked over to the fallen golem and slowly, agonizingly pulled out the spear from its head. He then teleported over to the last golem and killed it. "Or you could do that," said Tre'Vell. Derek teleported back over to them. "Now we can leave. Just let me get my book bag and grimoire."

***

Mayor Wright stared at her crystal ball, disappointment and anger dripping off her as she watched the boys walk back to their cars. She was positive that her golems would do the job, but they had gotten there too late. The diamond was now formed. Turns out her golems were no match for their boosted powers. This was a troubling development, to be sure. She angrily flung her arm out at the grandfather clock that stood in the corner and telekinetically tossed it across the room. Upon its collision with the opposite wall, it exploded into a million pieces, splinters of wood and shards of glass flying everywhere. Her plan B had failed. Derek and his group of cronies still lived. Simply unacceptable.

Angela quickly regained her composure and leaned back into her plush chair in contemplation. There was a silver lining to this dark cloud. She now had witnessed the diamond in action. She had to admit, they were impressive. What gave her pause was the thought that they would only grow closer, stronger, and more unified over time. This would make her task all the more difficult. But make no mistake, her task would get completed. A politician and witch as powerful as Angela Wright didn't reach that level without having multiple backup plans. Even now, in the ashes of this failed attempt, the seeds of a new plan were beginning to sprout. It would take some time for it to come together, but she had no doubt she could pull it off. By Christmas, the neophyte diamond would be no more!

Chapter 9

Thanksgiving

"So many choices, so little time," Bruce said to no one but himself. He was attempting to register for his classes for the spring semester. Much like at the beginning of the fall semester, athletes got first dibs on all the good classes by being the first ones scheduled to register. Since there was no football in the spring semester, he could afford to have a heavier workload than his current one. "Let's see. I already got Physical Science and Nutrition. Need three more classes. I wonder what everybody else is taking." Just then, Derek walked into their room.

"What's good with you?" asked Bruce.

"Huh? Oh, um, just got back from the physical trainer. Needed a massage," Derek answered as he tiredly plopped down on his bed. "What you doin'?"

"Registering for spring semester classes," he said. Derek's head perked up.

"Wait, that was today?"

Bruce chuckled. "Yeah. I already got two classes. I'm gonna take five."

"I totally spaced on that."

Bruce shook his head. "You ain't even start on it, have you?"

"Nah. The date just kind of snuck up on me. I haven't even looked at the classes available," said Derek.

Bruce warned, "You better get on that before the rest of the students can start registering. Then all the good classes gonna be taken up. We only get a day head start." Derek's head slumped back on the bed in frustration. "Yo man, you all right?"

"Why?"

"Because you been a little . . . off . . . the past couple of days. You forgot the registration date. You been going to sleep mad early. You been stuck in the trainer's room for the past couple of days. You just seem, I don't know, sluggish. You even seemed a couple of steps slow during the game Saturday. Like you physically and mentally beat down," Bruce said, concerned for his roommate.

"I'm fine. Just had a lot on my mind lately."

The truth was, he was both physically tired and mentally exhausted. On the physical front, his confrontation with the golems took a lot out of him. He was beat up. His whole body hurt, and it was taking some time for it to heal. He had tried the healing-water charm, but since nothing was technically injured, it had no meaningful effect. As bad as his physical condition was, his mental situation was worse. The linking ritual had done its job, but had some unforeseen consequences for Derek. His telepathy, which was very weak before the ritual, was much stronger now. Stronger to the point of being uncontrollable. He now frequently heard the thoughts of not only his family, who used to live out of his range, but also the thoughts of his friends and the rest of the diamond against his will. That was nine people's thoughts that would randomly and habitually encroach upon his own. These psychic assaults would happen at inopportune times: during class, at practice, during the game. There were a few times when, in addition to his own musings, he heard the thoughts of four, five, even six other people. During these episodes, he felt like his head was going to explode. The only time he got any relief was late at night when everyone was sleeping.

Earlier that day, he was overwhelmed during class. He was in the middle of a presentation when his head was bombarded with voices, reverberating off the walls of his skull. It was so bad that he had tears cascading down his face, like he had a severe migraine. The teacher excused him and allowed him to go to Student Health. The nurse did nothing but give him some aspirin, but that didn't help much. He just had to wait for the voices to subside. He looked in his grimoire for any potential relief, but found nothing particularly useful. He thought about getting help from his dad, who he was sure had experience with this sort of thing since his grandfather, who was currently deceased, used to be telepathic before he lost his powers. He didn't want to keep running back to his parents whenever he had a problem, however. This was something he wanted to solve on his own. He would just have to learn how to control this power like he learned to control his teleportation power. He hadn't heard anything too private up to that point, but he wanted to get a handle on the situation before he inevitably did. Unbeknownst to Derek, a couple of the other members of the diamond were also experiencing problems with their powers.

***

Omar finally caved and decided to go to Student Health. He had been sweating bullets off and on over the weekend, and it was unbearable. He felt like a furnace. He had never been so hot before in his life! He had hot flashes occasionally when he first came into his powers when he was a kid, but they were never this bad. He walked through the glass double doors and up to the secretary at the front desk.

"Can I help you?" she asked sweetly.

"Yeah. I set up an appointment."

"What's the name?"

"Omar Brutton," he answered.

"Okay. Let me check." The attendant looked at her computer screen. "Yes. Here it is. You have an appointment with Dr. Richards. You can have a seat in the waiting room over there while I tell him you're here. I'll call you when he's ready for you."

"Thanks."

Omar went over to the waiting room and took a seat by the water cooler. He immediately decided that he hated the wallpaper. It was a mustard yellow with red pinstripes that Omar thought was extremely tacky. There were a couple of other people spread out throughout the room. One guy was reading something on a tablet. There was a girl in the corner reading one of the magazines that were lying on the coffee table that was situated in the middle of the room. Another guy was sitting by the window, rapping along to a song he was listening to on his iPod, though Omar couldn't quite make out exactly which song.

After about fifteen minutes, the attendant told him the doctor was ready to see him in room 3. He thanked her and made his way down the hall to the room. Once he was in the small room, a nurse greeted him. She was a petite woman with a small salt-and-pepper afro. She took down his demographics and measured his vitals. She inputted the information on a laptop, told Omar the doctor would be meeting with him shortly, and left. The time alone in the room gave Omar some time to contemplate. He hoped that the doctor could help him with his hot flashes. He suspected they had something to do with the ritual, but he didn't know of a mystical remedy. Maybe the doctor could prescribe some nonmagical treatment.

After about ten minutes, a person that Omar assumed was the doctor walked in. He was a black man, similar height as Omar, with a neatly trimmed goatee and tidy haircut. He was wearing the typical doctor garb of a white lab coat, black slacks, and tie. Omar was struck by how young he looked. Omar thought that he didn't look much older than himself.

"Hello, Mr. Brutton. I'm Dr. Richards," he said.

"Omar," said Omar. They shook hands. Omar couldn't help himself and asked, "Can I ask you a question?"

The doctor nodded. "Sure."

"How old are you?" Omar asked.

The doctor laughed and answered, "I get that question a lot. I'm thirty-one, but most people say I don't look a day older than twenty-four. I take it as a compliment." The doctor sat down at the desk and perused the laptop. "So what seems to be the problem, Omar?"

"I been having these hot flashes the past couple of days."

"Hot flashes?"

"Yeah. Like, really hot. I be sweatin', thirsty. Honestly, I feel like I'm on fire sometimes." The doctor furrowed his brow and jotted down some notes as they were talking.

"Well, that certainly doesn't sound good. About how often do these hot flashes occur and about how long do they typically last?"

Omar had to think about it for a bit. "I would say I had about ten of them so far and they last about twenty to thirty minutes." The doctor took note of that information.

"About how long ago did they start, Omar?" Dr. Richards asked.

"Oh, maybe three days ago," he replied.

Dr. Richards said, "Now I need you to think. Was there anything strange that you ate? Anything that happened to you that was out of the ordinary?"

You mean besides performing a magic blood ritual that bonded me to three other people, then nearly getting killed by a couple of golems? Omar thought to himself. "Nah, not really," he answered.

"Well, your pulse and blood pressure is normal. Do you feel hot right now?" Dr. Richards asked. Omar shook his head. "Let's take your temperature anyway." He got a thermometer from the desk and inserted it into Omar's mouth. After a few moments, the thermometer started beeping, indicating that it was finished. Dr. Richards removed it. "Hmm. It says that your current temperature is 99.7."

"Is that bad?"

"It's a little above average, but since you said you don't feel hot right now, I don't think it's anything to worry about," the doctor said. He wrote down some more notes.

"So, Doc, what's wrong with me?"

"Well, Mr. Brutton, hot flashes like you have described are very rare in people your age, especially males. They can be caused by various factors, the most serious being cancer."

"Cancer?" Omar practically yelped.

"That's simply the most serious, but also the most unlikely. It's probably something as simple as an allergic reaction to something you ate. I want you to do me a favor. I want you to keep a diary of everything that you eat and when you eat it and document the exact times the hot flashes occur. Do that for a week. If you're still experiencing the hot flashes, then come back in and bring the documentation. We'll settle on a course of action based on what you tracked. Okay?"

"How's that help me during the week? I be really hot," asked Omar.

"Keep ice water on you. Maybe wear slightly thinner clothes. Try short sleeves and a coat. That way you can take off the coat if a hot flash comes. I also got a small portable fan if you want it," the doctor said.

"All right. Now you talkin'. Thanks."

Dr. Richards chuckled as they got up and shook hands again. "No problem, brotha."

***

Now he really was shocking people, and it was getting annoying. Ever since they did that ritual, his powers had gone wonky. His electricity was getting out of control. He had trouble managing the electricity that his body was generating. There were times when he tried to generate a current and nothing but a weak spark came out. Then there were times where his body seemingly couldn't contain the awesome energies lurking beneath the surface of his skin. He had shocked quite a few people he came into contact with over the weekend, and static cling was an issue at times. On Sunday, he had awoken to a bunch of dust bunnies clinging to his face and arms. Matthias also noticed that small metal objects, such as paperclips and coins, were attracted to him sometimes.

Given his maladies, Matthias was debating whether to even go to class that week. Until he got control over his powers, he didn't want to risk exposure. Skipping class would have only meant missing two days since their Thanksgiving break started Wednesday and lasted until the next Monday. In the end, he decided against it for two reasons: (1) two of his classes took attendance and (2) he had pre-break tests in three of his five classes. He'd try his best to avoid people as much as possible, get through those tests as quickly as he could, and get to the break. He just hoped that his powers went dormant while he was at tennis practice with his dad. His dad would definitely sense it and question him on it, and he wasn't in the mood to explain it to him. The last thing he wanted was an "I told you so" from his dad.

"Hello! Earth to Matt!" said Parker, one of his classmates. They were on their way to class. Matthias broke out of his reverie as he noticed her waving her hand in his face.

"Sorry about that shock. It's been happening a lot lately, for some reason. What were you saying?" said Matthias.

"That's okay. Not your fault. I asked if you were you ready for this test," she said.

"Well, I'm a little nervous about the last chapter we went over on Thursday. Hopefully it's not a lot about it on the test."

Parker nodded and said, "Kiss of death. Watch, I bet it'll be a whole two pages on it now. Thank you!" They both laughed. "So do you have any special plans for the break?"

"No. Just Thanksgiving with my mom and dad. Nothing terribly exciting, unfortunately."

"How about Black Friday? Gonna brave the crowds?"

"You know, my mom loves going out on Black Friday. I don't know why she torments herself. I got no intentions of doing that. Come Black Friday, I will be in my bed, sleeping," said Matthias.

"Where are you from anyway?" Parker asked.

"I'm from here, Pottington. You?"

"Chicago. Yeah, I'm going back home for Thanksgiving. O'Hare should be a real treat," she said sarcastically.

"I feel you," Matthias said as they arrived at their classroom and sat down at a computer.

The exam was a computer-based test. He panicked. What if he had a power surge? *Just stay calm, Matt. Concentrate on maintaining your power level like you used to and let's get through this test.* He closed his eyes, took some deep breaths, and began to do the test. He got through the majority of the test with no problems. As he got to the last page, he let out a sigh of relief. He had gotten through it.

Just before he was about to click the Submit button, a burst of electricity surged through Matthias's body and into the computer. The power surge blew the computer's circuits. "No!" yelled Matthias in disbelief. All his work, gone! Everyone who was left turned to him.

"Is there a problem?" the professor asked.

"Yes. My computer just went out. I just lost my exam!" said a distressed Matthias.

"Let me see," the professor said. After examining the computer, he said, "Yep. It looks like it's pretty much dead. You'll just have to stay over to finish it."

"I can't. I have another class. Can I come back after that?" Matthias asked.

"There's another couple of classes in this room for the rest of the day," the professor said.

"Well, what about tomorrow?" Matthias asked.

The professor shook his head. "I'm leaving tomorrow morning."

"Well, what am I supposed to do?"

"The only thing I can do is give you an assignment for you to do over the break in place of the exam. I want you to write a five- to seven-page paper on the factors that led to World War I. Do you accept that?"

Matthias threw up his hands. "I guess I don't have a choice, now, do I?"

"It's settled then. Have it in APA format. Use at least four sources, and it's due in class on Monday."

"Okay." A visibly frustrated Matthias walked out of the room. Great! Now he had work to do over the break.

****

Tre'Vell slowly walked toward the dining hall. Derek had invited him to dinner at the dining hall by the dorm where he, Omar, and Matthias lived. He told Derek that he didn't have a meal plan, but apparently, each student that had a meal plan got a couple of guest passes per semester that they could use for guests to get admittance to the dining halls for a meal and Derek offered to use one of his on Tre'Vell. He readily accepted. Tre'Vell wasn't one to pass up a free meal. He was on a budget, and any little bit helped.

As he walked through the front doors, he noticed Derek, Omar, and Matthias standing off to the side, probably waiting for him. Now he knew why Derek invited him to the dining hall. This more than likely had something to do with the diamond. Perhaps they learned who sent the golems after them? Or maybe something went wrong with the ritual? All Tre'Vell knew was that he was hungry!

"Took you long enough!" Derek complained.

"Whatever. Are we gonna go eat, or are y'all niggas gonna stand around here lookin' dumb?" Tre'Vell asked.

"How you gonna get in without us? I got your guest pass," Derek reminded him.

"Can we just go? You called me here to get somethin' to eat and I don't know about y'all, but I'm hungrier than a muhfucker!" Tre'Vell said, urging them upstairs. They proceeded up the steps and entered the dining area. After getting their food, they got a booth on the far wall.

"I'm sure y'all are wondering why I called y'all. Check that, I know for a fact that's what Matt's thinking at least," Derek started. Upon seeing the surprised look from Matthias that greeted him, Derek knew that he was right. "I also know that Omar and Matt have been experiencing some troubles with they powers."

"How you know that? I didn't tell you that," asked Omar.

"Remember when I told y'all that my telepathy was weak? That I could only read my family's mind and only if they let me?" They nodded. "Well, not anymore. Now I can read not just they minds, but y'alls too. I been hearing all of your thoughts off and on for days now," said Derek.

"Wait! Let me get this straight. You mean to tell me that you've been intruding on our personal thoughts for a couple of days? And you are just now deciding to tell us?" asked Matthias, practically hysterical.

"It ain't been on purpose! I thought I could get a handle on it pretty quick, so sue me," Derek said.

"But I thought your powers only worked on your family?" Omar asked.

"No, I said that my telepathy worked with people I was really close with. Up until now, it was just my mom, dad, sister, four of my closest friends, and Dodger. It must be a side effect of the ritual."

"Hmm. You readin' my thoughts. I don't know how I feel about that. Scratch that, yeah I do. That sucks. You need to stop, quick!" said Tre'Vell.

"It's not like I fully control it yet! I'm working on it. Besides, I ain't the only one having problems, remember? Omar going through menopause and shit," Derek protested.

"Menopause?" Matthias said in surprise, turning to Omar.

"I'm not going through menopause. It's just been difficult for me lately to regulate my body temp at times," he said.

"He's been having hot flashes. Lots of very, very hot flashes," Derek said with a smirk.

"It hasn't been that bad."

"You went to Student Health yesterday."

"Stop reading my mind. Matt's right. That shit's going to get fucking annoying."

"Well, at least you ain't Matt. Poor Matt over here got homework over the break because he blew up his computer during his test." Matthias glared daggers at Derek. "Sorry," Derek offered.

"Aw, man, that's fucked up," said Tre'Vell.

"Tell me about it. So all of us have been having trouble with our powers ever since we did that ritual. What about you, Tre'Vell?" Matthias asked.

Tre'Vell shook his head and took a bite of his food. "Nah. No problems with mine."

Derek said, "Lucky. Well, the good thing is we got about five days during our break to get them under control."

"Who says we'll ever get them under control? You did say that our individual magic would get less controllable, after all," said Omar.

"I think that was just our spells, not our active powers. Besides, that was supposed to happen over time," said Derek.

"Maybe we did something wrong. That ritual was really painful," said Matthias.

"Like I said back then, I did everything the ritual called for. And look, it helped us vanquish those golems. Let's be honest. We couldn't have done that without the power boost the ritual gave us. The ritual saved our lives. We'll get our powers under control," said an optimistic Derek.

"If you say so." Omar took a swig of his soda.

Deciding to shift gears, Derek asked, "So what time are y'all leaving tomorrow?"

Matthias answered first. "Pretty late. Probably around like five."

"I was going to fly back home tomorrow, but my mom went to go visit some family in Washington, so I guess I won't be doing that," said Omar.

"So what you gonna do?"

"One of the dudes on the team offered to let me stay with his family in New York over the break."

Derek thought about that for a minute as he began to finish off the last of his food. "I got an idea. Why don't you come stay with us?"

"Really? I don't know . . ."

"Yeah. There's no need for you to go all the way to New York. My sister ain't gonna come home for the break 'cuz her flight's been cancelled due to the storm, so we have an extra room. She won't mind, I promise."

Omar decided to take Derek up on his offer. "Okay. Thanks."

"What about you, Tre? I know you got your own place, but what you doing for the holiday?"

Tre'Vell looked solemn. "Nothin'. Probably just chill with my homie. I don't really got a family to celebrate holidays with."

"That's unacceptable. It's Thanksgiving! Come spend Thanksgiving with us!"

"Nah, I'm good, Derek," Tre'Vell said as he finished his meal.

"I insist. You shouldn't be alone on Thanksgiving. You can watch the games with us and taste my mom's cooking. She makes the best chicken and waffles."

That sounded tempting to Tre'Vell. "I do love me some chicken and waffles. A'ight. I guess I can stop by on Thanksgiving. As long as your mom and pops are good with it."

"Of course they'll be. They like meeting my friends. It's settled then."

****

Kelsey liked Thanksgiving. It was a time for her to reflect on everything that she had to be grateful for and reminded her that no matter how bad she had it, there were those that were less fortunate than her. There was a time not that long ago that she momentarily lost sight of that fact, so her mom made her volunteer at a mission the day before Thanksgiving and help hand out meals to needy families. That was a couple of years ago, and at first, she wasn't too enamored with the idea. For starters, the mission was in a high-poverty, high-crime neighborhood, and Kelsey wasn't too sure that her safety could be guaranteed. Secondly, she had plans that particular year, and her volunteer work would cut into those plans. Her reticence vanished, however, once she started to hand out the meals. The families that showed up were all extremely polite and warm. She was struck by how often the mothers and fathers would strike up a conversation with her, asking about how she was and blessing her for all of her help. Here these people were desperately in need of food, and they took the time away from their struggles to see if she and her family were all right. She couldn't count how many children's' faces lit up at the thought of having a nice warm meal to eat. It both lifted her spirits and deeply saddened her. In the end, she enjoyed the experience so much that she offered to volunteer again each Thanksgiving after that.

This year, there seemed to be more volunteers than before. She didn't mind. As a matter of fact, she welcomed all the help they could get. They would probably need the help, seeing as the line for the meals was longer than previous years. Soon, Kelsey ran out of turkeys at her table, so she went over to the truck to fetch some more. The person manning the back of the truck, where the turkeys were located, was inside it and the doors were closed. She banged on the doors. "Hey! Can I get a couple more turkeys please?" she yelled. The person inside told her to wait a minute while he brought them to her. After a few moments, the doors swung open, and the man appeared with the turkeys in a cooler.

"Here you go," the man said.

"Thanks," said Kelsey. "These turkeys are going pretty fast."

"Tell me about it. I been bringing turkeys out all morning. Don't I know you? I feel like I know you from somewhere," the man asked.

"You do look familiar, now that you mention it," Kelsey replied.

"I got it. I met you at the mall back in Delaware a couple months ago. Remember?"

"Oh yeah, you're right. Derek's friend, right?"

"Devon, yeah. And your name starts with a *K* . . . Kelsey!"

"Yup. Good memory," Kelsey said, giggling a little.

"Well, I never forget a pretty face."

Kelsey blushed. "So what are you doing down here in DC?" Kelsey asked.

"I'm visiting my dad for Thanksgiving. You?"

"I live here. I just go to college at Word U."

"Oh. Okay. What a coincidence to meet you again at a mission in DC."

"Yeah, I've volunteered for Thanksgiving here for the past couple of years. How about you? Have you done this before? I don't remember you from previous years."

"Nah, this is my first time. Just wanted to help out this year. I love to help people out in need during the holidays. I feel it keeps you grounded," Devon replied.

Kelsey began to see Devon in a whole new light. "I couldn't agree more."

Devon decided to make his move. "I know you shot me down back then, but I really would love to meet back up with you once we get back to Delaware. Take you out to a movie or something."

Kelsey pretended to briefly give it some thought before saying, "Okay. Here's my number." She handed him a piece of paper with her cell phone number on it. "Call me." Devon watched her as she walked off with the cooler of turkeys.

****

"That's him. Come on." Derek had just received a text message from his father, informing him he had arrived at their dorm and was waiting for them in front of the building. Omar followed him out of the room and down the stairs.

As they walked down the stairs, a thought popped into Omar's mind. "Don't the football team have a game this Saturday? How does that work if everybody is leaving for the holidays?" Omar asked.

"Actually, last week was our last game. We made the playoffs as a three seed. The playoffs start this Saturday, and we would have had a game if we didn't have a bye. Since our game isn't until next Saturday, Coach decided to give us the rest of the week off," Derek explained as they exited the building.

"Oh." When they got outside, Omar saw the same silver Camaro that Derek had at the cemetery. "You told your family that I'm coming, right?" Omar asked.

Derek nodded and said, "You can put your bag in the trunk and ride shotgun. My dad is big on guests taking the front seat." When they got up to the car, the door to the trunk popped open, and the boys placed their bags in it. Then Omar got in the front seat while Derek slid into the back.

"Dad, this is Omar. Omar, this is my dad," Derek introduced from the backseat.

Omar extended his hand. "It's nice to meet you, sir."

Stephen shook it firmly. "Likewise. And it's Stephen. I certainly don't need you to be callin' me 'sir' for the next couple days."

"Got it. Mr. Stephen it is." The car pulled out the complex. After a few moments, Omar said, "Thanks again for letting me stay at your house. That's good lookin' out."

"No problem. We can't have one of Derek's boys homeless for Thanksgiving. Besides, with my daughter not coming home this year, we had one less person to cook for, and Valerie loves to cook," Stephen said.

"How is Mom, anyway?" Derek asked.

"Same ol', same ol'. Ain't nothing new with that woman. She is mad you haven't called more often. She hasn't seen you since that time you stopped by the house to get some dog food. By the way, what was that for anyway?"

"Um, Devon had a pest problem," Derek answered, laughing.

"Pest problem? Never mind, I don't want to know. Anyway, I've had to take her keys away to prevent her from marching down to that school to see you a couple of times."

Derek shook his head. "Yup, that sounds like her."

"Mr. Stephen, do you mind if I crack the window? I know it's kind of chilly outside, but I'm a little warm," Omar asked, billowing his shirt.

"I don't care," he said. Omar cracked his window to let in some of the cool air. Derek laughed. Omar glared at him in the rearview mirror. "What's so funny back there?"

"Omar's going through menopause," Derek said through the laughter.

"What?"

"Man nigga, shut up with that menopause shit!" Omar said. Almost immediately, he noticed his linguistic slipup and sheepishly looked at Derek's dad. "Oops. Sorry about that. No disrespect, sir." Stephen waved it off.

"It's Stephen, remember? And you fine. I ain't no prude. We all men here. Although I wouldn't let my wife hear you using that language," he said.

"Yeah. My mom don't care if you not her child. She'll wash your mouth out regardless. I remember this one time I slipped and cussed in front of her. Oh man, she looked like she was gonna rip my tongue right out my mouth."

"I've got that look before," Stephen chuckled.

"Good to know. No foul language in front of Derek's mom," Omar said.

"So what did you mean, Derek?"

"Omar's powers been giving him hot flashes lately." Omar just stared out the window at the cars and buildings passing by.

"Derek told me you was a warlock."

"No, Dad, that was somebody else I was talking about. That was Matt."

"Oh. So what exactly is your power, Omar?"

"Pyrokinesis."

Stephen let out a whistle of appreciation. "The ability to control fire. Impressive. Have you always gotten hot flashes?"

"Not since I first got my powers when I was a kid. They just started happening the last couple days. This one isn't as bad as the ones I been getting though."

"That's weird. I wonder what caused those problems to just pop up like that." Derek and Omar shared a knowing look. "Maybe it's a allergy," Stephen offered.

"That's the same thing the doctor thought," Omar said.

"You went to the doctor's?" Stephen asked in slight surprise.

"Just to see if there was a mortal way to deal with them."

"Why would you do that? Ain't there something in your grimoire to help you deal?" Stephen asked. Omar suddenly found his shoes very interesting. "Was it something I said?"

"I don't have our family's grimoire. I accidentally torched it when I first came into my powers," he said solemnly.

Derek inched up to the armrest that sat between the driver's and passenger's seats. "You never told me that."

"You never asked. Although even if you did, I probably wouldn't have told you. It's not exactly my proudest moment."

On that note, the car pulled into the driveway. Omar got out of the car and looked at the house. The James family lived in a neighborhood made of colorful Victorian row houses. Each house was easily distinguishable from the houses on either side due to stark differences in color. Their house was a light blue with gray shingled roofs. A bay window slightly jutted out into the small yard. There was a small flight of steps that led to a small porch. Omar thought it was a pretty decent size. It wasn't too big, but it could comfortably fit a family of four.

After getting their bags from the trunk, they entered the house. "Mom, we home!" Derek yelled. He didn't receive a reply. His dad pointed out that she must have briefly stepped out since her car wasn't in the driveway. "Right. Come on. I'll take you to the room you'll be staying in," Derek said to Omar. He followed Derek up the stairs, which were next to the front entrance. At the top of the stairs was a hallway. "This is the bathroom," Derek said as they passed by the first door along the corridor on their right. They kept going. There was a door on the left. "This is my sister's room. She said you can sleep in her bed, but she don't want you spending more time than necessary in there. I told her nobody would want to spend time in her wack-ass room anyway." They both laughed at the comment. The next door up was on the right.

"This is my room. That last room is my parents'. We can put our stuff down in here."

His room was a little smaller than their dorm rooms, which was pretty good, considering that two people shared those rooms. There was a full-sized bed along one of the walls; a thirty-two-inch TV sitting atop a wooden dresser stashed in the corner; and posters of Adrian Peterson, Lebron James, Ryan Howard, and the Notorious B.I.G. adorned the walls. Omar felt something furry brush up against his leg. It nearly knocked Omar over with its strength.

"Dodger! What'd I tell you about that? That's not how you treat a guest, dog!" Derek admonished.

"That's cool. What breed is he?" Omar asked, petting him on the head.

"He's a mix between a German shepherd and a Labrador," Derek answered.

"I can definitely see the German shepherd in him," Omar said. Dodger was mostly black, with brown fur covering his legs, muzzle, and tip of his tail. He essentially had the body structure and fur pattern of a German shepherd with a Labrador's head.

"Why'd you name him Dodger?" Omar asked, curious.

Derek looked around the room and grabbed a baseball. He handed it to Omar and said, "Throw this at him."

"You want me to throw a baseball at your dog?" Derek nodded. "He won't bite me or anything, will he?" Omar asked hesitantly.

"I promise."

Omar threw the ball at Dodger. In seemingly the blink of an eye, Dodger dodged the projectile, and it landed harmlessly on the floor by the bed. "Okay, that is cool," said Omar.

"I can use my telepathy to communicate with him. He understands my every word, and I know what he's thinking too."

"You cannot."

"I'm dead serious."

"Prove it. Make him do something that's not basic."

"Okay. Let's see. Dodger, go to the poster of Adrian Peterson." Dodger just stood there, staring at Derek.

What are you doing? Go stand by AP!

Don't be showing me off!

Omar smirked. "I thought he understood your every word."

"Dodger, give me a high five!" said Derek, raising his hand.

Give me a high five, Dodger!

Nope.

Dammit, dog, you better get over here and give me a high five!

I think I'm gonna have some fun with this. Good luck looking like an idiot. He-he! Dodger sat down and started scratching himself.

"He's purposefully ignoring me to make me look bad!" Derek protested.

"Yeah, sure he is, buddy," said Omar, with a hint of sarcasm. Dodger got up and left the room.

"You better run," Derek grumbled. Dodger started barking and ran down the steps. "My mom's home." Derek and Omar went downstairs to meet her. They got to the bottom of the steps just as she entered the door. "Hi, Mom!" Valerie moved to hug her son. "This is my friend Omar."

"Well hello, baby," Valerie said.

"It's nice to meet you, Mrs. James," Omar said.

"Great. You guys are here just in time to unload the groceries from the car," she said.

"You joking, right?" She just stared at him. That told them all they needed to know.

****

"The food's done," said Bryant, poking his torso through the wall to Matthias's room. Matthias yelped in surprise. A few sparks of electricity shot from his body, and the light in the room flickered. Bryant knew that doing so would bug his older cousin to no end. Ever since he had gotten his powers a few years ago, the now thirteen-year-old found that his favorite hobby was annoying Matthias with it. Bryant had the ability to shift the cells of his body through solid objects, allowing him to pass through things like tables and walls similar to a ghost. When his body entered this state, it was practically invulnerable. This power first manifested itself when he fell though his room one night and landed on the couch that was situated directly beneath his bed in the living room below. It was an odd sensation, like he was floating through cool water. It didn't take him long to get the hang of it however, and once he got control of it, the torture of Matthias began in earnest.

"I really wish you wouldn't do that!" Matthias yelled at Bryant.

"That's why I do it! What was that?" Bryant asked, walking fully into the room.

"You surprised me, is all."

"But I done that before and you ain't did that. What's going on?"

"None of your business!"

"I'm telling, Uncle Isaac," said Bryant.

"If you do, I swear I'll fry you!" Matthias threatened.

"Oh please! We both know your powers won't work on me."

"Only when you shift. I'll catch you."

"If you want me to keep quiet, it'll cost you," Bryant said, holding his hand out.

Matthias shook his head. "Getting extorted by a thirteen-year-old. Fine." He took a few dollars out of his pocket and angrily handed them to Bryant. He stuffed them in his pocket.

"Good. My lips are sealed. So, what you doing?"

"Well, I was trying to write this paper that's due on Monday before I was so rudely interrupted!"

"I was just telling you that the food was ready, dang!"

"That's why we have doors!" said Matthias in exasperation.

Bryant said, "Doors are for normal people. And we definitely ain't normal." Matthias just rolled his eyes. "I'm surprised you got homework over Thanksgiving. I know I wouldn't be doing it."

"And that's why your grades are what they are and mine are what they are."

"You mean, that's why I'm popular and cool while you a nerd?"

"Whatever. Just get out, Bryant! I'll be downstairs in a minute." With that, Bryant shrugged his shoulders, shifted through the wall, and out of Matthias's room. "That's such an annoying power," Matthias mumbled to himself.

As Bryant descended the stairs, the smell of delicious turkey, stuffing, macaroni and cheese, and collard greens assaulted his nostrils. As he was making his way to the dining room, he heard the front door open and close. He went to go see who it was.

"Mommom! Poppop!" He ran over and gave them a big warm hug.

"Hey, baby!" said Vivian, hugging him back. "How have you been?"

"Great! Y'all got here just in time. Mom and Aunt Shawnette just got done cooking. Come on!"

Clarence said, "You ain't got to tell me twice!" They quickly put their coats in the coat closet beside the door and went into the kitchen area to greet everybody.

"Hi, Mom, Dad," Isaac said when he saw his parents walk into the dining room. He made sure to grab a seat where he could still see the big-screen TV that sat in the living room so he could continue to watch the football game.

"Hey, son," Clarence responded.

"You guys make it here okay?"

Clarence sat down at the table as Vivian went into the kitchen. "You know your mother. She always complaining about me driving too fast. She's always backseat driving from the front seat. I was *this* close from throwing her butt in the backseat where she belonged," he said, holding his fingers inches apart. Isaac shook his head at his father's familiar complaints about his mother.

In the kitchen, Mary and Shawnette were putting the finishing touches on dinner. They had cooked turkey, stuffing, macaroni and cheese, collard greens, ham, potato salad, corn, broccoli, lasagna, and sweet potato pie.

"Hello, hello, hello!" said Shawnette as Vivian walked into the kitchen.

"Hey, Mom!" Mary said, hugging her.

"Hi, Viv," Shawnette greeted.

"This smells wonderful! Let me help you take it out there," Vivian offered.

"That's okay, Mom. We got it."

Vivian grabbed the lasagna and said, "Nonsense. Come on here, now." Mary and Shawnette each grabbed a dish and followed Vivian out to the dining room.

Matthias came down the stairs to join everyone else for dinner. He saw his mom and dad, grandparents, aunt, and cousin sitting at the table. "It's about time you joined us, Matt," his mother scolded.

"Sorry, Mom. I was just working on my paper. It took me a little longer since SOMEBODY decided it would be a good idea to shift into my room unannounced," said Matthias, stealing a glance at Bryant.

"What did I tell you about using your power to sneak up on people?" Bryant's mom asked.

"You told me to tell him the food was done. That's all I did," he answered.

"I'm going to find a spell to keep you out if it kills me," Matthias said.

Clarence couldn't wait any longer and said, "Look, are we gonna bless this food already? I want to eat!"

Isaac said, "I agree. Matthias, why don't you do the honors?" Everyone stood up, clasped hands around the table, and bowed their heads.

"Heavenly Father, we thank you for bringing us all together on this day of Thanksgiving. We thank you for watching over us, Lord, and allowing us to reach this moment. We ask that you bless the food that we are about to ingest and know that we know that without you, dear Lord, that it would not be possible. We give you all the glory, God, and humbly request that you continue to confer whatever blessings that you deem fit on us. In Jesus's name we pray, amen."

Chapter 10

Finals

This rest of the week of practice was going to be intense. It needed to be intense. The Wildcats were preparing for the first round of the playoffs. Derek could already feel the intensity for the upcoming game. The upperclassmen were a little more uptight, and the coaches ran the practices even more focused than usual. Derek didn't know what they were so worried about. Word U was playing great the past couple of weeks. Besides, they were the higher seed and therefore had home-field advantage. There was no way they were going to lose the game. He didn't know what the big fuss was about. This was just another step on their way to the championship.

"That was a pretty brutal practice," Derek said. He was in the locker room getting changed after a particularly difficult and hard hitting practice.

"Yeah. I think coach is making up for the fact that we missed three days of practice last week. That and we got a playoff game coming up," said Josh Morris, a junior cornerback.

"Man, we got this. There ain't no way we gonna lose at home to Morlan State. It's in the bag," said Derek confidently.

"Never take your opponent too lightly, rook. That's how teams get upset. They go in cocky. Always respect your opponent," Josh said.

Derek said, "Look, all I'm saying is that as long as we take care of business, we shouldn't have any trouble winning the game. That ain't cocky, that's confident."

"And that's good. Take that confidence and apply it to every practice from here on out. We lost in the playoffs the past couple years to lower-ranked teams. I don't want that to happen again. All's I'm saying is I got postseason experience. I learned the hard way that every team is in the playoffs for a reason," said Josh.

"Fine. But if the rest of the week is as bad as today, we ain't gonna make it to Saturday in one piece. I mean, this is the hardest we hit since preseason. He got to let up, don't he?"

Josh chuckled. "Don't worry. If coach follows what he did the past couple years, the last few days will be mainly walkthroughs. I wouldn't count out tomorrow being the same as today, though. Of course, we ain't win the 'ship the past couple years, so who knows? He might change it up."

"Oh, he already has changed it up. He got me now."

"Better be careful. You don't want your mouth writing a check you can't cash," Josh cautioned. Derek just laughed. "So how was your Thanksgiving?" he asked as they walked out the facility.

"It was fine. My sister didn't come home, but I had a couple of my friends come over. How about you?"

"It was fun. It's the first time I been back home this semester, so that was good. See the fam again." The shuttle pulled up to the curb. "Yo, did you want a ride?"

"Nah, I'm straight. Good lookin' out, though," said Derek. He climbed onto the shuttle and headed back to his dorm.

****

Mayor Wright smiled as she lightly caressed the blue and gold police badge that she held in her hand. She didn't know why she hadn't thought of this before. *That's not true. It's because this is a drastic step,* she thought to herself as she placed the badge of the Pottington Police Department on the table in front of her. Drastic times called for drastic measures, however. Her golems failed. She needed a backup plan in case her next plan failed.

She covered the badge with lavender and pepper. Once she was done, she chanted, "Yobi crity hote ziran. Bilore astir vuty plyvetal shawti noir." The badge began to sizzle and emit a purplish-black smoke. The spell was working! She then conjured a set of iron shackles. She placed one end around her wrist and the other end around the badge.

> Magic forces, black and white
> Reaching out through space and light
> With urgent need, I call on ye
> Mind to mind, bend wills to me
> Public servants, heed my call
> Under my spell, you will fall.

The badge glowed a dull blue, indicating that the curse had worked. Of course, she would have to test it out. She removed the shackles and slowly lifted the badge. She could sense the dark magiks that were now trapped in the object. This was her meal ticket. There was no way that they would escape this. She actually had something much more insidious in mind for the diamond that would surely defeat them, but it was nice to have this as well. She knew that she was getting into dangerous territory, though. This spell could possibly create a trail of breadcrumbs that led right back to her if she was not careful. If it came down to it, she would have to tread carefully. As she got up and walked out of the room, she was confident that the curse wouldn't be necessary. The families of Derek, Omar, Tre'Vell, and Matthias wouldn't have to worry about making New Year's resolutions next year. They would be too swamped planning their funerals!

****

There were only two weeks left in the semester, so everyone was pretty excited about that. That also meant that the students were all done with spring semester registration. With the passing of the holiday break, the next thing that people looked forward to was finals. At least, that was what students at most colleges were preparing for. However, since the football team was in the playoffs, the campus was engulfed in playoff fever. The whole week, Derek and all the other members of the football team had people coming up to them wishing them luck. It was definitely a confidence booster. On his way to his English class, Derek saw Kelsey walking toward the building as well. He caught up to her.

"Hey, Kelsey!" he said, gaining her attention.

She spun around to discern the source of the greeting. She smiled when she saw Derek running up to her. "Hi, Derek. How was your Thanksgiving?"

"It was fine. Didn't really do much. But I enjoyed the time off, though. It was nice not having a paper due, or to study for a test, or football practice. At least for a few days," Derek said.

Kelsey nodded. "I know, right? We had the weirdest thing happen, though."

"What?"

"My mom and dad went shopping on Black Friday. They said they saw this one guy. It was this long line at Best Buy, and he was a couple of places in front of them near the middle. Well, when they got near the front, this guy just started peeing on the wall!" Kelsey explained.

"Ew. That's so nasty!"

Kelsey agreed. "I know! Apparently, he didn't want to lose his place in line and he really had to use the bathroom."

"Well, I guess so!" Derek said, laughing.

"Good luck," she offered.

"Thanks. We won't need it though," he bragged.

"I see that somebody's not nervous for their playoff game this Saturday," said Kelsey.

"Not in the least. You comin', right?"

Kelsey dug into her coat pocket and pulled out a ticket. "Just got my ticket today. The ticket-booth lady told me I was lucky because it was one of the last tickets they had. Those things sold out fast!"

"Well yeah. You should've known that was gonna happen. It's a playoff game!"

"I know. I was just so busy with my research paper that's due. I haven't even started it yet, and it's due next week! How bad is that?"

Derek shook his head. "Real bad. Why didn't you start it over the break? Why'd you wait so late?"

"I don't know. I'm a procrastinator," she said. She got a text message on her phone. She pulled it out, read it, and giggled. She quickly typed a reply and sent it off.

Derek's curiosity got the best of him. "Who was that?"

"Hmm? Oh, that was Devon."

"Devon? My boy, Devon?" Derek asked, needing clarification.

"Yeah."

"How he get your number?" Derek asked with a hint of jealousy.

"We met at a mission in DC over the break."

"Oh yeah. He told me he was heading down to DC. I forgot you lived there."

"Yup. He helped me hand out some turkeys. We exchanged numbers."

Derek tried to act nonchalant as he asked, "So what did he want?"

Kelsey saw right through his nonchalance. "Well, if you must know, he asked me if I wanted to go to the movies. Neither of us has seen *Thor* yet."

"Wow. So you gonna take him up on his offer?" Derek asked.

"Yes. I think I am. *Thor* looks really good." Kelsey thought she saw a slight look of disappointment flash across Derek's face. As quickly as it appeared, however, it was gone. "Is that okay?"

"Huh? Oh yeah, sure. Go enjoy yourself. Devon's cool peoples," Derek responded. "I guess." They walked inside the building.

"So you don't mind me dating your best friend?" Kelsey asked.

"I ain't say he was my best friend," Derek countered.

Undaunted, Kelsey asked, "Is he?"

"Well, yes, but I ain't say that though."

"I can tell these things. I pride myself on being pretty perceptive."

"I can see that."

"So you never answered my question."

"What was that?"

"Do you mind me going out with Devon?"

Of course I do! "No, not at all. Like I said, Devon's cool peoples," Derek said.

By this point in time, Derek realized that he clearly had feelings for Kelsey, and he thought that she knew that, especially if she was so perceptive. So what did this mean? Was she not interested in him like that? Or was she tired of waiting for him to make a move and decided to move on? Had he read the signals wrong? Were there even any signals to read? As he pondered these questions, they arrived at their classroom.

"Okay," she said. She opened the door to the class and walked inside. It would definitely be weird to see those two dating. Was it bad that he secretly hoped that they didn't work out? With that thought, he sighed and entered the classroom.

****

Rhonda yawned. It was getting a little late. She had gone to Matthias's room to study, and she guessed she lost track of time. They hadn't seen each other in over a week. She went to visit family in New Jersey for Thanksgiving, and Matthias stayed in Pottington with his own family. They had talked on the phone in the meantime, but talking over the phone wasn't the same as being in each other's' presence.

"Maybe we should stop, babe. You're yawning," Matthias said.

"I will. I only got one page left. Okay, how did you come up with that answer?"

"Did you distribute the 2x to both factors in the parentheses?" he asked.

Rhonda looked at her work. She was about to say "of course," but upon further inspection, she was crestfallen. "No. I only distributed it to the first one. That was a stupid mistake."

"Don't beat yourself up. A lot of people make that mistake," Matthias comforted.

"But it's a really stupid mistake. It's a mistake that can cost me on the finals. I can't afford to be making simple mistakes like this, or else it'll just lead to me making bigger mistakes," she said. She was beginning to get a little hysterical. "Bigger mistakes lead to a failing test. And a failing test leads to a failing grade. I'm struggling to hold a B minus as it is, and the finals is 30 percent of our final grade. You do the math because obviously I can't!"

Matthias grabbed her arms to calm her down. "Relax. Just like you told me earlier this semester, you'll do great. Take a deep breath." She did so. "And exhale." She did that as well. "Feel better?"

"No, I just feel tired. You got an energy drink?" she asked irritably.

"Let me check." Matthias looked in his refrigerator. "Nope. I'm going to run on over to the POD and cop us some. I'll be right back." He left the room.

Rhonda decided to take a little break while Matthias ran to the minimart. She searched in her purse for her cell phone in order to get on Facebook. "Crap! I must have left my cell phone in my room." She looked around the room and saw a tablet resting on the nightstand by his bed. Thinking she could use that to get on Facebook, Rhonda went over and grabbed it. When it asked her for a password, Rhonda was confident that she knew what it was. She typed in "Matty1994." That was it.

He's so predictable, she thought to herself. When the lock screen disappeared, Rhonda was expecting the usual home screen that was customary for tablets or some variation thereof. Instead, what she got was a strange page that looked like the cover to a book or something. It depicted the head of an elephant. The background was gray, and it had bronze bordering.

Rhonda was fascinated with this page. What was it? She swiped her finger across the screen, and a new page came forward. It simply had "Book of Magiks" printed across the screen in a fancy font. So this was a book. By the looks of things, it was a book on magic. Her interest piqued, Rhonda proceeded to flip through the e-book. On the subsequent pages were all types of spells, incantations, and pictures of strange creatures. What unsettled and confused her were additional entries that seemed out of place with the supernatural topics that were contained in the book. There were pages that contained pictures of people with Matthias's last name. Along with those pictures were things like "levels," "powers," "methods of death," and the like. What especially freaked her out was when she came across one such page and a very familiar face stared back at her—her boyfriend's father!

Before she could peruse the screen, she heard the door handle turn. She quickly locked the tablet and hurriedly placed it back on the desk. As Matthias handed her the energy drink, she decided she wouldn't bring up what she saw to Matthias, at least not yet. Something told her she had stumbled onto something she shouldn't have. But what?

****

This was Deandre's first basketball game. Tre'Vell decided to go to the basketball game with a group of people that included Matthias, Rhonda, and a few people from their classes. Not wanting to feel like an oddball, and knowing that halftime of the game was doubling as a pep rally for the football game that was taking place the next day, he brought Deandre along. After everybody exchanged pleasantries, they got settled in their seats in the student section behind the basketball hoop. Normally, the stands were nowhere near full capacity for an early

December game. The stands were filled to the brim on this Friday night, no doubt due to the pep rally.

"That's Omar right there," Tre'Vell said to Deandre, pointing to Omar.

"Number 7?" Deandre asked.

"Yeah."

The first half was a taut back-and-forth affair. The opposing team, the St. Alexander University Blue Jackets, got off to a hot start. The Wildcats kept pace, though. Every time it seemed as if the Blue Jackets were about to open up a big lead, Word U went on a run to pull them back to a one-possession or tied game. By the time the first half came to a close, the Blue Jackets led by four.

Once the buzzer sounded to signify halftime, a palpable buzz surged through the arena. "I'm so excited!" Rhonda said to Matthias. He smiled. The cheerleaders took the floor first and did a couple of routines to get the crowd fired up. Along with the cheerleaders, the school mascot, Willie the Wildcat, did a couple of skits that entailed him kicking, punching, stomping, and otherwise maiming a cardboard cutout of the opposing school's mascot. It was a little corny, but elicited a few chuckles among the crowd. Soon, the lights dimmed and the football team paraded to the center of the court to raucous cheers. Once the whole team was out there, Coach Steve took to the mike.

"What's up, everybody?"

The crowd collectively answered, "Nothing!"

"Good. I'm going to keep this short. We want to thank all of you for coming out tonight. Both us and the basketball team really appreciate you guys spending a Friday night with us. But the real work for us will take place tomorrow when we play Morlan State at Brooks Stadium. Now, one of their players already guaranteed a victory. That's right! They think that they're going to come into our house and rob the place!" The crowd booed vociferously.

"We need you guys to help us make sure that that won't happen. So here's what we want. We want to see every single one of you guys at that stadium tomorrow decked out in your silver and blue. Make life hell for them! Cheer your voices out! Make this a trip for them that they will never forget!" He walked away from the microphone, and the crowd went crazy. The captains took turns giving brief remarks before the football team took their seats in the stands while machines shot out shirts into the crowd.

With the conclusion of the rally, both teams emerged from the locker rooms and began their warm-ups. The second half went much like the first half. St. Alexander kept pushing ahead with Word University catching back up each time. Halfway through the half, tragedy struck. With the score tied, Word U grabbed the rebound from a missed shot and passed the ball to Omar. He walked it up the court and called for an isolation against his man. When his team cleared the top of the key, it was just Omar and his man. He began his drive to the basket. His defender was quick though and didn't allow him a direct path to the basket. Omar decided to shift direction with a crossover and try going to his left.

As soon as he made his cut, his leg gave out. An audible *gasp!* came from the crowd. The defender grabbed the vacated ball, ran down the court, and dunked it. No one really noticed, however, as all attention was fixed on Omar sprawled out on the court, grabbing the back of his leg in obvious pain. His teammates huddled around him as the coaches and trainer quickly made their way over to him. "Aw man. That looks like a hammy," said Tre'Vell. The crowd waited with bated breath as the trainers tended to Omar. Eventually, they got him to his feet and helped him limp off the court and into the locker room.

"I hope he's okay." Rhonda said in concern.

"I'm sure he'll be fine . . . eventually," said Matthias.

"Tough break," said Tre'Vell. Matthias turned toward him, incredulous. "No pun intended," Tre'Vell said.

With the pall that had befallen the arena, Word U lost the game 71–61. As the fans exited the stadium, Matthias's and Tre'Vell's thoughts were firmly planted on Omar and his well-being. They decided to stay at the arena and wait for Omar to emerge. The rest of the people in their group left, including Rhonda and Deandre. They went downstairs and waited in the lobby. Matthias shot Omar a text message.

> Matthias: Hope u alrite. Me n Tre waitn for u in the lobby

> Omar: Cool. They fixin me up now. Shuld be out in a couple mins

After about ten minutes had passed, Tre'Vell and Matthias saw Omar emerge from a set of double doors. He was on crutches. The injury must have been pretty serious. "What happened to you?" Tre'Vell asked.

"They said they probably think it's a bad hamstring pull. They want me to come in for a reevaluation tomorrow so they can see how it responds after I sleep on it," Omar explained.

Matthias said, "That's a bummer. It looked pretty bad when you went down."

"It hurt like hell. I just heard a *pop!* when I cut and just went down." He shook his head in frustration. "Ugh! I know this is going to keep me out for a while. Hamstrings are tricky."

"Hang in there. Let me give you a ride. We'll drop Tre off on our way back to the dorm."

****

You could cut the tension with a knife. At the beginning of the game, the fans inside the stadium were both rowdy and confident. They were so sure that their third-ranked team would steamroll Morlan State. The first quarter started off according to plan. Word U returned the opening kickoff for a touchdown. After forcing a quick three and out, they then marched down the field and scored a touchdown on a 6-yard run by Bruce. Toward the end of the quarter, Morlan State had reached the red zone. As they were about to go in for a touchdown, Word U forced a fumble at the goal line and recovered it at their 5-yard line. The first quarter came to a close with the score 14–0 Wildcats, and the rout was on. Or so they believed.

The second quarter saw a complete reversal of the first one. In their beginning drive of the quarter, the Wildcats were picked off. Morlan State got the ball at midfield and scored a touchdown. After trading three and outs, Word U drove down the field and got into enemy territory. On third down, Bruce had a long touchdown run called back due to a personal foul penalty. They would end up having to punt the ball. That was disastrous, as Morlan State returned the punt for an 80-yard touchdown. The score was tied 14–14. With five minutes left in the half, Word U had a good drive, but it stalled at Morlan State's 21-yard line. They attempted the field goal and missed wide left. With 1:47 left, Morlan State got the ball and went down the field. They kicked at 45-yard field goal and went into the half leading 17–14.

Seemingly emboldened by their lead and smelling the potential upset, Morlan State came out of the half on fire. A big kick return gave the offense the ball in Word U territory. The defense held them to a field goal, and it was 20–14 Morlan State. The Wildcats were beginning to feel the pressure of a choke. None of them believed that they wouldn't be up big by this point. They certainly didn't see themselves trailing by six in the third quarter. A couple of penalties, blown coverages, dropped passes, and missed assignments followed; and Morlan State entered the fourth quarter leading 26–14.

Now, the crowd was on pins and needles. The crowd's silence spoke volumes to the players. In a desperate attempt to rally the troops, Josh gathered his defensive teammates. "Come on! This comeback gotta start with us! We need a stop! Let's go!" On the ensuing drive, Morlan State got a good drive going, but the defense stood tall once Morlan State got past midfield and got off the field without giving up any points. With the ball now on their own 15-yard line, Word U began their comeback. After a few first downs, the crowd began to get back into it. With 6:43 left, the Wildcats scored a touchdown to cut the deficit to five. Word U recovered a surprise onside kick, and now the crowd was really into it. Their team was about to pull victory from the jaws of sure defeat! However, with 3:53 left in the game, Derek caught the ball at the 12-yard line. As he was fighting for extra yards, a defender jarred the ball loose and caused a fumble that Morlan State recovered. The crowd groaned. Their comeback attempt was thwarted!

With their hopes seemingly dashed, the defense took the field. With 1:54 left, hope was ejected back into the stadium. Josh intercepted a pass and returned it to their own 43-yard line. The crowd went wild. There was life! Nobody was more thankful than Derek, who got a chance to redeem himself. A couple of quick passes set up the Wildcats on the 24-yard line with fifteen seconds left. On the play, Derek got behind the defense because his defender slipped. Now wide open, he put his hand up. Lee saw and heaved a perfect pass to him. The crowd rose in anticipation. This was his chance! With the defender five yards behind him and nothing but grass in front, it was a sure game-winning touchdown. As the ball landed in his hands, the crowd cheered. It then gasped as it hit the turf. Derek had dropped the ball! He had dropped a wide-open pass that hit him right in the hands that would have been the game winner!

Derek was sick to his stomach. With only five seconds left, they were reduced to attempting a hail mary. Morlan State batted down the ball in the end zone and celebrated the huge upset. Word U walked off the field dejected. The crowd was stunned. The only sound that could be heard was the Morlan State Retrievers hugging, clapping, and cheering on the middle of the field. The Wildcats slowly began to trudge to the locker rooms as many people in the crowd refused to move, hoping beyond hope that if they stayed there, the scoreboard would cease to read 26–21 Morlan State.

The mood in the locker room matched the mood they just left in the stadium—a morgue. The football players moved around the space as if in a daze. Derek slumped in a seat by a locker and just stared off into space. His body was in the locker room, but his mind and soul were still out on that field, still playing in that game. He was in his own little world and barely registered Coach Steve's address to the team following their devastating loss.

"Well, there's not much to say. I'm sure that each and every one of you feels like absolute shit right now. What you're feeling right now is natural. You should feel that way. A game like that is supposed to hurt. It's supposed to feel like you just had your heart ripped from your chest and held up for the world to see. That's how you know you care. But listen to me here. There's not a single person in this room that should be ashamed of how they played out there. We win as a team, and we lose as a team. I saw effort. I saw fight. I saw a team that fell down by double digits and kept pushing. And that's something to be proud of. This game will sting for a while. For my seniors, your teammates, your coaching staff, and your school wants to thank you for your four years of blood, sweat, and tears you poured into this program. We had a good season, and we're sorry we couldn't script a better ending for you guys 'cuz you definitely deserved it. For everybody else, use this loss as motivation as you transition into the off-season. I love each and every one of you, and it was an honor to be your coach this year."

Unlike most other games, Coach Steve didn't leave the room after his speech. He decided to go around the room and personally address players who looked like they were truly struggling. Needless to say, he was going to be there for some time. Many players looked like they were on the verge of tears. Indeed, a few already were. When he got around to Derek, he could tell that he had his work cut out for him.

"Good game, Derek," the coach said as he patted Derek on the shoulder. Derek didn't move, smile, or otherwise acknowledge that Coach Steve was even in his presence. His gaze was fixed on the locker in front of him. He hadn't even yet begun to remove his uniform and pads. "I know how you feel, Mr. James." This seemed to get Derek's attention.

"Oh really? Can you tell me? 'Cuz I don't. I don't know how I feel," asked Derek.

Coach Steve pulled up a chair and sat opposite of Derek. "You feel embarrassed. You feel like a failure because you think you let your team down."

Derek scoffed and said, "Didn't I?"

"No, son. You didn't."

"Are you kidding me, coach? Did you watch the same game? How can you say I ain't let this team down when I cost us the game?"

"Because you didn't lose us this game."

"The ball was right there on the palms of my hands. There wasn't nobody around me. A catch like that I make in my sleep and I walk into the end zone. Everybody else did they jobs. The line blocked. Lee threw a perfect pass. All I had to do was do my job, and I didn't. If that ain't failure, what is it? I choked, coach."

"Derek, you have been one of the most remarkable freshmen I have ever had the pleasure of coaching. We wouldn't even have played in this game if it wasn't for you."

Tears began to pool in Derek's eyes. "And look how it ended. I embarrassed us in front of thousands of people. A fumble and dropped touchdown on back-to-back possessions to end the game? How can I look them dudes in the face ever again?"

Coach Steve leaned in and grabbed the back of Derek's neck to pull him closer. "Let me tell you something. Don't none of them boys blame you. Not a one. We was trailing when those things happened. Everybody played a part in the outcome. Like I said, we win as a team and lose as one."

"I know they blame me. I can feel they stares."

"Let me share a story with you. When I was in college, I was a lineman. On one play, I missed a block and got my quarterback blown up. He ended up breaking his leg on the hit. I felt so guilty I avoided him for that whole next week. I thought he hated me and I ain't blame him. Eventually, he came up to me on his crutches and asked me why I wasn't talking to him. When I told him, he just started laughing. I was worrying for nothing. He didn't blame me because things happen. People make mistakes. Nobody's perfect. All we can do is stay strong by sticking together, learn from our mistakes, and move forward," Coach Steve explained.

Derek nodded, but remained unconvinced. As his breathing became heavier and a stray tear rolled down his cheek, he said, "I just don't know how."

Coach Steve pulled the mercurial receiver into a close embrace. "Just let it out, son. Let it out." Derek finally broke down and sobbed into his coach's chest as he repeatedly mumbled, "It's all my fault."

****

Matthias raised his arms above his head and yawned as he began to wake. He slowly arose to a sitting position as he rubbed the last vestiges of sleep from his eyes. As the sun beamed in through his window, Matthias got a nagging feeling in the back of his head that something wasn't quite right. As the sleep-induced fog finally lifted, it hit him. He looked over at the clock on his desk and nearly fainted. In big red numbers, it read "7:50."

Shoot! His finals that morning started in fifteen minutes! How had he overslept? He swung his legs over the side of the bed as he wondered how his alarm hadn't gone off. He didn't have time to find out though.

Matthias threw on his sneakers, grabbed his keys, and ran out the door. The classroom he was going to was about a ten-minute drive away. In previous classes, the professor stressed that nobody would be let in late. The doors would closed at eight o'clock on the dot. If Matthias didn't make it there before the doors closed, he would fail the finals! He knew he would look like a fool showing up to class in his pajama pants and undershirt, but he didn't care. The most important thing was making it to his finals on time.

Matthias rushed to campus in record time, but couldn't find a parking space. Just his luck. He was forced to park a few blocks away from the building the class was in. He sprinted to the building, and his face fell. The door was closed. Knowing it was probably of no use but needing to try anyway, Matthias went into the room to try to convince his teacher to allow him to take the exam.

The lecture hall was set up like an amphitheater with the entrance at the top and the professor situated at a table at the bottom. As he descended the stairs, he could hear and feel the snickers as the students examined his attire. He approached the table the professor was sitting at out of breath.

"Can I help you?"

Matthias briefly paused to catch his breath. "I'm here to take the test."

The professor looked up at the clock. "You're late."

"Yeah, but only by like three minutes!"

"Refresh my memory. What did I say in the previous class?"

Matthias sighed. "That even if we were one minute late, we couldn't take the exam."

"Well, that settles it," the professor said.

"Please. This final is 25 percent of our grade. I'm only pulling a B in this class right now. If I get a zero on this, I might not pass this class. Please," Matthias pled.

"I feel bad for you, I really do. You certainly looked like you rushed right on over here," the professor said, appraising Matthias's odd look. "But I'm sorry. I cannot allow you to take this test. I made it explicitly clear that you cannot be late. All of your classmates somehow managed to make it here before the door closed. It wouldn't be fair to them to allow someone to come late and take the test when they were all here on time for it."

Matthias slumped his shoulders. "Can I at least do something to offset the F? Another assignment or something?"

"That also wouldn't be fair. Besides, your grades are due in a week, and I'll be honest, I don't feel like grading something that would be in-depth enough to be a suitable replacement of your final exam anyway."

Matthias threw his head back and grumbled out of frustration. This was the second exam that he had botched. The first one was mostly out of his control. His powers had caused that. This one was completely his fault. How could he do something as idiotic as oversleep his final exam? Who did that?

"I can't believe this," he said, mostly to himself.

The professor gave him a slight sympathetic smile. "If there is nothing else I can help you with, I'm going to have to ask you to exit the classroom at this time. You're causing a slight distraction to the class." Matthias turned around and scanned the hall in front of him. There were quite a few students with their attention fixed on him and the professor. He sadly trudged up the stairs and out of the lecture hall.

***

"Man, Deandre! Would you hurry up!" Tre'Vell yelled from the living room. Deandre was still in his room getting ready, and Tre'Vell didn't want them to miss their bus.

"Hold up. I'm almost done," he yelled back.

"Damn, what you doin' in there?" Tre'Vell looked down at his watch: nine thirty. Their bus left at nine forty. The stop was about a ten-minute walk from their apartment complex, and if they missed the bus, the next one didn't come for another hour. That was unacceptable, seeing as they both had a finals scheduled before then.

"All right, let's bounce," Deandre said as he emerged from his room.

"It's about time!" said Tre'Vell. They left the apartment and exited the building.

"So what class is your finals in?" Deandre asked as they walked to the bus stop.

"Intro to Psych. You?"

"Spanish," Deandre responded.

"How you think you gonna do?" Tre'Vell asked.

"Pretty good. Remember, we grew up around Spanish people so a lot of this stuff sounded familiar," he said.

"I'm glad you did good. My psych class raped me this semester. I need to ace this test just to pass the damn class."

Deandre laughed. "Took it up the ass, huh?"

Tre'Vell laughed along with him. "Nigga, stop laughin'. It ain't funny."

As they turned the corner, they saw a bus sitting about two blocks away. "What bus is that?" Deandre asked.

Tre'Vell looked at his watch. It was nine forty. "That's the 54!" The bus started to take off.

Deandre began to panic. "We ain't never gonna make it in time! Quick, do that thing!" Tre'Vell did a quick look-around. Nobody was around. He threw his hands at the bus, and it froze. Deandre and Tre'Vell took off for the bus to catch it before it unfroze.

When they got to the bus door, Tre'Vell unfroze the bus and banged on the door. "Hey, let us in!" The bus driver stopped the bus and opened up the door.

"It's a good thing you boys caught me because I was just about to take off. Where y'all come from anyway? There wasn't nobody at the stop just now?" the driver inquired.

Tre'Vell said, "We saw you pullin' off so we booked it from back there."

After they paid their fare and took their customary seats at the very back of the bus, Deandre leaned in. "Did I ever tell you how useful that thing is?" he said.

"I know, right?" Tre'Vell said. They each spent the rest of the bus ride doing some last-minute studying for their respective exams.

****

With the conclusion of the last day of final exams, the campus of Word U was again abuzz with activity. Everyone was leaving their dorms for the winter holidays, and they wouldn't be returning until the first week of February for the beginning of the spring semester. The only students that weren't leaving were those that were participating in winter sports and those that were taking classes during the winter session. Omar fell under the former category, and Matthias and Derek fell under the latter category respectively. Matthias and Derek decided to hang out with Monica in the RA's office on that day. This gave them something to do, and it also allowed them to say goodbye to their friends before they left for the winter as they turned in their keys.

"So how did your finals go?" Monica asked them.

"Ugh, don't ask!" replied Matthias as he spun around in his chair.

Monica laughed. "I take it you don't think you did too well?"

"One of them I didn't take at all," he said. Upon seeing her quizzical look, he expounded. "I overslept for one of them."

"Oh no. What happened?"

"I set my alarm for 7:00 p.m., not a.m. My professor didn't let me take the exam so I get a zero. I've already come to grips with the fact that I won't get a great final grade. I only hope that I can at least pull a C and pass the class."

Monica said, "Oh. I'm sorry." She turned to Derek. "What about you, Derek?"

"Okay, I guess. It was pretty hard to study for my first one 'cuz it was on Monday, and after what happened last Saturday, I ain't feel like studying much," he said.

"Understandable. How are you holding up after that?"

Derek said, "Honestly? Not great. I just can't believe I fumbled and dropped that pass. I feel like I let the school down."

Monica put her hand on his shoulder and said, "It'll be okay. You always got next year."

Matthias chimed in. "Yeah. Everybody makes mistakes. At least you put yourself in that position in the first place. We wouldn't have made the playoffs if it wasn't for you anyway. Anybody blaming you is a hater."

Just then, Porsche walked in to hand in her key. "Hi, guys. Just turning in my key and heading out."

Monica accepted her key and got her to sign out. "Okay. Have a great holiday. See you in February."

"You too. Bye y'all."

"Bye," Matthias and Derek said simultaneously.

"So what you gonna do this winter?" Matthias asked Monica.

"Well, like I said at the floor meeting, since we have so many students staying over the break, we need to have more than one RA for the winter session. Most dorms only have one RA on duty, and they get to go home until the New Year when classes start. Me and Dimere are going to be here. I get to go home for the next two weeks and he'll be here. The two weeks after that, he'll go home and I'll be here. Then we'll both be here for the remainder of the winter session. I'll be going back home and just relaxing with my family," she said.

Before Derek could ask his question, Omar and another boy walked into the office. They were each dressed in basketball shorts and a T-shirt. Omar had a basketball in his hand, and they were sweating profusely. "I'm 'bout to bounce," the boy said.

"Okay, Ryan. I just need you to give me your key and sign this," said Monica. While Ryan was doing that, she asked, "So where are you two coming from?"

"We just got done playing ball at the gym," Omar said.

Matthias and Derek looked at each other, confused. "I'm surprised you could play basketball so quickly after suffering a hamstring injury. I had one of those before, and it took a while. When you went down at that game last week, it looked pretty bad. I'm glad it wasn't serious," said Monica as Ryan left the office.

"Yup. You and me both," said Omar. He left the office.

"Huh. Quick healer," Derek commented.

"A little too quick if you ask me," Matthias said suspiciously. "I'll be right back." Matthias left the office and caught up to Omar. "Omar, hold up!"

Omar spun around. "What?"

"What's going on?"

"What you mean?" he asked innocently.

"You know what I mean. When we saw you after the game, you were on crutches. Now all of a sudden, you're playing basketball? And hard, judging by how much you're sweating."

"I don't know. Probably a combination of it not being as serious as first thought and the treatment this week. What can I say?" said Omar.

"I'm not buying it. What did you do?"

"Nothing, damn!"

"I could just get Derek to read your mind if you want," Matthias warned.

"No! Fine," said Omar. "I might have cast a spell," he mumbled.

"YOU DID WHAT?" Matthias yelled.

"Calm down. It ain't that serious."

"What spell did you cast? Where'd you get it from?"

"It was a healing hex from Derek's grimoire."

"How'd you even pull that off? He keeps it locked in his chest, and nobody else can touch it?"

"I asked him if I could see it, and when he pulled it out, he went to the bathroom. And I could touch it fine," Omar responded.

"Must be another side effect of the ritual," Matthias reasoned. "Wait, if you're talking about the spell I think you're talking about, you would have needed somebody else to cast the spell with you."

"I got Tre to help me," Omar said, shrugging.

"Why would you do that?"

"Um, because I was hurt. Look, why you making such a big deal out of this? It's not like you haven't cast similar spells before."

"That was because we got attacked by supernatural creatures. That's completely different from using your magic to heal an injury that occurred naturally," Matthias said.

"How?"

"Because it's not fair, especially in sports. Other players get hurt all the time and they don't have the option of just magically healing the injury. It gives you an unfair advantage," Matthias explained. "You basically just cheated."

"Well, I'm sorry to burst your bubble, Mom, but life ain't fair. I'm not gonna just sit here and suffer through an injury when I don't have to. What's the point of having magic if I can't use it for my benefit? Other people don't got that option? Tough."

"But—"

"Let's get one thing straight. Just because we linked now don't mean that I need your permission to use my magic how I see fit," said Omar.

"Wrong. You didn't use just your own magic, you stole a spell from Derek's grimoire to do it. Besides, that's exactly what it means. What you do affects all of us now. We have a shared destiny. You can't just go off doing whatever."

"Well, like I said, I got Tre to help me so it's not like I did it alone. But if it makes you feel better, I won't take any more spells from Derek's grimoire anymore. Now move. I gotta go take shower." With that, Omar shoved his way past Matthias and disappeared up the stairwell.

Chapter 11

Drawn

Tre'Vell closed his eyes and began to sing the lyrics as the instrumental played.

> Lately you've been questioning
> if I still see you the same way
> 'Cuz through these tryin' years
> we gonna both physically change
> Now, don't you know
> you'll always be the most beautiful
> woman I know
> So let me reassure you darlin' that
> my feelings are truly unconditional, see . . .

Clap! Clap! Clap! Tre'Vell immediately stopped singing just before he hit the chorus and opened his eyes to see who had interrupted him. As he peered out from the recording booth, he saw a girl standing in the studio. From what he could make out, she was about five feet ten and a little on the thin side, with braids cascading down her back.

"Musiq Soulchild. Not bad," the girl said with a small Southern drawl.

"Okay, how long you been there?" Tre'Vell asked, a little embarrassed.

"Not long. You left the door open, so I decided to stop on in. Sorry if I distracted you," she said.

Tre'Vell left the recording booth and entered the studio. "Nah, that's okay. I'm sorry you had to listen to me."

"Don't be. You were really good. And I like Musiq, so I don't say that lightly," she said.

"I'll take that. And what would be your name, pretty lady?"

"Ricquel. And you, kind sir?"

"Tre. So what brings you here to the studio? It can't be just to hear me. I ain't that good—yet," he said.

Ricquel laughed. "Actually, I was on my way to the music store that's here. I heard it's cheaper to buy albums from there than some place like Walmart or Target."

"What album was you lookin' at?"

"I can't seem to find that new Beyoncé album anywhere yet. I'm trying to buy two copies—one for me and one for my aunt for Christmas. Do you know if they got it in yet?" Ricquel asked.

"Since I work here, I can say that we just got it in yesterday," Tre'Vell replied.

Ricquel sighed with relief. "Good. I bought it on iTunes, but I want a physical copy. So I told you what I was doing here. What about you, Tre?"

"Well, like I just said, I work here."

"What was with the sangin' you was doing back there?"

Tre'Vell chuckled. "I'm workin' on an album. I ain't a good songwriter, at least not right now, so I'm doin' a cover album."

Ricquel was impressed. "Okay. You know, I'm just the opposite. I'm a singer-songwriter, but if I'm being honest, I'm more a writer than a singer. I'm certainly not as good as you. If you want, we could work together and I could write you a few songs for your album and you can duet with me on a couple songs. Win-win," she offered.

"I can dig that. Why don't you give me your number so I can call you to meet up?"

"How about you give me yours instead?" she countered. Tre'Vell shook his head and smirked before giving her his cell phone number. After she put it in her phone, she turned to leave. "I'll have my people call your people." She then walked out of the studio.

****

Derek teleported into the barbershop. Cedric, one of the barbers, was cutting Devon's hair. Lamar was lounging in his chair, scrolling through the texts on his cell phone. Raheem, one of his friends, was sitting in an empty barber's chair. There was nobody else in the shop, which Derek was grateful for. He was running late, and he knew that Lamar had somewhere to be afterward, so he had to be on time for his appointment. Not wanting to reschedule, he decided to teleport down to Sharp Cutz without thinking. He shuddered at what would have happened if there were people in there that didn't know about his secret and he would have had to explain himself.

"What's up, Cedric, Devon?" Derek asked. They both raised their hands as if to say hello.

"Now what if somebody was in here?" Raheem asked.

Derek shrugged and said, "So I took a risk." He went over to greet him. "What's been going on with you, Raheem?"

"Man, Christmas shoppin', what else?" he said.

"I heard that," Derek said. He went over to Lamar for his haircut. Lamar got up to let Derek sit down.

"You late," Lamar said as he draped the cape around Derek.

"That's why I 'ported. I was already running late, and if I didn't, I would've been like thirty minutes late," Derek said. Lamar nodded and began the haircut.

As he was cutting Devon's hair, Cedric asked, "Aye, Derek, you ain't never told me how your playoff game went."

Derek sighed as he prepared to relieve the gory details, but Raheem beat him to the punch. "They lost to sorry Morlan State. He had the chance to win the game and let it slip right through his fingers."

"Thanks, Rah," Derek said.

Raheem started laughing uproariously. "I mean, you should've seen him, Ced. Wide-open pass, ball right there, and dropped it. Lost them the game."

"I said THANK YOU, Raheem!" Derek reprimanded.

"I don't know how he dropped it. He did fumble right before that, though. He was probably high."

"Don't make me shut you up," Derek warned. Raheem stopped laughing.

"Calm down, nigga. You know I was only playing," he said.

"Man, that's rough. Get 'em next year," Cedric said.

Derek nodded. "So, Devon, I heard that you talkin' to Kelsey."

"Yeah. We went to the movies a couple weeks ago." He hesitated before asking, "You cool with that?"

"Yeah, yeah," Derek said a little quickly.

"No, he ain't," Raheem chimed in. Lamar chuckled and shook his head.

"You sure? I mean, I ain't trying to cockblock if you feelin' her. You saw her first. If you claim that, I'll back off."

"Nah, go 'head. I got plenty of other girls. Like I told you before, Kelsey's just a friend," he said.

Cedric finished cutting Devon's hair. A couple of minutes later, Lamar finished with Derek. "Lamar, before you leave, can you do another tarot reading for me?" Derek asked.

"Why?" Lamar said.

"Some things have happened recently, and I want to see if it's changed or not," Derek responded.

Lamar asked, "Like what?" Derek didn't answer immediately. "Look, if you want me to do the reading, you gotta tell me what's been going on."

Derek explained, "We been attacked by golems a couple of times, but we vanquished them. I just wanted to know if that ended the threat or not."

Raheem asked, "Golems? What's golems?"

Lamar looked concerned. "They supernatural rock monsters. Those things is hard to kill. How did y'all pull that off?"

"We found two other dudes and did that ritual you told us about. Gave us the power we needed to stop them," Derek said.

"You actually performed the ritual? How was it?" Lamar asked.

"Painful. So are you gonna do the reading or not?" asked Derek.

"Wait here."

Lamar disappeared into the back room. He emerged with a set of tarot cards and some candles. "Lock the door and close the blinds Cedric," Lamar commanded. He did as he was told. While he did that, Lamar pulled the coffee table that was sitting in the corner into the middle of the barbershop, and Derek turned off the lights. They all pulled chairs up to the table and watched with rapt attention. Lamar placed the five candles around the table in a circle and lit the flame on each one.

He held the deck of cards to his temple and whispered, "Show me Derek James's fortune." He then shuffled the deck and placed it on the table in the middle of the circle. "The past," he said. He flipped over the top card, and on it was a drawing of a rope in a knot.

"What's that mean?" Devon asked.

"This signifies that Derek made a meaningful connection of some sort, forged some bond. Probably the blood-bonding ritual he did," Lamar answered. His attention returned to the tarot cards. "The present," he said. He flipped over the top card, and a picture of a bird crying appeared. "A profound sadness," said Lamar.

"That was probably the football game," said Derek.

Lamar nodded and placed his hand on the top of the deck to pull the final card. Derek let out a nervous breath. This was the one he was truly anxious about. "The future," said Lamar. He overturned the card. On it was a drawing of a skeleton holding a scythe.

"Oh shit, that can't be good," Raheem commented.

"Death. The same as before," said Lamar. Derek's face fell. So nothing had changed. "I'm sorry, Derek," said Lamar.

"That's fine. It ain't your fault. Thanks for doing it for me. I'll catch y'all later." With that, Derek teleported out of the barbershop.

****

What a pleasant surprise. It was a couple of days before Christmas, and a blanket of stark white snow covered the landscape. The Word U campus, sparse and bare as it was, was absolutely beautiful. The students that remained on campus enthusiastically greeted the fluffy precipitation. Matthias looked outside his window. According to the news, eight inches had fallen overnight and that morning. It was the first big snow the state had gotten in a couple of years. The previous years had been practically devoid of snow. He planned on enjoying the snowfall, especially because he didn't have any classes to worry about at the current moment. He whipped out his cell phone and sent out a group text.

Matthias: Snowball fight at the park at 1. Spread the word

Omar: Aite

Derek: Definitely. Will do

Tre: Will be there

When one o'clock came, Matthias made his way to the park along with Omar. When they got there, they were somewhat surprised at how many students were there. Matthias only expected only about maybe ten to fifteen people: himself, Omar, Tre, Derek, and a few of their friends. As Matthias scanned the field that resided in the middle of the park, there had to be at least fifty people there. Their friends must have told some more friends and so on and so forth. The power of technology was fascinating sometimes.

They got to the front of the park. "Aren't you cold?" Matthias asked. Omar was dressed in nothing more than a pair of jeans and a thermal top. He didn't even have on a hat. This contrasted with Matthias, who had on a pair of sweatpants, a thick winter coat, a hat, and a pair of gloves.

Omar answered, "Nope. I use my powers to keep myself warm. I haven't had a winter coat since I was in elementary school. Saved my mom money on constantly having to buy coats every winter, let me tell you." As they made their way through the trees and to the field, Omar asked, "Does it freak you out that the last time we was in this park was when Tre was almost killed by those golems?"

Matthias answered, "It is kind of weird, isn't it?"

Omar spotted Derek standing with a few of his teammates, talking to some girls. He and Matthias smiled at each other, apparently each having the same idea. They each made a snowball and sneakily made their way toward him, hoping for an ambush. With their backs toward them, the group would never know what hit them! When they got close enough, they unleashed their snowballs. To their dismay, Derek ducked and the projectiles fell harmlessly to the ground in front of him. The others in his group turned around, gathered snowballs, and attempted to retaliate. This seemed to spark everybody else on the field, and the snowball fight began in earnest!

As his friends made their way into the fray in the middle of the field, Derek ran over to Omar and Matthias. "Thought you had me, didn't you?" he gloated smugly.

"There's no way you heard us. How'd you know to duck?" Matthias asked.

Derek tapped his head. "I heard your thoughts," he said.

"That ain't fair," Omar said.

"All's fair in love and war, and this is war!" said Derek. "Speaking of which, I can sense Tre's thoughts, meaning that he close to the park. Let's ambush him!"

Matthias and Omar grinned. They left the field and went into the wooded area that surrounded the park. They hid among the trees and waited for Tre'Vell to walk by. Sure enough, Tre'Vell soon walked into the park. As soon as he got to the spot that was in the middle of the three of them, they jumped out and pelted him with snowballs. "Aw shit! Stop!" he said laughingly. When they didn't make a move to stop, Tre'Vell threw up his hands and froze the snowballs that were on their way to him. The balls immediately stopped, suspended in midair.

"That's cheating!" said Derek.

"Says the guy that used his powers on us," said Omar.

"That was different. I used my powers to avoid a sneak attack. It was a preemptive strike. This is a cheap way to bail hisself out of trouble," countered Derek.

"So you sayin' my power is cheaper than yours?" asked Tre'Vell.

"No. I actually think your power is pretty cool. I wish I had it. I can think of a few useful things I could do with it. Of course, most of them deal with the opposite sex . . ."

"Why am I not surprised?"

"I'm just saying that y'all can counter my power by blocking me out if you tried. We can't get around yours. It's a cheat code."

"Well, that's not entirely accurate," said Matthias. The three of them gave him a questioning look. "Resumulous" he said and waved his hand at the suspended snowballs. They suddenly continued their path to Tre'Vell and pelted him.

"Ah! Hey, how you do that?" asked Tre'Vell as he wiped the snow from his face.

"I did a little research over the break on each of our powers. Came across that little spell to counteract yours," he said.

"That changes things," said Omar as he rubbed his hands together.

"That's not all I learned." Matthias pointed at the patch of snow-covered pine needles that hovered in the branches over Omar's head. "Nadai necral." The pile of snow fell from the branches and enveloped Omar. Tre'Vell and Derek snickered as Omar was covered in snow.

Omar melted the snow off him. As the steam billowed from his body, he said, "I'ma get you!"

Derek shouted, "MAGICAL SNOWBALL FIGHT!"

****

The Christmas holidays came and went with nothing remarkable happening. Omar had a couple of games to play and therefore could only fly out to his native Los Angeles for three days before he had to return to the campus. Tre'Vell went back to Baltimore for a few days to drop in on some old friends but quickly came back to Pottington in order to avoid any potential issues or unresolved conflicts. Derek spent Christmas with his family but decided to shuttle back and forth from his house and his dorm until his winter session classes were to begin in 2014. Matthias intended to spend the entire week after Christmas at home but changed his mind when he learned that his aunt had a conference to attend and therefore had to drop his annoying cousin off for the week.

Matthias's mother had gotten him the latest Mario game for his game system and had a blast playing it by himself for a day or two. He had heard that it was infinitely more fun with multiple players so he invited Tre'Vell, Derek, and Omar over to his dorm once they each got back in the area so they could play it as well. Derek was interested in playing it, thinking it looked like fun, but Omar and Tre'Vell were a little more skeptical. Omar and Tre'Vell were more into video games that dealt with sports, like *Madden*, or violence, like *Call of Duty*. Matthias convinced them to give it a shot after some persuasion. Just like Matthias thought, Omar and Tre'Vell had just as much fun playing the game as he and Derek. They spent about a good two hours laughing and joking as they made their way through the game.

"Smoke break," said Derek. He pulled a giant blunt from his coat pocket.

"Now that's what I'm talkin' about," said Tre'Vell.

"You are not about to smoke that in here," said Matthias.

"Why not? It ain't just for me. I brought it for all of us," said Derek.

"You might set off the smoke alarm."

"Can't you disable the alarm with your powers?"

"I guess. But what if the RA comes knocking because he smells it?"

"Dimere won't be in the building until tonight. I already talked to him. We in the clear."

"Any other objections you could think of?" Omar asked.

Matthias shook his head and reluctantly said, "No. None that I can think of." He sighed and conceded. "Go ahead."

While Omar used his power to light the blunt, Tre'Vell hooked up his iPod to Matthias's dock and started to play some music, a playlist mostly populated by Kendrick Lamar, J. Cole, Jay Z, Lil Wayne, Tupac, and Biggie. Derek took a few puffs before he passed it to Omar, who also took a drag. Tre'Vell got back to the futon and said, "Pass that shit over here." Omar took another drag before handing it to Tre'Vell, and he took a hit. He looked over to Matthias, who was watching the scene from his bed. Tre'Vell offered the blunt to Matthias, who declined. He shrugged and he, Derek, and Omar continued to pass it between each other.

After a few minutes of letting the music wash over them, Tre'Vell asked, "Who you think was better, Biggie or 'Pac?"

"B.I.G.," said Derek.

"You crazy? 'Pac, easy," countered Matthias. "'Pac's lyricism was on another level. That, and he rapped about better stuff."

"Are you kidding me right now? B.I.G.'s cadence was better than Tupac. Plus, he was more versatile. Most of 'Pac's shit was similar. Biggie could do party records right along with the hood shit," Derek argued.

"That's because he had Puff," said Matthias.

"Who you got now, Kendrick or J. Cole?" Omar asked.

"Not even a question," said Tre'Vell.

"I agree. Kendrick," Derek said at the same time that Tre'Vell said, "J. Cole."

"Yo, dawg, you cannot be serious right now. You honestly gonna sit here and say that J. Cole is a better MC than Kendrick Lamar with a straight face?"

"Nah. I just really fucks with J. Cole's last album. Kendrick killin' the game though. I'm waitin' for his next album," said Tre'Vell.

"All right, here goes a real hard one. Who would you rather do—Rihanna, Nicki Minaj, or Beyoncé?" asked Matthias.

"Aw shit."

"Now, we talking about like as a mistress or a one-nighter-type thing?" Tre'Vell asked.

"One time."

"I don't know. I gotta think about that one," said Derek.

"On the one hand, Rihanna a freak. She might can show me some things. But Nicki got that ass though and I'm a sucker for ass. I'ma have to go with her," said Omar.

"Give me the freak Rihanna. Nicki got ass, but it ain't all real. I think of Beyoncé more as sexy wifey material," said Tre'Vell.

"Yeah, but Beyoncé probably one of those chicks that a lady in the streets and a freak in the bed. You seen the album she just released? Talkin' about eating her Skittles and doing surfboards and shit. Making up new positions. I'm getting a boner just thinking about it. I might have to go with her," said Derek.

"What about you, Matt?" Tre'Vell asked.

"What you mean? You know Matt don't think none of them would be better in bed than his babe, Rhonda," Derek said teasingly.

"Even if I slept with them, I wouldn't know if they are or not," said Matthias.

"Not a good judge of talent?" Omar asked.

"No, it's just that I'm a virgin, so I don't have the experience to tell if they are better than average or not," said Matthias.

Tre'Vell asked, "Wait. Ain't you and your girl been together for a couple years?"

"Yeah."

"And you ain't hit that yet?"

"Nope."

"Wow! Why not? You scared or something?" Derek asked.

"What? No! Why are you guys making this such a big deal?"

"It's just I haven't met any guys that were virgins past the age of seventeen. I didn't think they existed anymore," said Derek.

"Well, how old were you when you lost it?" Matthias inquired.

"Twelve," he answered.

Tre'Vell shook his head. "Damn! Twelve? I thought I was young when I lost my V-card at fifteen," said Omar.

"Could you even . . . you know, . . . at that age?" Matthias asked.

"I hit puberty early for some odd reason. I could do that when I was ten. There's a funny story behind that too," said Derek.

Tre'Vell took another puff. "Well, what is it?"

Derek started laughing as he began to recall the memory. "I used to pee the bed until I was seven years old. One day, I woke up and my pants was wet. So I run to my parents' room and tell them I peed the bed again. My mom was like, 'I thought you were done doing that?' I said, 'I did too. But I think something is wrong, though.' They was like, 'What?' I said, 'My pee is a little sticky this time.' You should've seen they faces when they realized what happened. My dad took me in my room and tried to have the birds-and-the-bees talk. He was hella awkward."

The four of them laughed. "And on that note, I'll be back. I'm going to go to the POD. Any of you want anything?" Matthias asked.

Derek said, "Nah, I'm straight."

"Get me an Arizona Iced Tea," Omar said as he handed Matthias his student ID so he could use the points on it to get him the drink.

"Get me some PopTarts. I got the munchies," said Tre'Vell. He gave Matthias a $5 bill.

Matthias left the room and made the short trek to the campus convenience store. It was pretty empty, not just of people, but of groceries too. There wasn't much on the shelves. Matthias thought it looked like a Walmart right before a big snowstorm was about to hit. He walked up and down the aisles. Thankfully, he found some PopTarts for Tre'Vell. He went over to the refrigerated section and got himself some strawberries. They were his favorite fruit. He brought them up to the counter to check out.

"Will that be all, sir?" asked the student cashier.

"Yes," said Matthias. Then he remembered Omar. "Oh wait! I forgot something. I'll be right back." He jogged over to the coolers, grabbed an iced tea, and went back to the checkout. "Almost forgot this. Now I'm done."

Matthias paid for the items and left the store. When he got back into Garrette Hall, he decided to check his mail before going back up the steps. He hadn't checked it in a while and hoped that there wasn't anything in his mailbox that was important. He went over to the wall where all the student mailboxes were, which was directly opposite the RA office, and opened his up. He peered inside.

What's that? he wondered. He reached inside and grabbed the thin box inside. A note was attached to the top of the box.

Matt,

Merry Christmas baby. Saw this in the store and decided to get it for you. It looked like fun. I hope you enjoy it.

Mom

"Mom got me another Christmas present. Why didn't she just give it to me when I was home on Christmas?" Matthias opened the box to see what was inside. It was a video game. He pulled it out. *"Zombie Virus U!* I heard good things about this game." He made his way back up to his dorm.

"I was wondering where you was. It can't have taken that long to get to the store and back. I know there ain't nobody there," complained Tre'Vell.

"I stopped by my mailbox on the way back up here," Matthias explained as he handed Omar and Tre'Vell their things. "Apparently, my mom got me this game for Christmas and sent it to me in the mail."

Derek asked, "What is it?" Matthias flipped the game box over so the others could see.

"Zombie Virus U. Now that sounds like it's more up my alley. Pop it in," said Omar.

Matthias took the game out of the box and slipped it into the console. Once the main screen came up, he clicked on the icon of the game and the game started up. After some spooky animations and credits scrolled by, the title screen appeared. Matthias clicked on the Start option. Immediately, the screen went completely black.

"Uh, is that supposed to happen?" Omar asked. Matthias shrugged. Suddenly, the TV emitted a silver light that bathed the entire room in its glow.

"Okay, I'm pretty sure that's not supposed to happen!" said Derek.

The boys suddenly felt an odd tugging sensation. Before they knew it, they were floating through a corridor. The trip wasn't smooth by any means. They were bouncing along the corridor toward a bright light, crashing violently into the shimmering walls along the way. They had to close their eyes as they got closer to the light.

***

"Yes, Dr. Wallace. I agree."

"I'm happy to hear that, Mayor. Do you have any suggestions on how we could improve the program? If you do, I'm all ears."

"Actually . . ." Mayor Wright stopped midthought as she felt a tingling at the back of her mind.

"Yes? What is it?" asked Dr. Wallace.

That sensation can only mean one thing. My curse has been activated. The boys are in the game.

"Mayor Wright? Are you listening?"

It won't be long now. The boys' consciousnesses are trapped inside the game.

"Are you all right?"

There is but one way out for them now. But they'll encounter a couple of unpleasant surprises that won't allow that to happen. They will die in that game. And death in the mind will equal death in the body.

***

Derek regained consciousness and looked around. The others were still out of it. They all seemed to be lying in a plaza of some sort. There was a fountain to their left and pathways leading out into the city. But what city were they in? It looked like something out of a movie. The city was in shambles. Buildings were burned out, cars and trash cans were on fire, and debris was littered as far as the eye could see. But what unsettled Derek the most was the sound. To be more specific, it was the lack of sound. It was eerily quiet. The only sound that could be heard was the fountain, which made it seem even louder.

Derek tried to rouse his friends. "Omar, Matt, Tre, wake up! Wake up!" he said urgently as he shook them awake. They slowly came to.

"Ow, my head! What happened?" Omar asked, rubbing his head.

"I don't know," answered Derek.

Matthias took a look around. "Where the heck are we?"

"I was wondering the same thing. It looks like we in some sort of warzone or something," said Derek.

Tre'Vell said, "Do me a favor and pinch me."

"Why?"

"So I know I'm not dreamin'. This shit is crazy." They all stood up.

"Hello! Anybody out there!" Omar shouted into the distance. The echo ran along the empty streets, begging someone to respond. They heard none. "Where is everybody?"

"I don't know, but something's not right here," said Matthias.

"You think? What gave you that idea, brainiac?" said Tre'Vell sarcastically.

"No, I mean I'm getting a bad feeling about this. Like I know what's going on, but can't quite put my finger on it. What's the last thing you remember?"

"Well, we was chillin' in your crib when you came back with our stuff from the store."

"Yeah, and then you put in that game your mom got you for Christmas," said Omar, continuing Tre'Vell's memory.

"The screen went black, then real gray and the next thing I know, I'm waking up here," finished Derek.

Matthias walked slightly ahead and took in his surroundings a little more critically. "I think we're in London. See that tattered British flag hanging over there? And if you look out in the distance, that tall building over there is the ruins of what I think is Big Ben."

"So what, London all of a sudden looks like World War III? Did North Korea drop a nuke on it? And how did we get over here?" asked Derek.

Matthias remained silent as he began to put the pieces together. "Guys? LOOK OVER THERE!" yelled Omar, pointing to a couple of advancing figures in the distance. Matthias rejoined the group to see what Omar was talking about.

"So there are some people here after all. Maybe they can let us know what's going on," said Derek.

As Matthias got a better look at the figures, his heart filled with dread as he finally put two and two together. "I don't think those are people," he warned.

As the figures got closer, they noticed he was right. The beings' clothes were ripped, tattered, and shredded. Their hair was matted, and their skin was decayed and desiccated. Parts of bones were protruding through their thin skins, sticking out at odd, unnatural angles. A few of them even looked like they were missing body parts, like an eye, ear, nose, or arm. The beings slowly shuffled toward them, as if sizing them up.

"Now I definitely don't like this. Tre, freeze them," ordered Matthias.

Tre'Vell lifted his hands to freeze the beings, but they kept on moving toward them. "I can't," he said in alarm.

"I got them," said Omar. He tried to throw a stream of fire at them, but nothing came out. "I got nothing!"

Derek tried to teleport out, but couldn't. "I can't teleport!" This sudden outburst of activity seemed to spur the beings into action, and they took off toward the boys with a surprising and deceptive swiftness.

"Okay, clearly our powers aren't working but our legs are. Run! Run!" yelled Matthias and the group sprinted off in the opposite direction.

They ran out of the plaza and on to a trash-strewn street, passing downed power lines and flipped-over cars along the way. "Quick, let's duck into this alley!" yelled Derek. They dipped into an alley and pressed against the walls, melting into the scenery due to the darkness. The creatures that were chasing them sped past the alleyway and continued down the street. They had lost them.

"What's that sound?" Matthias asked. A faint crunching sound could be heard in the alley. They looked around to see where it was coming from. "Uh, guys? Look down there!" Matthias whispered, pointing at a spot a little deeper into the alley. Off to the side was another group of the creatures huddled around what appeared to be a human corpse. The corpse was missing a few appendages. One of the creatures yanked off the corpse's remaining hand. Blood started gurgling out of the wrist. The other creatures each snapped off a finger for itself and began to munch on it ravenously.

"Ew!" said Derek.

"I think I'm gon' be sick," said Tre'Vell as he covered his mouth. This seemed to alert the creatures to the diamond's presence. They looked up at the warlocks, blood staining their faces.

"Good job, big mouth!" scolded Omar. The creatures, eyeing a more appetizing meal, got up and ran after the warlocks. "That's our cue!" They ran out of the alley, again on the run.

"I know this sounds crazy, but I think we're in the game!" Matthias said as they continued to evade the hungry creatures chasing them.

"After what I seen lately, I'm beginnin' to think I'll believe anything," said Tre'Vell.

They rounded another corner. When they glanced behind them, the creatures were no longer in sight. "I think we lost 'em," said Derek. The group stopped running and began to walk along the sidewalk to catch their breath.

"Those things look like the zombies that were on the box to the game. The game is set in a postapocalyptic London as well. I think we somehow got sucked into the game when I started it up," explained Matthias.

"Your mom sure does have a sick sense of humor. No offense," said Omar.

Matthias shook his head. "No, my mom wouldn't do something like this. Besides, something like this takes a heck of a lot of magic. A lot more than my mom has at least. I don't know who did this, but it definitely wasn't her."

Tre'Vell asked, "I don't give a flyin' fuck how we got here. How do we get out?"

Matthias said, "I don't know."

They rounded another corner. Bad idea. They came face-to-face with the first group of zombies that were after them. "Oh shit!" Tre'Vell cursed under his breath. The zombies began to advance on the group. They turned to go escape the other way but saw that their path was blocked by the second group of zombies who had caught up to them by this point. Cornered, the diamond backed up until they came up against a wall.

"What now?" asked Derek.

"I say we fight our way out," said Tre'Vell.

"Yeah, that'll end well for us," Omar said sarcastically.

"I ain't scared. I looked down the barrel of a gun before. Barely avoided bullets flyin' past my head. If I'm goin' down, I'm goin' down swingin'," he said.

"No, Omar's right. We're outnumbered 15–4," said Matthias.

"What other choice we got? We don't got our powers and we surrounded!" Tre'Vell said.

As the zombies closed in on them, a smoke bomb flew in out of nowhere and filled the area with smoke. The zombies, as well as the warlocks, started choking on the noxious fumes. "Quick! In here!" said a nasal voice as the door on the side of the building opened up. The warlocks stumbled into the building and away from the zombies.

As they composed themselves, they looked to who just saved them. "Well, don't just stand there! Follow me!" The man opened another door and walked down the steps. They followed him down the stairwell. It was dark and dank with the faint smell of gasoline and stale crackers. Once they got to the bottom of the steps, they followed their savior into another room.

The room looked like a rudimentary command center. In the middle of the room was a panel with multiple monitors embedded on it showing scenes from locations all over the city. There was a trunk next to a small refrigerator, and a small cot was set up next to a bookcase. "Shut the door behind you," the man said in a heavy British accent. Once Derek did this, the man turned around to them, and they got a good look at him. He was about five feet nine, but he hunched over as he stood, so he appeared to be shorter than that. He had a long white beard that reached down to his chest. He had just one eye, as the other socket was empty. He was a squat man and walked with a pronounced limp. Omar thought it made him waddle, like a penguin.

"Are you blokes insane? You can't go walking around above ground out in the open like that! Bloody hell! You lot are lucky that I saw you and decided to help you," he said gruffly.

"Thank you. Who are you?"

"You can call me Jack," the man said.

"Nice to meet you, Jack. I'm Matthias and this is Derek, Omar, and Tre. How did you know where we were anyway, if I may ask?" asked Matthias.

"CCTV. I hacked the city's surveillance cameras and monitor the goings-on over here at this panel," he answered, pointing at the panel. "It helps me to stay one step ahead of the Yotes."

"Yotes?"

"Those zombies out there."

"Why did you call them Yotes?" Derek asked.

"You're joking right?" Upon seeing their looks, he said, "Because of the Yestitute virus, of course. It's what they were infected with."

"What you talkin' about?" asked Tre'Vell.

"Don't you know what's going on? Have you been living under a rock?"

"Our memories are kind of fuzzy. Could you fill us in?" asked Matthias.

"Fine. A couple months ago, a nasty virus started going around London called the Yestitute virus. It turned people into those flesh-eating zombies you saw out there. It spread like wildfire throughout the city, and nobody could find an antidote. In order to stop the virus from spreading further, Great Britain quarantined the city. Nobody was allowed in or out. The poor citizens that were left uninfected, such as myself, were left to fend for ourselves. The Yotes started getting hungry and feasting on the uninfected humans. There are hardly any people left. You lot are the first humans I've seen in about a month."

"How did you survive?"

"I was an engineer. I figured out a way to divert energy from outside the city into this safehouse. Whenever I have to venture out for food, I use the underground system, like the subway tunnels and sewer system. I noticed that the Yotes don't like going below ground for some reason. As I made my way around the city, I started to hack into the surveillance cameras and hook them up to my command center here so I would know which areas were safe to go to for food, weapons, and supplies. I got a small stockpile of food in the fridge and a few weapons in that trunk. Gotta keep going out for food and ammunition, though."

"So the government just left you guys here to die?"

"Sure 'nough did, the cowards. But I'm actually glad I found you guys. I've got a plan to escape the city, but I can't do it on my own. There's an electric barrier that surrounds the city, and it's controlled in two places: Big Ben and the Shard. If I could just hack into the systems, I could lower the barrier and escape," explained Jack.

"What's the catch?" asked Derek.

"I can't access the system without plugging this chip into the control panel located in the buildings. It has to be done at the same time, or the barrier won't come down. Unfortunately, those buildings are crawling with Yotes. With my pathetic speed and strength, there's no way I'd be able to make it into a building, plug in the hacking chip, go to the other building, plug in the hacking chip, and lower the barrier, all the while fending off a bunch of Yotes. You blokes look like you're pretty fit. I know it's going to be dangerous, but can I count on you guys to help me save whoever is left in London?"

"Un momento, por favor," said Omar as he huddled the others together. "We're probably going to have to do this to get out of the game."

"How do you figure that?" asked Matthias.

"Isn't that how these things tend to work out? We have to finish the game or complete some task? Don't you watch the movies?"

"Okay. But the question is, do we break up into groups of two or stick together and take each building one by one?" asked Derek.

"We're going to have to split up. That's the only way we can assure that the Yotes won't take out the chips when we leave," said Matthias. "Agreed?" They all nodded.

"Okay. We'll help," said Omar after they broke the huddle.

"Brilliant! Follow me." Jack hobbled over to the control panel. The boys went over to join him. "Now, this set of screens monitor Big Ben, and these ones look over the Shard. The control panel for Big Ben lies in a back room. The one in the Shard is on the fifth floor. I'll be directing you guys from here."

"Wait, you not comin' with us?" Tre'Vell asked.

"No, I'll just slow you down. I'll be more helpful if I monitor the situation from here. That way, I can let you guys know if there are any Yotes in the vicinity," Jack explained.

"Of course," Derek muttered.

"Here. Take these comlinks. They contain tracking chips that'll allow me to discern your location on this map. They'll also allow me to communicate with each of you." They each took a comlink and placed it in their ear. "Just to let you blokes know, I can try my best, but chances are that you'll have to fend off some Yotes. There's too much of them in those places to avoid." Jack waddled over to the trunk. "My weapons stash is pretty low—a handgun, a flare gun, a hatchet, a baseball bat, some smoke bombs, and a couple small explosives. I also got some flashlights. Power is out in much of the city."

"I call dibs on the gun!" said Derek.

"No, I'll take the gun. I got plenty of experience using one," said Tre'Vell as he grabbed the handgun from Derek.

"Fine, then I got the hatchet," said Derek. Omar picked up the flare gun, and Matthias picked up the bat. They each grabbed a flashlight.

"Since those two got nonlethal weapons, I'm going to give them the smoke bombs and explosives. Be judicious in how you use them because you don't have much of them. And Tre, you don't have much ammunition, so be accurate. Aim for the head. That's their weak spot. The Yotes are attracted to light. That's probably why they don't like to go underground. Try to stay away from the few areas that are still heavily lighted."

"Got it," said Omar.

"So who's going where?" asked Jack.

"Me and Tre will head to the Shard. Derek and Omar can go to Big Ben," said Matthias.

Jack hobbled back over to the control panel. "Here are the hacking chips." He handed one to Matthias and one to Omar. "When you get to the panels, put them in the USB port. I'll be in contact with you, and when the other team has also put their chip in place, I'll hack in and lower the barrier." He went over to a door. "This door leads to the sewers. You'll come to a fork in the road. The path on the left leads to Big Ben, the right one, the Shard. Be careful, and good luck."

Chapter 12

Undead

"God, it smells bad in here!" said Omar as he and Derek walked along the dark corridor, flashlights as the only source of light. The darkness seemed to be encroaching upon them, threatening to swallow them whole as they advanced into its depths. The flashlights only seemed to reach out a few feet in front of them. Even though Jack told them that the zombies didn't like venturing underground, the thought of a bunch of zombies potentially ambushing them from the darkness that surrounded them made Omar a little jumpy.

"Shh! Not so loud," Derek scolded. "We already got these flashlights. We don't need any zombies being attracted to our voices too."

"My bad," whispered Omar. "It's just I'm getting tired of being in these sewers."

"Well, we been walking for about twenty-five minutes. Jack said the building was about a thirty-five- to forty-minute walk from when we split up with Matt and Tre, so we got about ten to fifteen minutes left down here. I don't know what to tell you. Breathe through your mouth," offered Derek.

They continued to walk down the tunnel. They heard a strange sound ring out. "What was that?" asked Omar as he whipped the flashlight around, desperately searching for any Yotes. Derek did the same and discovered the source of the sound.

"Calm down. It's only a rat. See?"

"This is insane. I'm insane. I've been sucked into some game where I'm being attacked by man-eating zombies and I don't got no powers to protect myself. How did we get here, anyway?" Omar asked.

"I have no idea."

"Do you believe Matt when he said that his mom didn't do this? I mean, she is the one who sent the game to him. I don't know too many people that have 'being sucked into the game' as one of their complaints to customer service."

"It's hard to say, but why would she do it? What's her motivation? If she did, his family got some serious family therapy to go through."

"I've been thinking about something ever since we got here. What happens if we get hurt here? Or even die? Do you think that's it? Will it happen to us in real life? Are we really in the game, or is it just all in our minds and we really still laying back in Matt's room?" Omar pondered.

"I'm not sure, but something tells me it don't matter either way. Whether our bodies are physically in the game or in the room, I am pretty sure that the death will be permanent either way."

"Perfect."

Jack spoke to them through the comlink. "You two should be coming up to a path on your left. Take it. There should be a ladder that leads to a manhole that is located right in front of the Shard building."

Sure enough, the two warlocks came across an opening on their left that led to another path. They took it and tried to find the ladder. A rustling sound rang out. "What was that?" Omar asked skittishly, flailing the flashlight to and fro.

"Probably just another rat. Come on, help me find this ladder. It's on a wall somewhere," said Derek impatiently. He began to feel along the walls for the ladder.

"Fine. But I think—AAAH!" yelled Omar.

Derek quickly swiveled his flashlight around to see what was going on. Omar was struggling with a zombie as it was attempting to drag him to the water's edge, trying to pull him into the waste-filled river.

"What's going on? I see Omar going backward."

"A zombie's got him. Hold on," said Derek.

As he ran over to the zombie, he pulled out his hatchet. Before the creature could pull a kicking and screaming Omar into the water, Derek threw himself at the pair. He lunged for Omar's legs since the Yote had

Omar by the head and was already in the water. Derek got ahold of Omar's legs just before the zombie could pull Omar in.

"Pull me up! Pull me up!" screamed Omar, still struggling.

"I could if you would stop kicking your legs out!" said Derek.

Both Derek and the zombie struggled for control of Omar, resulting in a painful bout of tug-of-war. The Yote started to win, and Omar was being pulled farther and farther off the ledge. Soon, the zombie had Omar's forearms in the water. Derek quickly picked up the hatchet and launched it at the zombie. It buried itself firmly in the Yote's forehead. *Aaiii!* With a bloodcurdling scream, the zombie released Omar and slumped against the edge of the water, dead. Derek helped Omar pull himself up.

After taking a minute, Omar said, "Just another rat, huh?"

Derek responded, "So I was wrong. Sue me." He pulled the hatchet from the Yote's head. "At least you all right. Let's find the damn ladder so we can get out of this place."

***

Drip! Drip! Drip! The constant sound of water dripping from the ceiling was the only sound that greeted Tre'Vell and Matthias as they ventured through the sewer tunnel. The sound started about ten minutes into their walk and slowly increased in frequency as they continued on their journey. Matthias surmised that it was probably a good indication that they were getting closer to their destination. The Palace of Westminster was located near the River Thames. The dripping of the water was probably related to the proximity of the river.

As they continued to walk, Tre'Vell suddenly asked, "What if it don't work?"

"What if what don't work?"

"Lowerin' the barrier. What if we still stuck here even after it's down?" Tre'Vell asked.

Matthias remained quiet for some time as he pondered that ominous possibility. "I haven't allowed myself to consider that. If this doesn't work, then there must be something else we have to do. Some other task we have to accomplish."

"Like what?"

"I don't know. I wish I had played this game before so I would know what to expect," said Matthias.

"You two should be coming up to another split. The path on the right leads to the front of the palace. The one on the left leads to the back. It's easier to get to the control panel from the entrance on the south side of New Palace Yard located on the northern end of the palace, but the cameras are showing that there are a bunch of Yotes huddled around a few rubbish bins. It'll be safer if you go around the back way and use the Victoria Tower entrance on the southwest end," Jack instructed over the comlink.

When they reached the end of the path they were on, it broke off in two opposite directions, just as Jack said. They took the tunnel on the left. After a few minutes, Jack said, "Make the upcoming right turn. You should find a ladder that leads above ground on the wall on your left." They made the turn and found the ladder. Tre'Vell went up first. When he tried to push open the manhole cover, it wouldn't budge.

"This thing is locked tight," he said as he continued to struggle with the cover.

"Here, let me try," offered Matthias. Tre'Vell climbed down and let Matthias try to pry it open. He went up the ladder and tried to push open the cover with all his might, but he also couldn't get it to move an inch. "I have an idea. Let's both try to open it at the same time. You go up that side and I'll go up this one," he said. They both tried to open it, but it stood fast. "Jack, this thing isn't moving," said Matthias.

"Oh well. Looks like you'll just have to do this the hard way and take the front entrance."

"It just couldn't be easy, could it?" Tre'Vell asked as they walked to the other manhole cover.

"Of course not. Probably an obstacle built into the game," Matthias said.

They reached the ladder that led to the street and began to climb out. "Now when you reach the ground, you'll see a group of Yotes huddled around a few rubbish bins on your left, and directly in front of you will be the palace with Big Ben to your right. If you're quiet, you two should be able to sneak past them undetected while they're preoccupied with the person they're munching on."

"It'll be just like that time I snuck through the PR's territory to get to the park back in Baltimore," said Tre'Vell. Matthias gave him a look. "Well, it will be. Kinda."

Tre'Vell and Matthias slowly emerged from the sewer from the manhole. About one hundred yards in front of them stood the Palace of Westminster. It stood as a sentry along the banks of the River Thames. It was but a shell of what it was months prior, however. All the windows were broken, and trash was strewn all over the gardens that surrounded the building. From what they could make out in the darkness, it looked like there were dead bodies dangling out of many of the windows. The tallest tower, the Victoria Tower, wasn't much of a tower anymore. It had been reduced to barely more than half of its original height. There were huge chunks missing from the outer walls, giving the structure a swiss cheese–like appearance. Despite the devastation, the Elizabeth Tower, which housed Big Ben, miraculously stood unblemished.

Matthias and Tre'Vell began to silently creep toward the entrance. Tre'Vell held his breath as they crossed behind the group of zombies. Matthias could smell the rancid smell of decaying flesh assault his nostrils, and it nearly made him gag. Tre'Vell gave him a desperate look, his eyes imploring him to find a way to hold it in. Knowing that any sound could alert the zombies to their presence, he swallowed the gag before it could escape from his throat. Tre'Vell unwittingly let out a small sigh of relief, then panicked as he realized what he had just done! They both glanced back at the group of zombies behind them and were relieved that they hadn't heard it and were continuing to happily eat their meal.

They successfully crept past the Yotes and approached Elizabeth Tower. Matthias thought that the clock at the top of the tower appeared much higher up when they were directly in its path than it did from afar. There was a bunch of trash around the entrance, and Tre'Vell carefully stepped over a pile of soda cans. As they briskly and quietly walked up to the entrance, their hearts sank.

"Uh, Jack, we have a problem," said Matthias.

"What is it?"

"There's a bunch of rubble blocking the entrance. We can't get in," said Tre'Vell.

"Can you climb over it?"

"Nah. It goes up all the way to the ceiling, dawg. We ain't gettin' through."

"Well, as I see it, you got two choices. You can either go use the entrance under the Victoria Tower or you can use the explosives I gave you to blow through the rubble."

"Which do you suggest?" asked Matthias.

"That's not for me to decide. If you use the other entrance, you would be moving farther away from the control panel and would have to make it through the building and avoid any Yotes you might encounter. If you use the explosives, you would stay close to the control panel, but the explosion would attract all the Yotes in the vicinity. Those bloody blokes would be on you guys faster than you could say 'Queen Mum.' For what it's worth, my cameras aren't picking up any Yotes around the immediate vicinity of the other entrance."

"What you think we should do?" asked Tre'Vell.

Matthias responded, "Go to the other entrance. We should attract the least amount of attention as possible. Drawing all the zombies directly to us would be a bad idea. I would rather have to make my way through the building. At least that way, we would have an element of surprise and stealth."

Matthias turned around to begin making his way to Victoria Tower. Tre'Vell backpedaled in order to follow him. He forgot about the pile of cans behind him and accidentally knocked them over, sending a ruckus into the area. *Blong! Blong! Blong!* Matthias turned around in alarm, and Tre'Vell covered his forehead in exasperation. Both of their heads shot toward the group of zombies. They immediately stopped what they were doing and directed their attention toward the source of the racket. Matthias and Tre'Vell felt seven pairs of beady dead eyes bearing down on them.

"You idiot! Look what you did!" said Matthias. The Yotes began to snarl as they spotted their new prey. They took off toward the two warlocks.

"Oh shit!" cursed Tre'Vell.

"Come on!" said Matthias. He took off toward the other entrance, and Tre'Vell was close on his heels.

The Yotes were quickly gaining on them. "For the living dead, those things are fast! Ain't zombies supposed to be slow?" Tre'Vell commented.

"Apparently not," said Matthias as they turned the corner.

The sidewalk surrounding the palace was uneven on this side, and Matthias tripped over and banged his knee. "Ow!" he exclaimed in pain. Tre'Vell went back to tend to him. The zombies were getting dangerously close. He pulled out the gun. *Bang!* He shot one of them in the head, and it collapsed to the ground in a heap. Some of the Yotes that were trailing it tripped over their fallen comrade, which slowed the group up momentarily.

"Can you get up?" Tre'Vell asked.

Matthias tried to stand. With great effort, he was able to do so, but when he took a few steps, he stumbled. "Ah! My knee," he said.

"We don't got time for this," Tre'Vell said and draped Matthias's arm around his shoulder and helped him continue toward the entrance. The remaining zombies had gotten up by this point and were closing in on the two, helped by the injured Matthias, who was clearly slowing them down.

"They're gaining on us!" cried Matthias.

"Just a little bit farther," said Tre'Vell. They reached the entrance, opened the door, and entered the building. "We're gonna need something to hold the door so they can't get in," he said.

Matthias looked around and spotted a chair. "Use that chair. Hurry!"

Tre'Vell retrieved the chair and set it up against the double doors, jamming them shut. As soon as he did that, the doors started lurching and rattling as the zombies on the outside attempted to get in. The doors held, and eventually the zombies gave up. They had escaped—for now.

***

Omar and Derek emerged from the sewer. They looked up and saw the formerly gleaming tower rise above the surrounding buildings. "I'm guessing that's the Shard building," said Omar.

"Gee, I wonder whatever led you to that conclusion," said Derek.

The building looked like it was located on a block around the corner from their current location. They began to walk toward the building with Derek leading the way. As soon as he rounded the corner, Derek abruptly stopped and ran back behind the corner, shoving Omar and himself against the wall.

"What are you doing?" Omar asked.

"Shhh! There's a bunch of zombies at twelve o'clock," whispered Derek.

Omar peeked around the corner and sure enough, there were about fifteen zombies milling about toward the entrance of the building. "Great. Just great. Jack, is there another way into the building?"

"Not one that you can get to. You're going to have to find a way past those buggers," replied Jack.

"Why am I not surprised?" Omar asked rhetorically. "So how do you think we get past those things? I counted fifteen of them and there's two of us. I don't like those odds, and I don't really feel like pressing my luck."

"I agree. Our best chance is to probably sneak past them. If we only had a distraction of some sort," Derek reasoned.

An idea then popped into Omar's brain. "Wait. Didn't Jack say that the zombies are attracted to light?"

"Yeah. So?" Derek asked.

"Well I have the flare gun," said Omar.

"Okay, I get it," said Derek as he began to follow Omar's line of thinking. "Use the flare to attract them away from the building. Then use the smoke bombs to shield us running toward the building. Good thinking."

Omar took out the flare gun and loaded a cartridge into it. "Let's see. Where should I shoot this thing?" He scanned the street, looking for an appropriate target.

"That car over there. Aim the flare over there," Derek said, pointing to a flipped-over car on the side of the street.

Omar took aim and fired the gun. *Boosh!* Sparks flew out the car as the flare landed in the car's interior. The Yotes were startled at the sudden commotion. They saw the light emanating from the car and began to creep toward it, transfixed by the sparks flying from it. Once all of the zombies were amassed around the car, the warlocks pounced. "Okay. We got a clear path to the building. Throw the smoke bomb!" Derek said. Omar fished around for one of the bombs in his pocket. "Hurry up." Omar pulled the smoke bomb out and tossed it into the street near the zombies. *Whoosh!* The smoke bomb erupted, plunging the area in a sea of thick, silky fog. Derek was surprised at how effective and powerful the bomb was. It would give them the perfect shroud of secrecy.

"All right, let's go," said Derek. He and Omar sprinted from their spot and made a beeline for the door. Once they got there, they had to open the sliding door manually since the power was out. They pried the door open and walked inside. "Okay, Jack. We're in. Where do we go now?"

"The control panel is located in a former hotel suite on the fifth floor. The elevator lobby is to your right. I doubt it works, but you can try it anyway."

They went to the lobby and pushed the button to summon the elevator. To their surprise, the elevators were working! "Wait a minute. How do the elevators work if there's no power? The door didn't work," asked Omar.

"Who knows? Let's not look a gift horse in the mouth," replied Derek.

The bell rang out, indicating that the elevator had arrived on the ground floor. It opened up, and Omar and Matthias were greeted with a pile of mangled and dismembered bodies littering the floor of the elevator, blood staining the walls. "Nasty," said Derek. They hesitantly stepped into the car and around the bodies. Omar pushed the button to take them to the fifth floor. The elevator began to lurch up the building very slowly.

"I wonder how Tre and Matt are doing," said Omar.

"Let's just ask Jack. Hey, Jack, how are our friends doing?"

"They aren't doing so well. They had to take a detour around the palace. One of them hurt their leg as they were running from a mean group of Yotes."

"Why can't we talk to them again? I mean, we can talk to you," asked Omar.

"The comlinks I pilfered aren't synced with each other. Each of them are synced to my master link. The comlinks can only handle being synced to two other comlinks at one time. That would be me and your partner."

"Man, that's wack!" said Omar.

"What does 'wack' mean?"

"Just a saying we have in the States," said Derek. "It's like saying 'stupid.'" The elevator stopped a floor short of their intended destination. "Why is the elevator stopping on the fourth floor?" He got his answer as the door slowly opened. Waiting on the other side were two zombies!

"Oh snap!" cried Omar.

The foul creatures lunged into the car, each one targeting one of the boys. Derek was walloped by his and slammed into the corner. The zombie then attempted to leap onto Derek and smother him. As the zombie fell onto him, Derek caught it with his legs and pushed it into the opposite wall. He then pulled his hatchet out of his waistband and tried to hack it in the head. The Yote dodged the weapon at the last minute, and the hatchet lodged itself harmlessly into the wall of the elevator. "Crap!" said Derek. The zombie then wrapped its decayed hands around Derek's neck. The zombie was certainly stronger than it appeared!

While Derek was busy with his zombie, Omar was struggling with his. When the zombies entered the elevator, Omar stumbled back. He tripped over the dead bodies in the car and fell on top of them, their blood soaking his clothes. Seeing her opportunity, the zombie lunged on top of Omar. Omar momentarily kept her at arm's length before rolling over and tossing her to the side. Omar saw the hatchet lodged in the wall, grabbed it, and ran to the zombie, which was standing directly in front of the control panel of the elevator. He swiped the hatchet at the zombie, but missed and slammed the hatchet into the control panel, damaging it. "Ugh!" The zombie punched Omar in the face, causing him to stagger back. Omar lifted his arm to hack the zombie, but it caught his arm. They struggled for control before Omar kneed the zombie in the stomach, causing her to flinch and release her hold on his arm. Now freed, Omar hacked the Yote in the neck. *Aaiii!* Blood started to spew forth from the wound. With one final slash to the head, the zombie slumped against the wall, dead.

Derek was desperately attempting to break free of the Yotes' hold, but was finding that task impossible. The creature had a vise grip on his neck. He couldn't breathe, and his struggles was just using up more precious oxygen! His vision began to swim. Stars started to appear. Then the edges of his vision began to darken as he started to lose consciousness. He fought the encroaching darkness, knowing that if he succumbed to it, he was zombie food! As he was teetering on the edges of consciousness, the grip on his throat loosened before he could fall off that edge. He greedily gasped in air like it was going out of style. He looked up to see what happened. Omar had taken the hatchet and killed the Yote before it could kill him.

Breathing heavily, Omar offered him a hand. "You good?"

Derek took it and got up. "Yeah. Good looking out. That was too close. We gotta be more careful," he said.

"Yeah. That's going to be a little harder now, though," Omar said as he looked toward the control panel of the elevator. "I accidentally damaged the elevator as I was fighting that thing. The elevator is broken. Looks like we're going to have to get up to the next floor on foot."

"Awesome," Derek said. "Jack, the elevator's broke. Where's the stairwell that leads to the fifth floor?"

"On the opposite side of the building."

"Just couldn't be easy, could it?"

***

Matthias slowly limped along the hallway with Tre'Vell. Tre'Vell had his gun drawn in one hand and Matthias in the other. Each time they passed by a room, Tre'Vell waved his gun cautiously at the door, lest a zombie jump out and try to surprise them. No zombies had sprung up on them since they evaded the group of them outside.

"Jack, how do we get to the control panel?" Matthias whispered.

"Right now, you're walking down Chancellor's Corridor. At the end of that hallway will be a stairwell on your left. Go to the stairwell and take the exit on the other side. That'll lead you to St. Stephen's Hall. There are other ways to get to the tower, but I know there's no Yotes in that hall because I have a camera in that room. You guys are currently in a blind spot because you just walked out of range of one of the cameras, so I can't help you again until you reach St. Stephen's Hall. Once you get there, I'll give you further instructions."

Once Jack was done, Tre'Vell said, "So we on our own until we get to the end of this hallway. That's pretty far away. I don't like that."

Matthias said with a grimace, "I would say let's speed it up, but I don't think I can go much faster. My knee is getting worse." Just after he finished saying that, he felt a heavy body fall onto himself and Omar.

"What the heck?" he yelled as he and Tre'Vell were jarred apart. He hit the ground hard, which sent shots of pain into the injured knee. A zombie had fallen from the ceiling and ambushed them.

Tre'Vell was knocked to the opposite wall next to a still-shiny coat of armor. "Oof," he grunted. The zombie got up from the ground and advanced on Matthias, snarling all the way. Matthias dragged himself away from the approaching zombie in a futile attempt to get away. His back soon met the wall, telling him he had nowhere else to go.

"A little help here!" he yelled. On the other side of the hallway, Tre'Vell hastily pulled out his gun and shot the zombie. It halted momentarily before continuing on to Matthias. "You missed his head! Shoot him again! Hurry up!" he pleaded as the zombie was directly in front of him at that point. Tre'Vell shot the zombie again. *Bang!* Direct hit! This time, the zombie swayed on its feet before collapsing on top of Matthias, dead. Matthias used his good leg to shove the zombie off him. The Yote went crashing into the wall by Tre'Vell and into the coat of armor, sending the pieces of metal flying in multiple directions. The lower legs were the only things left in their original place.

"Cuttin' it a little close?" Tre'Vell said as he went over to help Matthias to his feet.

"I could ask you the same thing," he said. "Can't aim?"

Tre'Vell tried to explain himself. "I automatically went to the heart. Forgot in the heat of the moment."

"We can't afford for you to be forgetting. Remember, you have a limited number of shots. How many do you have left, anyway?"

"I started off with ten so I got about seven shots left," answered Tre'Vell.

"That's not good. We need to be more careful . . .," Matthias started to say before trailing off. "What is that?" he asked as he looked at something behind Tre'Vell.

Tre'Vell turned around to see what Matthias was talking about. Something was floating above the remnants of the coat of armor. They walked over to it. It looked to be an orb of some sort. It was pale white. It was so light that they could see inside the orb. Located inside was a small box. On the box was a red cross.

"What you think it is?" asked Tre'Vell.

Matthias was silent, trying to figure it out before realization dawned on him. "Let me get it!" He reached out his hand and grabbed the orb.

It momentarily shimmered in his grasp before it seeped into his skin. Matthias closed his eyes as he let the euphoric feeling it gave wash over him, traveling to every corner of his being.

"What's goin' on?" asked Tre'Vell.

"It was a health-up. My knee's as good as new," Matthias said when he opened his eyes. "Let's keep moving."

Tre'Vell and Matthias made it to the end of the corridor with no further issues. For that, Matthias was thankful. He couldn't shake the feeling in his gut, however, that the worst was yet to come. When they reached St. Stephen's Hall, they heard Jack's voice in their ear.

"Okay. Go across the hall into the big room at the end. That's Central Hall. Once in the middle of that hall, take the exit on your left."

Tre'Vell and Matthias walked through St. Stephens Hall and into Central Hall, again without incident. Tre'Vell thought it was very quiet. Too quiet, as the sounds of their footsteps were the only things heard in the building as they reverberated off the walls. Tre'Vell thought it was so quiet he could have sworn he could hear the sound of his own heartbeat. As he listened further, he thought he might have even been able to hear Matthias's. It was extremely unsettling. They took the exit that Jack instructed them to take.

"Good. Now you're currently in Commons Corridor. Ahead of you is Commons Lobby and past that is the House of Commons. Go through there. From there, there will be a court directly in front of you. All you have to do is go around that small court, take the hallway in front of you, and that will lead you to the Elizabeth Tower and the control panel. I have a camera online in Commons Lobby and I don't see any Yotes there, but that's the last camera I have on your path until you reach the control panel, so tread carefully."

They passed through the Commons Corridor and the Commons Lobby. Tre'Vell went to open the door to the House of Commons and gazed in horror at what was inside. The House of Commons was the chamber where the lower house of the British Parliament convened. It was a rectangular room with benches set up on both sides. Ornate chandeliers, which at the current time were dimly lit, hung from the ceiling. What scared Tre'Vell was the fact that the room was crawling with Yotes. There had to be more than forty in there, sprawled out on the benches and floor. The only thing that saved them was the fact that the zombies were all asleep. Tre'Vell quickly, but quietly, shut the door.

"What is it?" Matthias asked.

"Yotes."

"How many?"

"See for yourself."

Matthias cracked the door to scan the room and reclosed it after he got a sufficient glimpse. "A lot. Jack, is there any other way to get to the other side?"

"I'm afraid not. The other way is blocked."

"What we gonna do?" Tre'Vell asked. "I ain't got nearly enough bullets to kill all of them. Think we can sneak past them?"

Matthias said, "No. There's too many of them to step around. The way I see it, we only have one option."

Tre'Vell asked, "What's that?"

"We blow the place to smithereens," he answered.

"The bomb? Won't that just draw all the rest of those things from the rest of the building?"

"Yeah, but what other choice do we have? Hopefully, we can get by these guys and make it to the control panel before the other Yotes have a chance to make it here."

"Fine."

"Okay, on my count. You ready?" Matthias asked.

Tre'Vell pulled out an explosive. "Yeah."

Matthias began his countdown. "Three . . . two . . . one . . . Go!" he said as he opened the door.

Tre'Vell tossed the explosive into the middle of the room. Matthias quickly reclosed the door and braced himself for the tell-tale blast. *KABLOOM!* The blast was deafening, even with the door closed. It seemed to shake the very foundation of the Palace itself, like a miniearthquake. Matthias opened the door. The room was in shambles. Pieces of wood, metal, and glass were still flying everywhere. There was a gaping hole in the floor where the bomb landed. Only one of the chandeliers was still hanging up. Oddly enough, it still was emitting light although the room had darkened considerably. The bodies of Yotes were lying everywhere. There were bloody torsos, legs, and heads haphazardly strewn throughout the room. Even the walls and ceiling were not spared. Not all of the zombies were killed in the blast however. There was still a few stragglers left, yelping in shock and anger and moaning in agonizing pain.

"Okay, let's make a break for it!" said Matthias. He and Tre'Vell sprinted into the blast area to get to the other side. All the destruction made it difficult to go very fast, however, since they had to climb around and over benches, debris, and dead Yotes. It wasn't long before the surviving zombies noticed their presence and came at them.

"Looks like we gon' have to fight our way out!" said Tre'Vell as he pulled out his gun. A Yote knocked it out of his hand before he could use it. It skidded to the side. He was reduced to his hand-to-hand combat skills against the creatures. He delivered a powerful punch to one of them, knocking him to the ground. He was wrapped up from behind by one, his hands pinned to his sides. As another one approached, he kicked her with his legs, sending her flying back. He then thrust his elbow back, delivering a shot to his captor's abdomen. He loosened his grip on Tre'Vell, dropping him on the ground and allowing him to escape. Tre'Vell rolled on the ground, retrieving the gun. He shot two of the zombies in the head, killing them.

Matthias pulled out his baseball bat and charged at the zombies that were coming for him. He swung at a few of the zombies, decapitating them. Soon, he was outnumbered though, and the zombies began to overwhelm him. He used his bat as a barricade, attempting to keep a particularly angry-looking zombie from getting to him. As he struggled with the zombie, he heard a shot ring out, and the zombie was vanquished. Tre'Vell, after disposing of his zombies, was taking care of the ones around Matthias. One by one, the zombies fell until none were left.

"Thank you. I didn't think I was going to be able to handle them all," he said.

Tre'Vell said, "I got your back."

Tre'Vell had forgotten about the female Yote he had to deal with in his haste to help Matthias. This allowed her to sneak up on him. She grabbed a wooden stake from the pile of rubble and debris and walked up behind Tre'Vell. Matthias saw this unfolding before his eyes and attempted to warn him. "Tre! Behind you!" he yelled. But it was too late. Tre'Vell never saw the wooden weapon burst clean through his chest.

****

Mayor Wright stood in front of an armoire in her office. The six-foot-tall solid pine artifice was tucked away in the corner, inconspicuous to many people who entered the room. Most people thought nothing of the furniture piece. Mariah knew, however, that Angela liked to keep her mystical artifacts in the armoire. She knew Angela had a nearly identical one located at her home, but Mariah had never been privy to either of their contents. She saw this as an opportunity to finally see its contents. She walked over to where the mayor was standing. The armoire held all sorts of strange and weird objects: swords, amulets, small chests, and bottles containing colorful liquids and herbs. There was one thing that caught her attention though. She looked down at a clear glass jar that appeared to have four balls of light bouncing around in it.

"What's that?" she asked.

Mayor Wright picked up the jar and examined it carefully. "It's a part of the curse I cast."

This intrigued Mariah. "What curse?"

Mayor Wright held the jar up so that Mariah could get a better look. "I recently trapped four boys in a video game."

"That actually sounds like it could be fun," Mariah said as she tried to imagine what it would be like to be in a game such as *Super Mario*.

"Quite fun—for me at least. The game is designed to kill them."

"Kill them?" asked Mariah, hesitantly.

"Yes. These balls of light represent their life force. While they are trapped in the game, these balls of light remain trapped in the jar. When one of them dies in the game, one of the balls will dissipate. This will happen until there are no balls left, telling me that all four of them are dead," the mayor explained.

"Wait, you're trying to kill them?"

"Don't act so surprised, Mariah. You knew I had some special business to take care of."

"But I didn't know that the people you were trying to kill were just boys," said Mariah.

"They're not really boys. More like young men, actually."

"There's still something dirty about all this. To take someone's life so young . . ."

"Don't go soft on me now, Mariah. We must stand solid in our convictions, even in the face of difficult circumstances. This must be done. My very life depends on it."

****

"Tre!" yelled Matthias in shock and disbelief. He stood, feet firmly rooted to the floor, as Tre'Vell looked down at the massive wooden stake protruding from his chest. Blood started to pour from his mouth, a stream of life flowing forth from within him. Tre'Vell could no longer support himself and collapsed to the floor, his body struggling to hold on to what little life was left in it.

The sound of Tre'Vell hitting the floor seemed to awaken Matthias from his stupor. It was then that he remembered that there was still one last zombie in the room. He picked up his bat and charged at Tre'Vell's assailant in a blind rage. He had to get the creature away from Tre'Vell. He swung at the zombie, but couldn't connect for some reason. After a few hacks, the Yote was finally pushed back into a pile of rubble.

Matthias knelt down beside the dying Tre'Vell. "Just hold on. I'm going to get you out of here. Come on, let's get you up," he said.

Tre'Vell weakly shook his head, which Matthias took as an indication that he wouldn't be going anywhere. With his last reserve of strength, Tre'Vell pointed to the door, as if trying to urge Matthias to carry on. His head then rolled to the side as he took his last ragged breath. Tre'Vell's now glazed eyes told Matthias all he needed to know. His friend was now dead.

***

One of the balls of light that had been floating around in the jar suddenly went out. Only three balls of light remained. "Oh look, Angela. One of the lights disappeared."

"Perfect! My curse is working just as I predicted," Mayor Wright said with barely contained delight.

That can only mean one thing, Mariah thought with dread.

"One down. Three to go."

***

Matthias cradled Tre'Vell's lifeless husk of a body in his lap. He began to weep over his fallen comrade. Even though he had only known him for less than a couple of months, he had grown close to him. He considered Tre'Vell a dear friend—he considered every member of their nascent diamond a close friend now. He just couldn't believe that he was gone. Soon, to Matthias's dismay, Tre'Vell's body began to disappear. He tried to clutch his body tighter, as if that would prevent the body from going. Eventually, he was clutching nothing but air.

Once the body was gone, Matthias heard some movement from the rubble. The zombie was getting himself dislodged from the pile and would soon be after him again. Remembering Tre'Vell pointing to the door, he picked up his baseball bat and ran for the door, the Yote hot on his tail. He reached the door and exited the hall. Once he did, he closed the door and slid the bat between the handles on the door, locking the Yote on the inside. Once he felt he was safe, he slid down the wall in exhaustion and despair.

"Matt, you have to go! There's a bunch of Yotes closing in on your location!"

"My friend just fucking died! Give me a minute to compose myself!"

"Sorry to say, you don't have a bloody minute right now. You have to keep going."

Matthias slammed his fist into the wall. "This isn't right! Every game is beatable! If only I had saved that health-up," he said in frustration. He hadn't really needed that power-up. Tre'Vell could have used it to heal himself after he was impaled.

"You really don't have time to beat yourself up. The zombies are coming for you. Don't let your partner's death be in vain! Help me lower the barrier. That would be the best way to honor him. Complete the mission."

"Wait a minute," he said to himself through his tears of anger. "Game . . . power-up . . . mission. That's it! Jack, with Tre'Vell now dead, is it true that I'm no longer connected with his comlink?"

"Correct."

"Then that would mean that my comlink has room for another connection, right? One to replace his?"

"I suppose so."

"In that case, is there a way that you can patch me through to Omar and Derek?" Matthias asked frantically as he got up with renewed hope.

"Let me see. If I reconfigure some things, I may be able to temporarily connect you with one of them. Why? What are you thinking?"

"I need you to hook me up with Derek. Quick!"

***

Derek and Omar carefully made their way through the hallway. There were many doors on either side, and it made them skittish. A zombie could be lurking behind any or all of them, just waiting to chow down on their next meal. Their ambush in the elevator made them critically aware of that fact.

"How much further do we have to go, Jack?" asked Derek.

"There should be an office space coming up. The stairwell is on the other side. Go through that office and get to the stairs on the other side. Once you go up those steps, the control panel will be in a room in the office on the next floor."

The two of them made it through the building and arrived at the office. The door was locked, and they were surprised to find out that the door had a security lock that was still functioning.

"Jack, there's a pinpad here on the door," Derek said.

"I was afraid of that. It'll take the right combination to open the lock. Take the hacking chip and insert it in the slot under the pad. Maybe I can open it for you."

After Omar inserted the chip, Jack attempted to hack the door from his bunker. "Well, I've got good news and bad news. The bad news is that I can't open the door. The encryption is too good. The good news is that I was able to determine that it's a four-digit combination and each number is a digit between 0 and 4. You'll have to take it from there."

"Wonderful. Okay, let's see."

Derek punched some numbers on the pinpad. It glowed red, indicating the combination was incorrect. He tried another combination and it was also incorrect. He tried a few more combinations, but none of them worked. "This is going to take a while," he said. On the tenth incorrect attempt, a shrill bell sounded throughout the floor.

"Bloody hell. You guys set off the alarm! Those Yotes are surely going to come for you now. Get inside before they reach you!"

Now in a hurry, Derek tried a few more combinations, but was still unsuccessful. "What's taking so long?" Omar asked.

"Do you know how many potential combinations there are?" Derek shot back as he continued to work.

As Derek was focused squarely on the pinpad, Omar was keeping watch of the hallway in front of them. At the end of the hallway, in the direction from which they came, he saw a few zombies emerge, spot them, and begin to run down the hallway toward them. "Man, hurry up!" he said.

"I'm trying!" Derek said. The zombies were bearing down on them.

"Look, let me try. Move," he said. Derek moved from the pinpad and Omar put in a few combinations. With the zombies only a few doors away from them, the pinpad mercifully glowed green. Omar had finally placed the correct combination. "Yes!" he yelled in triumph. He and Derek quickly ran inside the office.

The two of them sprinted around cubicles and hurdled fallen debris and office furniture as they made their way through the office, the Yotes right behind them. "The stairwell should be coming up." They saw the door that led to the stairwell and were thankful that it didn't take a numeric combination like the front door to the office. They entered the stairwell and looked up at the winding stairs that led up quite a few levels, probably to the top of the building. As they began to climb the steps, a couple of Yotes were descending them, blocking their path. To make matters worse, they could hear the Yotes that were chasing them entering the stairwell. They were surrounded.

"What do we do?" asked Derek in a panic.

"I'ma toss a smoke bomb. Fog up the place," said Omar. He threw out a smoke bomb. Immediately the stairwell was enshrouded in a deep fog. The zombies stopped as they were unable to see. "Come on."

They ascended the steps until they reached the first few zombies that were blocking their path. After struggling with them for a bit, they tossed the Yotes over the railing, sending them careening to the bottom. They continued up the stairwell and tossed a few more zombies over the railing. By this point, the fog was beginning to dissipate. The zombies behind them could now see well enough to continue their chase up the steps. There were only two Yotes left in Omar's and Derek's way. Derek hacked one with his hatchet, killing it. Omar delivered a nice uppercut to the other one and tossed it down the stairs. With the group of zombies in hot pursuit behind them, Omar and Derek went through the door to the fifth floor.

"The room with the control panel should be at the end of the hallway once you make the upcoming right."

Derek and Omar made a right turn and were greeted by a group of zombies, way too many to fight. "Not today," said Derek. He and Omar turned back around and ran the other way. The group of zombies from the fourth floor had reached the fifth floor, spotted them, and joined the zombies on the fifth floor in chasing them. "This way!" yelled Derek as he made another left down a long hallway, Omar right with him.

"Let's hide in here," said Derek. He opened a door on his left. When he saw that there were a couple of zombies in there, he quickly slammed the door. "Or not." They kept running down the hallway. To their dismay, they could see that the hallway led to a dead end. What now? When they reached the end of the hallway, there was a room on their right. They quickly went inside and shut the door.

"We gotta barricade the door!" said Omar. They slid a bookcase in front of the door. As soon as they finished moving it into place, the zombies on the outside started banging on the door, attempting to get in.

"We trapped!" Omar said as he paced around in a circle.

"At least we safe," said Derek. "That's the most important thing."

"For now. But that bookcase ain't gonna hold them forever. We gon' die!"

"Get ahold of yourself and help me think!" said Derek.

"Derek? Derek, are you there?"

"Matt? Is that you?" Derek responded.

"Matt? What are you talking about?" Omar asked Derek.

"Matt's talking to me through my comlink," he answered. "How am I hearing you right now? And why can't O hear you?"

"No time to explain. I'm on a time limit so I need you to listen. Tre's dead."

"What?" Derek gasped. He sunk to the floor.

"What's going on? What he say?" Omar asked when he saw Derek's reaction to whatever Matthias was saying.

"He said that Tre's dead."

"What? How?"

"Matt, what happened?"

"He got impaled. But listen, I think there's a chance we can get him back."

"How?"

"Earlier, we found a power-up that healed my knee when it got banged up. It was a health-up. That reminded me that we are in a *game*. And if the game has power-ups, then it might have ways to gain extra lives. Because we are essentially playing a multiplayer co-op game, if one of us finds an extra life, it should pass to him and his life should be restored. But we have to save him before we lower the barrier. If not . . .," Matthias trailed off, but Derek didn't need him to complete the thought.

"How do we get extra lives?"

"We found the health-up in a coat of armor. It's logical to think that there might be an extra life hanging around in something like that. Keep an eye out for any place where one might be hiding and I'll do the same. We won't be able to communicate after this. Jack'll keep us both updated on our progress." With that, Matthias's link with Derek timed out.

"Matt? Matt?" There was no answer from Matthias.

"What'd he say?" asked Omar. Derek explained everything to Omar. "So we gotta find an extra life?"

"First things first. We have to find a way out of here or Matt's gonna have to find three extra lives," said Derek. He scanned the room for any potential point of exit. He saw an airshaft vent on the wall. "That air vent," he said, pointing to it on the wall. He and Omar walked over to it. It looked to be just big enough for them to fit in. Although Derek's muscular frame would be a particularly tight fit. "Jack, we found an air vent. Where does it lead?"

"Let me check . . . You're in luck. It leads directly to the room with the control panel."

"Good. Let's go."

***

After Matthias got done talking to Derek, he decided against continuing on the path that Jack told him to take to get to Elizabeth Tower and decided to take a detour.

"Where are you going? The control panel is in the opposite direction."

Matthias walked down the hallway. "I need to find an extra life," he said.

"What are you talking about? The zombies are going to be coming toward you any minute!"

"I'll only be a minute. I'm just gonna check out a couple of these rooms first," he answered.

He looked inside a few rooms, but found nothing of consequence. He went into a lecture hall. *There's got to be something in here.* He started to ransack the place, hoping to find what he was looking for. Even though he practically tore the room apart, there was no such luck.

"Look, you need to get a move on. My cameras are showing Yotes in your general vicinity. Those buggers are going to be on you soon!"

Matthias relented. "All right, I'm going," he said.

He turned around to leave the lecture hall, but something caught his eye. He looked up. Something was shining above bookcase that covered the height of the wall. Matthias thought that it was the biggest bookcase that he had ever seen. The wall had to be about twenty feet high, making the bookcase about eighteen feet tall. Lucky for Matthias, there was a ladder beside the bookcase that was tall enough to reach the top.

He climbed the ladder toward the top. This just had to be the extra life. That's how these games were normally designed. Useful items such as extra lives were located in obscure places to encourage exploration. When he got to the top, he found a shining toolbox. His face sagged. This surely was not an extra life. He grabbed the toolbox and noticed that he got some more ammunition for a gun that he didn't have. In his haste, he had left it in the room with the Yote. This power-up was useless. Hopes dashed, he descended the ladder and left the lecture hall. As he reentered the hallway, there was a group of zombies walking his way. They immediately noticed him and ran toward him, wanting a fresh meal. "Exploration expedition's over," he said to himself and ran toward the corridor that would lead to Big Ben.

"Take the upcoming left. That'll lead you to Elizabeth Tower. There's a door there that you can close to protect yourself. The control panel will be right there."

As he got toward the end of the corridor, bullets started to fly past him. One of the zombies must have had a gun, but he dare not turn back to look, lest that slow him down. He deftly avoided the gunfire, bullets whizzing by his ear, some coming dangerously close, and made the turn onto the corridor that led to Big Ben. The zombies were getting closer, but pure adrenaline was keeping Matthias from getting tired and letting them make up ground any faster. He was staying ahead. He reached Elizabeth Tower without being caught, slammed the door, and locked it. He bent over to catch his breath.

"Matt?"

***

"How long have we been crawling through this vent now?" Omar asked.

"Only about five minutes," Derek answered. Just as he thought, he was struggling to get through the vent. He was a little too thick for the small space. His back was scraping up against the roof of the vent. It was a tight squeeze.

"We almost there, Jack?" asked Omar impatiently.

"Just a little bit more. Turn left here. The exit vent should be right there."

Omar turned and saw the exit vent. "Good. We can finally get up out of here!"

He pulled off the cover on the vent and eased himself out the vent, dangling from his arms into the room below. He let go and landed on his feet. Just as Derek was about to do the same, something caught his eye. It was faint, but something seemed— off with the vent up ahead. The coloration of the vent up ahead was slightly different. It could be nothing, but he decided to check it out.

"What are you waiting for?" yelled Omar from below.

"I'm going to check something out up ahead. Hold on," Derek said.

He crawled to the end of the vent. As he got closer, he saw that there was a connecting vent that was perpendicular to the one he was on. In the other vent was a slightly glowing orb. Inside the white orb was a "+1."

This must be the extra life! he thought. He grabbed it. It quickly shone brighter before disappearing. "Jack, tell Matt I think I found the extra life." The vent was too tight for him to turn around, so he backed up the way he came and exited the vent that way.

"What did you do?" asked Omar.

Derek replied, "I found the extra life. It was further along in the vent."

"Good. So Tre's back alive?"

"Let's hope so. So this is the control panel for the barrier around the city," said Derek as he went over to the panel.

It looked like something out of a science fiction movie, which wasn't too far off from the case, seeing as they were in a video game. It was a cylindrical device about the size of a small car. It was covered in multicolored buttons of every size and shape. In the middle of the panels was a large antenna sticking up. *Probably emitting the wireless signal for the barrier*, Derek thought.

"What now, Jack?" Omar asked.

"You should see a large yellow button surrounded by three green buttons. Do you see it?"

Omar and Derek searched for it. "Found it," said Derek. Omar went over to the other side of the panel where Derek was.

"Push the yellow button, then the green button on its left."

Omar did this. A small box slowly rose from the top of the control panel. "Some box just came out the top."

"Good. It should be covered by a glass top. Lift that top and place the hacking chip into the USB drive."

Omar followed the instructions given. "Now what?" asked Derek.

"I'll check to see what's happening at the palace. Stand by."

***

Matthias looked up at the source of the voice. "Tre!"

"Where am I at?"

"Big Ben. The control panel is over there. It's good to have you back, man. I thought you were a goner."

"Not that I'm not happy, I am, but how am I back?"

"Well, when you . . . you know . . . I thought of the health-up that we found earlier and figured that if that's in the game, there might be a way to find extra lives and bring you back that way. I told Derek. He and Omar must have found one," Matthias explained.

"Good lookin' out. That was pretty smart."

"So where'd you go? How was it like being . . .," Matthias asked as he made a slashing gesture to his neck.

"I don't remember nothin', really. The last thing I remember was a sharp pain in my chest. Hurt like hell. I had a lot of blood in my mouth and you was kneelin' over me. The next thing I know, I see you just now."

"So you don't remember anything between then and now?"

"Nope."

"Well, that's good, I guess. Okay, let's put in this hacking chip."

Jack told them how to put in the hacking chip. When they did, Jack hacked into the mainframe and brought down the barrier that surrounded the city. "The barrier is gone. Thanks to you blokes, the humans remaining in London now have a real chance at survival. I'm going to get out of this blasted city as soon as I can. I would suggest you guys do the same."

After he was done addressing them, a purple portal appeared in each of the two locations. "I'm guessing that's our ticket home," said Omar.

"Hopefully," said Derek. He and Omar stepped into the portal.

At the same time, Matthias said, "That must be our way back to the real world. I hope Omar and Derek got this same portal."

"We won't know until we go through and see 'em on the other side," said Tre'Vell. They stepped through the portal.

Chapter 13

Fissure

"Are you sure you can do the job?" Mayor Wright inquired. Ever since her absorption curse failed, she was in a sour mood. It was 2014, and the warlocks remained alive. She began to feel her looming deadline closing in on her neck, threatening to strangle her.

"I've gotten husbands to cheat on their wives, clergymen to steal from their churches, men to kill their childhood friends. I've taken down multinational corporations and pitted nation against nation. Dissolving the bond of a newly formed group of friends is child's play. Hardly even a challenge, really," said the woman confidently.

"Yes, I can see that. Your résumé speaks volumes. Quite impressive," said Angela.

"Not that I'm ungrateful, but why did you think it prudent to enlist my services? It seems like overkill. I'm usually used for much larger jobs."

"The job I have in mind takes someone with your . . . special talents. You're discreet and effective, which is paramount to my plans. From what I've read, you are insidious and subtle, which should assist you. I don't care if it is overkill, as long as killing is the end result."

"Indeed I am. But can I ask you a question?" Mayor Wright nodded. "Why not just kill them yourself? Your reputation precedes you in the supernatural community. Surely Angela Wright is strong enough to take down a couple of inexperienced, juvenile warlocks," asked the woman.

"Two reasons. One, I'm not just an Ultimate witch, but I'm also a mayor, a well-known and highly visible public figure. I can't have a couple of homicides traced back to me. Doing it indirectly and through third parties is best. Two, there is a certain strength in numbers that they have that I do not possess despite my vast powers. They are not just a group of friends, they are a warlock's diamond. I have attacked them multiple times already, and they overcame them. What's worse, they are gaining confidence and experience with each victory over me. If I don't stop them soon, they will be nearly impossible for me to defeat. And I'm quickly running out of time."

"Meaning?"

"I've been given the assignment of killing them before May arrives, or else," Angela answered.

"By who?" asked the woman.

"An ancient entity that is not to be trifled with. One that it would be in my best interest to obey. She has the ability and complete eagerness to carry out her threat," answered Angela with a shudder.

"Wow. A being that makes even the mighty Angela Wright quake in her boots. Must be big time."

"She is, trust me. So what is your plan?" asked Mayor Wright.

"My way in is to ingratiate myself with one of the boys. To use my abilities to seduce and tempt him. My playing on his fears and insecurities will spread to the other boys, causing a schism, a fracture in their relationship. I've already begun my work on the one I'm targeting. Their breakup will be a mere formality. I assume that's why you called me. Dealing with them separately will be easier for you than attacking them as a group. The whole 'united we stand, divided we fall' thing?"

"Exactly. You work your magic, then I will finish the job," said Angela. The woman smiled and got up to leave. "Oh, and just so you know." The woman stopped and turned around. "It's of the utmost importance that my identity remain a secret to them. If you should do anything to alert them to my presence, I will kill you myself."

"Understood."

****

Derek walked into his dad's man cave with a purpose. The man cave was really just the den that was spruced up with memorabilia that he had collected through the years. His dad was sitting in his special recliner, watching TV. His dad didn't really like to be disturbed when he retreated to his man cave unless it was an emergency. Derek thought that what he had to discuss with him was an emergency.

"Dad, can I talk to you for a minute?"

His dad turned off the television. "Yeah. What's on your mind, son?"

"I have a lot to tell you, and I don't know where to start and I don't know how you'll take it," he said.

"I see. Well, how about you start at the beginning and we'll take it from there."

Derek took a deep breath. "Okay. A couple months ago when I went to get a cut, Lamar told me about the tarot reading he got for me."

"I told him not to bother you with that mess," Stephen said.

"He told me there was a way to protect myself."

"What he say?"

"That I could form a warlock's diamond with three other warlocks."

"WHAT? Please tell me you didn't, Derek."

"I did."

"I can't believe you tellin' me this," Stephen said as he shook his head. "Who you do the ritual with?"

"Omar and some other dudes I met at school. They names are Matt and Tre," Derek answered.

"Derek, do you realize what you done? Y'alls lives will never be the same!"

"I know that the ritual is permanent and links us together. We get stronger, but our individual spells get weaker and less controllable. That's why I did it. I can use the diamond's power to protect myself."

"No no no. That might be the case, but you put not only yours, but those other guys' lives in danger."

"How?"

"Whenever a diamond or coven is made, it sends out a magical signal throughout the area—a jolt of magical energy that many different types of mystical beings can sense. I felt it, but I didn't know what it was. That signal acts like a beacon, drawing supernatural beings to the source of the energy. That would be y'all."

"What's that mean?"

"It means that for the rest of your natural-born life, all manner of magical beings, both benevolent and malevolent, will be attracted to you," said Stephen.

"That might explain the attacks," Derek muttered.

"Attacks? What attacks?"

"Shortly before we did the ritual, Matt and Omar saw Tre getting attacked by a couple of golems. He got away, obviously, but then a little while later, me, Tre, and Matt were all attacked by golems. This is one of the reasons why we ultimately decided to do the ritual," Derek explained.

"No. Up to that point, you guys hadn't done the ritual yet, so the golems wouldn't be attracted because of that. But golems are homemade assassins. Somebody made those things and sent them out to kill you."

"That's what we thought when we read the entry in the grimoire."

"I'm the one that put it in there," Stephen revealed. "I came across some in the late eighties."

"Well, on the night that we did the ritual, all of them attacked us at the same time. We vanquished them—barely. Got beat up pretty good though."

"Derek, why didn't you come to me with any of this as it was happening?"

"'Cuz I wanted to do it on my own. I'm eighteen, a grown man now. I feel like I should start handling things on my own instead of having to run back home to daddy. Besides, you don't even have your powers anymore. What could you have done?"

"Just because I don't have my powers no more don't mean I'm useless. I still got all the knowledge I gained in my life. If you had come to me earlier, I could have warned you about the bonding ritual. I also could have told you about the warding spell that could have kept the golems away from y'all," said Stephen.

"Warding spell? The book ain't mention nothing about a warding spell," said Derek in surprise.

"That's because I found it after I made the entry on golems in the grimoire. I just didn't feel the need to update the entry."

"I guess I really messed up, huh?"

"Well, yes. But the most important thing is that y'all are safe for now, I suppose."

"Actually, that's not all that's happened to us," said Derek.

"Do I even want to know?"

"A couple days ago, the four of us got sucked into a game that Matt's mom sent to him for Christmas, or so we thought. He swears his mom didn't send the game."

"What game was it?"

"Zombie Virus U. We had to fight all these zombies and we ain't even have our magic," said Derek.

"But I assume everything turned out all right?" asked Stephen.

"Yeah. We beat the game and got out. Tre was killed temporarily, but we got him back," Derek answered.

"Has that been it so far?" Stephen asked hesitantly.

"Yeah. That's been it."

"It takes someone with a whole hell of a lot of magic to pull off a curse like that. That's a lot of effort to take you guys out. Someone very powerful has it in for you guys," said Stephen as he furrowed his brow in thought.

"We figured as much. It's probably the same person that made the golems. Looks like Lamar's reading was correct. There is death in my future."

"Perhaps. Or you doing that ritual in an attempt to avert the future the tarot cards predicted could have had the opposite effect and might actually contribute to it coming true by drawing an unnatural amount of supernatural beings and phenomena to you," his dad reasoned.

"True," Derek conceded.

"Well, what's done is done. No use crying over spilled milk now. You guys need to be extra careful from now on. Especially if there's someone after you."

****

"Out, 15–0." Matthias was beginning to ramp up his training for the upcoming spring college tennis season. The new year marked a turning point in his regimen. Now he would begin playing his dad in competitive matches. And by competitive, he truly meant *competitive*. His father never gave him an inch in their matches, and he always struggled to win them in the beginning. Today, they were just playing a set. They would eventually work up to multiple set matches.

After Isaac held his first service game at love, Matthias won the first point of his first service game with an unreturned serve. On the next point, his dad hit a second serve return winner with a beautiful backhand down the line: fifteen all. "You gonna have to come with a better serve than that, Matt." Seemingly spurred on by that, Matthias hit an ace out wide to go up 30–15. The next point involved a rally. After a crosscourt forehand exchange, Matthias redirected the ball down the line with his forehand for a winner. Now 40–15, he hit another unreturned serve to get on the board and even up the set at one apiece.

Isaac hit an ace out wide to go up 15–0. "Come on, Matt, you didn't even make an effort on that one!"

"I didn't read it," Matthias answered.

On the next point, Isaac had to hit a second serve. Matthias hit a great, deep return that he was sure would earn him the point. Isaac retrieved it though and put it back in play down the middle of the court. He wasn't quite preparing to have to hit another shot. He hit a forehand long. "Ugh!" Isaac led 30–0. Isaac hit a serve up the T. Matthias hit a blistering forehand return winner, as if taking out his anger at the previous point on the ball. During the next point, Matthias sliced a backhand deep in the court to the corner. His father had to scramble just to get the ball back. Matthias slipped into the net and put the volley away for the winner and evened up the score at 30–30. On the ensuing point, Matthias decided to hit a drop shot. Isaac got to the ball and pushed it all the way back to the baseline. Matthias lifted a high-arching lob to the open court behind Isaac and went up 30–40. Isaac could only clap his racket to applaud the shot. "Too good," he said." On break point, he decided to do a serve-and-volley, catching Matthias by surprise and erasing the break point. At deuce, he hit two unreturnable serves to win the game and go up 2–1 in the set.

Matthias quickly held his next game at love with a couple of backhand winners and two unforced forehand errors into the net from his dad. He followed that outstanding game up with an error-filled return game to again let his dad pull ahead 3–2. On his service game, he started it out with an ace down the middle. His dad pounced on his next serve and smacked it crosscourt for a return winner. After trading backhand errors on the next two points, Isaac ended a twelve-stroke rally by hitting a backhand volley for a winner to go ahead 30–40 and earn a break point. Matthias erased it when his dad hit a return long. Matthias hit a drop shot winner for advantage and then won the game after a brief six-stroke rally with a backhand down the line winner. Three all.

Matthias went up 0–30 on Isaac's service game, but couldn't capitalize. His father held the game by drawing a couple of errors and closing it with a volley that Matthias missed the passing shot on. Matthias evened up the score with a love service game. Now 4–4, Isaac began his service game with a double fault, his first of the set, to give his son a 0–15 lead. Seeing his chance to get a break and serve out the set, Matthias dug in. On the next point, the two engaged in a grinding all-court twenty-one-stroke rally. When Isaac seemingly hit a great approach shot to the corner, Matthias had to scramble to retrieve it. Isaac moved to the net to cover the potential crossing pass. Matthias had other plans and hit a bending forehand on the run down the line that landed just in to win the point and go up 0–30.

"Great shot, son," complimented Isaac. On the next point, Isaac directed a shot to Matthias's backhand. Matthias decided to run around it, and he hit a blistering inside-out crosscourt forehand to go up 0–40 and earn three break points.

"Come on!" yelled Matthias.

"Don't get too happy just yet," warned Isaac.

On the next point, Isaac redirected a backhand down the line that his son couldn't put back in play to erase the first break point. At 15–40, Matthias hit a flat crosscourt backhand that he thought got him the break.

"Out," called Isaac.

"What? That ball was in!" complained Matthias.

"I'm telling you it was out. I wouldn't cheat you out of a point," said his father. Matthias stood there in disbelief. "Thirty to forty," said Isaac as he went back to the baseline as he prepared to serve. Even though he saw a second serve, Matthias hit it into the net to even the game at forty all. He had blown his chance. Crestfallen, he quickly dropped the next two points to lose the game and let his dad go ahead 5–4.

Now serving to stay in the match, his dad jumped ahead 0–30. Matthias hit a backhand slice to get his dad off the court and then followed it up with a forehand winner to the open court to get to 15–30. The next point saw both of them at the net going volley for volley before

Isaac hit a lob that Matthias smashed. He smashed it right back to his dad, though, and Isaac easily hit it to the open court to go up 15–40. Now down match points, Matthias hit an ace down the middle to get the game to 30–40. On the second match point, Matthias missed the first serve. On the second serve, the tennis ball hit the top of the net, bounded high up into the air, and landed outside the service box. Double fault. Matthias groaned. Game. Set. Match.

They met at the net. "Good game, son. I think that's the closest you've come to beating me in our first match of the season. Can't double-fault on match point, though. Like I always tell you."

"Make your opponent hit the shot. I know," Matthias said impatiently. He had heard it plenty of times before and didn't feel like hearing it again.

"Well, smart-ass, if you know, then why didn't you do it?"

"Do you think I wanted to double-fault? I tried to. I just clipped the top of the net. I'm not match tough yet. That's why it's called practice," Matthias grinded out to his father, coach, and hitting partner.

Isaac was slightly taken aback by the small venom in his son's voice. "Why you so mad? What's the matter?"

"Nothing," Matthias answered shortly.

It wasn't just frustration with the loss. Ever since the incident with the video game, he was a little shook. He had almost died in that game. Witnessing Tre'Vell get impaled was an image that caused nightmares for the couple of days after they escaped. Even though they eventually got him back, it illuminated the fact that their lives were very much in real danger.

****

He looked around, trying to spot her in the crowd of tables. Ricquel had asked Tre'Vell to meet her at the establishment. He assumed it was to discuss their working together. That was something he was looking forward to. After he scanned the busy tables, he spotted her in a booth in the corner by the window. He made his way over to her. She saw him as he approached her.

"Well, hello there," she said.

Tre'Vell sat down. "What's poppin'?"

"Nothing. I'm glad to see you, Tre. You're looking good."

"Thank you. You ain't too hard on the eyes yourself," said Tre'Vell.

"I try. So you must be wondering why I asked you to come here," Ricquel started.

"Can't say it didn't cross my mind, although I'm glad you did. Wanted to talk about the album?"

"Actually, no. We've got time for that. No, I asked you to come here so we could break the ice. I mean, if we're going to be working together, I figured we should properly get to know each other. Right?"

"I couldn't agree more," said Tre'Vell.

Just then the waitress came over and asked them for their drinks. After ordering their beverages, Ricquel asked, "So how have you been? What's been going on in your life? Anything interesting?"

Tre'Vell thought back to the video game that he got trapped in. "You got no idea," he said with a wry smile.

"I bet."

When the waitress returned with their drinks, they placed their food orders with her and she left. Tre'Vell had ordered a root beer float and indulged. He soon felt Ricquel's curious gaze on him. "What?"

"I don't know. There's something . . . different about you. I get the sense that you're out of the ordinary," she said.

"Oh. I don't know. I guess it could be my devilish good looks and charm," he joked.

Ricquel laughed. "Yeah. Or it could have something to do with the fact that you're a warlock."

Tre'Vell nearly choked on his float. "Huh?" he spit out in a panic.

Ricquel placed her hand on his and giggled. "Calm down. I know."

"How?" he asked suspiciously. He was on high alert.

"Because I'm a witch."

"Oh," he said as he let out a sigh of relief and let himself relax. "That still don't explain how you know I'm a warlock."

"Isn't it obvious?" she asked. He shook his head. "Magic," she said, as if it were the most obvious thing in the world.

Tre'Vell laughed. "Does it got somethin' to do with your power? Is that how you know?"

Ricquel shrugged flirtatiously. "Maybe. I guess you'll just have wait and see if I decide to tell you later."

Tre'Vell said suggestively, "I'll show you mine if you show me yours."

"Who said I'm interested in seeing yours?" Ricquel asked.

"I did. Come on, girl, we both know you want to."

"Please! Boy, you aren't all that."

"If you saw what I can do, you wouldn't say that."

"Maybe you can show me in a place a little more . . . private."

Tre'Vell raised his eyebrows and asked, "You want us to go someplace more 'private'?"

"Depending on how the rest of the meal goes, I just might."

The waitress brought their food to them, and the rest of the evening went off without a hitch.

****

A huge roar erupted through the sports bar. The bar was packed to the brim and filled with patrons that were watching the playoff game between the hometown Eagles and Saints. It was a tight low-scoring game for the majority of the first half, and that eruption meant that the Eagles had pulled ahead. Derek decided to watch the game at the bar with his friends Devon, Raheem, and Dominique. He set up the outing with his friends for two reasons. Since they no longer went to the same school, they found it difficult to get everyone's schedules to match up and, as a result, hadn't hung out nearly as often as they used to. Even now, Tyrone, the fifth member of their quintet, couldn't make it because he had to work. Derek missed his buddies. This was also an opportunity to get his mind off his magical issues. As the four of them were laughing over a story that Derek was telling, a woman in a miniskirt walked by their table.

"How much you wanna bet that she ain't wearing any panties?" Dominique asked.

"You don't think she ain't wearing any panties?" Raheem said.

"Not a chance in hell."

"How you figure?"

"She got 'hoe' written all over her. She got the uniform down pat," Dominique reasoned.

Raheem said, "I don't think so."

"How much you wanna bet?"

"Ten bucks says she got panties on," Raheem offered.

"You on," said Dominique. They shook on it.

"So how we gonna settle this? Just walk up to her and ask," Raheem said.

"I was thinking we could get our good buddy over here to help," said Dominique as he looked over at Derek.

Derek was confused. "What you looking at me for?"

"You can . . .," he said as he waved his fingers toward the woman, who was standing near the bar.

Once he realized what Dominique was insinuating, he chuckled and shook his head. "No."

"That's a good idea!" said Devon.

"No, it's not. Y'all know I'm not supposed to use my magic like that!"

"If you can't use it for that, what can you use it for? Live a little," said Raheem. "How else we gonna know?"

"It's just for fun. It ain't like we asking you to rob a bank or nothing," said Dominique.

"All right, all right, all right!" Derek said as he relented although he didn't really put much effort into his resistance. Truth be told, he was curious to see if she had on underwear as well. Derek glanced around to make sure no one was watching him. He stared at the woman's skirt and whispered, "Aero pritus." A small gust of wind swirled around the bottom of the bar, blowing the woman's skirt up. Surprised, the woman quickly moved to put it back down.

"Hah! I told you! No panties!" Dominique exclaimed in triumph as he high-fived Devon.

Raheem shook his head. "You know what she here for. And it ain't to watch the game."

"Pay up!" said Dominique. He extended his hand.

Raheem reached in his pocket and pulled out $10. "Gladly. It was worth it to see that!"

Buzz! Devon's phone indicated that he received a text message. Devon picked it up. "Who that?" asked Dominique as he put the $10 in his pocket.

"My girl," he said. He typed something up.

"Kelsey? What does she want?" Derek asked.

"We was supposed to go to this spoken-word thing that she wanted to go to tonight, but I skipped out on it." ǀ

"You blew her off for us?"

"Why not? We always said, 'Bros before hoes,'" said Raheem. "Not that I'm calling your girlfriend a hoe, of course. I'm sure she a very nice girl and far from it," he quickly added to Devon.

"Well, I didn't exactly tell her I was chilling with you guys."

"What you tell her?"

"That I had to take my sister to her basketball game."

"But you don't even have a sister," said Dominique.

"I know that. You know that. But she don't know that."

"So you lied to her," said Derek.

"Lie is such a harsh word," said Devon. They all shared a laugh.

Derek said, "She's gonna be so mad when she finds out."

"How she gonna find out? I won't tell her. You won't tell her. And I know Dom and Rah won't."

"Because they always find out when you keep secrets. I seen it happen to too many dudes before. That's why I don't do girlfriends. That way, I ain't got to lie about nothing."

"No, you don't do girlfriends because you a thot and therefore wouldn't be able to hold one down," said Dominique.

"Exactly. That way, I can fuck as many girls as I want and don't have to worry about sneaking behind anybody's back. I'm upfront about it. Honesty is the best policy in that case," said Derek.

Devon disagreed. "Nobody can handle the truth all the time. It might work for you, but in this case, I think it's best to keep her in the dark. What she don't know can't hurt her." The noise level in the bar began to rise as the second half of the game began. "The game's starting back up."

Taking that as Devon's sign to drop the conversation, the four of them turned their attention back to the football game. What he heard about Devon and Kelsey didn't exactly bother Derek. He certainly wasn't rooting for them to fail. Devon was his boy, and Kelsey was a pretty good friend. He would be lying to himself, however, if he said that the thought of them potentially going through a rocky period in their relationship was causing him great distress though.

****

He made sure to bundle up. He dressed in multiple layers in anticipation of the frigid temperatures that were going to greet him when he left the dorm on his way to the bus that was going to take him to the main campus for his history class. All week, it was unseasonably cold, with high temperatures in the teens. Today was expected to be the coldest day of the year. The temperature was not expected to reach double digits. Derek had lived in Delaware his whole life, and he could not remember it being so cold for such a long period of time. The temperatures had remained below thirty degrees for about two weeks, and it was expected to stay that way for at least another week. Earlier, Derek decided to teleport to his class to avoid the weather, but when he teleported into one of the stalls in the bathroom, there was another person in the adjacent stall! He had to jump through hoops to explain that one away. He decided against doing that again, at least for a while, just to be safe.

Derek opened the door, and sure enough, the frigid air hit him like a ton of bricks. It was like stepping into an icebox. The wind made it feel like it was zero degrees outside. Why didn't they just cancel classes? he wondered. He briskly walked to the bus stop. When he got there, Omar was already there waiting for him. They had the same class, and they decided to ride the bus together. Derek was surprised to see him dressed in only a light jacket. No hat, no gloves, and no heavy coat. Only a jacket.

"You look cold," Omar commented amusedly.

"Man, I'm freezing my ass off! Ain't you cold?" Derek asked.

"Nope."

"You're kidding, right?" asked Derek incredulously. "How you not cold? It's like negative degrees out here right now!"

Omar responded, "I'm using my powers to keep myself warm. I'm nice and toasty right now."

"I'm really wishing I had that power right about now. I got on two layers, a big ol' coat, and a hat and gloves, and I'm still cold."

They saw the bus bound around the corner in the distance and were glad that it was on time. The last thing they needed to do was to wait for a late bus on a day like this. The bus pulled up to their stop, and they quickly hopped on. It was nice and warm on it, much to Derek's relief. There weren't many students on the bus. Derek saw only three other people. Omar and Derek grabbed a seat near the very back of the bus.

"So how you been? I feel like we haven't really talked that much since we got trapped in that video game," Omar said.

"Yeah, that was weird, wasn't it? We still never found out who sent that game to Matt, did we?"

"Well, if we're sure his mom didn't send it—" Omar started.

"And I'm pretty sure she didn't," said Derek as he interjected.

"Then no," continued Omar. "But I'm willing to bet it was the same person that sent those golems."

"I agree."

"But why would somebody be out to get us? And why magically? It just doesn't make sense," Omar pondered aloud. Derek got really quiet and took great interest in the buildings passing by out the window. Omar noticed this. "Derek?"

"Hmm?"

"What is it?"

"What's what?"

He was being evasive. Omar got suspicious. "What do you know?"

"I can tell you what I don't know—what you're talking about."

"The hell you don't. You're not answering the question. Do you know who's after us? If you know something, you need to tell me, seeing as my life could be in danger and all."

"Fine. There's something about the ritual that I didn't know," said Derek.

Omar didn't like the sound of that. "What?"

"Warlock diamonds attract paranormal activity."

"What do you mean 'attract paranormal activity'?"

"We now emit a special signal that many magical beings and mystical phenomena can sense. They drawn to the source of that signal. Each of us."

Omar chuckled in disbelief. "Hold on a minute. So you telling me that the reason we've been attacked is because you got us to cast that stupid spell to protect us from attacks?"

"Yep," he said quietly.

"And how long does this last, although I already got a pretty good idea."

"It lasts as long as the ritual is in effect."

"So the rest of our lives."

"Yeah."

Omar could only shake his head in disgust and scoff. "Unbelievable."

****

Rhonda and Matthias were dancing to the lively club music that was blaring throughout the space. They decided to go to a nightclub in Philadelphia with Omar and Derek. Tre'Vell was going to meet them there with his date. Apparently, she was a witch. He seemed excited to introduce them to her, Matthias thought. Rhonda and Matthias had migrated to the middle of the dancefloor when they arrived in the club. They agreed to meet by a spot just to the side of the bar when Tre'Vell arrived. He told Omar that he would send him a text message when he got there. Until then, the four of them had split up, with Matthias and Rhonda going off together.

Chris Brown's "Love More" came on. Rhonda and Matthias grooved to the upbeat song and briefly lost themselves in the music. After the DJ played a few more current popular R&B and hip-hop tunes, Matthias and Rhonda decided to take a break. They squeezed through the packed crowd and went to the meeting spot.

"It's so hot in here," said Rhonda. "I'm sweating out my hair."

Matthias laughed. "That's a good thing. Means you're enjoying yourself," he said.

Rhonda playfully slapped him on the arm. Matthias scanned the room. "Who are you looking for?"

"Omar and Derek."

After some time, Rhonda said, "There goes Omar over there." She pointed him out in the crowd. He was grinding on some girl while "Show Me" from Kid Ink was currently playing. Once the song stopped, he made his way over to Matthias and Rhonda.

"I got the text from Tre. He's going to be here soon," he said.

"Oh good. Where's Derek? We need to get him over here so he can meet Tre's date," Rhonda said.

"He over there," said Omar. He pointed out Derek. He was making out with a girl on the opposite side of the club.

"Should we interrupt him?" Rhonda asked.

"You can try to pry his lips off hers if you want to," Omar said.

"I think I will." Rhonda went off to get Derek.

Not too long after Rhonda left, Tre'Vell and Ricquel showed up. "What's poppin', Matt, Omar?"

"Nothing. Just chillin'," said Omar.

"This is Ricquel. Ricquel, this is Matt and Omar."

They shook hands. "How you doin'?" greeted Omar.

"I'm fine. It's nice to meet you. So these are the warlocks that Tre's told me about," Ricquel said. "I thought you said there were three?" she asked Tre'Vell.

Matthias said, "There is. The other one is Derek."

"Where is Derek, anyway?" Tre'Vell asked.

Omar said, "Over there making out with some chick. Rhonda went to go get him, but I guess she ain't have too much success."

"I see them. I'll go get them." She left the group.

"So how you been?" Matthias asked.

"Could be better," Tre'Vell said.

Matthias countered, "Could be worse too. I mean, you were dead after all."

"That's true," Tre'Vell agreed. "That was trippy."

"Speaking of that game, guess what Derek told me a couple of days ago," said Omar.

"What he say now?"

"There was something about the ritual that he didn't know about. It seems our little spell had some other side effects. We now each emit a special magical signal that attracts supernatural activity that lasts for the rest of our lives."

"So what you're saying is . . ."

"Is that gives us an explanation for what's been happening to us. The golems, the zombie video game, whoever's behind it. And we can expect similar things to happen to us in the future. Probably worse."

Tre'Vell said, "Please tell me you jokin' right now."

"Afraid not."

"That doesn't explain the golem attacks before we became a diamond, though," Matthias opined.

"Maybe whoever's pulling the strings knew we were going to perform the ritual and wanted to stop it? I don't know. But even if the previous monsters wasn't because of the spell, the rest will be. Think of all the monsters and other magical creatures we might have to face."

Tre'Vell rubbed his temples in frustration. "I knew I shouldn't have did this. Messin' around with Derek's just put me in even more trouble than I was in before." He walked off.

Derek walked up to them. "Where's Rhonda and Ricquel?" Matthias asked.

"They went to the bathroom. Where's Tre?"

"He stalked off in anger," said Matthias.

"Why?"

"Probably because I told them what you told me last week," Omar said.

"What? What you do that for?"

"I thought it was only right. It affects them too. They ought to know."

"And I'm glad he did. Derek, do you know what you've done?"

"Just like I told him, I didn't know about the signal. And I didn't do it alone. Each one of us agreed to do the spell. It wouldn't have worked otherwise," Derek said, defending himself.

"We did it because you practically begged us to. All because of that stupid tarot reading. What did I tell you about tarot readings? Looks like I was closer to the truth than I initially thought," said Matthias.

"Look. This ain't the time nor place to be talking about this. We'll discuss it later. Now if you'll excuse me, I'ma find myself a bad bitch and go have some fun."

Chapter 14

Splinter

Omar panted heavily as he darted through the trees. He had to find a place to hide, a place that offered protection. He glanced behind him. He didn't see it. Maybe he lost it. He dared not stop, just in case he hadn't. After running along a beaten path, he came to a riverbank. He surveyed the area. Good! There was a small opening in a huge rock formation at the end of the bank. Omar heard a rustling in the brush behind him. Out popped the monster that was chasing him! It spotted him and came charging for him. Omar picked up the pace and headed for the rocks.

From the distance, the opening looked just big enough for him to crawl through and small enough to prevent the beast from following him. It was a race to the end. With the creature quickly gaining on him, Omar reached the rock formation. He got on all fours and crawled into the opening. As soon as he moved toward the back, he felt the enclave rattle as the monster crashed into it. The creature couldn't fit in. It was too big. Omar relaxed, but quickly retensed up as the creature stuck its arm into the tiny cave. Its arm stopped just short of Omar as he was just out of its reach. The creature lowered its head to the ground and gazed menacingly at Omar before raising it again and backing away beyond Omar's line of sight. He didn't know if the beast had given up and left or if it was just waiting him out, knowing that Omar couldn't stay in there forever. Omar didn't want to take the chance of it being the latter.

"What now?"

**

Matthias's phone started ringing. "I wonder who that is." He went over to pick up his phone from the dresser. It was Omar. "Hey, Omar. What's up?"

"Matt? You gotta help me!"

"What's going on?"

"Something is after me! It almost got me, but I got away. But I'm trapped, though. I can't get out! It's gonna kill me!"

"Slow down. What happened?"

"I was walking and this . . . monster grabbed me from behind with its claws and started to fly off with me. When it was over a clearing, I burned its claws and it let go of its hold on me, dropping me to the ground. I shot fire at it from the ground, but kept missing and set some trees on fire, so I stopped 'cuz I didn't want to start a wildfire. It came at me again, and I shot a couple of fireballs at it. I burned its wings, and it crashed to the ground. It then started chasing me through the woods. I found this little opening in some rocks and now it's got me cornered."

"What does the monster look like?"

"It's huge. Bigger than me. It looks like its body is a lion and its head, front legs, and wings are an eagle."

"That sounds like a gryphon. I'm going to look it up in my grimoire and call Derek so we can help. Where are you now?"

"Black Clay Creek State Park. Matt, hurry up! It keeps trying to get in and I'm not sure how much longer I can hold it off with my powers!"

Matthias called Derek and told him to come to his room immediately. While he was waiting for Derek to arrive, Matthias pulled out his grimoire tablet and toggled through its contents. Derek teleported into Matthias's room just as Matthias reached the page he was looking for. He went over to where Matthias was sitting.

"What's up? What's the big emergency?"

"Omar just called me and said he was being chased by this monster in Black Clay Creek State Park."

"What's he doing there?"

"He didn't say, and I really didn't think to ask. I was more concerned about his safety. The monster's got him cornered, and he's not sure how much longer he can hold him off."

"Did he say what's after him?"

"Well, from what he described, I'm pretty sure it's this," he said as he pointed down at his grimoire.

Gryphons

Mythical creatures indigenous to parts of Africa and Asia, mostly the peaks of Mount Kilimanjaro and Mount Everest. Standing about seven feet tall when they're on all fours, these creatures are distinctive for their body composition. They have the hind body of a lion and the torso, head, and wings of an eagle. This combination has led many ancient cultures to consider it the king of all creatures of the land and sea. Because of this, it is believed to be an emissary of the divine.

"What's a gryphon doing all the way over here?" Derek wondered aloud.

"Who cares? It's over here and after Omar," Matthias said impatiently.

"Does it have a way to stop it?" Derek asked.

Matthias scanned the rest of the page. "There's a killing curse here. But it's going to take all four of us to say it for it to work."

"Great. Okay, here's what we'll do. I'll teleport you to Omar. You need to find a way to distract it while I go get Tre so Omar can get out of wherever he's hiding. I'll teleport back in with Tre, and we'll say the spell."

"How are you going to pull that off? You don't know where Omar is, and I thought you couldn't teleport with anybody else tagging along."

"Before the bonding ritual, I couldn't. Now, I can have a passenger. And I don't need to know exactly where Omar is. By using my telepathy to lock in on him, I can teleport to him instead of to a particular location. That's another side effect of the ritual. Now, write the curse down as I let them in on what's going on. Hurry."

Matthias fetched a piece of paper to write the spell down. As he was busy doing that, Derek reached out to Tre'Vell telepathically.

Tre.

Derek? That you?

Yeah. Look, I gotta keep this short 'cuz we don't got a lot of time. Omar's in trouble at Black Clay Creek. He's being chased by a gryphon. Me and Matt got a killing curse, but it requires all of us to say it. I'm gonna teleport to where you are to pick you up. Go somewhere I can 'port into safely and use the connection to call me back when you ready. Hurry up.

Matt. It's Derek. We got a plan. I'ma bring Matt to you and he'll explain it. Just be ready to come out on his mark.

"Okay. Tre's ready. Let's go. Take my hand." Matthias grabbed Derek's hand, and he teleported them out. Shortly thereafter, they arrived in Black Clay Creek State Park along the riverbank.

"Woah," Matthias said as he put a hand to his head to steady himself.

"What's wrong?" asked Derek.

"I feel like my insides are, like, squeezed or something."

"That's how I felt when I first teleported. It'll wear off. Look over there," Derek said as he pointed to where a large gryphon was repeatedly attempting to get inside of a small hole in the rock formation while small bursts of fire erupted from it, trying to keep it at bay. "Okay, I'm going to get Tre. Try to get him out of there," said Derek and he teleported out.

"How am I supposed to do that?" he yelled. That seemed to catch the gryphon's attention, and it turned around to face Matthias.

The gryphon kept looking back and forth between Matthias and the hole where Matthias assumed Omar was. It was as if he wanted to go after Matthias but was unsure if he should leave Omar. Matthias decided to goad it. He unleashed a stream of electricity at it. This did nothing but anger it. With a terrifying *screeeeech!* it ran at Matthias.

"Omar! Quick, while it's focused on me, get out!" Matthias yelled. He looked at the river. "Agueus liberan."

A stream of water arose from the river and snaked toward Matthias's outstretched arm. He then redirected the stream toward the approaching gryphon. It got drenched. He then bombarded it with electricity. At first, it cried out in pain before it seemed to shake off the assault and continue. Matthias's attack was no longer effective.

While the gryphon was preoccupied with Matthias, Omar cautiously emerged from his hiding place. He saw the gryphon shirk off Matthias's attack. He formed a fire spear and hurled it at the gryphon, hoping to kill it. At the last second, the gryphon turned around and snatched the spear out of the air with its talon. It then chucked it at Matthias. The fire spear went straight through his shoulder and embedded itself in the tree behind him before dissipating and setting the tree ablaze. Matthias fell to his knees and clutched his shoulder as the singed flesh caused pain to shoot down his arm.

Seeing its opportunity, the gryphon soared high up into the air, its wings now healed from the burns that Omar inflicted earlier, and dove straight at Matthias. Omar ran at Matthias in an attempt to protect him. As he ran, he realized that he wasn't going to get there in time.

***

Derek teleported into a tiny bathroom. Tre'Vell was standing right in front of the door, but the small space meant that he appeared directly in front of him. Any closer and they would be practically face-to-face. "Um, what am I doing in here?"

"You said go someplace where you could teleport into," said Tre'"Vell.

Derek responded, "And this is the best you could come up with? Kind of small, don't you think?"

"It works, don't it?"

"Where are we anyway?"

"A lounge. Some industry people are in the crowd. My turn to perform is comin' up. I can't leave or I'll be taken off the list. This better be quick," Tre'Vell said.

"Okay, come on." He took Tre'Vell's hand, but thought of something. "Wait. Did anybody see you come in here?"

"Yeah. The door opens straight to the room."

"Lock the door. Just in case somebody comes before we get back," Derek said.

"Oh. Good thinkin'." Tre'Vell turned around and locked the door.

"Ready?" Derek asked. Tre'Vell nodded. "Now I gotta warn you. You might feel a bit weird after we get to the park. Teleporting can be a little disorienting at first."

"Can we just go? I'm on a deadline!" rushed Tre'Vell. Derek teleported them out.

***

The gryphon was closing in on Matthias, whose shoulder injury kept him rooted to the spot he was in. Omar watched with dread as he realized that he wasn't going to get there before the gryphon. What would he even do if he did? As he was running, Omar noticed that the gryphon suddenly slowed down considerably. Its trajectory remained unchanged; it was just moving slower, like a video being played in slow motion. Omar looked around to see what caused it. That's when he noticed Derek and Tre'Vell standing some distance behind him. They must have teleported in and froze the gryphon. But why didn't the beast come to a complete stop? Maybe the monster was too powerful to be fully contained by Tre'Vell's magic. In any case, the gryphon's slowed descent allowed Omar to beat it to Matthias.

"You all right?" Omar asked.

"My shoulder is burned. Do you think I'm okay?"

"I was just trying to be helpful. You ain't have to get smart. Here, let me help you up." Omar said as he gave Matthias a hand to his feet.

Just then, Derek and Tre'Vell teleported over to them. When he got a look at his injury, Derek asked Matthias, "What happened to you?"

"Omar. That's what."

Tre'Vell and Derek looked at Omar. "I was aiming for the monster. It ain't my fault that he caught my spear and threw it at you!"

Tre'Vell grew impatient. "Whatever. Can we just say the fuckin' spell before my freeze wears off?"

Matthias pulled out the piece of paper with the killing curse on it. "We all have to say the spell together."

In unison, they chanted "Ghanki holne tyck poit zyck. Gryphon reivis waba destructe. Waba destructe. Waba destructe." The gryphon squawked and shuddered before falling to the ground with a *thud!* It continued to convulse on the ground before inching toward the group. It didn't get very far before it finally succumbed to the curse and exploded in a plume of purple fire. Feathers, fur, and specks of golden light rained down around them, and the monster was vanquished.

"Great! Now get me back, Derek. Come on!" Tre'Vell urged as he grabbed Derek's hand.

"I'll be back." He and Tre'Vell teleported out.

Matthias cried out in pain. "Ahh!" He clutched his shoulder.

"You gonna need to get that checked out," Omar said in concern.

"No, I won't. Follow me." They walked over to the river. "Cup some water in your hand," Matthias instructed. Omar did as he was told. Matthias held his hand over the water. *"Rigomortis inglotum.* Now pour the water over my wound." Omar did and watched in fascination as the skin stitched itself back together.

"Wow. What did you do?"

"Healing charm. Simple, really." He swung his arm around to test his shoulder. "There. Good as new. So how and why are you here in the first place?"

"I was with a friend. He got a physical science class, and I was helping him with a project. As a matter of fact, he probably wondering where the hell I am. I'm surprised he ain't text me yet. I better get back to our meeting spot before he gets nervous," said Omar. He walked off in search of his friend.

Derek reappeared in the park. "Where Omar at?"

"He came here with a friend so he went to go find him. Let's get back to the dorm. Off to your room we go!" Derek teleported them out.

****

Rhonda waltzed through the aisles. There were many trinkets on the shelves, but nothing that really caught her eye. The few things that looked sort of interesting were out of her price range. This was a sports memorabilia store! Couldn't she find something that was both interesting and affordable? Was that too much to ask? Eventually, she settled on buying a Dodger-themed baseball that was signed by a couple of stars from the team. For having signatures from such prominent players, it was surprisingly affordable: only $300. The price left her a little skeptical about its authenticity, but what Matthias didn't know wouldn't hurt him.

"Rhonda? Is that you?" she heard a voice call out. She looked to see who it was.

"Ricquel? What are you doing here?"

Ricquel closed the distance between them. "Just browsing. I was just walking through the mall and decided to stop in since I haven't been in here before. What are you doing here?"

Rhonda said, "Just buying Matt a present. Our anniversary is tomorrow."

"Can I see what you got?" Rhonda showed her the baseball. "I bet he'll love that."

"I hope so. He likes the Dodgers," Rhonda said.

"You know what would be really good?"

"What?"

"If you surprised him with the gift. It would add a lot more to the presentation," Ricquel said.

"How so?"

Ricquel explained her train of thought. "Like if you could sneak into his room while he's not there and decorate the room with balloons and candles and stuff. And when he walks in, you could be there waiting for him, dressed in something nice, if you catch my drift."

"Hmm. I do have a key to his room. That's a good idea. But how would I get him out the room is the question."

"Well, I could help. I'm going to be with Tre tomorrow. I'm sure we could distract him around a certain time. Keep him busy for you."

"You would do that?"

Ricquel waved her off. "Yeah sure. It won't be any trouble at all."

"Thank you so much, Ricquel." Ricquel nodded before turning around to leave. "Before you go, can I ask you something?"

"What is it?"

"I don't know why I'm asking you this since I barely know you, but let's just say hypothetically you saw your boyfriend do something that was . . . weird. Like really freaky, but you're not quite sure what you saw. What would you do?"

"I would decide if it's worth bringing up to him first. No need to bother him with something that's not important. But if it really began to bother me, I would just ask him. In most cases, there's a perfectly good explanation. Why?"

Rhonda shook her head. "Just something with Matt dealing with something I found and something I saw him do. But you're right. I'm sure there's a perfectly good explanation. Thanks for the advice. And for all your help too."

"No problem. Just promise me you'll really surprise him."

****

When they reappeared, Matthias took stock of his surroundings. This wasn't Derek's room. There were scented candles lit around the room although not so much that it would set off the sprinklers. The window had a "Happy Anniversary" streamer draped along it. There were balloons situated around the room, and the lights were dimmed. Through it all, he recognized the layout of the furniture. They were in his room.

"This isn't your room," he told Derek. Before Derek had a chance to answer him, they heard a voice from behind them.

"WHAT. THE. HELL!" They turned around to find a shocked Rhonda standing in front of the door with a box in her hands.

"Rhonda!" said Matthias in surprise.

"What . . . how . . . why . . ."

"Rhonda, I can explain," Matthias said.

She shot her hand out. "What was that? Where did you come from?" she asked in a panic.

"If you just calm down, I can explain everything to you."

"I mean, you just appeared out of thin air! Who are you? What are you?"

"You know who I am. I'm your boyfriend. Here," he said as he began to walk toward her.

"Don't you come near me! Take one more step and I swear I'll scream."

"I didn't want you to find out this way," he muttered to himself.

"What? That you were some kind of . . . of . . . freak?" By this point, Rhonda was on the verge of hysteria.

"No. That I'm a . . ." He looked toward Derek, who merely shrugged. "A warlock."

When she heard that, Rhonda could only shake her head at the absurdity, but because she couldn't come up with another plausible explanation, she took his word for it. She backed up toward the door. "I gotta go."

"Babe, please don't go," Matthias pleaded.

Rhonda tossed her box toward him, and it landed at his feet. "Happy anniversary." With that, she left the room in a rush.

Matthias reached down and picked up the box. Inside it was a blue-and-white baseball with "Dodgers" written across it in manuscript. He rotated the ball and noticed the signatures of many players on it that he followed and cheered for. In another moment, he would have greatly appreciated the gift. In this moment, however, he could only focus on what had just transpired. In the span of minutes, his entire world felt like it had come crashing down.

He wanted to yell. He wanted to desperately run after her, to reassure her that everything was okay. But he couldn't do that because he wasn't sure they ever would be. The shock of what just happened had him rooted to the spot. All sorts of emotions were churning within: disappointment, shame, sadness, frustration. But the emotion that had won the tug-of-war was anger. And Matthias focused his anger on the most convenient target at that time.

"Look what you did, you idiot!" Matthias yelled at Derek.

"What I did? How is this my fault?"

"Are you serious? You teleported us to my room . . . against my wishes and exposed us to my girlfriend. I told you to go to your room!"

"How was I supposed to know that your girl was waiting in here? You could have said something!"

"I didn't know either! She probably wanted to surprise me for the anniversary of our first date. Didn't you think to mind-scan the room before you teleported into it!"

"No, because I know you don't have a roommate. Why would somebody be in your room? I don't mind-scan my house when I teleport in."

"Great. Now I have to find a way to fix the mess you made."

"Maybe I can go after her. Explain everything," he offered.

Matthias said, "No! I think you've done enough damage for one day. You know what? Just get out."

Derek slightly hung his head and slowly walked to the door. "For what it's worth, I'm sorry." He left the room and closed the door behind him, leaving a devastated Matthias in his wake.

****

"Stop. Stop." Ricquel turned off the music. Tre'Vell ceased his singing and sighed. He knew why she had stopped him. Ricquel leaned back in her chair in frustration before returning it to its original position. "You didn't hit that note. Let's try it again." She restarted the track, and Tre'Vell began to sing the lyrics before he again reached for the high note. "Stop! You missed the note again. Don't tell me you can't hit that note," she said.

"I can hit that note," he shot back.

Ricquel asked, "Yeah, I know. I've heard you hit it before. Do I need to change it? Make it lower? Change the key?"

Tre'Vell shook his head. "No. It fits the song."

"Well, thank you, captain obvious. I know that, that's why I arranged it that way. But if you can't hit it, I'm going to have to take it out," she said.

"I'll get it," he reassured her.

"I'm concerned. It's not just this note and it's not just this song. You've been off the past couple of sessions. You've been sharp, flat, off-key, forgetting lyrics. What's going on? Is something wrong?"

Tre'Vell took off his headphones. He walked out of the recording booth and joined her in the studio. "I don't know. I guess I'm just mad that I missed my chance at the lounge. That could've been my big break."

Ricquel asked," Why did you miss it, anyway? I knew you were there. I dropped you off."

Tre'Vell chuckled and said, "It's a long story."

"Pull up a seat. I got time," said Ricquel.

"You won't believe me if I told you," said Tre'Vell.

"Try me," she said. He grabbed a chair from outside the studio and began his tale.

"Just before it was my turn to go up, Derek calls me in my head and tells me to go to a place he can 'port in."

Ricquel stopped him. "Wait. Derek's one of those warlocks I met at the club, right?"

"Yes."

"And when you say 'called you in your head' . . ."

"That's one of his powers. I think he calls it tele something."

"Telepathy?" Ricquel offered.

"Yeah. That's it, I think."

"You said 'powers,' plural. So he's got more than one? What level is he?"

"He can teleport. That's what he wanted to do. And he a level 4, he said," Tre'Vell answered.

"Okay. Keep going."

"So like I was sayin', he tells me to go someplace so he could pick me up 'cuz we had to help Omar."

"What was wrong?"

"The nigga was bein' chased by a monster, go figure."

"Oh my god! What did it look like?" Ricquel asked in concern.

Tre'Vell said, "It was like a crazy mix between a lion and an eagle. And it was fuckin' huge!"

"So what happened? Is he okay?"

"Yeah, he'll be a'ight. We killed the thing with a spell that Matt had. It was him who was hurt."

Ricquel asked in confusion, "Wait, I thought that Omar was the one being chased?"

"He was. Derek dropped Matt off first before he picked me up. He hurt his shoulder before me and Derek got there," Tre'Vell explained.

"Oh, I get it now. I assume you didn't make it back for your performance."

"Hell no. I can't tell you how pissed I was."

"It seems like you might have saved his life. That's got to count for something, right?"

Tre'Vell grumbled. "It ain't just that. The past couple months have been one big mess."

"How so?"

"I met them dudes just a couple months ago. Back then, I didn't know anything about magic or being a warlock."

"What? How's that possible?"

"I'm an orphan. When I was little, my mom abandoned me and my dad was killed. Neither of them told me about my heritage. I'm not even sure which one was magical. I ain't even get my powers 'til a few years ago."

"I'm sorry," said Ricquel.

Tre'Vell waved her apology off. "Around then, I was attacked by monsters. I used my power to get away, but Omar and Matt saw me. They found me and introduced me to magic."

"You got lucky they saw you."

"Luck ain't have nothin' to do with it. They was lookin' for another warlock so they could complete they little diamond," Tre'Vell countered.

"Diamond?"

"They group. Anyway, at first, I refused. But after I was attacked again and they helped save me, I agreed. We was attacked one night by a bunch of golems, and they almost killed us."

"That's quite a story."

"If only that was the end. Not long after Christmas, we got sucked into a video game."

"What?"

"Yup. Some zombie game. We got out, but not before I died."

"Excuse me?"

"One of the zombies rammed a wood stake right through my chest," Tre'Vell said, unconsciously rubbing his chest.

"I don't believe it."

"They got me back right before they got out, but it was still pretty scary."

"I bet."

"So as you can see, my anger was built up. Not just 'cuz of the missed show," he finally said.

"From what it sounds like, those guys are more trouble than they're worth," said Ricquel.

"What you mean?"

Ricquel explained. "Think about it. That all started around the time you met them. That can't be a coincidence."

Tre'Vell thought about that. "Now that you mention it, I think they did mention somethin' about Derek bein' in danger. A tarot reading."

"So basically, they asked you to join them to protect him."

"When you put it like that, it sounds kinda bad."

"That's what it is. They've asked you to put your life in danger to protect a guy you barely know. That ain't right."

"No, it ain't. Is it?"

Ricquel said, "I would stay away from them from now on if I was you."

"I don't know," he said uncertainly.

She got up and went over to where Tre'Vell was sitting. "I mean it. You've already been attacked by golems, sucked into a video game and died, and had to miss an important show to vanquish what sounds like a gryphon. Who knows what else'll happen to you if you stay with them." She stared deep into his eyes and caressed his chin. "I just don't want to see anything bad happen to you. Is that so bad? Break it off with them. For me?"

"Well, how can I argue with that?" he said. Ricquel smiled and gave him a deep, passionate kiss.

****

"Thanks for giving me a ride, Ty," said Derek as they got out of the car. Tyrone joined him on the sidewalk as they began making their way to Sharp Cutz. It was another cold day, and Ty didn't want Derek to be waiting at the bus stop. He was more than glad to give his friend a ride. Once Derek told him what he was going to the barbershop for, he was even more intrigued. When Derek told his circle of friends about his being a warlock, he wasn't as freaked out as the others. Tyrone immediately thought it was cool and had a lot of questions, which Derek answered to the best of his ability. Ty was instrumental in getting the others on board and assuaging any reticence they may have had. Truth was, Ty was fascinated with magic from the moment Derek introduced him to it.

"No problem. So explain to me again what's going on," he said.

"Me and a couple of my boys was trapped inside this game"—he held up the copy of Zombie Virus U—"and we barely got out. The game was cursed by somebody and sent to us. I told my dad and he said that somebody must be after us. Lamar said that I could perform a divination ritual on this game to find out whose curse it was," said Derek.

"Oh. How does it work?" asked Tyrone.

"When a witch or warlock casts a spell on a person or object, they leave a residue. A divination ritual can detect that residue and determine from whom the spell was cast. It'll give us an image of who's behind this," Derek explained.

As they approached the front of the barbershop, Tyrone asked, "What you gonna do when you find out?"

Derek pondered that question as they reached the door. "Huh! I don't know. I haven't even thought that far. I'll cross that bridge when I get to it."

"Well, you better put on your walking shoes 'cuz that bridge is coming up pretty soon," said Tyrone. Derek opened the door, and they walked in the barbershop.

They walked into a surprisingly busy barbershop. All four of the barbers had men in their chairs, and there were about six men waiting for their turn to get a cut. They greeted all the barbers before they reached Lamar. He told them he had to finish the guy he was on and another guy that had scheduled an appointment. Once he was done with them, he would be ready for Derek. Ty and Derek took seats and waited for Lamar to get done.

About thirty minutes later, Lamar summoned them into the back room of the shop and locked the door behind them. Derek had never been to this room. It looked like a basement. There were a couple of bookcases along the wall with various mystical tomes, artifacts, herbs, and miscellaneous supplies. "Do you have the game?" asked Lamar. Derek nodded and handed him the CD. Lamar took it and went over to a desk. Ty and Derek followed.

He pulled some papers out of the drawer. "Let's see here. Where's those divination instructions?" He rustled through some of the papers before finding it. "Aha! Here it is. Now, what ingredients do we need?" After looking over the list, he said, "This stuff is pretty basic." He flitted across the room, grabbing ingredients, and returned to the desk with a gray candle, a strange candleholder with a small tray above it, and a cup filled with a light blue powder.

"Dim the lights," Lamar instructed. Tyrone turned down the lights. Lamar placed the candle in the candleholder in the spot under the tray that was situated at the top. He covered the bottom of the tray with some of the blue powder. He put the CD on the tray and lit the candle. The flame soon spread around the tray like a Bunsen burner. Lamar handed Derek the parchment that had the incantation on it. "Get ready." Soon, the powder in the tray began to crackle and emit a white smoke into the air. "Pour some of the powder into your hands and recite the activation incantation." Derek scooped some of the light blue powder from the cup into his hands and chanted "Divinio revelus por bach lau vivi ati." The powder briefly glowed before returning to normal.

"Now blow it into the air above the divining tube." Derek took a deep breath and blew the powder into the air. It began to interact with the smoke coming from the divining tube. "The last part is the revelation spell. Once you say it, an image should start to coalesce in that cloud of smoke. That would be the person who cast the spell," said Lamar.

"Pictura imaginus liken harpe matvu imunde," chanted Derek. Static electricity erupted from the cloud. No image appeared.

"This is bad," said Lamar.

"What happened? What's bad?" asked Tyrone.

"The spell caster can't be divined. Whoever cast this spell must have found a way to conceal their magic," said Lamar.

Derek asked, "How is that possible?"

Lamar replied, "Only Ultimates can conceal their magical signatures. You don't have enough power by yourself to break through the protection. You need somebody else to say the spell with you."

Derek turned the lights back on, grabbed the supplies, and put them in a plastic bag. "What are you doing?" asked Ty.

"I'm taking the stuff so I can get the boys to cast the spell with me," said Derek.

Lamar chimed in with, "Good idea. Casting the spell with other warlocks should give you enough power."

Derek nodded before saying, "Okay. I'm out. Thanks for the stuff, Lamar. I owe you one."

Tyrone asked, "You need a ride home?"

"Nah. There ain't nobody in my room right now so it's safe to 'port there. Although I guess I better walk out the shop so anybody that's still out there don't get suspicious."

***

"Good, you finally here," said Derek as Tre'Vell walked in the door.

"You lucky I came at all! What you want now, Derek?"

"I found a way to trace the magic of the person that sent us that video game, but I need your help. Just thought y'all might want to know."

"Well, you thought wrong," Tre'Vell replied.

"How?" Omar asked.

"A divination ritual."

Matthias asked, "Why don't you just cast it? I don't get why you need our help for a divination ritual?"

"I already tried, at the barbershop. It didn't work. Somebody blocked their curse from being traced. Lamar said that only Ultimates can do that. Clearly I don't have enough power by myself to overcome the magic of a level 5, especially since it was weakened by the ritual," Derek explained.

"Didn't y'all tell me that an Ultimate is, like, the strongest? So rare that there only a few in the whole world?" Tre'Vell said.

"Yeah. So?"

"So? So I don't want anythin' to do with them. I ain't going to go pokin' the bear," said Tre'Vell.

"The bear's already awake and chasing you, Tre."

"Wrong! They after you. We just gettin' caught in the crossfire. This all got started because of you and your protection. It ain't have nothin' to do with us. Being around you is liable to get me killed, and I ain't finna take the risk that my death will be permanent this time. Man, I'm out! Good luck with everythin'." Tre'Vell walked toward the door.

"When we formed the diamond, we all walked through a one-way door. You can't just up and leave!" said Derek.

"Watch me," countered Tre'Vell. He walked out the door.

Silence reigned for a few moments. "Well, hopefully we won't need him to cast the spell," Derek said.

"He's right, you know," said Omar.

"What!"

"Think about it. This all started the moment I met you. I was perfectly fine before. Since then, I been attacked by golems, sucked into a game and had to fend off man-eating zombies, and nearly been picked apart by a gryphon. I can't shake the feeling that this is only the beginning. Diamond or no, I gotta look out for numero uno. *Hasta luego*, homie." Omar also got up and walked out.

Matthias arose. "Matt, please don't go. I can't do this without your help," Derek pleaded.

"It's not just what they said. You're reckless and don't think about the consequences of your actions. Tre told me he missed a very important performance because of the gryphon thing. And you exposed me to Rhonda and now she won't talk to me," Matthias said.

"I already apologized for Rhonda, and I don't see how you can pin the gryphon thing on me. The spell required all four of us, and Omar would have died otherwise. I don't see what the big deal is. All I need is for you to help me find out who cast that curse on the video game."

"And what will you do when you find that out? If it is an Ultimate that is behind everything, what do you hope to do? What if this is all somehow related to the diamond? You have to admit, the timing lines up for that."

"The diamond is the only thing that protected us in those situations. Why am I the only thing that can see that?"

"That's a good question. And it's one that you're going to have to answer on your own." Matthias exited the room.

Once Matthias left, Derek remained to marinate in his thoughts in the empty room. What now? There was a potential Ultimate after him, and his brother warlocks had abandoned him. Did they have a point? In his zeal to prevent his barber's tarot reading from coming to pass, had he ignored the danger he put them in? Had he irrevocably damaged their lives for his own selfish reasons?

Whatever the answer to those questions were, one thing was clear to him. Their diamond was on the rocks.

Chapter 15

Suspicion

"Hmm. This smells good," said Angela as she inhaled the succulent aroma wafting from the dish in front of her. The waiter had just brought their food out. She had ordered a delicious-looking chicken parmesan dish. She absolutely loved Italian food, and the restaurant she was dining at, the Silver Dove, was known for having great Italian food. She had eaten there before and couldn't tell if she preferred the Silver Dove or the Olive Garden. In the end, she decided that both of them were excellent, and you couldn't go wrong with either one. She had to admit, though, that the Silver Dove was slightly pricier. She wasn't paying for the meal, though, so what did she care?

"Wow, that does look good!" said John, her date. Even though she was the mayor, Angela was still a woman in her thirties looking for love. Her responsibilities and ambitious climb to the political top left precious little room for romance. Her magical identity also made her hesitant in venturing out into the dating pool. A few months ago, John asked her out. Wanting a respite from all the craziness, she decided to take him up on his offer. She was pleasantly surprised that John turned out to be just what the doctor ordered. He was a physical therapist in his late twenties. Angela thought he was funny and quite handsome. She enjoyed spending time with him. He served his purpose: being a distraction, a break from her work.

"What did you end up getting?" she asked.

"Shrimp and fettuccine alfredo," John said.

"That looks great." Angela took a sip of her drink. John made no attempt to begin eating his food. "What's wrong?" she asked.

John said, "Nothing. Just waiting for you to start on your food before I dig in. A gentleman always waits for his lady to eat before he does."

"Aww, you didn't have to do that. But I think it's sweet nonetheless. I guess I better start because I don't want to leave you hungry," Angela said. She picked up her knife and fork and began to cut the chicken. She looked up toward the front door in the background as she took a bite of her food. She began to choke as she saw one of the senators standing there, staring intently at her.

"Are you okay?" John asked.

"Yes," she said, her eyes still on the senator. He gave a head nod toward the door, indicating that he wanted her to follow him outside. "Listen, I have to go to the ladies' room."

"Didn't you go before the food got here?" he asked, confused.

Angela got up. "Yeah. I guess that soda went right through me, huh? I'll be right back." She walked past the senator and out the door. He followed her. "Can't you see that I'm out? Couldn't this wait?" Angela asked.

"I don't care where you are, witch. Wherever you are, whatever you're doing, we will find you. She will find you. And you will wait on us, not the other way around. You would do best to remember that!" the senator said.

"Now that you're through with your grandstanding, what is it that you want? I know there has to be some reason why you pulled me away from my date."

"Your attacks have been unsuccessful. The boy still lives."

"Clearly. In order to destroy Derek, I had to first separate him from his little circle of protection he surrounded himself with. Mission accomplished. Now that they are apart, divided, they should be much easier prey. The task will get done. Don't you worry."

"Oh, it isn't I who should be worried, it's you. I came to tell you that she is getting restless and dismayed at your lack of progress. She believes that you haven't been as committed to the cause as you should have been. As such, she has empowered me to take steps to . . . encourage you to pick up the pace."

That worried Angela. "What have you done?"

The senator took out a bracelet. Angela noticed it immediately. It was the one her mother possessed. "What have you done to her?"

"She is unharmed for now. She will be released the moment you are successful and not a minute before."

Angela was steamed. "How dare you threaten my family? If one hair on her head is out of place, so help me God, I will turn you into a snake. You must forget who exactly it is that you're dealing with. I am Angela Wright!"

The senator looked slightly unsettled. He quickly recovered. "Let's get one thing straight. Your threats don't scare me, witch. Powerful though you may be, I answer to an even higher being than you. If you want to see your mother alive and well, then I suggest you GET THE JOB DONE!"

The senator took some dust out of his pocket and tossed it up into the air. As it fell around him, he slowly began to disappear until he was gone. The senator had just upped the stakes. With her mother's life in danger in addition to her own, the situation had just gotten a lot direr. She had to shift her timetable forward. On that thought, she went back into the restaurant to enjoy the rest of her date.

***

This Move-In Day was much more low-key than the first one. Students were simply returning from their winter break for the spring semester. There was no congestion. No furniture being shuffled into the dorms. It certainly wasn't nearly as hot. It was actually quite nippy, which was to be expected at the beginning of February. Derek was just happy to have the campus bustling again. He looked forward to catching up with his friends and find out what they were up to over the break. After the winter session he had, he needed something to pick him up. He went down the hall to Turquoise's room. He knocked on the door. There was no answer. He knocked again and waited. Again, there was no answer.

"Turk, you in there? It's Derek." There was no response. *She must not be in yet.* He turned to leave, but heard a voice from behind him.

"Derek, was you looking for me?" said Turquoise, walking down the hallway to her room.

Derek turned to face her. She looked a little different from the last time he saw her. She had let her hair grow down to her shoulders, added light brown highlights, and had on a pair of stylish purple glasses.

"I was just coming to check on you. To see how your break went and everything," he said.

She closed the remaining distance between them. "It was great. You?"

"It was . . . interesting, certainly eventful," he replied.

"Wasn't you here for winter session?" she asked as she opened her door. They both walked in.

"Yup."

"Then how interesting could taking classes with nobody on campus be?"

Derek grew a wry smile. "You have no idea." He quickly dropped the smile as he reran the events of the previous month in his head.

Turquoise saw this. "What's wrong?"

"Nothing. I like what you did with your hair."

Noticing this change of the subject for what it was, she decided to go with it. "Thanks. I wanted to do something different. New look for a new semester."

"You didn't wear glasses last semester. Where they come from?"

"I wore contacts. Got these glasses for Christmas."

"Oh. They look nice."

Turquoise said, "Thanks. So what classes you taking this semester? You declare a major yet?"

"Let's see. I'm takin' Psyc 100; Leadership; Urban Communities; Crowds, Cults, and Revolutions; and Earth Science."

"What professor you got for psych?"

"Brown."

"Okay, good. I heard he a great teacher. As long as you ain't have Gozi. I heard that she a bitch," said Turquoise. "Do you at least have any idea yet about your major? Have you ruled out anything? Looking at anything?"

"I think that I want something to do with people. I'm a people person. So no business administration or engineering or nothing like that. I'ma schedule a appointment with my guidance counselor next month to go over things. Hopefully, I'll have a better idea by then," Derek responded.

"That's good. Well, I gotta go meet somebody." They both left her room. "Talk to you later."

***

"I don't want to hear it, Devon!" said Kelsey as she walked out of the mall. Devon was trailing behind her.

"Hold on!" he yelled after her. She kept walking. "Would you just wait a minute!" She stopped.

"What?" she asked angrily. "What do you possibly have to say for yourself?"

"I don't know what I did to make you so mad."

Kelsey scoffed and asked, "Are you serious?"

"Dead serious."

"So you think what happened with that girl back there was okay?"

"Nothing happened. What are you talking about?"

"Oh, so you think that flirting with another girl is no big deal?"

"I wasn't flirting with her," he protested.

"So her complimenting you on how you look and you doing the same was what?"

"Nah, you got it all wrong. See, I was just being nice. She gave me a compliment and I returned it."

"It wasn't just that. She was all up on you, and I didn't exactly see you trying to push her away."

"Oh my god, that was nothing. Trust me."

"How can I trust you when you don't always tell the truth?"

"When have I ever lied to you?"

"When you blew me off to go hang out with your friends at a sports bar," she said. Devon got a sheepish look on his face. He was busted. "You told me you had to watch your sister. Ergo, you lied."

"How you find out about that?" he asked.

"That's not important. It's things like that that make it kind of hard to trust you in situations like this."

"I just went to go chill with my boys. We ain't hang out in a while, and that was one of the few days all of us was free. It wasn't that serious."

Kelsey countered, "Well, you obviously thought it was serious or else you wouldn't have lied."

Silence.

"I thought so." Frustrated with Devon, she started to walk away again.

"You drove us here. How am I going to get home?"

"Catch the bus," said Kelsey.

***

"Well, look who decided to call me."

"Yup. Got the itch to check in on my little brother. I feel like we haven't talked in god knows how long."

"That's 'cuz you didn't make it home for Thanksgiving. Or Christmas. Or New Year's—"

"Okay, okay. I get the point. I've been AWOL."

"And why is that?"

"I've just been so busy with school. I also got this good internship in this hospital, and that's been eating up my free time."

"At least you on your way. I feel like I'm still stuck trying to figure things out."

"Still haven't decided on a major yet?"

"Nope."

"Well, Derek, all I can say is keep trying different things. I'm sure something will grab you eventually."

"That's the best you got?"

"That's the best I got."

"I think you losing your touch, sis."

"Nah. I'm just getting old." They both laughed. "How are Mom and Dad doing?"

"You didn't call them?"

"No. I called you first."

"They fine. Nothing new to report. Mom complained about not seeing you in forever. Said she was going to sneak out to Cali and kidnap you to bring you home for the winter."

"That sounds about right."

"Why didn't you come home for at least a few weeks this winter, anyway? You can't say school because y'all was on break."

"Well, like I said, I had that internship. I also was enjoying the weather out here. I heard it was brutal over there."

"Yeah. It has been a pretty bad winter."

Naomi noticed a change in her brother's tone. He sounded unusually melancholy. "Derek, what's wrong? I know it ain't about the weather."

"It's nothing I can't handle."

"Derek, I know you. You don't sound like that unless something is really bothering you. Tell me. I moved away, not out of your life."

"It's about magic," he warned.

"I'm listening."

Derek sighed. "Okay. Last semester, I met these guys. They're warlocks. Remember when I told you about the tarot reading? Well, me and these guys formed a warlock's diamond as a precaution—"

"What's a warlock's diamond?"

"It's this blood ritual that binds us together for life. It makes us stronger."

"Okay. Go on."

"Anyway, we started getting attacked. First it was golems, then we got sucked into Zombie Virus U, then by a gryphon. After the gryphon thing, they blamed me for everything and now don't want anything to do with me. But there's still somebody after us, and I can't find out who without they help."

"Why would they blame you?"

"Well, the diamond ritual was my idea. What I didn't know at the time was that forming a diamond would make us magical targets. See, we now attract magical things to us. That could be an explanation of everything that happened to us. They said I was selfish and didn't care about what happened to they lives as long as it was for my own benefit. And I can't say they don't have a point."

"I see. Looks like you got yourself into some trouble. Gotta man up and fix it."

"Is that supposed to make me feel better?"

"Oddly, yes. You made a mess. You have it in you to clean it up. You can't do that moping around. Go talk to them. It might hurt your ego, but apologize. Go to each of them and iron things out. Your problem isn't magical, it's normal."

"But—"

"But nothing. Go get your friends back."

He sighed. "I'll try. Thanks, Naomi. I guess you ain't lost your touch, after all."

***

"Matt? What are you doing home?" Shawnette asked in surprise.

"Hi, Mom. I ran out of money and I needed to wash my clothes."

"I don't know why you didn't always wash your clothes here and save your money in the first place," said Shawnette.

"Because it don't cost that much to wash my clothes on campus. I would probably waste more money on gas going back and forth."

"If you say so. Can I ask you something?"

"Sure, Mom. What?"

"Now I don't want you to think I'm prying, but you might know about this. I saw Rhonda at the grocery store the other day. When I went to go say hi to her, she blew me off. What was worse is the look she gave me. Like she was almost afraid of me or something. You know anything about that?"

Matthias sighed. "Rhonda isn't talking to me anymore."

Shawnette furrowed her brow. "Why not?"

"Probably because she found out I was a warlock. She probably assumed it extended to my family too," said Matthias.

"Oh no. How did she find out? Did you finally tell her?"

"No, I didn't. It was Derek's fault. He teleported us into my room and Rhonda was there waiting for me, trying to surprise me for our anniversary."

Shawnette was confused. "Who's Derek?"

"Oh, Mom. There's so much about my life that has happened recently that you have no idea about. I don't even know how to tell you. Derek is this warlock I met at the beginning of the school year."

"And why did he teleport you into your room?"

"We just got done helping Omar and Tre—"

"And who's that?"

"Two other warlocks we met. Anyway, he teleported us in and she saw us. I tried to explain things to her, but she was pretty emotional and ran out. I've been trying to get in contact with her, but she won't answer the phone and she won't answer the door when I go to her dorm."

"And you blame Derek for driving her away from you."

"Well, yeah. Don't you? He outed me to my girlfriend," said Matthias.

"From what you told me, he's partially to blame, but you can't overlook the role you played in this."

Matthias asked, "How do you figure?"

"How long have you known Rhonda? A couple years, right?" Matthias nodded. "When you first started to get serious with her, what did I tell you? I said that you should tell her your secret, did I not?"

"Yeah, but Dad said I shouldn't and I agreed. There was no point in risking it if I didn't have to," Matthias said.

Shawnette said, "When were you going to wait 'til your wedding day? Were you ever going to tell her? If you had told her then, you could have controlled the conversation. By letting it linger, you allowed her to fall into the truth suddenly and unexpectedly. You lost control of the situation. You strung her along, and it blew up in your face. Derek may have lit the match, but you made the bomb, Matt."

"I really don't need a lecture right now, Mom."

"I really think you do. You can't put the all of the blame on your friend. The first thing you need to do is stop being mad at him and take some personal responsibility. Then you need to find Rhonda and talk to her before she does something we'll all regret later."

***

Omar groaned as he spied the line of people that filled the pathway leading up to Russell Dining Hall. He hadn't been to this dining hall yet, but he heard great things from people who had. Apparently, they had the best food on campus. Unfortunately, because of this reputation, it got pretty crowded, especially for dinner. Practice had run over, which was the reason why he was running late. On a normal day, he would have been at the dining hall by 5:30 p.m. Today, he didn't get there until slightly after six. He entered the line at the back. He peered over the line. At this rate, he wouldn't get into the building until 6:15 p.m. That meant that he probably wouldn't sit down to eat until sometime between 6:30 and 6:45 p.m., probably closer to the latter. He didn't like that because he sure was starving!

When he finally got his food, he searched for a seat. Every table and booth was taken! Just his luck. He was about to give up on finding a seat and go to one of the standing rest tables, when he heard somebody call his name. "Omar! Omar! Over here!" He whipped his head around trying to find the person calling him and soon saw who it was. His friend Nita was waving at him from a table. She was by herself and had a seat open across from her. He was saved!

"Hi, Omar," said Nita.

"What's going on? I'm so glad you found me. I ain't have nowhere to sit!"

Nita laughed. "I know. It is pretty crowded. But I didn't want you to keep looking for a seat. You looked like a lost puppy."

"I did not! Girl, stop lying!"

"What? You did!" she said. They both laughed. "So what are you doing down here? Aren't you normally up on Liberty?"

"Yeah, but I just decided to try out Russell for dinner. I heard so much about it I just had to see for myself," Omar said.

"How do you like it? Does it live up to your expectations?"

"I like it. The food is pretty good—for a dining hall at least. It's a little too overcrowded for my taste though."

"Yeah, you came right smack dab in the middle of rush hour."

"I know. I was going to be here earlier, but practice ran longer than normal. I guess coach decided to do some extra drills since we on a bit of a losing streak," said Omar.

As she took a bite of what little was left of her food, Nita asked, "How's your classes going so far this semester?"

Omar said, "Well, since classes just started not too long ago, they going good so far. Don't anticipate that staying that way for too much longer. I just know those papers and tests are coming."

"I heard that."

Omar's cell phone, which he had placed on the table, rang. He looked down at it. It was Derek. He rolled his eyes and ignored the call. "Aren't you going to get that?" Nita asked.

"Nah," said Omar. He pushed the Ignore button. "It ain't nobody important."

***

Derek had taken his sister's words to heart. After some soul-searching, he realized that the accusations levied against him were true. He had acted rashly on multiple occasions, and it had not only cost him but the others as well. His decisions would affect them for the rest of their lives, and for that, he was sorry. Once he got past that stage, however, he resolved to do something about it. Despite everything, he knew that what he said during the argument was correct. Their lives were currently under attack from someone who was very powerful and very secretive. They had to find out who it was, and the answer to the questions lay with the divination ritual. He just knew it. He didn't know what he was going to do when he found out who it was, but it was at least a start. First things first, though. He had to cast the spell, and to do that, he was going to need his diamond.

He decided to talk to Tre'Vell first since he was the one who levied the initial misgivings. That wasn't easy, seeing as Tre'Vell was seemingly avoiding him. He had sent him texts, with no answer. Going to his apartment was useless because he didn't have a key to his building. And after what happened with Matthias's girlfriend, Derek dared not teleport in unexpectedly again. No, he had to confront him at a place and time where he knew Tre'Vell would have to be. Derek decided to go down to the studio on a day when he knew Tre'Vell would be there.

When he walked into the lobby of the theater, he hurriedly went over to the receptionist. "Can you call Tre? I need to talk to him," he asked.

The receptionist said, "I'm sorry. He just left not too long ago. Said he had to leave early for something. You can leave a message with me if you want, and I'll try my best to get it to him when he's back in."

Derek said, "Yeah. Can you just tell him that I'm trying to get in contact with him? My name's Derek."

She wrote herself a note and promised to get it to Tre'Vell. Derek turned around to walk out, but saw a girl walking across the lobby. He thought she looked familiar before remembering where he had seen her before.

"Excuse me!" he said to her, getting her attention. He walked over to her. "Ain't you friends with Tre? Tre Hinton?"

"Well, I would say I'm more than his friend, but yeah, I know him," she said.

"I think I remember you from when he brought you to the club a few weeks ago. I'm Derek."

"Oh yes! I remember now too. My name's Ricquel. What can I do for you, Derek?"

"Is it safe to say you stay in pretty close contact with Tre?" he asked. She nodded. "Well, I was wondering if you could get him to meet up with me or call me. I think he been ducking me."

"I don't think I can do that."

"I'm sure he'll listen to you," said Derek.

"Let me rephrase that. I won't do that."

"Why not?"

"Because I'm not going to try to make him change his mind on a decision he made. I trust his judgment. And based on what he told me about you, I think he made a pretty good one. He clearly doesn't want to associate with you anymore. I would leave it at that. Now if you'll excuse me, Derek, I got somewhere to be," Ricquel said.

She pushed her way past Derek. As she did so, she bumped into him. Derek momentarily looked down at his chest as he steadied himself. When he did, he couldn't shake the feeling that something was off. His shirt was a little wrinkled, but nothing too egregious. He spotted a small rip in his jeans that wasn't there when he put them on.

Maybe that's it, he thought to himself as the white diamonds in his amulet sparkled in the light. Derek squinted his eyes. Why did that seem odd to him? Wait! Wasn't Ricquel supposed to be a witch?

***

Tre'Vell glanced down at his watch as he walked into his apartment building. Good, he was a little early. When he left work, he was afraid that he would be late meeting up with Deandre. He had lost track of time working with Ricquel. He had to admit, it was really easy to do that when he was with her. Tre wasn't a sappy dude by any stretch of the imagination, but he was at the point where he was thinking about her when they weren't together, counting down the minutes to when they would be. He had never felt this way about anybody before. It surprised him how quickly his feelings for Ricquel progressed and how strong they became. Due to his upbringing, Tre'Vell was normally a very guarded fellow, slow to warm to somebody. But she just had an effect on him, and it hit him hard. He couldn't explain it, but whatever it was, he liked it. It was different.

As he approached Deandre's room, Tre'Vell heard Deandre's voice through the door. He seemed to be shouting something unintelligible.

Tre'Vell also heard some type of banging sound. Tre'Vell knocked on the door.

"Deandre? What's goin' on in there?" The sounds stopped, and Deandre opened the door.

"You early. You never early. As a matter of fact, you late most of the time," Deandre said, letting his friend in.

"What was that noise I heard?"

"I was practicing my step."

"What step you talkin' about?"

"I'm pledging," revealed Deandre.

"A fraternity? Which one?"

"Alpha Xi Omicron. It's a new one on campus."

Tre'Vell shook his head. "So you pledgin' a frat. Wow."

"You sound so surprised."

"I just didn't take you for bein' the frat type."

"You should pledge with me," said Deandre.

"Nope. You couldn't pay me to join a fraternity. That's all you," said Tre'Vell.

"You going to at least come to my probate, right?"

"I'll think about it while we on our way." They left the apartment.

***

"Lamar, I need help."

"What's up?"

"Is there any other way of tracing the magic of that game?"

"Nah. Not that I know of."

"Then is there at least another way of strengthening the spell?"

"The only way I know of is with another witch or warlock. Why?"

"'Cuz it don't look like I'm going to get that help."

"What about your boys in the diamond?"

"They ain't fuckin' with me right now. I been trying to call them, text them, but they ain't answering. I went down to Tre's work, but he left before I got there. I went to Omar's ball game and got front-row seats in the student section, but he ain't even look my way. Tried to get his attention, but he ignored me."

"Man, that's just cold. Maybe you should ask your dad if he knows something."

"It's only so much I can ask without him getting suspicious about why I'm asking. That's an option, but I was hoping it could be a last resort."

"Well, you might be down to that because I don't got nothing else for you."

Derek sighed and rubbed the bridge of his nose. "I need my diamond," he muttered.

"Well, maybe you can start with just one of us and go from there," said a voice behind him. Derek turned around and saw Matthias standing there.

"Lamar, let me hit you up later." Derek hung up the phone. "Matt. What you doin' here?"

"Taking advice."

"I gotta admit, you the last one I expected to be talking to me after what I did, exposing you to your girl and all."

"Yeah. Well, a very wise person gave me a different perspective on the situation," Matthias said.

Derek said, "I really am sorry. This is all my fault."

"I thought so too. But what happened with Rhonda is also partially my fault. I never told her about magic even though I had ample opportunities in the past. If I had told her, she wouldn't have gotten caught off guard like that."

"So that means I'm off the hook?" Derek asked optimistically.

Matthias chuckled. "Hardly. All it means is that you aren't the only one to blame. So what does this spell take to cast?"

"I have everything. It don't take much. I just need you to say the incantation with me to give it a little more juice. Hopefully, it'll work with the both of us saying the chant. Lock my door."

Matthias locked the door. While he was doing that, Derek went over to his closet and pulled out the chest that held his grimoire and mystical contraband. He pulled out the parchment that held the divination spell and the supplies necessary to cast it. He placed the candle, divining tube, and small plastic bag filled with the blue powder on the desk. "Dim the lights while I set this up, please," he said. Matthias did as he was asked while Derek placed the candle in the divining tube and filled the tray above it with a layer of the blue powder. He then fetched the game CD from the drawer and placed it on the tray.

Matthias asked, "You know how to do this, right?" Derek nodded and lit the candle. Once the white smoke began to rise from the tube, Derek told Matthias to hold out his hands and dumped some of the blue powder into them. He then recited the activation spell. "Divinio revelus por bach lau vivi ati." It briefly glowed. He told Matthias to blow the powder into the air above the divination tube where the smoke was swirling, which he did. "Now, say this incantation with me," said Derek. Together, they chanted "Pictura imaginus liken harpe matvu imunde."

"Now what?" asked Matthias.

"An image should appear in the smoke. When I tried this before, the picture was being blocked by something," answered Derek.

Soon, an image began to materialize in the smoke. "I see something," said Matthias as he squinted into the mist, trying to discern who the rapidly clearing image was. The person in the cloud appeared to be a woman, a young woman. Her skin was a smooth shade of brown, and she had braids flowing down her back. "Why does she look familiar?" Matthias asked, racking his brain for the answer.

"This don't make any sense," said Derek.

"What doesn't? Do you know her?" asked Matthias.

"Yeah. And you do too. That's Tre's girl, Ricquel. We met her at the club, remember?"

"Oh yeah! The witch."

"About that. I just ran into her the other day. My amulet was white when I was talking to her," Derek said.

"But your amulet detects witches," said Matthias.

Derek said, "Exactly. Which means she ain't no witch."

"But she told Tre she was a witch. Why would she lie to him?"

"You're really asking me why a woman that trapped us in a game with man-eating zombies where we nearly died would lie?" Derek asked incredulously.

"Good point. But how could she put the curse on the game if she isn't a witch?" Matthias wondered.

"I don't know. Maybe it wasn't a curse, but something else."

"Like what?"

"Hell if I know. But I do know that she got a lot of explaining to do."

Chapter 16

Reconnection

Valerie approached the top of the steps in a red sequined dress that hugged her every curve. To combat the cold, she put on a white faux fur coat. She topped the ensemble off with a pair of red high heels and a glittering diamond necklace. Stephen said that he would be taking her out for Valentine's Day. She had tried to pry their destination from him, but he was tight-lipped. She didn't really expect much else. If there was one thing Stephen James was good at, it was keeping secrets. Being what he was, she understood why that was the case. It definitely caused friction between them when they first started dating, though. Eventually, especially when he revealed his magical secret to her, they made some compromises. Stephen kept her in the loop about everything nonmagical, and Valerie trusted him to tell her about magical issues on a need-to-know basis. That understanding had allowed their marriage to flourish for over twenty years.

As Valerie descended the stairs, roses began to materialize along her path. The moment she hit the bottom of the steps, the lights dimmed; and the candles, which were placed all along the downstairs floor, magically began to light. Stephen, appearing in a white tuxedo, emerged from the living room.

"Stephen, what is this?" Valerie asked in amazement.

"Your Valentine's gift," he answered. He held out his hand for her to take and she did.

He led her through the house and out to the backyard. In the backyard was a brick path that led to a small gazebo that protected a dining table. This surprised Valerie because neither the path nor the gazebo, which twinkled against the night sky, were normally there.

"Isn't it a little cold to be eating outside?" she asked.

"Just trust me, Val," said Stephen. When they entered the gazebo, Valerie noticed a spike in the temperature within the gazebo. It was as if there was an invisible barrier keeping the cold out and a comfortable warmth in.

"I thought we were going out for Valentine's Day?" she asked.

"We are out. Out in the backyard," Stephen responded cheekily.

"Cute." Stephen pulled out her seat, and Valerie sat down at the table. Once he sat down, she asked, "How did you pull all this off?"

"Magic," he said simply.

Valerie laughed. "I do believe that is an improper use of your magic," she protested halfheartedly.

"If I can't use it to show my beautiful wife a good time on the day of love, what can I use it for?" he countered. "I'll be fine for the night." He snapped his fingers, and their food appeared on the table in a swirl of white lights.

Valerie surveyed the food. There were stuffed shells, shrimp scampi, mixed vegetables, chocolate-covered strawberries, and a bottle of champagne. "Oooh. This looks delicious. You've really outdone yourself."

Stephen popped the bottle of champagne and filled their glasses. "I can never outdo myself when it comes to you, babe. You deserve this and so much more."

"What made you come up with this idea?"

"Well, it's our first V-Day where the kids are both out of the house in years, and I wanted to celebrate that freedom."

"What do you think they're doing right now? Do you think they have any plans?"

"I don't know. They aren't having a better time than us though."

She raised her glass and said, "With all this effort, you might just get lucky tonight, kind sir."

Stephen said, "I'll certainly toast to that."

***

"Do you really think this will work?" Derek asked as Matthias unfurled the map of the city onto the table beside his grimoire tablet.

"It should. It's a simple locator charm. My dad's cast it to find me before when I got lost. All you have to do is cover the map in something. That's what I got the pepper for. Then you have to have an image of who you want to find in your mind when you say the spell. The location of the person you're trying to find will clear on the map," Matthias explained.

Derek poured the pepper on the map to the point where it was completely covered. "Now get an image of Ricquel in your mind. Make it clear. The clearer it is, the more specific the spell is. We'll both cast it to make it stronger," said Matthias. Derek closed his eyes and thought about Ricquel, recalling the way she looked during their last encounter. "You got a good image?" asked Matthias. Derek nodded. "Okay. Now for the spell."

They chanted, "Brevus matus buscar itve." Soon, the pepper began to migrate away from a singular spot on the map.

Derek peered at the location. Matthias said, "The 500 block of Madison Street. Isn't there a supermarket there?"

Derek said, "Yeah. I think it's a Super G. It's close enough for me to make the trip by 'porting." He held out his hand for Matthias to take.

"You want to go right now?"

"Yeah. If we drive, she could leave before we get there. This way is a lot faster."

"What'll we do when we find her?"

"We'll ask her what's up. If she the one that sent us the game."

"And what if she doesn't want to answer. Or how do we know if she does answer if it'll be the truth?"

"Well then, I'll use my telepathy to read her mind," Derek said.

"Sounds kind of sketchy to me," said Matthias, doubtful.

"You got a better plan?"

"Unfortunately, no," said Matthias. Derek held out his hand again. Matthias took it and said, "Do me a favor and at least make sure you teleport us into a vacant area."

"Will do." Derek teleported them out.

***

Pretzels. Pretzels. Where were the pretzels? Ricquel knew they sold them because she remembered buying some a few months ago. But they weren't in the aisle with the rest of the snacks. Maybe they discontinued them? But why would they stop selling pretzels? It was a common snack, like chips or cookies. She went up and down the aisle again, carefully perusing the shelves to double-check. She didn't see any.

Ricquel began to leave the aisle to go check another one when she heard somebody call her name. Oh great! It was two of Tre'Vell's warlock buddies. What were they doing here? And how did they even find her? She contemplated ignoring them, but thought better of it, lest she raise suspicion.

"Derek. So nice to see you again," she said sarcastically.

"We on to you!" he said.

"On to what?" she asked innocently.

"Don't play dumb with me. I ain't in the mood!" said Derek.

"Let me handle this," Matthias said to Derek. "What Derek is saying is that he doesn't believe that you have been truthful about your status as a witch," he said to Ricquel.

"Are you accusing me of lying about being a witch?"

"Damn right," said Derek.

"And how would you know if I'm a witch or not? Like I told Tre, I'm a witch. That's how I found him in the first place. I have the power to detect mystical beings and objects," Ricquel said.

"You lying. Know how I know? Because the diamonds on my cross was white around you."

"So."

"So my cross is an amulet that detects witches and warlocks. The diamonds turn black around them. Meaning that you ain't no witch!" Derek accused.

Ricquel was busted! If they ever found out what she truly was, her cover would be completely blown! "You ever think maybe your amulet is broken, genius?"

"I can assure you it ain't broke!"

"Whatever. It's not my problem," she said and made a turn to leave.

Matthias said, "Wait! There's something else. We recently got cursed into a video game. We cast a divination spell on the game, and it told us you cast the spell. Now why would that be the case?"

Ricquel laughed. "So let me get this straight. First, you call me a liar and accuse me of not being a witch. Then you turn around and accuse me of casting a curse that drew you into a game? You realize that don't make sense, right?"

"I noticed you ain't answer the question," Derek grounded out.

"That's because . . .," Ricquel started before she paused. What was that? She hadn't felt it before and could barely feel it now, but something was definitely there, niggling at the back of her consciousness. Someone was snooping around in her head! She threw up a mental block, putting a wall between the invader and the rest of her thoughts. She saw Derek get a concerned look on his face and look at Matthias. She smirked.

"Like I was saying, that's because the question is ridiculous, and I won't dignify it with an answer. Now if there isn't any other outlandish accusations you want to levy my way, I have to go. You've wasted enough of my time already!" Ricquel quickly walked off.

She had no idea why the spell had led them to her. It was Angela that cast the curse, after all. In any case, they were getting dangerously close to finding them out. The good thing was that she had done her job and broke up the diamond although it appeared that Derek and Matthias had reconciled. She would have to keep her distance from them from now on, Tre'Vell included.

Once she was gone, Matthias turned to Derek. "What happened?"

"I don't know. It's like she blocked me somehow."

"What did you get before she blocked you?"

"Not much. I couldn't see anything about the game, but she's definitely lying about being a witch," Derek said.

Matthias asked, "Well, what is she then?"

"Do you know what a chimera is?"

***

Why did he take this class? He didn't need it for his major; it fulfilled a breadth requirement. When he saw History of Rock as a class offering, Tre'Vell jumped at what he saw as an easy A. Little did he know that his first paper was going to be a seven- to eight-page examination on the career of Chuck Berry. Tre'Vell admired Chuck Berry and his role in creating rock 'n' roll, but he was currently sitting in the library struggling to flesh out the paper that was due the next day.

He had two more pages to write and was out of ideas. The sad thing was that this was only the first paper. The syllabus that was handed out at the beginning of the semester showed that there were five more papers that he would have to write in addition to three tests. He thought about just dropping the class, but it was too late to get into another class that wasn't just as taxing. Besides, he liked the subject matter.

Tre. Tre. Can you hear me?

Derek, stay out my head.

I need to talk to you.

I don't got nothin' to say to you.

Where you at right now?

Not that it's your business, but at the library tryin' to get this paper done.

The paper can wait. Is Ricquel around?

What? Nah, I ain't even seen her in a couple days.

That's a good thing. Trust me.

What you talkin' about now?

Look, dawg, she ain't who she say she is. She trouble.

And how would you know?

I asked her. She ain't a witch. She a chimera.

And she just told you this 'cuz you asked her?

Well nah. I used my telepathy to read her mind. You need to stay away from her from now on.

Why? 'Cuz you say so?

No. Me and Matt looked up what a chimera is in his grimoire. She a seductress. She probably been using her powers to seduce you this whole time. When me and Matt cast the divination spell, it led us straight to her.

I don't believe you.

Don't you get it? She the one who been behind everything this whole time.

That don't make no sense. I ain't even meet Ri until after we did the ritual.

It makes perfect sense. She tried to kill us, but her golems and game curse failed so she decided to take matters in her own hands. She probably been seducing you into liking her and not trusting us. Why? I don't know, but I can only guess it's to break us up, making it easier to pick us off one by one. We need to come together and come up with a plan.

You know how paranoid you sound right now? Ri ain't been seducin'
nobody. She cool peoples. I mean, she been helpin' me with my music and
everythin'. Get the fuck out of here with that shit.

Look. Whatever problems you got with me, we can hash it out later.
This is about more than just you and me. This is about Omar and Matt
too. Ricquel is out to get us, whether you want to believe it or not, and we
will find a way to stop her. We would like you to help us since it affects you
too, but it ain't necessary. I tell you one thing, though. You better not tell
her we coming and you better not get in our way.

What's that supposed to be? Some kind of weak-ass threat?

Take it for whatever you need to. All I'm telling you is to either help us
or stay out the way.

***

Omar walked down the street on the blustery, cold evening. He had
missed the shuttle, and since it was the weekend, that would be the last
shuttle for the night. This had forced him to walk the distance to his
friend's off-campus apartment. He didn't feel great about walking by
himself at night, especially the semilong distance it was from his dorm
to his friend's place. He was having a get-together, though, and he didn't
want to miss it. Hopefully, he could get somebody to drop him off, and
he wouldn't have to make the trip back late at night.

He passed by a few convenience stores, pawnshops, and liquor stores
along the way. The street was practically devoid of life, which struck
Omar as odd. It was night, but it wasn't too late yet. There should have
been at least some people out and about. He literally hadn't encountered
a single person on his trek. He glanced behind him and noticed a police
car creeping down the street behind him. He didn't think much of it,
but when he took a peek behind him a few moments later, the car was
still there. Omar thought that was strange. The cop should have passed
him by now or turned off onto another street. That was, unless it was
following him. Omar picked up his pace. The squad car pulled up
behind him and rolled down its window.

"You there!" said the cop sitting in the passenger seat.

"Can I help you, Officer?" Omar asked.

"Yeah. We'd like to talk to you," he said. Both of the cops parked
the car and got out of the vehicle.

Omar's instincts were on high alert. Something about this didn't feel right. Omar already was uneasy around cops. Ever since his older brother was arrested and forcefully taken from their home when Omar was a kid, he harbored a grudge against them. Omar thought about taking off, but that would only make them think he was doing something wrong, which he wasn't. He decided to play it cool for now.

"About?"

"We got a call about a guy matching your description robbing a store a few blocks from here," one of the cops said.

"And what description was that?"

"Young black male, about six feet tall with dreadlocks and a blue jacket." Omar had to seriously refrain from rolling his eyes at the description given. That could be anybody. "Where were you just coming from?"

"My dorm," Omar answered.

"So you're a student?"

"Yeah."

"And where were you heading to?"

"My friend's crib," answered Omar. "Not that it's any of your business," he mumbled under his breath.

The cops gave each other a look. "We're going to need you to get up against the wall."

"What for? Am I under arrest?"

"Are you giving us lip, boy? Just do what we tell you and get against the wall!"

"Man, I don't got to do nothing!" he said, but the cops shoved him against the wall.

"What you doing? You can't do this!" Omar yelled as the cops began frisking him.

"Quiet, punk!" As the cops continued to frisk him, Omar thought that he was just glad his mother wasn't here to see this because this was embarrassing. "He don't got anything on him," he heard one of them say behind him. "Where'd you hide the stuff you stole?"

"I didn't steal nothing!" Omar protested.

"Liar! I can't stand you niggers. You're a fucking menace to society! You're under arrest for suspicion of a robbery."

Omar couldn't believe what was happening! The cops read him his Miranda rights as they roughly put the handcuffs on him. Once they were on, Omar expected them to lead him to their car and put him in. Instead, one of the cops shoved him to the ground. He didn't even have time to process what had happened before the cops started kicking him. He kicked his legs out and tripped the cops, knocking them to the ground. While they were down, he used the wall to struggle to his feet. He used his power to burn off the chain that held the pair of handcuffs together, freeing his arms. He then took off running.

He heard gunshots being fired behind him. As bullets ricocheted around him, he felt a sharp pain in his shoulder. "Ahhh!" he screamed as he clutched it. He had been hit! He scampered around a corner and quickly took refuge beside a set of steps, hoping the cops wouldn't notice him and run right past him. To his lasting relief, they did. Once they were out of sight, Omar tried to relax, which wasn't easy with his shoulder in the condition it was in.

What the hell was that about? The cops just went h-a-m on him! That's why Omar didn't like cops! They were racist as fuck! Deep down, he thought a lot of them felt that way about young black men, and given the chance, many of them probably wished they could put a bullet in brothers just like him. But he was just walking, minding his own business! Now, he was a fugitive of the law! The good thing was that they didn't have a name or a photograph. They didn't really have anything except a description, and that wasn't very specific. As he started to lose feeling in his arm, his thoughts snapped back to his physical condition. He might bleed out if he didn't get his arm taken care of, as it was bleeding profusely. He took off his jacket and shirt, exposing his unnaturally warm body to the frigid night air. The bullet was still lodged in his shoulder, so he couldn't put much pressure on it to stop the bleeding. He wrapped his shirt around it as tight as he could to at least stem the tide of blood escaping from it. What now? He could only think of one person to call for help.

***

"What are we doing here?" Matthias asked over the loud music.

"I told you. It's my friend's birthday, and I thought we should come," said Derek in response.

"Okay, I get why you're here, but why am I? I don't know this person."

"I didn't want to come by myself. Besides, I thought with what happened with Rhonda, this would be a good chance to get back out there."

"Me and Rhonda will be fine eventually. Once we just sit down and talk everything out, we'll be okay."

"It never hurts to have a backup plan."

"Shouldn't we be worrying about Ricquel? And I have a test on Monday. I need to be studying."

"Both Ricquel and your damn test can wait for a night." They both made their way through the throngs of people in an attempt to find Derek's friend. When they did, Matthias was surprised to see who it was.

"Oh my gosh! Derek, I'm glad you made it."

"Hi, Layshawn! Oh course I made it. I ain't seen you since graduation! How you been?"

"I been fine. Doing my college thing. How about you?" asked Layshawn.

"Struggling with school. But I'm surviving."

"I heard that. You still playing football?"

"You know it. I got to. I'm on scholarship. You know I been trying to find you in this crowd for a minute!"

"How long you been here?" Layshawn asked.

"About a half hour."

"Why didn't you just text me?"

"I lost your number."

"Oh well, that explains it." Layshawn looked at Matthias. "Who's your friend?"

"Oh yeah! Layshawn, this is Matt. Matt, Layshawn." They shook hands. Just then, a girl pushed her way through the crowd.

"Lay! It's some people fighting in your living room!" she said. Layshawn, Matthias, and Derek followed the girl to the living room. At the scene were about five guys fighting, throwing each other around the room.

"Ya'll need to get out of here with that mess! Y'all messing up my house! Stop!" she yelled. The boys continued to fight.

"Let's break this up. Come on," said Derek. He and Matthias went in to the scrum to try to separate the combatants.

"Ayo, man, get the fuck off me!" said one of the guys as Matthias tried to get him off another guy. He punched Matthias in the face, and Matthias fell back. Derek saw this and went over to protect Matthias. Soon, Matthias and Derek were fighting right alongside the other guys.

Soon, the cops came to the house. "We got a noise complaint for this house. We also were told there may be underage drinking taking place," the cops said. They saw the fight taking place in the living room and sprang into action. "Break it up! Break it up!"

After some time, they got the guys to calm down. "Listen! Party's over! I suggest everyone leaves before we start busting people for underage drinking," the cops said. That spurred all the partygoers into action. They got out of that house as quickly as humanly possible.

When the fighters went to leave, the cops said, "Not you guys. You guys come with us!" When they got outside, two of the cops took the five other guys to their car, and one of the cops took Derek and Matthias to his squad car.

"Wait here while we sort all this out," he said and migrated over to the other squad car.

"How did we end up here?" Matthias asked.

"We tried to be good Samaritans and it backfired," said Derek.

"See. I just wanted to study for my test, but no. You had to drag me down to a party for somebody that I don't even know. Now, we might be arrested for disorderly conduct or worse, assault."

Derek said, "Calm down. See over there? It looks like they letting us go." Over at the other car, the boys who were fighting were walking away, and the cop was heading back over to them. "So you letting us go?" asked Derek when the officer reached them.

"You're under arrest," he said and snapped a pair of handcuffs on both of them.

"Hold on! What's going on? You let them go!" said Matthias. "I hope they didn't tell you we started it. We were just trying to break it up."

"Quiet!" He shoved them into the back of the car and went back over to the other cops.

"I don't get it. Why did they get to just leave and we get arrested?" asked Matthias.

"Something's not right," Derek muttered.

"I'll say."

"No. I mean, I can't read their thoughts."

"I didn't know mortals could shield their thoughts," said a confused Matthias.

"In most cases, they can't."

"What does that mean? Do you think it's a blocking spell?"

"Either that or they ain't mortal. I don't know, but whichever it is, I don't like it. I'm getting us out of here!" Derek maneuvered himself so that his hands, which were still in the cuffs, were touching Matthias. He concentrated, attempting to teleport them out, but soon scrunched his face.

"What's wrong?"

"I can't teleport! Okay, now I reeeally don't like this," said Derek in alarm.

"It must be the handcuffs. They must be blocking your powers somehow," reasoned Matthias.

"How much do you want to bet this has something to do with Ricquel?" asked Derek.

"Probably. We need to find a way out of here. They're coming back over here. And if I'm not mistaken, they're reaching for their guns!" said Matthias.

"Shit! Think of something!" yelled Derek.

Matthias said, "I could zap them."

Derek said, "The car is made of metal. You'll probably zap us too! Ain't you supposed to know that, genius?"

"Well, I don't hear you coming up with anything!"

"We get out and make a run for it."

"In handcuffs? Yes, your plan's so much better than mine," said Matthias sarcastically.

"Just get out!" said Derek. Matthias opened the door, and they both awkwardly stumbled out of the car.

"Freeze!" said one of the cops. Derek and Matthias made a break for it. The cops started shooting at them. They ducked behind a car for protection from the oncoming bullets. The barrage of bullets pelted the car.

"This won't protect us for long! What now?"

"I need to get these cuffs off so I can teleport us out of here, but I'm sure the cop who cuffed us got the key. We need to get it. Now that we out the cop car, zap 'em just enough to knock them out."

Matthias nodded. He quickly arose from their hiding spot and let loose a stream of medium-voltage electricity. The cops were electrocuted and fell to the ground in a heap, unconscious. "Let's go!" The two of them ran over to the cops. Matthias searched the cop's pockets and belt for a key. "Aha! I think I found it," he said. They got up and went over to the car to separate from the unconscious cops. Matthias used the key to unlock Derek's handcuffs.

"Thank God!" Derek said. He then unlocked Matthias's cuffs. As soon as he did, Derek got a phone call. "It's Omar."

"Hello? . . . You're what? . . . You all right? . . . Where you now? . . . Okay. I'm on my way. Just hang in there." He hung up. "We need to get to Omar, quick."

Unbeknownst to them, the cops had regained consciousness while Derek was on the phone, and they were just about on their feet. Matthias noticed at the last minute that the cops were just about to fire on them. "Get us out of here, Derek!" Derek grabbed Matthias and teleported them out just as the cops unleashed a hail of bullets at them.

***

Tre'Vell looked up at the neon sign that towered above him that read "Robinson Records." He and Ricquel had finished work on about half of his album. He got a text from her to meet her at the small independent record label. Apparently, she used some of her connections to get him a meeting with the owners of the label. After he missed his chance at the lounge, he didn't think he'd get another one anytime soon. But somehow, Ricquel worked her magic and pulled through. He had never heard of the label, but that wasn't important. If he handled this meeting correctly, this could be his big break. He sent her a quick text message to let her know he had arrived, just as she asked.

He walked in but didn't see anybody at the receptionist's desk. When he walked over to it, he saw a small note. It was addressed to him and read, "Mr. Hinton, welcome to Ramos Records. Our receptionist has gone home for the night. Come up to the second floor and take the first door on your right. Ricquel has told us many good things about you, and we look forward to meeting with you to discuss your future."

Tre'Vell shrugged. He walked up the stairs and entered the room in question. He was confused. The room was unremarkable. There was a solitary wooden table and two chairs. Nothing else: No windows, no recording equipment, no other furnishings. Tre'Vell didn't know exactly what he was expecting, but he was sure it wasn't that. Another thing that surprised him was that there wasn't anybody in the room waiting for him. Perhaps they were preparing for his arrival and would be joining him shortly? Yeah, that had to be it. Tre'Vell sat down in one of the seats and waited for the label executives.

About ten minutes later, nobody had come. What was taking so long? He was just about on the verge of getting up and taking a look around the building to see if he could find anybody when about five police officers abruptly entered the room.

"What's goin' on?" he asked.

"We got a report of a break-in."

"A break-in? What are you talkin' about? I got a meeting here with the label execs."

"Nobody else is in the building."

"What? That can't be!" said Tre'Vell.

"Keep your hands where we can see them!" said one of the cops as they quickly drew their guns.

"Woah, woah, woah! Take it easy! There must be some kind of mistake," Tre'Vell said, his hands quickly moving in front of him in a reflexively defensive maneuver.

With Tre'Vell's sudden movement, the officers sprung into action and unleashed a torrent of bullets at a shocked Tre'Vell. "What the hell!" he yelled in surprise. He barely had enough time to react to the firing squad. As the bullets were hurtling toward him in the blink of an eye, he froze the scene just before they could find their mark. He tried—and failed—to take a calming breath as the ten bullets stopped mere inches from his body. Panicking, he ran out from behind the desk and past the officers, who were frozen in midshot.

When he left the room, a police officer emerged from the adjacent room simultaneously and pointed his gun at him. "He's over here!" the officer yelled. In a flash, Tre'Vell grabbed the officer's hands and struggled to avoid being shot as the gun fired off a few shots. Tre'Vell kicked the cop in the groin, causing him to fall to the ground and let go of the gun. He picked up the gun and gave the cop one last kick. Down the hall, another group of officers had appeared and opened fire. Tre'Vell ran toward the door that led to the stairs. He fired off a few shots behind him, never taking his eyes off the door. He ducked into the stairwell and narrowly avoided a few shots whizzing by over his head as he descended the stairs to the first floor.

Another cop was ascending the stairs from the ground level. "Oh great!" Tre'Vell froze him as the officer was raising his gun. Tre'Vell opened the door, and another cop was waiting for him on the other side. He pushed Tre'Vell back and punched him in the jaw. "Oof!" Tre'Vell staggered backward to the railing. The cop rushed him. After trading a few blows, the cop got the warlock to the ground. He pulled his gun and pointed it at Tre'Vell. Tre'Vell swung his leg out and tripped up the cop before he could pull the trigger. The cop fell, and Tre'Vell got to his feet. The officer staggered to his feet right in front of the stairs just as the other officer unfroze and started to climb the stairs toward them. Tre'Vell kicked him in the chest, sending him tumbling down the stairs and barreling into the other cop. Both of them crashed at the bottom of the stairwell in a heap.

Tre'Vell quickly exited the stairwell and practically ran toward the door. "Freeze!" yelled a cop that was standing near the wall. Without breaking his stride, Tre'Vell lifted his arm toward the cop and froze him. He walked out the door and up to the curb of the sidewalk. "Taxi! Taxi!" he yelled as he gestured for one of the oncoming taxi cabs to pull over for him. He just hoped that one of them would stop for him. He wasn't sure it would happen, him being a young black guy, looking like he did, and it being night. Luckily, one did pull over. He quickly got in.

"Where you headed, boss?" the driver asked.

"Take me to Word U. And step on it!" said Tre'Vell.

"You got it," said the driver.

As he pulled off, Tre'Vell whipped out his phone. "Where you at? . . . He all right? . . . Good. Y'all meet me at the library. I got to tell y'all about somethin'." Tre'Vell hung up the phone. He now had to admit that Derek may have been onto something with that whole Ricquel conspiracy theory thing.

***

Derek and Matthias teleported onto a deserted street to find Omar hunched against a wall tucked away in a corner. He looked terrible. They could see beads of sweat trickling down his face and bare chest despite the cold weather. A deep gash adorned his shoulder, where they assumed he had been shot. "You look terrible, dawg. What happened?" asked Derek.

"What do it look like happened? I been shot! Damn! Asking stupid questions!" said an irritable Omar.

"I meant, how it happen?"

"You ain't going to believe this," started Omar.

Derek and Matthias looked at each other. "After what we just went through, try us," said Matthias.

"I was walking to my friend's house when I got stopped by these cops," said Omar. At the mention of the word *cops*, Matthias and Derek stiffened, but Omar was in too much pain to notice. "They said I robbed a store. When I tried to tell them I didn't, they just went ham and started shooting! I busted it out of there and lost them, but obviously got hit."

"That sounds a lot like what just happened to us. We were at this party and got into it with these dudes. The cops came and shut down the party and arrested us. Then they opened fire on us. Had no choice but to use our powers to get away," said Matthias.

"Don't forget about them being able to block their thoughts and the magic handcuffs that prevented me from teleporting," added Derek.

"Look, this swapping stories is all well and good. But in case nobody noticed, I'VE BEEN SHOT! Can we deal with that right now? Is there any way we can heal it up? What about that healing charm?"

Matthias said, "That was designed to heal minor injuries. I don't know if a gunshot wound counts as minor."

"Well, it can't hurt to try," said Omar.

"I'm going to get us out of here. Should we go back to get your car?" he asked Matthias.

He thought about it before answering, "No. I'll go pick it up later. Just in case the cops are still in that area. It's parked in a safe area for now."

"Okay. I'll take Omar first, then come back to pick you up." Derek teleported out with Omar then reappeared shortly to retrieve Matthias. He teleported them into a room that looked quite familiar to Matthias.

"Are we in the library?"

"Yeah," said Derek as he walked over to where Omar was sitting. "Why?"

"Tre's going to meet up with us. Now the first thing we have to do is remove the bullet. Matt, go get some water while I think of a way to do it." Matt left the room and returned a short time later with a cup of water.

"Any ideas?" Matthias asked.

"Nope. We're just going to have to pull it out," said Derek.

"In that case, I'll do it myself," said Omar. His fingers hovered over the wound before he quickly plunged them into the flesh. "Ahhh!" he screamed in pain as he dug into his shoulder toward the location of the bullet. Blood oozed out as he pulled the bullet out. He tossed it on the table and took quite a few quick, deep breaths.

"All right, cast the charm," Derek ordered. Matthias did so and poured the water over Omar's shoulder. The bleeding slowly stopped, and the wound closed slightly, but not totally.

Matthias asked, "How does it feel?"

Omar rotated his shoulder and said, "It still hurts pretty bad. But it's definitely a lot better than it was. I'll live."

Just then, Tre'Vell burst into the room. "You will never guess what just happened!" He looked at Omar. "I thought Derek said you got shot?"

"Healing charm," Omar said simply.

Tre'Vell nodded in understanding. "I can't believe what I just went through!"

"Let me guess. Did it have something to do with cops?" Derek asked.

Tre'Vell looked surprised. "Yeah."

"And they just randomly opened fire on you?"

"Again, yeah. How you know?"

"Because the same thing just happened to Omar, and me and Matthias. Obviously, that can't be a coincidence."

"No, it can't. The question is, why would the cops try to kill us?" asked Matthias.

"I bet you this has something to do with Ricquel," said Derek.

"As much as it pains me to say this, you might be onto something," said Tre'Vell.

Omar asked, "Why do you say that?"

"Because Ri told me she got a meeting for me with these executives at this indie label to discuss my album, but when I got there, nobody was there. I texted her to let her know I got there, and the cops showed up not too long after."

"I'ma kill her!"

"We don't have proof. All we know is that she is a chimera and *might* have set Tre up. We need something a bit more concrete than suspicions," said Matthias.

"Like what?"

"We need answers. And I think . . . no, I *know* that she's got them. It's just a matter of getting them out of her."

"And how do you propose that we do that exactly? She can block my telepathy. And even if she couldn't, I'm sure she'll be ready for that now."

"I actually have an idea. But it's going to take Tre's help to pull off," said Matthias as he looked toward Tre'Vell.

Tre'Vell took a deep breath before saying, "Count me in."

***

Ricquel hesitantly entered through the doors of the building. She had to admit that she was both surprised and concerned when she got a call from Tre'Vell. She was surprised because she was sure that Angela was going to make her move when she told Ricquel to lure him to the music label building. She didn't know exactly what that move was, but by the way Angela made it sound, he wouldn't be around to call her. She was concerned because it was possible that if he indeed survived, he correctly sniffed out her involvement.

She started to ignore the call, but decided to answer to see what he wanted. She was relieved when he told her that he had a bunch of pictures that he was thinking of using for his album cover and wanted her to meet up with him to get her opinion of them. She was trying to keep her distance from him, but if he didn't suspect anything, then what could be the harm? If she declined, that in and of itself could raise suspicion, she reasoned.

Tre'Vell was standing in the hallway, waiting for her. "Hey, Ri. How you been?"

"Fine. Just been busy working on an assignment for work."

"What kind of assignment?" he asked, trying to sound curious.

"Oh, a long-term project. Very, very delicate."

"Yeah, I bet," he mumbled.

"Hmm?"

"Nothin'. I feel like I ain't seen you in forever."

"Well, like I said, I've been busy."

"Okay. Well, those pictures I was talkin' about is in here." They went into the room. On one of the tables was a portfolio filled with a few images.

"Let's take a look at these," she said. She flipped through a couple of the pictures. "What was that?"

"What was what?"

"That sound."

"What sound?"

"It was like a pop, or vacuum, or something. Didn't you hear it?"

Tre'Vell shook his head. "Nah, I ain't hear nothin'."

Ricquel shook her head and went back to examining the photos. "I think I like this one the best. Goes with the whole vibe of the album, you know what I mean?" She heard another sound. "Okay, I know I heard it that time," she said as she turned around.

When she turned around, she was immediately met by Matthias, blowing some type of powder into her face. "What? What is that?" she asked in surprise.

"Slumber dust," he said.

Ricquel began to sway on her feet. "I gotta . . .," she began as she stumbled toward the door. She didn't get a chance to finish as she slumped to the floor, knocked out cold.

***

When Ricquel began to awaken from her slumber, she was tied to a chair in the middle of a room. She didn't know where she was. The room was devoid of anything to clue her in either. There were no windows, nothing on the walls, and no furniture, save for the chair she was currently strapped to. She had no idea how long she had even been out for. How had she gotten herself in this predicament?

"She's waking up," said a voice behind her. Derek walked into her view from behind her.

"What are you up to, Derek? Why have you tied me up?"

"Ah, ah, ah. We'll be the ones asking the questions around here," he replied.

"We?" she asked. Omar, Matthias, and Tre'Vell soon came into view.

"Oh goody," she said as she rolled her eyes. "The Four Stooges."

"Sorry for the extreme measures, but this is the only way I could think of to get the answers from you that we're looking for," said Matthias.

"You'll get nothing from me," she said defiantly. "I've faced a lot worse things than you four. So do your worst."

"Did you have anything to do with those cops shooting at us?" Omar asked.

Ricquel opened her mouth to deny any involvement, but what came out was, "Yes." Her mouth was left agape in shock.

"Surprised? We cast a truth spell on you while you were asleep. Everytime we ask you a direct question, you'll be compelled to answer with the truth. No lies," said Matthias.

"Well, aren't you clever," said Ricquel.

"So I've been told. Now how were you involved with those shootings, exactly?"

"I lured Tre to the music studio. I didn't do anything to you three, though."

Derek stepped up and asked, "When I asked you before if you cast that curse on the game, you said no. Was that the truth?"

"It was. I didn't cast the curse."

"Then why did the divination spell lead us to you. Would you know why?"

"I don't know. Maybe the real person that cast the spell rigged it so it would give you my face instead of theirs. But I don't really know why."

It was Tre'Vell's turn. "We know you a chimera. I met you before Christmas. Have you been just seducin' me this whole time? Did you ever really like me?"

"No. It was all a ruse."

"Why?" asked Derek.

"I was given the task to split you guys up. To create a schism, making each of you more vulnerable and susceptible to attack. I saw my opening with Tre and took it."

"You bitch!" said Tre'Vell angrily. He made a move toward her, but Matthias held out a hand to stop him.

"You said 'given the task.' Who gave you the task?" he asked.

Ricquel tried her best to be evasive. "The same person that made the golems, that made the cursed game, that sent the gryphon, and was behind the police officer attack. At least, I suspect."

"Who was it? Give us a name."

Ricquel tried her hardest to resist the spell. "I can't. She said she'd kill me if I let you find out her identity."

"If you don't tell us, we'll kill you!" said Omar.

"Please!"

"One last time. Who sent you?" asked Matthias through squinted eyes.

Ricquel clenched her teeth in a desperate attempt to prevent herself from spilling the beans. The spell won the battle, and she eventually succumbed. "The mayor of Pottington, Angela Wright!"

Derek prepared to ask a follow-up question when all of a sudden, Ricquel spontaneously combusted. The fire seemed to erupt from inside her very being, engulfing her whole body. Her bloodcurdling screams filled the emptiness that surrounded them. The four warlocks watched in shocked terror as the woman in front of them was burned to a crisp by the flames, leaving only a charred, bloodied mess of a corpse in their wake.

A dumbfounded Derek looked at Omar. He threw up his hands. "Wasn't me," said Omar. Silence reigned as they each contemplated what just happened and the revelations that were revealed. Who would have guessed that the person after them would be the leader of the very city that they called home?

Chapter 17

Preparation

Angela could sense them coming. Even if her telepathy hadn't alerted her to their approaching presence, the ominous, dark aura that emanated forth from them threatened to swallow her whole. She could tell that this wouldn't be a pleasant experience. With them, however, it never was. She briefly thought about leaving, but thought better of it. They would track her down eventually. More importantly, she would track her down, and that would only create more problems for her. No, she would listen to what they had to say. She hoped listening was all she would be doing.

Without pleasantries, the two senators barged into her office. "Gentlemen! What an unpleasant and unwelcome surprise."

"You know you've really done it now, don't you?" one of them said.

"And what have I done exactly? Please enlighten me, Alex," Angela said. She was attempting to pull off a more confident vibe than she was feeling at the moment.

"Nothing. Exactly nothing. The deadline approaches, and the task has not been completed," said the John, other senator.

Angela was incredulous. "Nothing? Nothing? I have been up to my pointy hat in mystical activity, trying to find a way to do what was asked of me."

"Not what was asked, what was required. According to her, you have not done nearly enough!"

"Are you kidding? I have—"

"She knows what you have done. She has always known. The golems, the absorption spell, the gryphon, the chimera, and the obedience spell. All of those have failed. And failed miserably."

"I was close. I can tell I'm getting closer."

"Close isn't good enough. We thought that the prospect of saving your dear mother would be incentive enough, but clearly it is not. Maybe we need to up the ante . . ."

"Don't! I have a few more ideas and—"

"No. You've got one more chance, witch! One final attempt to kill Derek and his pals. Or . . ."

Suddenly, Angela's mind was bombarded with a psychic attack. The agonizing screams of her mother drowned out every other thought. It was overwhelming! She fell to the floor, sobbing. Images of her mother's mangled, nearly unrecognizable body soon joined the chorus of screams. It was just too much to bear!

"And once she is finished with her, you're next! We suggest you make this last attempt your best one, Angela. Quite literally, your very lives depend on it."

***

Omar pulled his headphones over his ears and let the music from his iPod pull him into the zone. Things had not gone well for the basketball team. They had suffered a rash of injuries to key players and therefore had not had the year that they were anticipating. They currently resided in last place in the conference standings. They had to win this game, on the road, against Castle College. If they lost this game, they would fail to qualify for the conference tournament, and any hope of earning their league's automatic bid to the postseason tournament would be extinguished.

Once the game started, Word U was put into an early hole. Castle College opened the game with fifteen consecutive points. The head coach called timeout. "Come on, guys, what's going on out there? We just lettin' these guys run up and down the floor! We already got three turnovers! Omar, what are you doing out there? You got two of them!"

Omar said, "I'm sorry, coach. I guess I got a lot on my mind right now."

The coach responded, "You got to leave that stuff behind and get your head in the game, son. All right, here's what we gonna do. Jackson, set the screen for Omar when you get the inbound from Peppers. Omar, roll to the basket for the easy lay-in. Let's go!"

The Wildcats went on a run of their own to cut the deficit to five. Then Castle College went on another run to push the lead back up to fifteen. The score was 30–15 with 10:00 left in the half. Omar missed a couple of wide-open shots during the run to contribute to the deficit growing. At 30–15, Omar was removed from the game.

"Coach, what's up? Why you pullin' me?" he asked, upset.

"Because you stink out there. You missin' wide-open layups, you're turning the ball over. We trailin' by fifteen, and we got to get back in this game and hopefully cut the deficit to single digits by halftime. We can't do that with the way you playing right now. Take a seat."

Omar angrily took a seat at the end of the bench. He couldn't believe that Coach Spinder pulled him from the game! Who was he kidding? Yes, he could. The truth was, coach was right. He was a big reason why they were losing the way that they were. He was missing shots that he could make in his sleep. The team was out of sync both offensively and defensively. As the point guard, that failure reflected on him. It was his job to be an extension of the coach on the floor and get his teammates in the best position to make plays, and he wasn't doing it. But he could still lead his team, even from the bench, by being a good and supportive teammate. If he was reduced to being a cheerleader for the time being, he would be the best cheerleader on the team. His team could use the encouragement. Their season was on the line, and they didn't want to go out by being blown off the court.

When halftime came, the Wildcats had successfully cut their deficit to eight. It was a tough situation to be in, especially on the road, but manageable. When they got back to the locker room, the coach pulled Omar aside.

"What's going on, Omar? Where's your head at? Because it definitely wasn't on that court out there!" he asked.

Omar said, "It's just some stuff going on in my life right now, coach."

"Is it anything you want to talk about?" Coach Spinder asked.

Omar shook his head and said, "Nah, not really. There's nothing you can do about it, and talking ain't going to do nothing."

The coach put a hand on Omar's shoulder. "Do I need to sit you for the rest of the game? Because the way that you playing just won't cut it, and our season's on the line."

Again, Omar shook his head. "Nah, I'll be good. Put me back in. I promise I won't let y'all down."

The coach nodded. "Good because we need you out there. We don't have a chance in hell of winning this game without you playing at your best, making plays."

Once the second half started, Omar played like a man possessed. He was flying around the court. His energy, particularly on the defensive end, was infectious, and the team fed off him. They rode the wave to a twelve-point run to kick off the half and take their first lead at 55–51. The run was capped off by a three-pointer by Omar, and when he hit the shot, the bench went wild. After Castle College called a timeout, momentum swung right back to their side. Over the next seven minutes, they outscored Word U 16–5. With 7:48 left in the game, Castle College led 67–60.

Not to be deterred, over the next five minutes, the Wildcats clawed their way back into the game. With 2:30 left, the score was tied 75–75. The teams traded baskets from there. With less than a minute left and the score tied 81–81, Omar thought he blocked a ball cleanly, but was called for the foul. It was his fourth of the game and meant that with one more, he would be ejected. Omar had to pull his shirt over his head in frustration at the call as the shooter sank both free throws to give Castle College the 83–81 edge.

Omar walked the ball up the court. After a couple of passes around the perimeter, one of the Word U players hit a clutch three-pointer. "That's what I'm talkin' about, Milton!" yelled Omar in celebration as the team went over to hug their teammate as Castle College called a timeout. With an 84–83 lead, the Wildcats were only fifteen seconds away from victory. On the inbounds, however, Word U lost sight of the opposing power forward. He received the inbounds pass and rolled right to the basket for an easy layup to put Castle College on top 85–84. Word U opted not to take a timeout and, instead, quickly tossed the ball inbounds in an attempt to catch their opponent napping. Omar got the ball and saw a clear lane to the basket. At the last minute, just as he was going up for the shot at the basket, a Castle College player slid in front of Omar, and both of them went to the ground. The ball went in the hoop, and the bench was ecstatic! Their elation quickly went away when they realized that the referee waved the shot off. Offensive foul! Not only did the basket not count, but Castle College also got two free throws at the other end.

The foul was Omar's fifth, so he was done for the night. "Are you fucking kidding me, ref? He slid right under me!" Omar yelled as he tried to plead his case to the referee, who was making his way to the scorer's table. "Man, this is some fucking bullshit!" he screamed. His teammates tried to calm him down, but Omar wasn't having it and continued to berate the referee. He eventually crossed the line. The referee blew the whistle.

"Technical foul, number 7. Abusive language."

Omar was beside himself. "Oh my god! Do you got it out for me?"

The coach quickly came over to lead Omar away. When he put his arm around Omar, he quickly retracted it. "Omar, you're burning up! You okay?" he asked in concern.

Omar had to get his temper in check. It was causing his powers to go a little haywire. "I'm fine, coach," he said as he quickly made his way to the bench.

With only seven seconds left in the game, with three free throws, and already up by one, Castle College had the opportunity to close out the game. The shooter hit the first shot to give them a two-point lead. Omar lowered his head. He just couldn't bear to watch their season come to an end! He sank the second free throw. This was it. If he hit the last free throw, the game was over! Just when he had given up hope, it came roaring back. He missed the last free throw! Word U grabbed the rebound and raced down the floor. With two seconds on the clock, Milton broke free for an open corner three-pointer to tie the game and send it to overtime! When Milton released the ball, Omar thought it looked good. The ball clanked off the rim and fell harmlessly to the floor as the buzzer sounded. Omar collapsed to the floor in anguish. The game, and their season, was over!

*****

Derek walked into Sharp Cutz and was surprised at how empty it was. Nobody else was in the barbershop except for Lamar and

Dominique. Dominique was getting a haircut from Lamar, but it looked like they had just gotten started.

"Do I want to know?" he asked.

Lamar shook his head. "Nope. You should have hit me up. I would have told you that nobody was going to be in the shop today. The only reason why I'm here is 'cuz Dom here said that he really needed a cut."

"Got a date. Gotta look sharp," said Dominique.

"I just figured I would be able to walk in and get a cut eventually. I wasn't in a hurry or nothing," said Derek. "You got time to cut me after Dom, or should I come back another time?"

Lamar looked at his watch and said, "I can squeeze you in."

Derek took a seat. "Actually, since we alone, this is the perfect time to get your opinion on something."

"Like what?"

"Remember that tarot reading you did for me?"

"Yeah."

"And remember that divination spell?"

"The one that didn't work? Sure do."

"Well, I got Matt to cast it with me and it worked!"

"So who did it lead you to? Anybody you know?"

"Yeah. It showed us this girl that Tre was talking to. But get this—she wasn't the one that put the spell on the game."

"Really? Then who was it?"

"She said it was Angela Wright."

"What?" Lamar asked in surprise. "The mayor, Angela Wright?" Derek nodded. "Are you sure she telling the truth?"

"Yeah. We cast a truth spell on her."

"Hmm. Why would the mayor cast a spell on a game to suck you into it?"

"We don't know. But there's more to the story. She also told us that the mayor is the one behind all the attacks. The golems, the game, the gryphon, the cops—"

"Cops?"

"Oh yeah. I forgot you don't know about that. Let's just say all four of us had experiences with trigger-happy cops last week."

"And how does the girl know about all of this?" Lamar asked.

Derek responded, "'Cuz she was sent by the mayor. See, she a chimera that the mayor sent to split the diamond up."

"Ah! A seductress. I see."

"What should we do? The mayor obviously is a really powerful witch if she could pull all this stuff off, and for whatever reason, she wants us dead."

"And she clearly has control of the police. You can't count on them to help."

Dominique scoffed. "When could we ever?"

"I'm pretty sure now that the tarot cards was trying to tell me that I die by her hand," said Derek. "I'm surprised we lasted this long."

"I say you fight back. Stop letting her have the chance to go after y'all and y'all go after her. Four warlocks against one witch. I would like those odds," said Dominique.

"Gee, why didn't I think of that? Let's just go after the mayor," Derek said sarcastically. He shook his head, mocking his friend's ridiculous idea.

"Dom might have a point, Derek. If she willing to go through everything you say she has to take you out, I think it's safe to say that she won't stop until y'all kicks rocks. I don't know how you guys can pull it off, but y'all might have to stop the mayor yourselves."

***

"You can't seriously be considering this," said Mariah as she trailed behind Angela.

"I'm dead serious, Mariah. I can assure you," said Angela.

"But why?"

Mariah stopped dead in her tracks as Angela came to an abrupt stop and swung around to face her. "I already told you. They have my mother. As far as I'm concerned, it's them or her. That's not such a difficult decision, don't you think?"

"But how far are you willing to take this? Making golems, casting curses on video games, sending gryphons are all well and good. But kidnapping an innocent girl who is not a part of this in the least? That's wrong, Angie," said Mariah.

"The timeline has been moved up! I've got one last chance! The indirect method up until now has failed. It's time I dealt with them personally, on my terms, and on my turf. Kidnapping Matt's girlfriend will lure them to me."

"And then what? It'll be four against one. To make matters worse, they're a diamond now. They've overcome everything you've thrown against them so far. What makes you think you will be able to stop them? What makes you think they won't kill you instead?" asked Mariah in concern.

Angela laughed. "Thanks for your concern. It's touching, really, but I think I'll be just fine. I am Angela Wright, mayor of Pottington and one of the most powerful beings on this planet. I am an Ultimate, a witch of the highest level. I'm sure I can handle four inexperienced teenaged warlocks."

"You know that if you kill them, people will come looking, and they'll eventually come to you. Do you really want innocent blood on your hands?" Angela sighed. "I can't let you do this!"

Angela grabbed Mariah's shoulders, desperately trying to make her understand her predicament. "Now is not the time to get soft on me, Mariah. What part of this don't you understand? It's either me and my mom, or them. Now I feel bad for them, I really do, but I have no other choice."

Mariah said, "Like you said before, you're an Ultimate witch. Why don't you just go rescue your mom yourself?"

Angela grumbled in frustration and began to walk away. Mariah began to follow. "She would be dead before I had the chance to get anywhere near her."

"I've never seen you get pushed around this much. Whoever this person is, she's yanking you around like a dog on a leash. Making you do things that go against your very nature. If she says jump, you're asking how high. How can one person make one of the most powerful witches on the planet cower in fear?" Mariah questioned.

Angela stared off into the distance. "A person who isn't a 'person' at all."

Mariah asked, "Then what is she?"

Angela paused before replying, "Evil incarnate."

The gravity of that statement hit Mariah before she said, "This is madness."

Angela sadly said, "I couldn't agree more."

***

Matthias had to admit, the airport was more congested than he anticipated. He and his father just got done getting through the security line. There was a person that had a bunch of large bottles of liquids in his carry-on bag, and that held up the long lines a bit. Now that they were past the checkpoint, they were slowly making their way to their departure gate. Matthias's phone started to ring. It was Derek.

"Hello?"

"We need to talk. You got a minute?"

Matthias glanced at his father. "No, not really."

"Why not?"

"I'm with my dad."

"Doing what?"

"We're at the airport."

"Airport? What you doing there?"

"I got a tournament in Florida."

"For tennis? In March? I didn't even know that you was off campus."

"What are you talking about? I told you I was going away last week."

"You did? Must have forgot."

"Obviously."

"Well, I need to talk to you. It's about our mayor situation."

Matthias lowered his voice to barely above a whisper. "I said I can't talk right now, especially about that. Why don't you call Omar or Tre?"

"I already did. But Omar told me to get your opinion, and Tre's still a little new to magic."

"Well, it's going to have to wait until I get back. I'm going to be back on Tuesday."

"Why do it sound like you whispering?"

"Because I don't want my dad to hear. I don't need him asking questions. Especially if I don't have the answers."

"All the more reason for us to come up with some as soon as possible. How about we just talk telepathically?"

"No. My dad might be able to sense that. Besides, I want to begin focusing on my tennis. Just be patient. Our problems will still be there when I get back. If anything funny happens, call me and I'll do the same. Got it?"

Derek relented. "Fine. Catch you when you get back." He hung up.

Matthias put his phone away. "Who was that?" Isaac asked as they got in line to board their flight.

"Oh, it was Derek," Matthias responded.

"What did he want?"

Matthias groped for a viable explanation. "Uh. Just school stuff."

"He called you on a Friday evening about school stuff?"

"Well, see, it's not really school stuff. More like, girl stuff, who is at school. Yeah! He likes this girl, but she's going out with one of his friends. But they're on the rocks, so he wanted to know if he should make his move now or not."

"Ah, to be single again. Glad I don't have to worry about that type of stuff anymore. Okay, put that stuff out you mind. From now on, I want your mind on tennis. There's no room for distractions."

"Yes, sir," said Matthias. They both handed the attendant their boarding passes and boarded the plane.

***

Derek kept glancing down at his notes as he prepared to finish the paper that he was writing. He had to write a paper examining Sigmund Freud's psychoanalytic theory for his psychology class. Derek thought that Freud was a flake, but he was an interesting flake. Freud had all sorts of beliefs and theories that didn't make sense when held up to modern knowledge, but Derek thought that his theory of the id, ego, and superego had some interesting applications. As a matter of fact, the entire class was something that he genuinely looked forward to attending every other day. It was one of the highlights of his week and by far the class that had stimulated his mind the most since he began the school year. Getting into people's minds and examining their thought processes came naturally to him. Maybe it was a byproduct of his telepathy?

As Derek was typing up his paper, he got a Skype call. He answered it, and the image of his father appeared on his laptop's screen. "Hi, Dad."

"Anybody in the room with you?"

"Nah. Bruce is at the dining hall. Why?"

"Good. Now what's this I hear about you and the mayor?" Stephen asked in an accusatory tone.

Derek sighed. "Lamar. What he tell you?"

"That she's been attacking you and you're thinking about confronting her yourself."

"Can't he keep anything to himself?" Derek wondered aloud.

"So it's true? Derek, what's been going on?"

"After the golem incident that I told you about last year, a couple more things happened to us."

"Like?"

Derek said, "We got sucked into and trapped in Zombie Virus U, attacked by a gryphon, shot at by cops, and seduced by a chimera that was pretending to be Tre's girlfriend."

"And how is all that connected to the mayor?"

"We cast a truth spell on the chimera, and she told us—right before she burst into flames."

"And you thought you would just, what, stop her yourself?"

"Well, we haven't gotten together and talked it through yet, but yeah, that's the general idea," answered Derek.

"Nope. I forbid it," said Stephen.

"Dad,"

"I'm serious, Derek. Y'all just chill. I'll deal with it."

"You and Mom are on vacation in Jamaica."

"We can come home."

"Don't. You and Mom been planning this vacation for months. I would hate for it to end early because of me."

"You think we'll be able to enjoy ourselves knowing what's going on back home? I need to be doing everything in my power to stop the witch that's trying to kill you."

"No offense, but that's not a whole lot of power right now," Derek countered.

"Careful, boy," warned Stephen.

"She a level 5 witch and you don't have your powers anymore, Dad. What can you realistically do?"

"I've lived my life. It's better for me to risk mine than for you to risk yours," his dad replied.

"When I left the house at the beginning of the school year, you gave me the grimoire because you said that you thought I was ready for the responsibility. That it was the beginning of the process of me becoming my own man. Well, this is just another step in that process. I have to begin taking care of things like this without you, especially since I'm the one with the powers now," said Derek.

"Like I said before, you might got the powers now, but not the experience to deal with something like this alone," said Stephen.

"I'm not alone. I got Omar, Matt, and Tre to back me up. We a diamond now, remember. You just gotta have faith that we have the power to get this done."

Stephen shook his head. "It'll take more than just power to deal with this. It'll take tact. You're talking about the mayor of Pottington. She a huge political figure with loads of clout and protection in addition to being an Ultimate."

"We'll figure it out, Dad, I promise," said Derek, trying to assure his dad. "You ain't raise no punk." Stephen had to smile a little at that.

Knock! Knock! Knock! "Somebody's at my door. Gotta go, Dad. Don't worry and enjoy your vacation." He exited out of the call and went over to open his door. Monica was standing on the other side. "Monica! Come in, come in."

She held her palm up. "No, I'm good. Thanks," she said, declining his invitation.

"Okay. So to what do I owe this pleasure?" he asked, leaning up against the door frame.

"I was just letting you know that you came in second place for our floor's Black History Month contest. Congratulations."

"Thanks. I thought y'all had already did the judging and I didn't place."

"No, we just did it today. You would have known that if you hadn't missed my floor meeting for March," she said disapprovingly.

"You had that already?"

"Yes. It was Friday evening. I made it then so nobody would have an excuse like they have a class or lab or something. So, what's your excuse? It had better not be one of those."

"No excuse. I just spaced. Got a lot on my plate lately. I'm sorry. I'll be sure to make it next time," Derek said.

"You better." She started to walk away. "Oh, and by the way, you might want to put on a shirt and some pants to answer the door next time."

Derek looked down at his body, which was devoid of any article of clothing, save for the blue pair of boxers he was wearing. "Why, when I know that you enjoy the view?"

Monica laughed as she continued to walk away.

***

An extremely small crowd began to gather in the gymnasium. Tre'Vell was among the small throng of people hustling into the gym in an attempt to get out of the cold temperatures outside. It was early March, but judging by the weather, you would have thought that it was mid-January. It had snowed half a foot a few days ago, and they were predicting another couple of inches in a few more days. When were warmer temperatures coming? This current weather pattern was just depressing.

Tre'Vell was surprised at the small turnout for the probate. True to his promise, he was there to support Deandre during the fledgling fraternity's step show. By the looks of things, he wasn't the only person doing that. It seemed that the only people that were there were friends of the pledges. It sure was sparse. It was also a little dark. Tre'Vell turned to one of the few people in the gym. "Couldn't they have at least turned on a few more of the lights?" he asked. The person just shrugged.

A man addressed the crowd. "How is everybody this evening?" He got a smattering of responses. "All, right, all right, all right. I know it's cold outside so let's get this thing started! We don't want to keep you guys too long. The men of Alpha Xi Omicron and the ladies of Rho Tau Nu would like to thank you in coming out and supporting our pledges. We have a great show planned for you. First up will be the pledges of Rho Tau Nu, and after them will be the pledges for Alpha Xi Omicron. Enjoy the show, everybody?"

The ladies ran out onto the floor in front of the small crowd and spent the next fifteen minutes clapping, stepping, singing, and dancing, drawing cheers from the crowd. When they were done, it was the guys' turn. Tre'Vell watched as Deandre led his fellow pledges out on the floor. Deandre got a call and response going with the members of the crowd before the pledges spent the remaining fifteen minutes stepping, dancing, shouting, and marching. Tre'Vell wasn't expecting much, but he was pleasantly surprised at how much he enjoyed the show. He thought it was thoroughly entertaining.

When the probate was over and everybody began to disperse, he called Deandre over to him. "Tre! Man, thanks for coming!"

"No problem. I told you I'd be here. You did your thing out there, boy! I'm proud of you!" said Tre'Vell as him embraced Deandre.

"Thanks," said Deandre.

They slowly began to make their way out of the gym. "So this mean you in the fraternity now?" he asked Deandre.

"Nah, not yet. This was only the first part. The actual initiation is in a few more weeks. We got a couple more things we have to do to get in," he answered. Tre'Vell nodded in understanding. "So how's life treating you? Even though we live in the same building, it's like we ain't talked in a good minute."

Tre'Vell said, "Eh. Just doin' my thing. Tryin' to get these classes right. Gettin' the grind started again."

"Yeah. I been so focused on pledging lately. Hey, what's up with that girl you was seeing?"

"Ricquel? It didn't work out. We broke up."

"Really? What happened?"

"Bitch was playing me. When I found out, she told me, right to my face, that she never even liked me. She was just using me to get to some of my boys."

"Ouch. That's cold," sympathized Deandre.

"Yup. You could say that relationship . . . went up in flames," said Tre'Vell, smirking at how literal that statement truly was.

"Dang. I'm sorry, dude. Well, you know what they say. There's plenty of other fish in the sea."

Tre'Vell looked at him funnily. "You know, I never did like fish."

"It's a figure of speech, dawg."

"A figure of speech, huh? You just learn about those in English class?" Tre'Vell joked. They both shared a hearty laugh as they ventured out into the cold night.

***

Rhonda was running a little late. She was on her way to meet Matthias. She now had plenty of time to digest what happened in his dorm that fateful day. She had avoided him like the plague since then. It was by far the longest time they went without seeing each other since they had met. Over that time, Rhonda realized that despite what she had seen, she missed Matthias dearly and decided to meet up with him so they could try to iron things out. Matthias seemed genuinely excited when she called him. They knew that the things that they needed to talk about were best said in person, so they decided to meet up when Matthias got back from his tennis tournament. Besides that, Rhonda didn't want to distract him during the tournament. She knew how tough of a coach his father was. In her rush, Rhonda bumped into somebody. The contact caused the lady to drop her briefcase, and all the papers went flying out.

"Oh, I'm so sorry!" said Rhonda.

"That's okay," said the lady. The lady bent down to collect the papers.

"Here, let me help you with that," said Rhonda as she also bent down and helped the lady collect her wayward papers.

When they were finished, she handed her collection of papers to the lady. "Thank you," the lady said.

"No problem. It's the least I could do after I bumped into you," said Rhonda. "I'm Rhonda, by the way."

"I know who you are," said the lady. "Rhonda Little. You're Matthias Johnson's girlfriend. As a matter of fact, you are on your way to see him right now."

It was at that time that Rhonda got a good look at who she had bumped into. "I'm sorry, do I know you?" Rhonda asked.

"I don't know. Do you?" the lady asked. Her tone sent an involuntary shiver down Rhonda's spine.

***

Matthias was dumbfounded. He couldn't describe how happy he was when Rhonda called him over the weekend and told him that she was finally ready to talk to him. With everything that had been happening lately, he eased his chase of her. He figured that pursuing her would do no good and that she would contact him when she was ready. His magical situation caused him to give her space, which was probably for the best anyway. However, Rhonda was supposed to meet him, but never showed up. She had never called to let him know either. He tried calling her, multiple times, but never got an answer. It had been two days, and he hadn't heard a peep from her. This was unlike her.

While he was in class, he felt his phone vibrate in his pocket. Normally, he just ignored his phone in class, but he pulled it out to see what it was. He was relieved when the caller ID indicated that it was Rhonda who was calling. Matthias quickly but quietly got up and excused himself from the room. Once outside, he answered the phone.

"Rhonda! Thank God, you finally called!"

"Expecting someone different, I see."

Matthias didn't recognize the voice on the other end, but he knew it wasn't Rhonda. "Who is this?"

"I'm sorry. I forgot that even though I've been preoccupied with you for the past couple of months, we've never actually met. It seems like we should know each other by now. I certainly feel like I know you and your warlock buddies."

"Wait! You're the mayor, aren't you? Angela Wright!"

"There you go."

"What have you done now? Where's Rhonda?"

"Oh, she's right here keeping me company. Say hello, Rhonda."

"Matt?"

"Rhonda?"

"Matt? What's going on? She's got me tied up!"

"That's enough out of you," Angela said.

"Don't hurt her."

"I won't. She's just a means to an end. I'm not after her, I'm after you four."

"What do you want?"

"I want you, Tre'Vell, Omar, and especially Derek to meet me at city hall this Saturday at two o'clock. Alone. Do this, and I will release your darling Rhonda."

"Fine. Just tell me one thing. Why are you doing all this? Not just this, but everything. The golems, the game, the gryphon, the cops, the chimera. Why are you after us? What did we ever do to you?"

"You might find out on Saturday. Two o'clock. Don't be late."

***

"Hey, Derek! Wait up!" yelled Travis. Derek looked behind himself and saw his teammate running up behind him. Derek had just finished eating lunch for the day and was on his way to see his guidance counselor so that they could discuss his plans for declaring a major. The good thing was that he was finished with classes for the day and had some time to relax when he was done with the meeting. He wanted to be prepared for the meeting with some ideas for a major and was engrossed deep in thought on the walk to the Office of Academic Affairs, which was the building where the guidance counselors resided. Travis had interrupted his train of thought.

"What's going on, Travis?" said Derek.

Travis said, "On my way to class."

"Oh yeah? Which one?"

"Chemistry."

"Wow. I didn't know you was taking that," Derek commented.

"Yup. So where you off to? Class?"

"Nah. I'm going to see my guidance counselor."

"What for?" asked Travis.

"I'm trying to declare a major."

"You ain't did that yet?" Travis asked in surprise.

"Nope. Couldn't decide which one to pick," answered Derek.

"You got any ideas?"

"I actually do have a few now. Hopefully, my counselor can help me decide on one. I do know that I need to declare one before next year."

"Why?"

"'Cuz most majors are three-year programs, and that's without a soft fall semester schedule, which I need because of football. If I wait much past this semester, I'm probably not going to graduate on time," Derek explained.

"You can always take classes over the summer," Travis offered.

"But that's not covered in my scholarship, and I'd rather not have to come out of pocket. This school ain't too cheap," said Derek.

"Well, you better hope you don't have to change your major then."

"I know. That's one of the reasons I waited to declare. I want to make sure I pick the right one the first time so I don't gotta change it and delay my graduation."

"Okay. Well, my class is down this way so I'll catch up with you later," said Travis. He walked off.

Derek continued walking. When he reached his destination, the Office of Academic Affairs, he walked in. He went up to one of the receptionists. "Hello. Can I help you?" she asked sweetly.

"Yeah. I have an appointment with my guidance counselor," Derek responded.

"All right. Can I have your student ID?" she asked. Derek pulled out his wallet and retrieved his ID card from it. He handed it over to the receptionist, and she scanned the barcode on the back. After looking at the screen on the computer in front of her, she said, "Derek James. Yes, I see that you have an appointment for one thirty with Darrelle Ross. If you take a seat over there, I'll let him know that you're here and he'll come out to get you when he's ready," she said. Derek nodded a thank-you and took a seat.

Derek sat down, idly picked up the copy of *Sports Illustrated* that rested on the coffee table, and began to skim through it. After about ten minutes, he heard someone call his name, "Derek." Derek looked in the corner from whence it came and saw a large man standing there. He got up and went over to him.

"Hello, Derek. I'm Darrelle," the man said and held out his hand.

Derek took it and gave him a firm handshake. "Nice to finally meet you, sir," he said.

Darrelle said, "Please, call me Darrelle. Well, let's go on back to my desk so we can talk." Darrelle led Derek through the hallway that led to his cubicle.

Once they sat down, Darrelle said, "Let me pull up your account. All right, now what would you like to discuss with me, Derek?"

"I want to declare a major, and I wanted some help in picking one."

"Do you want help with the process, or actually determining which one you want to declare?"

"Both. But mainly the second option."

Darrelle asked, "Okay. Well, what is it that you like to do?"

Derek said, "I'm on the football team, but I can't major in that."

"You're right about that, but have you thought about majoring in one of the more physical majors? Something like exercise science?"

"Yeah, but I don't really want to major in something like that."

"What else are you interested in?"

"I like music, but I don't see a future career in the field. It's more just a hobby. I like to listen to it, that's all."

"Out of any of the classes that you've taken, have any of them caught your eye? Piqued your interest more than the others?" Darrelle inquired.

"Well, I really enjoy the Intro to Psych class that I'm in right now."

"Good. What about it do you like?"

"I like the different theories and stuff on why and how people think and act the way they do."

"Maybe you should major in that. Seems like you have a budding passion for the subject."

"What can I do with a psych degree?" Derek wondered.

"Plenty of things. Psychology degrees are very versatile. You could get into law. You can get into business or finance—occupational or organizational psychology. You could be a therapist, researcher, guidance counselor, social worker. You just have to be a people person, obviously."

"Oh, I am. With most of those, don't you need a graduate degree?"

"Yes. A master's would suffice for most of those, and that would only be about two more years. Of course, if you wanted to get into law, that would be much longer."

"Would I have to have an idea about what area of psych I wanted to be in? 'Cuz I don't know."

"Not at first. Most people discover things like that as they're matriculating through the program. Psychology is a great major because it's very customizable. Once you get past the prerequisites, you can tailor the program to your interests."

"What's the prereqs?"

"Psych Statistics and Research Methods."

"That's it?"

"That's it."

"I like the sound of that."

"I could register you for the major right now if you want," offered Darrelle.

"Yeah, let's do that."

"Okay. Did you want to make your degree program a bachelor of science or a bachelor of arts?" Darelle asked.

Derek asked, "What's the difference?"

"A BS degree is more science intensive. You'll be taking more classes like chemistry and biology. If you think you might want to get into psychiatry or if you want to do research on the physical processes of the brain, you'd pick this," Darrelle explained.

"Let's *not* go with that one."

Darrelle chuckled. "All right, Derek. You are now enrolled in the bachelor of arts degree program for psychology. The prerequisites are Intro to Psych, Statistics, and Research Methods. You're currently taking Psych 100. When it's time for you to register for your classes for next school year, I would enroll in the Statistics and Research Methods courses. That way, you have the rest of the courses for the major open to you from there on."

"Okay. Cool." Derek rose from his seat. "Thank you so much for helping me. I was lost before I talked to you."

"That's what I'm here for. Glad I could help you out, young brotha. Take it easy. And keep in touch."

***

Matthias walked into the room in the library in a rush. He quickly closed the door behind him. "What you need us for, Matt? You sounded all panicked and shit on the phone," asked Omar.

"This has something to do with the mayor, don't it?" asked Derek.

"Did you?" Matthias began to ask.

"No. Just a feeling," Derek replied.

Just then, Tre'Vell walked in, completing the group. "So what's so important that I had to rush on over here for?"

Matthias ran his hand over his head and said, "The mayor's got Rhonda!"

The tone suddenly got very serious. "Woah!" said Tre'Vell.

"How do you know?" asked Omar.

"She called me using Rhonda's phone and told me," Matthias answered as he sank down in one of the chairs that surrounded the table in the middle of the room.

"Did she say why?" asked Derek.

"No, just that she wanted the four of us to meet her at city hall, alone, this Saturday at two o'clock. If we don't show up, then . . .," Matt trailed off ominously.

"Obviously, that's a trap. She's using Rhonda to lure us to her on her turf where she's the most comfortable. How much you wanna bet that she'll try to kill us the moment we get there?" said Derek.

"I agree, but what choice do we have?"

Tre'Vell chimed in with, "We could always just not show up."

Matthias vehemently shook his head. "Not an option. If we don't go, Rhonda's going to die. The only reason that she's caught up in this mess is because of me, or us rather. The mayor's after us, not her. I would never be able to live with myself if something happened to her because of me and I was able to stop it."

"Okay. Say, we do go. What then?"

Derek said, "Omar's got a point. I was talking to Lamar about this, and he raised a good point when he said that the mayor is a huge political figure. We can't just kill her."

"Why not?" asked Tre'Vell. "She tryin' to kill us. We just defendin' ourselves."

"Because if the mayor disappears, it would cause a manhunt that I'm sure would be somehow traced back to us. And we can't show up in a court of law and say, 'Well, she was a witch and we had to kill her in magical self-defense.' Somehow, I don't think that will fly," explained Derek.

"Derek's right. I don't fancy going to prison. I don't think that's a good trade-off. We need to go into that meeting with a plan, but that plan can't involve killing her. Any ideas, anybody?" said Omar.

"Derek, did you bring your grimoire like I asked? Because I brought mine, and I was hoping that we could use them to help us brainstorm some ways on how to deal with the mayor," asked Matthias.

"Oh shoot! I forgot it in my room! Y'all get started and I'll 'port right to my room, get it, and be right back." Derek teleported out.

Matthias pulled his grimoire out of his backpack and began to scroll through it. "How about a protection spell of some sort?" offered Omar.

"That could work," said Tre'ell.

"No, it wouldn't," said Matthias.

"Why not?"

"Because even if we could find a protection charm powerful enough, it would only extend to ourselves. What about Rhonda?"

"Oh yeah. I forgot about her that fast," remarked Tre'Vell.

"Any plan that we have can't be just about saving ourselves. It has to be about eliminating, or at least minimizing, the mayor as a threat from now on," said Matthias.

"How about this? We threaten to expose her if she doesn't leave us alone and release Rhonda. I'm sure there's a spell in there that could help us do it," said Omar.

"That won't work either. We couldn't expose her without exposing ourselves too. Besides, she could just kill us to prevent us from leaking her activities to the press, if that would even do any good."

Tre'Vell asked, "What do you mean?"

"I mean, what if she has control of the press too? She has control of the police so I don't think that's too much of a leap in logic. At this point, we have to assume that she has every government official under her control."

"Why you keep shooting down my ideas?" Omar whined.

"I'm not trying to, but we have to get this right. Our lives, and Rhonda's, are on the line."

"It's too bad my powers won't work on her. I could just put the whammy on her and we could use a spell to make the effect permanent or some shit like that. Know what I'm sayin?" said Tre'Vell.

"That would be nice. Man, it just can't be that easy, can it?" Omar mused.

Matthias looked around. "Shouldn't Derek be back by now?"

Omar, as if noticing Derek's extended absence for the first time, said, "He has been gone a while."

Just then, Derek teleported back in, grimoire in hand. "What took you so long?" asked Matthias. "You should have popped into your room, got the book, and popped back in."

"Um, I picked up my book and dropped it. When I went to go pick it up, it was opened on a page about disempowerment. Let me see if I can find it again," said Derek. Something about the way he said it made Matthias slightly suspicious, but he decided to drop it. He plopped the book down on the table and riffled through its pages. "Here we go." He passed the book to the others so they could read the entry.

Disempowerment

A witch or warlock is genetically bound to their magic. The only way to forcefully remove the magic of a witch or warlock is through disempowerment. The person performing the disempowerment must be stronger than the one being disempowered. This is a three-step process: separating them from their magic, removing their magic, and then placing it in a mystic containment unit.

The first step is separating them from their magic, which entails destroying the genetic bonds that bind their magic to them. You can do this by getting them to drink a potion made from the ingredients and process listed at the bottom of the page. It's important to note that they will still be able to use their magic whilst separated from them.

The second step is calling for their magic. This is accomplished by using an item that has great meaning to the person being disempowered; a significant and prized personal belonging. Once you are in possession of this object, recite the spell listed at the bottom of this page. If the spell is recited before the witch or warlock has been separated from their magic, the entire person will be drawn to you, not just their magic.

The final step is creating a unit that can hold the person's magic. This is called a mystic containment unit. Choose a sturdy and secure, yet small storage unit such as a box or jar. Bless it using the blood of the person being disempowered and the spell listed at the bottom of the page. When calling for their magic, place the containment unit next to the personal belonging. As you chant the spell, the being's magic will begin to flow forth from their body and toward their personal belonging. It will be redirected into the mystic containment unit. If you do not have a containment unit, or the unit isn't strong enough to hold the being's magic, it will return to the being's body and rebond with them, in which case, the entire process will have to be started over from the beginning.

If this process is successful, the being will, for all intents and purposes, become a mortal. Their powers will be locked away in the mystic containment unit. Even though they will not be able to access the magic contained in the unit, certain other types of mystical beings, with the power and certain knowledge of the occult, can. Mystic containment units are extremely rare and coveted objects, especially those that already house someone's magic. If you create or come across one, guard it accordingly.

"This is a brilliant idea!" said Matthias. "We disempower her so that she can't come after us anymore and we spare her life so we don't get caught up in a murder of the mayor!"

"What's to stop her from squealing to the press after we disempower her?" asked Omar.

"She wouldn't dare. Not unless she wanted to explain her involvement, and I doubt she'll be so willing to spill her guts," said Derek. "I've been thinking about this. Why didn't she just come after us herself before? Why go through all this trouble to attack us in a roundabout way? She must be just as concerned about murder as we are. The attacks were just her way of trying to get rid of us without it being traced back to her. She don't want her involvement to come to light. I don't think that'll change just because she don't have her magic anymore."

"Now it's my turn to rain on your parade, Matt. I see two problems—one, how are we going to get a prized personal possession, and two, how are we going to make the containment unit without her blood?" asked Omar.

"Well, we're going to city hall. I'm sure she has something we can use for the spell in her office or something. And we can get some of her blood when we subdue her, assuming we can," answered Matthias.

"That sounds sketchy," said Tre'Vell.

"Sketchy is all we have," Matthias responded.

Derek nervously cleared his throat, which didn't go unnoticed by Matthias. "Okay. So we all clear on what we have to do? We go to the meeting and ask for Rhonda back and for her to stop attacking us. If she proves hostile, we subdue the mayor and disempower her."

"And if that don't work?" asked Omar.

"Then we're probably dead."

Chapter 18

Confrontation

"Well, this certainly looks delicious," said Angela. She gazed down at the spread of food that covered the table: pancakes, waffles, eggs, bacon, french toast, muffins, bagels, and glasses of apple juice. She rubbed her hands together, mouth already salivating at the thought of the scrumptious-smelling breakfast tickling her taste buds. She was usually so busy that she didn't have an opportunity to partake in a big breakfast like this. Today was an important day, however. It was a good day. She anticipated that it would be made even better with the events that would be taking place later on. She was so excited that she decided to share her breakfast banquet with a couple of guests.

"You're certainly in a chipper mood," said Rhonda.

"Why wouldn't I be? Today, I facilitate the safe return of my mother," said Angela triumphantly.

"And how do you intend on doing that?" Rhonda asked.

Mariah decided to answer her question. "By killing your boyfriend and his friends," she said quietly.

Rhonda whipped her head to Mariah in shock. "What?" She turned back to Angela. "Why?" she asked her forcefully.

Just to show she wasn't bothered by Rhonda's tone, Angela calmly took a bite of her waffles, savoring the bite. When she was done chewing, she said, "Like I just said, because it's the only way to save my mom's life." Just as Rhonda opened her mouth to follow up, Angela said, "And don't ask me why."

Mariah said, "How are you so sure that you can pull it off?"

"The odds are stacked in my favor," Angela responded as she took a gulp of her drink.

"How do you figure?"

"I know their plan. They intend on disempowering me."

Mariah asked, "How do you know that?"

"Because I read Matt's mind."

"You can channel someone's thoughts from that far away?"

"Not normally. Usually, the distance from city hall to the campus of Word University is out of my range. But I used the relationship between Rhonda here and her man to strengthen my connection."

Bitch!

"Now that's not a nice thought. I would like to think that I'm much prettier than a female dog," scolded Angela. She smiled at Rhonda's shocked expression. "You haven't touched any of your food."

"I don't know what's in this food. It could be poisoned," said Rhonda.

"If I wanted to kill you, I wouldn't resort to something as backhanded as poison. That's not my style," said Angela.

"You don't seem too worried about that plan," observed Mariah.

"They won't be able to pull it off. I know this spell all too well, as you know. It's very complex. They won't be able to get the main ingredients that they need. How will they get one of my items of great personal significance and some of my blood? Even if they were to find a way to get those things, I'm a level 5 witch, and none of them are. They won't be able to draw my magic out of me, nor make a containment unit strong enough to house it. And if by some minor miracle they were, they won't be able to subdue me long enough to get the potion down my throat and cast the spell," boasted Angela.

"Not alone, maybe. But with the power of the diamond, they just might. It would be wise not to be too overconfident," said Mariah.

"Doubtful."

Rhonda interrupted their conversation. "Just answer me one thing. You kidnapped me a couple of days ago, but you haven't treated me like a prisoner. I've been able to shower, watch TV, you've kept me pretty well-fed. Other than not being able to leave or otherwise communicate with the outside world, I've been fine. Why?"

Angela took some time before candidly answering, "Because I'm not after you. You're simply a means to an end. I know you might not believe me, but I'm not the bad guy here. This goes over all of our heads. What I'm doing brings me no joy. I look at you and see a little bit of myself when I was around your age. A part of me is sad that you are about to suffer a great loss in your life, and I guess I don't see the need to add more to your pain."

Mariah was surprised at the candor Angela displayed. This was more like the Angie that she was used to. She knew that Angela was under the gun, but Mariah couldn't, under any circumstances, condone cold-blooded murder, and there was a time in her life where Angela would have felt the same thing. What mysterious force caused Angela to act so out of character? Mariah contemplated this as she watched Angela finish off her apple juice.

***

The drive to Center City was quiet, reflective, and somber. Each young man in the vehicle was locked in his own thoughts. Derek's mind kept focusing on the tarot reading that seemingly got this whole thing started. Death was in his future. It was obvious to him now that this meeting with the mayor was where that death happened. The question was, whose?

Omar reflected on the year as a whole. The past couple of months seemed liked a course in Advanced Mysticism for him and the others, which he thought was sort of fitting since this was their first year in college. Everything that they had been through were tests of their mettle, and they passed all of them with flying colors. They were coming up on the final exam, however, and Omar had a sinking feeling in his gut that somebody was going to fail. On this test though, there wouldn't be an opportunity to take the class over again.

Tre'Vell leaned up against the window as he thought back to that fateful night that he was attacked by that golem. His life sure had changed since that moment. He had learned of, seen, and experienced things that he could have never in his wildest dreams imagined existed. Tre'Vell was wary of his new magical world at first, but now wanted to explore it more. He came to realize that it was an intrinsic part of who he was. Now, that world that he was introduced to was being threatened by the mayor. He wouldn't let her get away with it. The code of the streets said that you don't let anyone disrespect you and get away with it, and even though Tre'Vell was attempting to turn over a new leaf, he still respected that rule.

Matthias, the driver, remained focused on the task at hand. As the most logically based of the group, he didn't see a need to allow sentimentality to cloud the end goal. They were going to city hall to rescue his girlfriend and end the threat of the mayor. Nothing else mattered. He knew it wouldn't be easy. It was very possible that one or all of them wouldn't be making the drive back home. None of them knew what to expect when they got to city hall. They had a plan but couldn't be sure that it would work. It was the best plan they could come up with however, especially on such short notice. But Matthias knew one thing. He would gladly lay down his life if it meant that Rhonda would be safe.

Omar broke the silence. "Why didn't you just teleport us down there, Derek?" he asked.

"It's outside my range. Even if it wasn't, I could only carry one of you at a time, and I think it's best that we stick together as much as possible," answered Derek.

Matthias said, "Well, while we're on our way, let's go over everything. Do we have the potion?"

"Yup. Right here," said Tre'Vell as he held up the vial that contained the bluish-green liquid. It sparkled in the sunlight.

Matthias looked in the rearview mirror. "And, Derek, do you have the spell?"

"Got the instructions right here in my pocket," he said.

"What's our actual plan when we get there?" Omar asked.

"I'm sure she'll be waiting for us. We give her a chance to give us Rhonda. If she proves hostile, and she's given us no reason to believe she won't be, we do whatever we can to incapacitate her. Our powers, the spells we went over, anything. We don't know what powers she has, but I'm sure she has a couple of surprises in store for us," said Matthias.

"Since I can teleport, I got the slumber dust. I'll teleport in front of her, hopefully surprising her long enough to knock her out with it," Derek continued.

Tre'Vell picked up from there. "That's where I come in. I'll force the potion down her throat while she sleep. We find some possession of hers, Matt uses the knife—"

"Athame," Matthias corrected.

Tre'Vell rolled his eyes. "Athame, to get some of her blood, and we cast the spell."

Omar said, "That takes care of the mayor, but what about Rhonda? How we find her?"

"That's easy. Rhonda should be somewhere in the building, or at least in the vicinity. Derek can do a mind scan. If that doesn't work, we can always cast a locator spell," Matthias replied.

They soon arrived at their destination, driving by the statues that stood sentry in front of city hall. Matthias parked on the next block over to avoid the parking meters. With the serious business that was about to take place inside the building, it seemed silly to be worrying about a parking fine, but Matthias just didn't want to put money in the meter. He was cheap in that way. Before they got out the car, Matthias bowed his head and closed his eyes.

"What are you doing?" asked Omar.

Matthias quietly said, "I'm praying." Once he was finished, they got out of the car.

As they briskly walked toward the entrance to city hall, Tre'Vell said, "I didn't know you was religious."

"Yeah?"

"Christian?"

"Yes, sir."

"Can I ask why?"

"It's how I was raised. I fully believe that Jesus died on the cross to atone for our sins. And that living our lives believing in and following God Almighty will lead to everlasting life," said Matthias.

"Sounds like wishful thinking to me," said Tre'Vell.

"I take it that you are a nonbeliever?"

"I seen too many bad things happen to good people to believe in the fairy tales that exist in the Bible. I would think that you of all people wouldn't submit to that stuff."

"Why?"

"Because you a warlock. You know, magic and monsters and shit. I'm pretty sure that's not in the Bible, and if it is, it ain't positive."

"Well, it says that in the beginning, God created all things on earth and in heaven. That includes warlocks and witches and monsters and every other mystical creature. We are all God's creations," said Derek, deciding to interrupt their conversation.

"You a Christian too?" asked Tre'Vell.

"Well, I'm not as strong with my beliefs as Matt, but I do believe in a higher power—a grand design. My amulet proves that my family has always believed in him to some degree," Derek replied.

Tre'Vell shook his head as they approached the door. "I just don't understand how you could believe in somethin' you can't see or even really prove one way or the other."

Matthias said, "If you could prove his existence, then it wouldn't be called faith."

The four of them walked up to the door. Omar prepared to knock, but the door opened before his fist had a chance to connect with the door. They walked in and were almost immediately met with a floating golden orb of light. They all tensed up, expecting the worst, before they collectively heard a voice ring out in their heads.

Welcome to city hall, gentlemen. I take it you all got here safely, and alone, as per my request. Don't be alarmed at the orb that floats in front of you. Follow it and it will lead you to the place that we will be meeting. I look forward to meeting each of you in person, shortly.

"This is *so* a trap," commented Omar.

"Definitely. But for now, we play along. Derek, can you pick up anything on her thoughts?" Matthias asked.

"Nah. She blocking me. I got nothing," Derek replied.

Matthias said, "Too bad. Well, let's go. Everybody keep an eye out as we're walking for anything you think can be used for the disempowerment spell."

The floating orb began to float down the hallway, and the boys followed behind it as it led them to their destination. "Derek, can you at least sense for Rhonda's thoughts? Is she close by?" Matthias asked.

Derek did a mind sweep for Rhonda. He said, "No. The only people's thoughts I hear in the building is you guys'."

The four of them cautiously trailed behind the orb, on high alert for any sudden movements or potential surprise attacks. As the orb led them up an ornate staircase, Omar said, "Wait! The mayor just talked to us in our heads. That must mean she's a telepath!"

Tre'Vell said, "So?"

Matthias picked up on Omar's train of thought. "He means that if she's telepathic, she could have read our thoughts, found out about our plan, and performed countermeasures," he finished.

"Even if she did, it wouldn't matter. This is our plan, and we have to stick it out 'til the end. I think I would have sensed if someone was channeling one of you guys' thoughts anyway, and I'm shielding mines," said Derek.

Eventually, the orb meandered down a long corridor and then disappeared behind a closed door. "Two guesses what's behind door number 1," said Omar. Derek slowly opened the door.

The room was an office. They saw a desk with papers and documents strewn about and a laptop resting on it. Along the wall were pictures of various dignitaries and a couple of framed diplomas. An armoire was tucked in the back corner and a coat rack stood in the corner nearest the door. Along the back wall was a huge window that spanned most of the length and height of the wall that overlooked the city. What concerned them the most was the woman who stood at the window, her back turned toward them.

"Greetings. You have no idea how happy I am to finally meet all of you."

***

The two senators purposefully walked through their dank surroundings. The corridor was dimly lit with the light from torches that were stationed along the walls. The shadows cast from the flames hungrily devoured their guests, gleefully anticipating the senators' every step as they journeyed through the corridor. They reached the end of the path and entered through the wooden door that separated the room from the depressing corridor. The room they entered was even more depressing. The rancid odors of hopelessness and despair blanketed all who entered the room to the extent that they lingered when they departed. The senators made their way to a hooded figure that sat at a table situated off to the side. The figure was hunched over a bowl that was filled nearly to the brim with human blood.

"What is it?" the figure asked. She seemed none too pleased that she had been interrupted.

"Our apologies for interrupting your unholy communion, mistress, but we have news of the witch," one of the senators said.

"What could possibly be so important that you felt the need to disrupt my communications with the other side, Asmodeus?" she asked.

"The witch was successful in luring the warlocks to her. She is in the process of disposing of them herself as we speak," one of them said timidly. He desperately wanted to avoid incurring her wrath.

"I'm well aware of the development! Tell me something I don't know!" she raged.

Benzor decided to speak up and lend his partner a helping hand. "I sensed an undulation in the mystical slipstream that surrounded one of the warlocks."

"Really? Now that is interesting," said the hooded figure.

"Should we alert the witch?"

"No. She thinks she's so powerful, let her figure it out." She got up from her seat and practically glided over to an older woman that was chained up to a chair in the corner.

"Please!" she screamed. "Let me go!"

"I can't do that. On second thought, I take that back. I won't do that."

"You could at least give me something more to eat. What scraps you've given me aren't enough! I'm weak."

"Compared to me, you are, always were, and will forever be weak, no matter the circumstances."

"What do you want with me? Do you want money?"

"What I want is so much more important than something as frivolous as money."

"What do you plan on doing with me?" the woman asked with dread.

"Well, if your daughter fails with her assignment, I'm going to kill you, right in front of her. Then she'll be next," the hooded figure answered.

The woman began to weep, begging for mercy as best as she could. "No, not my daughter! Please spare her and just take me!"

"I'm afraid that's not how it works. But don't worry. You'll know your fates in a relatively quick time frame."

***

"Okay, we're here. Where's Rhonda? Hand her over. Now!" demanded Matthias.

"So direct. Didn't your mother ever tell you to respect your elders?" taunted Angela.

"It's hard to respect somebody that's spent the last couple of months trying to kill us," said Derek.

"Now I wonder who told you that. Competent help can be so hard to find," said Angela.

"I'll ask again. Where's Rhonda?" said Matthias.

Angela was briefly annoyed with Matthias's defiant tone, but recovered. She turned to address them. "Ms. Little will be released when we are done here and not a moment sooner, understand?" She took their silence as a yes and went back over to the window and gazed out of it once more. "Beautiful, isn't it? This city has come so far in such a short amount of time," she mused.

"Enough small talk. We here. What you want with us?" asked Tre'Vell.

Angela spun around and smirked. She noticed Omar's eyes wandering around the office. "Looking for something?" she asked him.

"Just admiring your office," he said.

"I'll bet." Angela gestured to the middle of the office. Four cushioned wooden chairs materialized out of thin air, one behind each of the warlocks. "Please, have a seat."

"Nah, we're good. Thanks," said Omar.

Angela frowned and said, "Such insolence from the younger generation." She used a "come hither" gesture with her hand and telekinetically yanked the chairs forward. With their legs swept out from under them, the boys collapsed into the chairs. "That's more like it." They attempted to rise from their seats, but found that some invisible force was keeping them seated. "Ah, ah, ah! Stay down," she said.

"What game are you playing? Why do you want us dead?" asked Derek.

Angela walked up to Derek, looked down at him, and said, "I don't."

"But you've been trying to kill us for months!" said Omar.

"That may be true, but it is not I that wants you dead. I'm simply carrying out the wishes of someone else."

"Like who?" asked Tre'Vell.

"Their identity isn't important to you at the current moment. I should be your primary concern right now."

"Whoever it is, they must be so mad that you've failed so spectacularly up to this point," taunted Matthias.

Angela went over to Matthias and placed both of her hands on the arms of his chair. "What was that?"

"We crushed your golems, escaped your video game curse, killed your gyphon, outran your cops, and outwitted your chimera." Matthias could see that he was getting to the mayor. She was beginning to focus more and more of her attention on him, loosening her control on the others. "Face it. We've beaten you at every step. It must be pretty embarrassing, seeing as you're a level 5 witch and all."

"You'll pay for those words," she said.

"I doubt it," said Matthias.

Suspicious, Angela attempted to read Matthias's mind to find out what he was getting at. She felt a presence behind her and quickly got up to face it. As soon as she turned around, Derek blew slumber dust in her face. "What?" she said as she staggered back in surprise.

The mayor's hold on them disappeared. Omar, Tre'Vell, and Matthias got out of their chairs. Matthias quickly jumped into action. "Derek, get the knife out the bag so we can draw some blood. Omar, Tre, fan out and find something we can use for the spell. She has to have something in here."

Before any of them could execute their marching orders, the mayor recovered from the surprise attack. "Slumber dust. You'll have to do better than that." She swept her arm toward them, telekinetically sending the four of them hurtling through the drywall and into the hallway.

"Go find Rhonda! We'll hold her off!" said Derek. Matthias nodded, got up, and quickly ran off in search of his girlfriend.

"And just how do you expect us to do that?" asked Omar from across the hall, sprawled out against the wall with bits of drywall peppering his outfit.

"By any means necessary," said Tre'Vell.

The mayor walked out of her office and into the hallway. "Come on!" yelled Derek. They got up and took off down the hallway.

Annoyed, the mayor chased after them. "It's pointless! There's no escape!" she yelled. She waved her hand and tossed Derek off to the side.

"Keep going. I'll get Derek," said Omar. Tre'Vell kept running, and Omar stooped down by Derek and quickly helped him to his feet.

"Anime," said Angela. The statues that stood at the other end of the hallway ahead of them came to life and began advancing on Tre'Vell. He froze them, but they were blocking his path.

The mayor clenched both of her fists. Both Omar and Derek started coughing and choking as their passageways were being constricted. They fell to their knees as they clutched their necks, trying in vain to alleviate the pressure on their throats. Omar threw a fireball at Angela. "Ow!" she cried as it hit its mark on her hand. Her grip on Omar loosened. Omar let loose a stream of fire at the mayor. Angela, thinking fast, conjured up a shield to protect her from the flames. This action caused her to release her grip on Derek as she hid behind the shield. "I'll keep her busy. You go with Tre!" said Omar. Derek looked ahead where Tre'Vell was, placed his hand on Omar's shoulder, and teleported them to him. With Omar gone, the flames stopped.

"You're only delaying the inevitable. Give up now, and I promise to make your deaths quick and painless," Angela offered.

"Fuck you!" shouted Tre'Vell.

"Suit yourself," she said.

Angela reared back and hurled her shield at the trio, using her telekinesis to give it even more speed and force. *Zoom!* It sliced through the air, seeking its target. Tre'Vell lifted his arms and froze it in midflight. "That's a really annoying power," the mayor said to herself. She used her telekinesis to counteract Tre'Vell's power, and the shield continued on its path. "In here!" yelled Derek. The three of them opened the door on their left and went inside just as the shield flew past the area they just vacated. It cut right through the stone statues and embedded itself into the wall.

Perfect, thought Angela. The room they stumbled into was a huge banquet hall. On the other end, the double doors that were the exit were wide open.

"We need to find a way to get this potion in her so we can do the spell. We can't do nothin' if we keep runnin'," said Tre'Vell.

Derek said, "Our first priority is to stay alive. We also can't do nothing if we dead." Just as they approached the door, it slammed shut. Omar shook the handle and tried to yank the doors open. They wouldn't budge.

"There's nowhere left to run now," said Angela from the opposite side of the banquet hall. She slammed the doors behind her shut. They were now trapped with her. "You don't think I know what you plan on doing? You want to perform a disempowerment. All this running was probably a way to delay me long enough for Matt to find his girlfriend and something of mine to use for the spell. Am I right?" She chuckled. "It's not a fair question, really, because I know that I'm right. Sorry to tell you that spell won't work for you. And that mistake will cost you dearly!"

"I'm tired of this. It's time we fought back! I'm takin' her down," said Tre'Vell.

"No! Wait!" said Omar.

Tre'Vell ran at the mayor. "Idiot," she muttered. She flung him across the room. Derek noticed that he was heading straight for the window. He was going to crash through it and fall a couple of stories to his doom! Derek quickly teleported between Tre'Vell and the window. Tre'Vell crashed into Derek, and they both fell to the ground in front of the window, Tre'Vell sprawled out on top of Derek.

Angela quickly focused her attention back on Omar. She used her telekinesis to raise him in the air and pin him squarely to the wall. She used her free hand to levitate the knives that were on one of the banquet tables. The gleaming missiles briefly hovered ominously over the table before launching toward a prone Omar.

"No!" yelled Tre'Vell. He threw up his hand, freezing the knives in time before they could slice and dice Omar. Omar let out a sigh of relief.

Angela huffed, saying, "You are really trying my patience!"

Derek teleported behind the mayor and kicked her, sending her to the ground. Omar fell to the ground, crashing through a table on the way down. The mayor quickly recovered and got to her feet and started to spar with Derek. After trading a few kicks and punches, Derek kneed Angela away from him. Seeing an opportunity to strike, Omar sent a powerful fireball at her. At the same time, Tre'Vell started to make his way over to the action to offer Derek some help. The mayor, reading Omar's mind before he could send off his fireball, redirected the attack toward the oncoming Tre'Vell. The fireball hit him squarely in the chest, singeing his shirt and sending him hurtling backward into the wall. He violently banged his head and fell to the floor, unconscious. The potion vial slipped out of his pocket and rolled along the floor.

Derek came at Angela again while Omar went over to tend to Tre'Vell. *Please don't be dead. Again*, hoped Omar. When he got to Tre'Vell, he checked for a pulse and was relieved when he found a steady one. He was just knocked out, thank God! Derek wrapped Angela in a bear hug, teleported out with her, and reappeared near a window. The mayor kicked Derek in the groin, which sent him stumbling back in pain. Angela then delivered an uppercut punch, backed up with a jolt of telekinesis. Derek flew back and went crashing out the window!

"*Ay díos mío!* Derek!" shouted Omar. Angela turned around with a satisfied smirk. "That's one down," she said. She pulled the vial across the room until it rolled under her foot. She crushed the vial, and the potion spilled onto the floor. "And there goes your plan. No potion, no disempowerment. Now, do you understand the folly of your actions? The inevitability of your fate?" In a rage, Omar unfurled a great stream of fire at Angela. Anticipating this, the mayor pulled a banquet table in front of her to block the fire. Omar kept the attack coming, but eventually Angela sent the table at Omar. He dodged the table by jumping to the side. "Concelios," he chanted. Omar disappeared from sight.

"Ah, smart boy. That hex turns both your mind and thoughts invisible," said Angela. She scanned the area, attempting to see if she could detect a hint of his location. She sent a telekinetic wave out. A table flipped over and some dinnerware crashed to the floor, but no sign of Omar. She saw Tre'Vell still unconscious on the floor and got an idea.

"If you won't show yourself, I'll draw you out." She conjured an athame and threw it at a still-prone Tre'Vell. Angela heard a gasp from the corner and saw a fireball make its way from the area. It connected with the athame before it could strike Tre'Vell and knocked it to the floor. "There you are!" she said. She clenched her fist, strangling Omar. Quickly losing air, Omar was unable to hold his hex. It wore off as he fell to the ground. Omar fought to bring air to his lungs, but was losing that struggle. The edges of his vision began to darken. Angela heard a noise behind her.

***

Derek went flying through the window. "Aaaahhh!" Before he could fall to his death, he desperately reached his arm out. He grabbed the ledge and caught himself. With his body dangling from the ledge and certain death awaiting him if he let go, Derek's arms began to tire. He had to pull himself up! Imagining that he was in the weight room doing pull-ups, Derek slowly pulled his considerable body weight up. Before he could finish, the ledge gave a little and one of his arms went flying! Legs flailing away, Derek eventually resteadied himself and grabbed hold of the ledge again with both hands. He then carefully began to pull himself up. He grabbed the windowsill and pulled himself through the window.

Once he got through the window, he took a few breaths. He saw Angela strangling Omar in the corner. Derek noticed a sword on display on the wall next to him behind a protective glass box. He broke it, grabbed the sword, and tried to sneak up on the mayor. Just before he could bring the blade down on her, Angela conjured a sword of her own and spun around to block the attack.

Omar hungrily gobbled up air. He then scampered over to Tre'Vell while the mayor was busy with Derek. He thought for sure that Derek was a goner! How did he survive the fall? However he did it, Omar was glad that he stepped in when he did because he wasn't sure how much longer he could have held on to consciousness. "Tre'Vell concelios," he chanted and Tre'Vell's body turned invisible. He dragged his body over to the corner out of harm's way. The spell should protect him until he regained consciousness as long as Omar could maintain it.

Angela and Derek were locked in an epic swordfight. For every strike that Derek attempted, Angela parried and vice versa. They both ducked and weaved from each other's attacks. Angela flipped onto a table and Derek did the same. They continued their fight on the table. Eventually, Derek knocked Angela's sword out of her hand and onto the ground. She went to pick it up, but Omar quickly ran and grabbed it before she had the chance.

Derek and Omar thought they had the upper hand since they now both had a sword and Angela did not. She taunted them with a "come on" gesture with her hands. They both attacked her, but they couldn't touch her. She easily evaded their attacks by hopping over their swipes, contorting her body and ducking their stabs. Omar succeeded in kicking her to the ground and Derek went to her other side. Angela flipped to her feet, and just as Derek and Omar brought their swords down on her simultaneously, she caught both of their blades, one in each hand. To them, it appeared that she caught them with her bare hands, but she used her telekinesis to keep a sliver of space between the swords and her hands. She brought the tips of the swords to her eye level and said, nonplussed, "Unimpressive." She spun around, causing them to release their grips on their swords and go flying in opposite directions. She nonchalantly tossed the swords to the ground. Omar's hex on Tre'Vell wore off as Tre'Vell finally began to regain his consciousness in the corner. She sensed someone about to enter and tossed her hand out to the door as soon as it opened.

***

Matthias rushed out the door and practically hopped down the steps. He didn't really like leaving his friends alone with the mayor, but he had to find Rhonda. At least they had powers to protect themselves. Rhonda didn't. Who knows what the mayor was doing to her. He knew that she said that Rhonda would be relatively unharmed, but Matthias was definitely not going to take her word for it. Besides finding Rhonda, Matthias had to find an item to use for the disempowerment spell, and that might very well take some time. He just had to hope that they could survive long enough for him to accomplish both objectives. He knew it wouldn't be easy for them. The mayor was a level 5 witch, meaning they needed all the help they could get. All the more reason for him to find Rhonda as quickly as possible.

He came to a split in the hallway with three different paths available. "Great. Which way?" He looked around, trying to make a decision. "What the heck. Eenie meenie miney moe. Catch a tiger by its toe. If it hollers, let him go. Eenie meenie miney moe. Old black Joe." His finger, which had been rotating among the paths, landed on the path to his right when he stopped. "Right it is." He took off running down the hallway. "Rhonda! Rhonda! Rhonda, can you hear me? Are you there?" He got no response. She wasn't there.

He turned back around and tried the opposite hallway. "Rhonda! It's me, Matt! You there?" Again, only silence answered him. He got to the end of that corridor and slammed his fist against the wall in frustration. He took the stairwell down another flight of steps. Maybe this floor would yield more luck. He ran the halls, yelling for his girlfriend, hoping to hear a response. Each time, his hopes were dashed. This was taking too long. This place was too big. He would never find her in time looking for her like this. There had to be a way of expediting the search. He just had to think. He wished he had brought the map from Derek's bag, although he realized it wouldn't do him any good. The map was one of the city, not city hall. A locator spell would have told him she was at city hall if she were here but wouldn't have told him what room she was in specifically.

He examined the lobby he was currently in, and something caught his eye. On the wall was a layout of the building and a red star indicating his current location. Next to it was a potted plant. Perfect! He used the flowerpot to break the glass that the layout was behind, pulled the map from the shards, and spread it out on the floor. He then used the dirt from the pot to cover the map. He hoped that this worked. The last time he cast this spell, he did it with Derek. Now he was doing it solo. "Brevus matus buscar itve," he chanted. The dirt began to shift along the map, and the dirt that covered one room completely removed itself. 'Yes!" He took note of which room it was before wiping all the dirt off the map. According to the layout, he wasn't very far from her location. He just had to go down another level, and she was on the sixth room on the left.

When he reached the room, he found that it was locked with an electronic lock that needed a keycard to open. Not for him, though. He sent a jolt of electricity through the lock, which short-circuited it. The lock opened. Matthias shoved the door open. His heart fluttered as he saw Rhonda pacing around the back of the room.

"Rhonda!" he exclaimed.

"Matt!" Rhonda said as she ran over to her boyfriend. "I'm sooo glad to see you!" She jumped into his arms, and they both shared a loving embrace.

"Are you all right? Did she hurt you?" he asked as he examined her for any bumps or bruises.

"No, I'm okay. What about you? She said she was going to kill you. I was so scared . . ."

"Shh. It's okay. I'm fine. For now at least."

"How did you find me?"

"I'll explain everything later. Right now, we have to get you out of here. Come on!" He led her out the room, and they went up the steps.

When they reached the lobby on the floor, Matthias turned to Rhonda. "I need you to find your way out of here."

"My way? Wait, aren't you coming with me?"

"No. I'm going back upstairs."

"You're going back to the woman who's trying to kill you? Why?"

"Derek, Omar, and Tre are up there with her, and they're going to need my help. I can't just abandon them."

"But—"

"Look, I'll be fine. I just need you to get out. It'll give me peace of mind to know that you're out of harm's way. Can you do that for me?"

"Yeah."

"Good. When you get out, shoot me a text. If you run into any problems, call me. I'll meet you outside when we're done." They shared one last hug.

"Be safe," she whispered. She then took off running down a hallway. Matthias went off in search of the central stairwell that would lead him back up to where his friends were.

Rhonda walked for a few minutes, looking for any sign that she was approaching an exit. She went up to the next level and ran around, took a couple of left turns, a couple of rights. She eventually saw a door that led outside. She ran to the door in earnest. Just before she was about there, she heard a voice ring out.

"Stop right there! Don't take another step!" Rhonda stopped dead in her tracks and turned around. A woman was quickly approaching.

"What are you doing here?" Rhonda asked in surprise.

"Trying to stop you from going through that door," the woman said.

"Why?"

"Because it's booby-trapped, that's why. All the exits that lead outside are. Watch." The woman picked up a box that was lying on the ground and tossed it at the door. When the box reached just beyond where Rhonda was standing, sharp metal spikes shot out from the walls on either side.

"Woah!" screamed Rhonda as she jumped back. If she had taken just one more step, she would have been skewered alive!

"Thank you for saving my life," Rhonda said.

The woman said, "My pleasure. Just sit tight right here. I have to go take care of something."

"But my boyfriend—"

"Trust me, if you want to help him, you'll stay right here. You'll only distract him if you go to him right now. You'll be safe here. I promise. I'll be back." The woman took off in the opposite direction and disappeared into an elevator.

***

Angela sensed the approaching thoughts of Matthias, no doubt trying to surprise her. Utterly useless. As soon as the door opened, she flung out her hand. It was Matthias who was caught off guard. Now in the mayor's clutches, he was hurled toward the corner and right into Tre'Vell, who had made his way to his feet. They both tumbled to the floor.

"How great of you to join us, young Matthias. Find what—or should I say who you were looking for?" she asked.

"Seeing as you can read my mind, I'm sure you know by now that I did. Must cut you up that the girl you kidnapped is now safely outside. Put another one in the win column for us," Matthias boasted.

Angela could only let out a hearty laugh at Matthias's naiveté. "My, my. You are certainly a mouthy one, aren't you? Are you completely sure that she made it out the building? Did you see her actually walk out the door? All the exits are magically rigged to impale anyone that attempts to get out." Matthias's face paled. "Did you actually think I would let her go before we were done here? I must admit, I am somewhat surprised you found her. But I have learned my lesson not to underestimate you and took the necessary precautions in the off chance you did. But now that you're here, I can get on with it."

Angela waved her arm at Matthias, sending him flying through the air. He landed where Derek and Omar were standing with a *thud!* She then performed a series of circular gestures with hands, conjuring a magically reinforced steel cage around the three of them. The mayor then turned her attention on Tre'Vell. She extended her arm, slowing dragging him along the ground toward her.

"Go get him, Derek!" said Omar. Derek teleported out only to reappear in the same spot.

"What happened?" asked Matthias.

"I don't know," he said, confused.

"The cage is magic proof. No magic can pass through its bars," Angela said. Omar, Derek, and Matthias were helpless as they watched Tre'Vell being dragged feet first toward the mayor. He flailed his arms, desperately trying to resist her telekinetic pull, but it was of no use. When he was at her feet, he found that he couldn't move away! She was holding him in place. "When I learned that you guys formed a warlock's diamond, I was slightly worried that I wouldn't be able to accomplish the task set forth before me. I've heard great stories about the strength of covens and diamonds. They're legendary, really. Looks like I had nothing to fear after all." Without taking her eyes off of the boy at her feet, she extended her hand. One of the swords floated across the room and into her waiting palm. "Or maybe I'm just that good."

She raised the sword above her head, preparing to bring it down and end Tre'Vell's life. He put his arm up in an attempt to freeze her, knowing that it wouldn't work but not having any other course of action. Just as he thought, his powers were ineffective on Angela. Tre'Vell closed his eyes and waited for the blade to pierce his body. He was about to die for the second time that year. As he waited for the end to come, he realized he was somewhat lucky. Everybody else only died once.

Just as Angela was about to kill Tre'Vell, she was hit on the back of the head and fell to the ground, knocked out. Tre'Vell opened his eyes when he heard the mayor hit the ground. He looked up to see what happened. A woman was standing there by the door, holding a giant book in one hand and a paperweight in the other. At first, he was too stunned to speak, but eventually found his voice.

"Who are you?" he asked.

"I'm the woman that just saved your ass," she said.

"It's about time! Cutting it kind of close, don't you think?" said Derek.

"You know her?" asked Matthias.

The woman walked over to the cage and unlocked the door, letting them out. "This is Mariah, the mayor's assistant."

"Friend or foe?" asked Matthias suspiciously.

"Are you kidding? Did you not see what I did back there?" she asked incredulously.

"She's definitely here to help us. She's the one that helped me plan this whole thing," said Derek.

"Plan what whole thing?" asked Omar as Tre'Vell made his way over to the group assembled by the cage.

"Using the disempowerment spell on the mayor."

"When she have time to do that?" asked Tre'Vell.

"Remember when I teleported out to get my grimoire?"

***

Earlier . . .

Derek arrived in his dorm room and went over to his closet. He pulled out his chest and opened it using the amulet on his chain. Sitting right there was his grimoire, just as he expected. He pulled it out, closed the chest, and placed it back in his closet. He was going to teleport back to the library, but paused when he felt someone attempting to telepathically communicate with him.

Derek? Derek, can you hear me?

Yeah. Who is this?

My name is Mariah.

How you doing this? You a witch?

No. Just a mortal. I'm the mayor's personal assistant.

This put Derek on high alert. *Her assistant?*

Sensing his hesitancy, Mariah said, *Don't worry. I'm not here to hurt you. I just want to talk. To help.*

Why would the mayor's personal assistant want to help us?

Angie's under the gun right now, but I can't condone her killing innocent boys. She needs to be stopped, but I also don't want her to get hurt either.

Okay. What did you have in mind?

Have you ever heard of a disempowerment curse?

Can't say that I have.

About a decade ago, Angie cast it on her boyfriend at the time. It's a spell that will remove her magic. Without it, she will no longer be a threat to you guys.

Hmmm. That sounds intriguing. What do we need to cast the spell?

It was a while ago since she cast the spell, so I don't remember all the spell's requirements unfortunately. Can you check your grimoire to see if the spell is in there?

Hold on. Derek rustled through his grimoire for a couple of minutes before finding something. *I think I found it! Let's see. We need to make her drink a potion. We also need some of her blood and an item of great personal significance.* How we gonna get that?

I can get the item for you. I already have an idea for what you can use. Fine. What do you need from us?

When you make the potion, give me a batch. I'll try to slip it to her. I also need you guys to keep her busy for as long as you can so I can get the item. She keeps it locked up pretty tight, and it'll take me some time to get it. Once I do, I'll try to sneak up on her while she's focused on you guys.

Sounds like a plan. We'll get on it.

Do me a favor and don't mention where you got the spell from to the others. Pitch it to them like it was your idea or something.

Good idea. I better get back before they start to worry. Thank you again, Mariah. For all of your help.

Don't mention it. Literally.

***

"So that's what took you so long," said Omar.

"I don't get it. Why didn't you want him to tell us he got the idea from you?" asked Matthias.

Mariah said, "Because you have to remember that Angela is telepathic. She would have read your minds and figured out my involvement. If she did that, I never would have been able to help you."

"But she could have just read your minds though," said Matthias.

"Derek is telepathic himself so I knew he could shield his thoughts from her. And Angie trusts me. She wouldn't think to read my mind for something like that. As it was, she read Matthias's mind beforehand and found out about the spell and cast a spell on her armoire where she keeps her mystical artifacts that sends her a mental alert when it's opened. That's why I needed you guys to distract her so she couldn't focus on me breaking into her armoire and getting this," she said and held up the book.

"Look, this is all well and good, but can we just cast the damn spell before she wakes up!" said Tre'Vell.

"Right. Tre, where's the potion?" asked Matthias.

"It's in my . . .," he trailed off when he reached into his pocket and didn't feel the potion vial. "It was in my pocket."

"She crushed it when you were unconscious," said Omar. Matthias and Tre'Vell groaned.

"Not to worry. I slipped her some of the potion that Derek gave me. I spiked her drink at breakfast," said Mariah.

"Oh good. And am I correct in assuming that book is her grimoire?"

"Yup. Her most precious possession."

"Well, all right then. Let's do this."

Matthias went over to Derek's backpack and took out the small metal box that was to be the mystic containment unit. He went over to the mayor, picked up the sword that was resting next to her, and cut her arm, letting the blood drip onto the box. He went back over to the group, and they said the incantation to create the containment unit.

"Contanus myste rivulet. Myskina binvic mordu." The box levitated out of Matthias's hands and hovered in the air and briefly did a few twirls before returning to his hand. "Now for the final step. Mariah, if you could come stand by me," said Matthias. With Angela's grimoire in hand, she went to go stand beside Matthias. "All together now." Derek held out the paper with the spell on it for all four of them to read. "Slante istante vrabem denph feng," they chanted.

Nothing happened at first. They continued to repeat the incantation, with the urgency in their voices rising with each chant. After a couple of rounds of the chant, they started to make headway. Sparkling cerulean lights began to slowly spew forth from her body. Now was the most crucial point in the spell. They had to draw the magic into the containment unit. They continued to chant. The lights lingered above Angela's body as if they were desperately trying to stay with their master. Soon though, the lights slowly made their way toward the grimoire. When they got close to the grimoire, they made the detour to the containment unit. The diamond stopped chanting once all the lights were trapped inside the unit. The box glowed bright blue and began to violently shake. Time seemed to stop as they waited with bated breath to see if the mystic containment unit would hold. They let out a collective sigh of relief when the unit settled down and returned to its former state. It worked!

"It's finally over!" said Derek.

"Now that Angie has been depowered, all of her spells have been reversed so it's safe for you guys to leave now. Rhonda is safe downstairs waiting for you guys. I stopped her before the spikes could impale her," said Mariah.

"Thank you so much, Mariah. Not just for helping us stop your boss, but saving my girlfriend too. You took a big risk," said Matthias.

Mariah nodded in appreciation. "You guys better get out of here before she wakes up." Matthias offered her the mystic containment unit. "You keep it. You would be able to protect it better than I ever could. Put it in a safe place," she said.

"We will." The four of them turned and walked toward the door.

"Wait." She walked back over to them. "I want you guys to have this." She gave them the mayor's grimoire.

Tre'Vell grabbed it from her. "Why you givin' us this?" he asked.

"I'm not a witch so I don't have any use for it. I have a feeling that you guys might need this in the future. There are a lot of powerful spells and information on rare creatures in there. I hope it helps you."

"Thanks," said Tre'Vell.

"Now go on and get out of here. And good luck with your studies."

***

Angela hurriedly went to her office and closed the door. She had been betrayed. Just when she was mere moments from victory, and thereby saving both herself and her mother, someone had conked her on the back of the head. It had to be Mariah! She was the only one who could have passed through the building undetected. When she awoke, Mariah and the boys were gone, she found that her arm was cut, and that her powers were gone. Mariah must have helped the boys get the item that they needed to cast the disempowerment curse! Of all the people to betray her!

She didn't have much time to ponder that fact. She needed to hightail it out of there. Whatever the circumstances behind it were, Angela had failed. Now, she would surely be coming for her. Angela knew that running was useless, especially now that she was disempowered, but she had to try. It wouldn't be enough to leave the city or even the country. Angela had to leave the entire hemisphere. Maybe she would disappear to Monaco. She liked it there. Angela quickly gathered her things and bolted for the door. When she opened it, a cloaked figure was standing on the other side.

"You!" said Angela as she backed away.

"Going somewhere?" asked the figure.

"As a matter of fact, I was," said Angela as she continued to backpedal.

"*Was* being the operative word in that sentence," said the figure.

"You don't scare me. If I still had my powers . . ."

The cloaked figure laughed a shrill laugh. "You'd what? Wave your fingers at me? Your false bravado amuses me, but your soul glistens with the sweat of fear." The cloaked figure began to advance on the retreating mayor. "It is practically dripping off you, pooling at your feet and reflecting your fear for all to see. As well it should. You failed in accomplishing the task I had assigned you. Now, it's time to pay the piper."

This is what Angela had feared would happen for months. Ever since she received that letter all those months ago, the prospect of exactly this moment coming to pass haunted her, driving her to attempt to do unspeakable evils to avoid it. The cloaked figure slowly lowered her hood. Angela knew what was coming next.

"Please! I tried my best! Spare me!" Angela begged, cowering against the wall.

"You didn't try hard enough, Angela. This is the ultimate fate of all who oppose me, of all who disappoint me." The woman closed her eyes, and when she reopened them, the entirety of the eyes, both the corneas and the irises, were as black as coal. Staring into them was like staring into the depths of a bottomless pit of endless despair. "Now, gaze into . . . my . . . eyes. And face what you fear the most!"

Angela's heart began to race uncontrollably as terrifying images began to assault her eyes. "No! . . . No! . . . Noooooooooooooooo!"

Chapter 19

Resolution?

Derek saw his dad pull up to his dorm building. Dressed in his red-and-white Phillies gear, he went out the doors and got in his dad's car. They were on their way to the Phillies' home opener. Ever since Derek was old enough to understand the game, he and his dad had made it a tradition to attend the Phillies home opener. They never missed a year. Even though Derek's favorite team was the Cardinals, his dad bled Phillies red. Derek liked the Phillies too. He especially liked the fact that the team had great success with players like Jimmy Rollins and Ryan Howard. He wished them well, just not when they were playing the Cardinals.

Once they were on their way to Philadelphia, Stephen asked, "Whatever happened with your situation with the mayor?"

"Well, we won."

"I can see that, seein' as you coming to the game with me today. I meant, how did it go down?"

"We decided to disempower her," Derek replied.

"Disempowerment? Interesting. What made y'all come up with that?"

"We knew that we couldn't kill her because she the mayor, but we had to find a way to stop her. But we can't take all the credit. Her assistant, Mariah, reached out to me telepathically and suggested it."

"Still, a disempowerment is tough to pull off, and from what you told me, the mayor is a really high-level witch. How'd y'all pull it off?"

"Well, the mayor kidnapped Rhonda and told Matt that she wanted us to meet her at city hall," Derek began.

"Who's Rhonda again?" asked Derek's father.

"Matt's girlfriend. Anyway, Mariah slipped her the separating potion before we got there. We had to keep her busy while Matt went off to find Rhonda and Mariah got the mayor's grimoire for us to use for the spell."

"By 'keep her busy', you mean . . ."

"We fought her. Actually, that's not accurate. We survived her. She easily used her powers to counter ours, and our spells didn't really help us for long."

"What powers she have?" Stephen asked.

"Telepathy, telekinesis, and conjuration. And she was really good at using them, let me tell you. We barely survived."

"What happened?"

"Her assistant snuck up behind her and knocked her out just before she was about to chop off Tre's neck, just like we planned. While she was knocked out, we cast the spell," Derek answered.

"I wonder. If she was telepathic, why didn't she use it to find out what you guys and her assistant were up to?"

"Because we didn't know. At least, Matt, Omar, and Tre didn't. When Mariah and I came up with the plan, we didn't tell them for that reason. We figured that I could shield my thoughts and the mayor wouldn't think to read Mariah's thoughts because she trusted her."

"Wow, that's good thinking. I'm so proud of the way you and your friends handled that, Derek." He glanced over and gave his son a playful, loving rub on his head.

"Thanks, Dad."

"I can't say that I would have handled it any better. Which makes me and your mother's decision much easier," said Stephen.

"What you mean?" Derek asked.

"We're moving. To Chicago."

Derek was shocked. "When?"

"At the end of the summer. We about to put the house on the market," Stephen said.

"Why?"

"Your mom got offered a promotion. With everything that was happening with you—the diamond, the mayor—I didn't think we should go. I thought I was needed here to protect you, help you, guide you. But you showed that you really don't need none of that from me no more. With how y'all dealt with the mayor, you showed that y'all clearly have things covered. Y'all showed smarts, strength, resiliency, and great courage. As long as y'all stick together, you should be fine."

Derek's mind was still trying to process everything. "What about Dodger? He my familiar. We can't be that far apart for that long," said Derek.

"You'll have to find a place to live next year that'll let you have pets. If you can't, then he'll have no choice but to come with us. Like I said, we ain't moving 'til the end of the summer, so you got time," said Stephen.

Derek got quiet as he thought about what his father had just said. His compliments and vote of confidence meant a lot to him. He felt that with those words, his father was acknowledging that Derek was now a man. He was a young man, but he had matured to the point where he could handle himself and any problems that he encountered, and all of that meant the world to Derek. But he had a predicament on his hands, and that put a slight damper on things. He needed to find a place to live for the upcoming school year that would let him keep Dodger with him. Dodger was his familiar, his animal guide. They had been through so much together. They had grown up together. From the minute that a seven-year-old Derek found the magical beast as a stray puppy, huddled under a park bench that protected it from a thunderstorm that popped up, the two had an instant bond. In some ways, Dodger was his best friend. Living half the country apart for an entire school year was out of the question. He would rather transfer to a school in Chicago than do that. Of course, because of the diamond, that would be untenable because he also couldn't live that far away from Omar, Tre'Vell, and Matthias. What if they needed him? Derek had to figure this out.

***

Rhonda and Derek looked around the dining hall for a suitable place to sit, eat, and talk. The good thing was that they showed up at the facility a little later in its operating hours, so there weren't as much people there as it were during the rush hour. They saw a booth by a window that didn't have anyone around it, so they picked that one.

Once they sat down to eat, Matthias decided to get the conversation going. "So I guess we've got some things to talk about."

"Yes. Yes we do," said Rhonda.

"Where do you want to start?" asked Matthias.

"From the beginning, I guess. What are you? What did I see that day in your dorm?"

Matthias took a deep breath. On the one hand, he was glad that he was finally getting the chance to explain everything to Rhonda. On the other hand, he was extremely nervous because he wasn't sure how she would take it. "Omar, Derek, Tre, and I are warlocks. Magic is very real. We can cast spells . . . the works. We also each have an active power, something that we can do without the need of a spell. Derek has the ability to teleport. That's what you saw. He was teleporting me and him into my room."

"What's your power?"

"It's called electrokinesis. I can control electricity."

"So that must be what I saw that day. I could have sworn that I saw some electricity running from your finger to your laptop, but I just assumed it was static or something, like you said," said Rhonda. Matthias nodded.

Rhonda took a bite of her lasagna. "Where did you get your magic, these powers? Where does it come from?"

"It runs in my family. I've had them since I was a kid," Matthias replied.

"So that means that you've had them since we first met."

"Yes."

"Since you said it runs in your family, I'm assuming that if you had kids . . ."

"They would most likely be witches and warlocks too. I mean, I guess it's possible that they wouldn't inherit the gene that would allow them to harness magic, but that's extremely unlikely. In my whole family's history, we only know of one person that was born into it that wasn't magical," said Matthias.

Rhonda took that in as she took a swig of her drink. "What was with that funky tablet? Was it a book or something? It had a picture of your dad in it and said it was a 'Book of Magiks'?"

"Right. That was my family's grimoire. Every magical family has a book that is passed down from generation to generation. Each one adds whatever spells, potions, info on any monsters, mystical objects, they come across. It's a chronicle of my family's magical history. I found a spell to link it to the tablet. That makes it much more portable. I can easily carry that around while I leave the book, which is a lot bigger, at home," Matthias explained.

Rhonda finished her lasagna and took a few bites of her broccoli. "Let's move on to the mayor. Why did she want to kill you?"

Matthias said, "I honestly don't know. She said something about saving her mom and that she didn't want to kill us, but she had to. I guess somebody else was pulling the strings. Of course, she could have been lying. I don't know exactly what to trust from her."

"What happened back at city hall? How did y'all stop her?"

"We cast a disempowerment curse. That removed her magic."

"So she was a witch?" Rhonda asked. Matthias nodded. "And that other woman? The one that helped me?"

"She wasn't a witch, just a normal person. She actually helped us out with casting the spell," said Matthias as he took a bite of steak.

"Oh okay. Good. So now that she doesn't have any more magic . . ."

"She is no longer a threat to me, or you, or anyone else. We don't have to worry about her anymore. I'm so sorry that you got sucked into my mess. She only took you to get to us."

"Was that the first time you guys heard from her?"

"No. She's been trying to kill us for months. It started with a couple of golems she sent after us—"

"Golems?" Rhonda asked, confused.

"Creatures made from dirt, rock, and trees. So we killed those things, but then she sent us a cursed zombie game that sucked us into it, but we got out of that too. We killed the gryphon she sent after Omar, found the chimera she sent to seduce Tre, and escaped the cops, whom she had control of and ordered to shoot us," Matthias told her.

"And all this has been happening for the past couple of months?" Rhonda asked. Matthias nodded. "Now I know what she was talking about," she mumbled.

"What who was talking about?"

"The mayor. On our way to city hall that day, she said that if you had lived, the rest of your life would be as hectic as it's been lately anyway. I didn't know what she was trying to say, and when I pressed her on it further, she didn't elaborate."

"Yeah. Omar, Tre, Derek, and I performed a blood ritual last year that bonded us together for life. It makes us collectively stronger. We cast it to protect us from what we would learn later was the mayor, but it had a side effect. We're going to attract a lot of magical forces to us from here on out."

"And that's irreversible," said Rhonda.

"It's irreversible," confirmed Matthias. Rhonda remained silent for a while as she ate some of her cheesecake. "Well, that's pretty much everything. What's your reaction?"

"I'm still trying to process everything. I just don't see how you could keep something like this from me. For this long."

"I was just trying to protect you, to keep you apart from all this. I didn't know how you'd take it. It's really important that this stays a secret as much as possible. If the existence of magic—real magic—got out to the general public, who knows what would happen. Can I trust you to keep it?"

Rhonda said, "Despite everything, I do still care for you, Matt. Even if I didn't, I certainly don't wish you, your family, or friends any harm. If you say that it's that important to you, your secret is safe with me."

Matthias let out a breath that he didn't even know he was holding. "So this means that you're okay with everything? That we can make this work?"

"I have to be honest. I don't know, Matt. After hearing what your life is like, and is going to be like from now on, I don't know if I want that for myself. And I'm not sure that I want my future kids around that either. How can I relate to them when they're magical and I'm not? How do I teach them? Protect them?"

Matthias lowered his head. That wasn't the answer that he wanted to hear, but it also wasn't one that he wasn't expecting. "So are you breaking up with me?" he asked.

Rhonda finished the last few bites of her dessert before answering. "I'm not saying that. I love you. You know that. Look, this is a lot to process right now. I just need a little time to sort through everything. Is that all right with you?"

"Of course, I understand. I'll give you your space. You have my number and know where I live. Take all the time you need and get back to me when you're ready." Rhonda nodded and got up from the table. Matthias watched as she went to put her tray away and leave the dining hall. Matthias had finally bared his soul to Rhonda. Now, everything else was up to her.

***

Asmodeus and Benzor walked the halls of the capitol building. There were reporters, media outlets, and government officials running to and fro. When the mayor was found dead in her office, the political machine was sent into a frenzy. It was uncommon for a mayor to die in office, and it sent everybody scrambling to figure out how it went down. From what was found at the scene of the crime, it looked like a struggle had taken place, but there was no sign of who was the culprit. They found weapons, but forensics had revealed only the mayor's fingerprints on them. They were stumped.

The senators walked up to the governor's office and knocked on the door. "You can enter," they heard. They opened the door and walked inside. The governor was seated behind her desk, her back turned to them. The large back of her seat obscured her from their vision.

"I'm sure you've heard the news," said Asmodeus.

"I have. Seems as if Mayor Wright has met a rather premature end. Tragic, really," said the governor.

"We assume that you had something to do with that," said Benzor.

"What makes you think that?" asked the governor.

"We saw the body. It looked like some of your work."

The governor spun around to face the two senators. When she was finally facing them, they saw that her eyes were jet-black. "It was some of my best work. Her fears were particularly delicious."

"What about her mother? Was she dealt with in a similar way?" asked Asmodeus.

"No. I planned on feeding her to you two, my pets. You beasts are always so . . . ravenous. I'm sure her screams will serve as a fitting side dish to the main course," answered the governor.

"Thank you, mistress. We look forward to the meal. What are you going to do now? The witch failed," asked Benzor.

"Thank you for stating the obvious," she quipped. "You know, good help can be so hard to find, gentlemen. Kill four little warlocks. That's all I asked of her, and she couldn't even do that."

"From what we witnessed, she blew her chance when she didn't go after them fully until the very end. By that point, the warlocks were already a diamond and were gaining both experience and confidence in their abilities. It only helped that they overcame her at every turn leading up to their confrontation," said Benzor.

"Which is why I wanted to give her a little . . . incentive. Clearly, that didn't work. It was a mistake to entrust a mortal with this, and it's a mistake that I will not make again."

"Does this mean what I think it means?" asked Asmodeus.

"It would be best if I entered my hat into the ring and got rid of them myself. You know what the humans say—if you want something done, you must do it yourself," said the governor.

Benzor had to wonder why his master wanted those warlocks dead so much. It was rare that she deemed any situation serious enough to warrant her dealing with it personally. "Will you be attacking them soon while they're still licking their wounds?"

"Oh no, at least not yet. I have something much more insidious up my sleeve. And ultimately, a much more effective way to deal with them." The governor leaned forward on her desk and rested her chin on her hands, whose fingers were weaved together. The senators thought they saw a gleam in her pitch-black eyes as she said ominously, "It's a long-term job. But the beauty of it is that they will never see it coming."

***

Derek could hear the thumping bass from where he was standing in line outside of the arena. He was in line to enter the arena for the spring concert that the student union put on every year. Word University's spring concert was known for being top-notch. They always seemed to get big acts to headline the concert. This year was no different. They got Ludacris to headline it this year. Not only that, Miguel was opening up. Derek got his tickets as soon as they went on sale a month ago. Since students received a discount on tickets and got the chance to get theirs before they went on sale to the general public, Derek got tickets for both himself and his buddies. The good thing was that all of them could make it. It was one of the few times that Derek, Raheem, Tyrone, Dominique, and Devon would be able to all get together; and they weren't going to waste it. They expected this concert to be jumping.

"So how you and Kelsey doing?" Derek asked Devon.

"We broke up, as if you didn't already know," said Devon.

"Wow. I'm sorry to hear that," said Derek.

"No, you not!" said Devon.

"Yes I am!" Derek protested. After Devon gave him a knowing look, he capitulated. "Okay, okay. So I'm not exactly disappointed either," he said.

"You not gonna try and get with her, are you?" asked Raheem.

"What? No!" said Derek.

"Good. 'Cuz you know our code as it pertains to bitches. We can't mess with a girl that one of us has been with before," reminded Raheem.

"And you especially can't fuck 'em," chimed in Dominique.

"I know the rules. I came up with them! And I will honor the code. But Kelsey was my friend before Devon went out with her and I'ma keep that friendship," said Derek.

"But what happens when she comes to you 'cuz she on the rebound? We all know you don't got the best self-control when it comes to the ladies," said Tyrone.

"Who you kidding? Derek wants to fuck anything with boobs and an ass. I can't imagine how he'll restrain hisself if she comes to him all vulnerable and shit," teased Dominique.

"Nothing will happen between me and Kelsey," Derek grounded out. "Come on, Devon. You know I wouldn't do you dirty like that," he said.

"I know. I ain't sweatin' it. There's plenty of other fish in the sea," he said.

"Oh shit! They checking people at the door," said Tyrone.

There were security guards at the entrance, and they were checking people's tickets and searching them, for weapons and contraband, no doubt. They each brought some marijuana to smoke during the concert, but that plan was in jeopardy.

"What we gonna do now? How we gonna get the weed past the security?" asked Devon.

Derek said, "I got it covered. Don't worry. Give me y'all joints." They each dug in their pockets and pulled out their individual stash, handing them to Derek. "Stand around me so nobody sees," he said. They did so.

"What you finna do?" asked Tyrone.

"Hiding the stuff," Derek answered. He held the weed in his hands and closed them. "Concelio." When he reopened his hands, the joints were gone.

"Where'd they go?" asked Dominique.

"Nowhere. I just made them invisible," answered Derek. He gave his friends their joints back. It was amazing! They could feel the joints in their hands, but all they saw when they looked at them were their palms. "Obviously, you can't see them, but you can still feel them. Hold them in your hands. They'll feel them if they pat you down, but won't check your hands. I'll lift the charm when we get inside," said Derek.

"Cool," said Raheem.

When they got through the security entrance undetected and inside the building, they went to go find their seats. After settling in, they each went off to go to the bathroom and get refreshments. As Derek was walking along the concourse, he spotted Tre'Vell standing in line for some concessions. He went over to greet him.

"Yo, Tre. What's up?"

Tre'Vell briefly stopped talking to the guy he was talking to and turned around to discover the source of the greeting. "Derek! Nothin' much, man." They shook hands and gave each other a brief and light embrace. "Just hyped for this concert. Luda should have everybody turnt up!"

"I heard that."

"Oh, Derek, this my boy Deandre," said Tre'Vell, pointing to his companion.

The boy nodded and said, "Whazzup?"

"What's goin' on?" Derek replied. He turned back to Tre'Vell. "Tre, let me ask you something. What's your plans for housing next year?"

"What you mean?"

"Well, everybody's applying for housing next year. The deadline to apply to get into the dorms is next week."

"Ain't really thought about it. Why? What you gonna do?"

"My original plan was to stay in the dorms, but my parents are moving to Chicago. I wanted to keep my dog with me here in Delaware, but I had to find a place that would let me have pets."

"Don't you got family or some friends you can stay with?"

"Not nobody that's close to campus, no. And I don't want to take a couple busses to and from class every day. That'd be hard with my football schedule anyway. We usually have early morning weight lifting before the busses start running."

"So what, you wanna crash with me or somethin?"

"Not exactly. More like . . . I want you to crash with me."

"What?"

"I found this three-story house that's just off campus. It's four bedroom and two and a half bath. It even got a basement and everything. I just need three roommates. I already asked Omar and Matt and they agreed. We need one last roommate. So . . ."

Tre'Vel cut him off. "No."

"But you didn't even let me finish."

"Don't need to. I ain't moving in with y'all."

"Why not?"

"I already got a place to stay next year. I like the apartment I'm in now."

"You have to admit, it'd be perfect. Especially with what each of us can do. We wouldn't have to hide anything. Know what I mean?" Derek had to be careful with what he said. He wasn't sure what Deandre knew about them.

"With everything that's happened this year, it'd be a bad idea to move in together. I don't want to be no closer to y'all. It's hard enough to keep my space from y'all as it is. I can only imagine what it'd be like if I was right down the hall from you."

"But where am I going to live?"

"Don't know. Ain't my problem though. Now it sounds like the concert's about to start 'cuz I can hear Miguel. Let's go, De." Tre'Vell and Deandre walked off.

Derek sighed. He thought he had found a perfect situation when he found that the house was up for rent. With four people contributing, the rent and utilities were pretty affordable too. The only one holding them up was Tre'Vell. Derek didn't understand why he was so hesitant. It was perfect. If he rented the house with them, they could freely practice magic in the house. They wouldn't have to hide anything. Plus, Dodger wasn't a regular dog. He was a familiar. It'd be awkward to explain to a nonmagical roommate why he was talking to his dog, why he treated him the way he did. To someone who didn't understand their relationship, Derek would look weird. If push came to shove, he would ask one of his friends if they would do it, but the logistics for each of them didn't quite work out conveniently. They were a last resort. In more ways than one, Tre'Vell was the best option. Derek shook his head and made his way back to his seat as Miguel started to sing and the concert began.

***

Mark, the founder of Alpha Xi Omicron, paced in front of the three men who were being inducted into the fraternity. Today was the induction ceremony. For their fraternity, it was historic because it was the very first induction ceremony. The brothers who were already in the fraternity were standing off to the side, spectating. Deandre, who was standing in the middle, could barely contain his excitement. He had grown up without the traditional family structure. He had lived with his grandmother since he was nine. His mother died of cancer, and his father was in and out of prison. He didn't have any siblings, so it was just him and his grandmother. Growing up, he longed for a family. He wanted that emotional fulfillment that he didn't really have at home. That was one of the reasons that the gang that he joined with Tre'Vell was so alluring to him. It wasn't the illegal activities that he partook in, which he always detested, but the camaraderie. They protected him, raised him, and showed him love. The fraternity was Deandre's way of trading in one family unit for another.

Mark began to speak to the pledges. "I want to congratulate each of you for making it this far. Alpha Xi Omicron is predicated on the pillars of perseverance, excellence, and loyalty. Perseverance in the face of seemingly insurmountable odds. No matter how hard something seems, an Omicron man never gives up. He will keep coming until he succeeds. Excellence from top to bottom. An Omicron man excels in everything that he does. Second is the first loser. His best is *the* best. Lastly, but most importantly, is loyalty. Alpha Xi Omicron is not just a fraternity, but a family. We are all brothers. An Omicron man is dedicated to not just the community in which he lives and is a part of, but to his brethren. You three have shown your adherence and faith in these pillars, and because of that, you have been chosen to become new members of our family."

Three fraternity members approached the table that Mark stood behind. On the table was a chalice and nine ropes: three red, three green, and three blue. Each of the brothers, who had a rope of each color draped around their shoulders, approached the table. They picked up one of each of the ropes and walked over to the pledges. Each one picked a pledge and stood behind him. Mark said, "The blue rope signifies excellence, to remind you to never settle for less than your best." The brothers draped the blue ropes around the shoulders of the pledges. "The green rope signifies perseverance, to remind you to never give up." A green rope was draped around each of the pledges. "The red rope signifies loyalty, to remind you to always stand side by side with your brothers." The red ropes were draped around them.

Mark grabbed the chalice that was on the table. "The last step is the communion. We drink from the same chalice to seal our bond with each other and the ideals of the fraternity. Brother Tim, will you step forward." The student to Deandre's left walked to the table, took the chalice, and drank from it. He then retreated back to his spot. "Brother Deandre, will you step forward." Deandre walked up to the table, grabbed the chalice, and drank. He thought it tasted like wine, but there was a strange coppery hint to it. He went back to the spot he was standing in previously.

Once the last inductee, Justin, drank from the chalice, Mark addressed the gathering once more. "You are now brothers of Alpha Xi Omicron!" The current members who were standing off to the side yelped out, "Alpha Xi Omi-Crooooooon!" Mark said, "Welcome to the family . . . forever!"

Just then, the brothers who were still standing behind Mark, Deandre, and Justin, reached up to their heads and shoulders and snapped the inductees' necks! All three of them fell to the floor, dead.

***

A light breeze tickled Rhonda's skin as she typed away on her laptop. She had a paper due, her last paper for the semester. The only things left after this were a couple of projects and the final exams. The good thing was that the paper was an opinion piece. Rhonda liked opinion papers because there was no right or wrong answer. As long as she could back up her opinions with researched facts, at which she was very good, finishing this paper should be a breeze, no pun intended.

It was a nice day outside, which was a welcome and long-overdue change. Here it was the beginning of May, and the weather only recently began to break. The year had been unusually cold up to that point. It was as if Old Man Winter did not want to let go. It had snowed in late March, and the temperature remained in the forties and fifties into late April. Today, it was in the upper seventies and sunny, or at least, it was earlier. Because of that, she decided to enjoy the rare weather and type her paper outside in the park. She walked along the path, found a bench, and began typing away. Now, the dusk of early evening was approaching. The temperature was quickly dropping, and the sunlight was rapidly fading. As Rhonda looked up into the twilight, she could begin to make out the stars. Rhonda needed to complete the last few paragraphs and head inside.

Another gust of wind ran through the trees around the park. This one was a little more forceful than the previous one and seemed to linger. A few leaves kicked up and onto her laptop. Rhonda looked up into the wind, trying to assess whether she should cut her paper short and go inside early. When she did, she saw something peculiar. Off in the distance, something black seemed to be traveling in the sky. It didn't look to have any particular shape, like it was massless. If she didn't know any better, Rhonda would have thought it was a cloud of black smoke. But it wasn't hovering in the sky, it was moving, and quite quickly at that. But clouds weren't black, and they definitely didn't move like that. She closed her laptop when she realized that the cloud was coming in her direction!

As it began to get dangerously close, Rhonda got up and ran. When she glanced behind her, the cloud was following her. What the hell? Not looking at where she was going, Rhonda tripped on a rock and fell to the ground. The black cloud circled around her, surrounded her. The noxious, sulfuric smell of brimstone assaulted her nostrils. She got up. What did it want? Soon, as if to answer her question, the cloud invaded her mouth and entered her body. Rhonda fell to the ground and convulsed. Soon her body calmed as the convulsions ceased. Lying prone, back to the ground, Rhonda quickly opened her eyes, which were entirely jet-black. She slowly arose to her feet. She lightly twisted her neck and looked at her hands, wiggling her fingers. Satisfied, she said, "This will have to do."

***

Deandre slowly opened his eyes. Where was he? He was lying in a strange bed in a room that he didn't immediately recognize. He looked around, trying to get his bearings. There was a large flat-screen TV mounted to the wall with a Playstation 4 sitting on the floor under it. To his left was a side table with a lamp and digital clock on it. To his right was a five-drawer dresser with some grooming items on it like cologne, deodorant, and hair grease. The digital clock, which read 9:51, was the only way that Deandre was able to tell what time of day it was because there wasn't a window in the room.

Deandre tried to shake the cobwebs out of his brain as he attempted to recall how he got here. What was the last thing he remembered? He was at the induction ceremony. Demeco put the ropes around his shoulders. Mark welcomed them to the family and then he felt a sharp pain in his neck. That was the last thing he could recall before waking up in this room. Deandre panicked when he realized that. What happened to him? He began to hyperventilate, but panicked even more when he realized that he wasn't breathing! He heard somebody opening the door. Demeco poked his head around the door.

"Good, you finally up," he said. He came in the room.

"Demeco?" asked Deandre.

"Yup. How ya doin'? Happy birthday, lil' bro!"

"Where the fuck am I? What's going on? And did you just say happy birthday? It ain't nowhere near my birthday," said Deandre.

"First off, you at our house. Second, I'm here to help you recover from your transition. And third, it is your birthday. You was just born," answered Demeco.

"Transition? Born? What are you talking about?"

"Your transition to vampirism."

"Vampirism?"

"Yeah. See, you drank some of Mark's blood at the induction ceremony. He a vampire. We all vampires. When a human dies within an hour of drinking the blood of a vampire, his body undergoes a transition. If his body survives that transition, he wakes up a vampire. He's reborn into his new life," Demeco explained.

"Vampires? That's crazy. There ain't no such thing. Vampires don't really exist!"

"Really? How do you think you woke up after I snapped your neck? How do you explain the fact that you ain't breathin'? Vampires don't breathe. And all those scents you smellin'? Those beats you hearin'? That's comin' from all those people outside the walls of this house. It's their heartbeat, their blood."

"I . . . I still don't believe you. This got to be some sick joke or something!"

Demeco sat down on the edge of the bed and said, "Okay. I'm going to show you my face. My real face. Maybe that'll convince you."

Deandre looked on as Demeco's face morphed before his very eyes! He grew an extremely pronounced brow ridge, forming the shape of a *V*. His ears grew pointed, and his nostrils flared out. The pupils of his eyes turned bloodred. Most convincing was the set of fangs that descended from his gums and replaced his teeth.

Deandre was at a loss for words. All he could say was, "Woah!"

"Now do you believe me?" asked Demeco. Deandre nodded. "Good."

"Can I do that?" Deandre asked, pointing to Demeco's face.

"Yeah. This actually our natural face. We just use our more human-lookin' face when we out in public or around outsiders. But when we here, we almost always use our real face. I only came in here with my human face so I wouldn't scare you before you understood what was goin' on."

Deandre nodded in understanding. His initial fear and skepticism was passing and being replaced with curiosity. "What else can you do? I do? Can I turn into a bat?"

"No."

"Do I sleep in a coffin?"

"No. Both those things are myths perpetrated by pop culture." Demeco smiled. It seemed like Deandre was already warming up to his new life despite his cool blood. "Well, you a hunter now. You much stronger, faster, and durable than humans. We'll have to test you out to see just how much. Some vamps are stronger than others. Some are faster. Some are more durable. You also have enhanced senses of sight, sound, and hearing. Helps you track, kill, and eat your food. Of course, you eat it using these things." He pointed to his fangs.

"I figured that," said Deandre.

"There's a couple of other things. You will age extremely slowly from here on end. Many vamps can live for centuries before they die of old age, depending on how old they were when they were born. We have the power of hypnosis."

"Wow really? How do that work?"

"Just look into somebody's eyes and really want them to listen to what you tell them. It's all about desire on your part. If you want it bad enough, they'll listen to you most of the time. That power only works on humans, though. Makes it much easier to eat them, let me tell ya, lil' bro."

"That's the second time you called me lil' bro. We ain't related though."

"Wrong. We was both sired by Mark. He was the one whose blood we drank to begin our transition. That makes him our dad, our creator. That makes us brothers. I'm the bigger one because I was born first, of course."

"Why did Mark, I mean Dad, turn me?" Deandre asked.

"He saw somethin' in you that he admired. That was why we put you through all the hazing rituals. Unfortunately, you the only one of the three we turned to survive the transition. The others never woke up. The fraternity is just a front for our family. It's a way for us to recruit without drawing suspicion," explained Demeco. "One last thing. We very sensitive to UV light. Stay in it for any length of time and we'll start to burn, flames and all. It's one of the only ways we can die. That, wood through the heart, and beheading."

"If we can't go in the sunlight, how do y'all attend class? I know y'all do 'cuz I've seen it," asked Deandre.

Demeco held up his necklace, which had had an orange pendant on it. "This. It's a magical amulet that protects us from sunlight. All of us have one. Dad got some witch he's known from way back to make them for us. But she died a couple of weeks ago so you'll have to share mine until Dad finds another witch to make one for you."

"Witch?" Deandre sighed. "Well, if vampires exist, why can't witches, I guess? Who was it?"

"I don't know. I never met her, and Dad never told us. Apparently, she suffered a heart attack, and her hair was turned white. It was like she was scared to death. Really weird . . ."

"That is weird," agreed Deandre. A thought popped in his head. "Let me ask you something. I got a friend. Do you think he could join our family?"

"Um. You have to ask Dad, but I doubt it. Dad's really, really careful about who we turn. Besides, the less contact you have with people from your human life, the better."

"Why?"

"Humans have a conscience. The further removed from your human life you get, the more and more of that conscience that's left in you that will fade. Makes it easier on you to eat them if you don't have to think about what you doing to them. They our food source, nothin' more, nothin' less, and you shouldn't feel bad about eating them. They don't feel bad about eating other animals, do they? Of course not, because that's just the food chain. Being around people from your previous life can bring that conscience back, make you conflicted."

"Oh. Got it. I have to make an exception for Tre, though. We been through too much for me to cut out on him."

"As long as it's just one, I guess you'll be fine. Just always remember what you are and what he is. Don't let your friendship cloud your judgment."

Deandre nodded. "Man, he gonna freak when he learns what I am!"

"Hold up! I never said anythin' about tellin' him that you a vamp! Uh-uh. No way!"

"He'll be cool about it. Sure he might be scared at first, but he'll come around. Besides, he might be more open to it than you might think."

"What's that mean?"

"Tre can do this weird thing where he can use his hands to, like, stop things from moving completely. We didn't know what the hell it was. I just knew it was cool. Came in handy a few times too."

Demeco furrowed his brow, which was hard to tell since he was still in his vamp face. "Stop things completely? Almost like he can stop time?"

Deandre shrugged his shoulders and said, "I guess."

"That sounds dangerously close to a warlock. Now I'm sure you shouldn't associate with the guy!"

"What? Why not?"

"Witches and warlocks are immune to our hypnosis, which makes them very dangerous. Warlocks are tricky because they are drawn to power by their very nature. They aren't to be trusted."

"But what about that witch that Dad got to make the amulets?"

"He knew her for years. He could trust her."

"Well, I've known Tre for years and can trust him. If he is a warlock like you say, he won't be a threat to me or any of you," Deandre protested.

"Oh yeah? And how will he deal with you eating people?" countered Demeco.

"We've seen and done some pretty bad things in our past. If I know him—and I do—he won't care. He'll understand that it's something that we have to do to survive. As long as I don't try to eat him or anybody he cares about, we'll be cool. And I would never even think about eating him, no matter how hungry I got."

"It ain't me you gonna have to convince, it's Dad," said Demeco. *Grrrrrrr!* Deandre's stomach began to loudly growl. "Speaking of hungry. I completely forgot that all newbie vampires are ravenous for their first meal. You must be starving."

Deandre nodded. "I ain't felt this hungry in years!"

Demeco got up from the bed. "Come on. Dad brought home somebody to eat just for you. He makes it a point to bring home a couple of people for us to eat when we get an addition to our family. It's like a feast, a special occasion. And by our tradition, for your first meal, you get an entire person to yourself and we wait until you drain him. Until you learn how to hunt, it'll be the biggest meal you'll eat."

Deandre liked the sound of that. At the thought of satisfying his hunger, his face morphed into his vamp face. He really did have a real family now. He had a house, a dad, brothers. He had people that cared about him. It was what he always wanted. So what if they killed people and drank their blood? In Deandre's burgeoning new mind, that was a small price to pay for everything that he was gaining: immortality, a new family, new abilities, a new life. He just hoped that he would be able to share it with Tre'Vell somehow.

***

Matthias finished the fifteen-stroke rally with a forehand winner down the line. He was competing in the conference championships and had advanced to the semifinals of the tournament. He had already helped his team advance to the doubles championship earlier that day. In the tournament, schools had to use each of their players in doubles play in at least one round of round-robin play. Because of that, coaches had to manage when and how they would deploy their best players, who were usually also competing in singles play. The points for doubles counted just as much as the points for singles when it came to determining which school won the team championship. Head coaches had to determine when to use their star player in the doubles matches so as to maximize their chances of winning in singles and getting the most points possible in doubles.

Matthias was the only player on the team who had their own coach. The head coach of Word U decided to hold back on using Matthias in the earlier doubles matches because Matthias didn't have much practice playing doubles with his teammates. It was a constant power struggle between the head coach and Matthias's dad about that issue, but Matthias was such a good singles player—the most talented player that he had ever been around—that the head coach eventually conceded. Since the team advanced past round-robin play and made it to the semifinals of the doubles, Matthias had to play in either the semifinals or finals. If he didn't play in the semifinals and Word U lost, the team would be docked points because he would never have played. Unfortunately, their doubles match was scheduled right before the semifinals of singles play on the same day. So there was a choice: they could either take the chance and hold Matthias back from doubles play to give him the full rest for singles or play him in the doubles and hope he had enough left to win his singles match.

In the end, Matthias decided to play both matches. He wanted to be the team player. He wasn't selfish. He didn't want to potentially cost his team the chance to win the conference title just to give himself the best chance to win the singles. They won their doubles match in three tight and long sets, but now he was locked in a dogfight in his singles match. The first two sets went to tiebreaks. Matthias won the first one 9–7, but his opponent won the second one 10–8. They were now in the third and decisive set. After the fifteen-stroke rally that Matthias won, he was leading 15–0 in the first game.

"Good shot, Matt," said Omar. He was attending the game with Monica. It was Omar's first time watching a tennis match of any kind.

He had to admit, it wasn't an unpleasant experience. He liked the one-on-one nature of the sport. There were no teammates to bail you out if you made a mistake. The rules and idiosyncrasies of the sport had to be explained to him, and Monica obliged throughout the match, for which Omar was grateful. Omar was a quick study though, and by the time the third set came around, he knew enough to be fully invested in the match.

Matthias got a couple of errors to close out the first game at love. His opponent hit a couple of aces and backhand winners to even the set at one apiece. In his service game, Matthias fell behind 0–30. His opponent gave him a gift by hitting a second serve return long to make the score 15–30. Matthias won the next two points to go up 40–30, but lost a ten-stroke rally to even the score at deuce. His opponent hit a return winner to go up advantage. One point from being broken, Matthias hit an ace to erase the break point. Then he won the next two points with a crosscourt forehand and backhand down the line. It was tough, but he held to go up 2–1.

Matthias's opponent won his service game relatively simply, only losing one point. On his service game, Matthias committed three unforced errors to go down 0–40. Fatigue was clearly becoming a factor. The match was just under two hours long at that point. Matthias's opponent seemed emboldened when he noticed that Matthias's shots were getting shorter and shorter. Clearly, he wasn't moving as well, and his strokes weren't penetrating the court as much as they were earlier in the match. Matthias took a deep breath before serving.

"Come on," said Omar. Matthias hit a good first serve out wide, but his opponent anticipated that shot, inched out wide, and hit a booming crosscourt backhand whizzing by Matthias. "Out!" yelled the linesman. Matthias let out a breath as the shot landed just inches wide. Given new life, Matthias rallied to tie the score at forty all by winning a couple of long rallies. On the deuce point, Matthias won a point by scrambling to recover a beautiful drop shot and hitting a volley winner. A service winner gave him the game and he went up 3–2.

Despite winning the game, Matthias had to expend a lot of energy, energy that he was quickly running out of. Sensing this, his opponent altered his tactics. He began to take some pace of the ball and utilize spin and angles more. He kept hitting shots to opposite sides of the court, forcing Matthias to run from side to side, which served to wear him down. The shots weren't particularly great shots and were normally balls that Matthias would get to easily and pound. He lost the game at love, and the score was tied 3–3.

Matthias was thankful for the changeover, as he was sucking wind at that point, but it was all too brief. On the first point of the next game, his opponent took immediate control of the point by hitting a great, deep return that Matthias barely got a racket on. It landed back in the court, but his opponent won the point with a forehand: 0–15. Matthias lost the next two points on a backhand error and a lob winner. Matthias was drawn into the net by a drop shot and didn't even make an attempt to chase down the lob. Once again, he was down 0–40 and faced break points.

Matthias lowered his head in dejection. Seeing his friend needing any kind of positive energy, Omar yelled out, "Keep your head up, Matt! Take it a point at a time!" Matthias reared back and fired a serve up the T. He knew he hit a good serve and wasn't expecting it back, so he was surprised and caught off guard when his opponent returned it in play. A long back-and-forth rally ensued. Matthias ended it by unloading on a forehand down the line. "Come on!" Matthias yelled, trying to get himself up. That was one break point saved. On the next point, Matthias hit a drop shot to draw his opponent to the net, then hit the passing shot for the winner. That was two break points saved. Now 30–40, Matthias was just one point from evening the score at forty, but finally ran out of steam. A grueling twenty-one-stroke rally ended when his opponent hit a backhand crosscourt that Matthias dumped into the net. Matthias was broken.

"It ain't over yet!" yelled Omar. Despite being a novice to the sport, even Omar could tell that Matthias was fading. He used up a lot of energy and grit during that last point, and he looked spent. Matthias, knowing that he was practically running on empty, felt that the only shot he had left was to just go for broke on every shot. He hit two blistering return winners to go up 0–30 on his opponent's serve. This got the small crown back into it. His opponent hit a couple of drop shots that Matthias didn't have the legs to get to, and at 40–30, Matthias hit a backhand long to lose the game and fall down 5–3.

Dejected, Matthias hung his head. That last push was Matthias's last hurrah. He dropped his service game at love to lose the match 7–6 (7), 6–7 (8), 6–3. After the meeting at the net, Matthias walked over to his chair and plopped down. His team came over to see how he was doing and cheer him up, but he needed no encouragement. What he needed was rest. Matthias knew what happened and was fine with it. He felt that the only reason he lost was because he played doubles earlier that day and his opponent did not. Because of that, he got tired earlier in the match than normal and his opponent was smart enough to recognize that and take advantage. Matthias had no regrets, however. His team earned enough points to clinch the team championship with their win in doubles play. He could settle for that with his head held high.

***

Omar, Derek, Matthias, and Tre'Vell ambled down the street toward the basketball court, Omar dribbling the ball along the way. The semester's classes were done, and it was the day before final exams began. The four of them decided to get a couple games of two-on-two in before hitting the books to study for their respective tests. Omar was the one that brought up the idea, but with the way the day progressed, he was kind of rethinking it. The day started off with temperatures in the sixties, but by the time they began their walk, the sun was blaring and temperatures were soaring into the low eighties. The humidity, which was normally very high in that area, made it feel like it was in the low nineties. It was the hottest day of the year by far. The weird thing was that it was cloudy, blustery, and cold just a week or two ago. It seemed like the region went straight from winter to summer. One day it was cold, the next day it was hot. The pleasantness of spring was pretty much skipped altogether. What strange weather they were having that year!

"Man, when did it get so hot?" asked Matthias as he used his shirt to wipe away some of the sweat that was trickling down his face.

"This did seem to come out of nowhere, didn't it?" said Omar.

"Maybe we should shelve this for another day, fellas," said Matthias.

"Oh come on! Don't be a pussy! It ain't *that hot*," said Tre'Vell.

"If I pass out and need to go to the hospital before my finals, I'm going to kill you guys!" huffed Matthias.

"Who y'all got in the playoffs?" asked Tre'Vell.

"In the West, I got the Thunder. In the East, I'm rolling with the Heat," said Derek.

"I got news for you. The Spurs is going to win the West," said Omar.

"Nigga, is you high? They ain't beating KD and Westbrook. It ain't happenin'. Thunder in six," said Tre'Vell.

"I love they ball movement. I think they got a better team than the Thunder. Why you think they finished with a better record? Plus, I don't trust Westbrook not to take some stupid-ass shot or have some dumb turnover to lose them a game or two," answered Omar.

"I don't know anybody that's not picking the Heat in the East," said Matthias.

"God, the Pacers' got to be the sorriest one seed I ever seen. If they don't get swept, I'll be shocked," said Derek.

"You know what? Ever since it got out that Paul George knocked up that stripper, his game ain't been the same," said Omar.

"Should've wrapped it up! I don't know why these niggas always be hittin' it raw. Then they get hit with that child support and baby-mama drama! I couldn't do it," said Tre'Vell.

"Well, sometimes you be in the heat of the moment and don't be thinking about putting a rubber on. Besides, sometimes it be so good that you want to feel it fully and let's be honest. No matter how thin a condom is, it never feels as good as when you up in there raw," said Derek.

Matthias chuckled. "Speaking from experience?"

Derek responded to his ribbing, "I always use a condom . . . mostly. Look, if you sure she ain't got nothing, you don't got to wear a condom. Your pull out game just gotta be on point, though. Or else you got a situation that he dealin' with now."

"No matter what happened, the Pacers wasn't beating the Heat anyway. LeBron is a beast. I'll believe he'll lose when it actually happens," said Matthias.

"He'll lose to KD. It's his time," argued Tre'Vell.

"How he going to lose to Durant when Durant won't even get past the Spurs?" countered Omar.

"You'll see."

There was a brief lull before Omar asked, "Aye, did y'all hear about the mayor dying?"

"I know! That shit was crazy! They said on the news that it was a suicide," said Tre'Vell.

"The way they described her body when they found it, I highly doubt it was a suicide. She didn't seem like that type of person to kill herself," said Derek.

Matthias said, "I agree. Somebody murdered her."

"I wonder who did it?" wondered Tre'Vell.

"Well, if you remember, she did say that somebody else put her up to it. Maybe it was that person, for failing," said Derek.

"This is bad."

"Why you say that?" Omar asked Matthias.

"Because the press will be searching for answers, and that search could lead them straight to us."

"But we ain't kill her," said Tre'Vell.

"But we were there fighting her right before she died. If they find that out, they'll come snooping and we'll have some explaining to do. Even if they find out that we didn't kill her, any investigation could expose our magic and *that* would be disastrous," said Derek.

"I bet you it was her assistant, like the butler. It's always the butler," commented Omar.

"It could have been, but I really didn't get that vibe from her," said Derek.

"Well, whoever it was, that's tomorrow's problem. We'll deal with it when we have to. But I must say that those tarot cards weren't wrong, Derek. There certainly was death in your future. It just wasn't yours," Matthias pointed out.

"Yeah, I guess you right. Ricquel. The mayor . . ."

"Don't forget Tre," said Omar. Tre'Vell gave him an annoyed look. "What? You might have come back, but you did technically die."

"I'm just glad that it's all over and we all made it okay," said Derek.

Tre'Vell's cell phone rang. He answered it and seemed to have a conversation that started off well enough. He then quickly became annoyed then agitated. He hung up the phone. "What was that all about?" Omar asked as they approached the basketball court.

"That was my landlord. He said I can't renew my lease when it's up at the end of next month," Tre'Vell seethed. They could practically see the steam rising from his head, which could have been an indication of his level of anger or how hot it was outside. Either one was a possibility really, even a combination of the two.

"Did he say why?" Matthias asked they stepped on the court. The asphalt surface made it feel even hotter. It was like stepping onto a hotplate. The boys decided to take off their shirts since it was scorching and they were already drenched anyway.

"He found somebody willing to pay more," Tre'Vell said angrily.

"He can't do that? Give you such short notice!"

"He can and he did!"

Derek saw an opening and jumped in. "Aw, man, that sucks! Too bad you don't have a place to stay . . ."

"I think that's his not-so-subtle way of reextending his invitation to room with us," said Matthias.

"I'm sure I can find another place," Tre'Vell said.

"One that's in your price range, is close to campus or on the bus route, and is available right now? Good luck finding it. Really," said Derek cheekily.

Omar chuckled. "Look, it's no pressure. Yeah, we need a roommate, but whatever is good for you. I'm sure we can find another roommate."

Tre'Vell let out a long sigh before relenting. "Fine! I'll room with y'all. You lucky I needed a place to stay."

"Now that that's out the way, can we get these games started? The sooner we start, the sooner we can finish and get out of this heat," said Matthias. The four boys tossed their shirts to the benches and took to the court to begin their spirited games of pickup ball.

Epilogue

Derek finished neatly folding the last of his clothes and gently placed them in the plastic tote. Moving-Out Day was finally here and he had spent the morning preparing to move out of the place he called home for the past nine months. That entailed packing his clothes and personal items, sweeping the floors, cleaning the bathroom, yanking down his posters, and unhooking and unplugging his appliances. Knowing what to expect this time around, his finals went much smoother than during the fall semester. He glanced at the time on his cell phone. His mother wouldn't be arriving for about another hour. Since his television was unplugged along with all his other devices, he decided to turn in his key and check out down at the RA's office so that he could leave right when his mother pulled up.

Derek migrated his way through the hustle and bustle of students and parents entering and exiting the building with various boxes and electrical appliances in hand. The day wasn't quite as chaotic as Move-In Day was because some students had already moved out when they finished their last finals on a previous day during the week. When he reached the office, he poked his head in the threshold.

"Knock, knock!" he said. Inside the office were all of the building's RAs, including Monica.

"Hi, Derek. Please come in!" she said. Derek walked into the office. A couple of students were just hanging out, probably enjoying the last moments of the school year with their RAs before the summer break. He walked up to the table where Monica was situated.

"So are you checking out on me?" she asked.

"Yeah, but I won't be leaving for another fifty minutes or so. I just wanted to turn in my stuff early so I could just go when my mom shows up. That all right?"

"Did you check off all the points on your checkout list that was posted on your door?"

"Yes I did. The dorm is spotless."

"Then it's all right. Do you have your key?" Derek removed his key from his key ring and handed it to Monica. She recorded the number on it in her book. "Okay, I just need you to sign here and you're free to go."

Derek bent down and signed the sheet of paper and handed it back to Monica. "There you go."

"Thank you. Well, it was certainly an . . . experience to have you as my resident this year, Derek. I hope you have a fun summer. Don't get into too much trouble." She smiled.

"Now that you ain't my RA no more, do you think I can get your number?" he asked hopefully.

"No."

"Why not? Come on, I know you was checking me out!"

"How about you shoot me a friend request on Facebook and I'll accept it. We'll start from there and see where it takes us."

"I'll definitely do that." He turned around and left the office, going back up to his dorm room. About thirty minutes later, he heard a knock on his door. It was Omar and Matthias.

"We just came to say that we're leaving," said Matthias.

"Cool. Well, y'all have a good summer. If you need anything, you know how to get in touch. See y'all at our new house in a couple months."

"You too. Don't do anything I wouldn't do," said Matthias.

Derek wrinkled his nose. "No can do. Then I wouldn't have any fun."

The three of them shared a laugh. Omar and Matthias nodded and turned to leave. Omar turned back round. "Derek, at least do me a favor."

"What?"

"Stay out of trouble."

"Monica said the same thing. I'll try. Can't make any promises though." They shook their heads and walked off down the hall.

Derek surfed the Internet while waiting for his mother to arrive. When she did about ten minutes later, she sent him a text telling him she was there and coming up to help him move his things. Just like Move-In Day, she insisted that he not use his powers to help himself. She just insisted on doing things the hard way! He didn't know why she didn't send his dad to help him move out. Part of him thought that she just wanted the exercise. Yeah, that was it.

When they had everything loaded up in the vehicle, Derek all of a sudden remembered that he left his backpack in the room and forgot to sign the checklist that was taped to his door. He ran back up the stairs, fetched his backpack, signed the checklist, and closed the door. As he walked back down the steps, he realized that was probably the final time that he would be making that particular trek, which caused him to get slightly contemplative.

So many things had happened during the previous nine months that he lived in the dorm. So much had changed since he first made the trek up those stairs. He had finally decided on a major. He met plenty of new interesting people and made a boatload of new friends. His powers and mystical knowledge had expanded and evolved. He survived multiple attacks on his life. And he met three other warlocks with whom he now shared a deep, irrevocable, and life-altering magical bond. Something told Derek that what happened with the mayor was only the beginning of the trials and tribulations that he, Tre'Vell, Omar, and Matthias were going to face. Whatever that thing was, it was trying to let him know that it was just the tip of the iceberg, as if wanting to prepare him for what was to come. As Derek walked out of the dorm, he turned to get one last good look at it. One year down, three more to go.